DAVID QUAMMEN

The Zolta
CONFIGURATION

A TOM DOHERTY ASSOCIATES BOOK

This is a work of fiction. All the characters and events portrayed in this book are fictional, and any resemblance to real people or incidents is purely coincidental.

THE ZOLTA CONFIGURATION

Copyright © 1983 by David Quammen

All rights reserved, including the right to reproduce this book or portions thereof in any form.

Reprinted by arrangement with Doubleday & Company, Inc.

A TOR Book

Published by Tom Doherty Associates,
8-10 West 36 Street,
New York, N.Y. 10018

First TOR printing: December 1984

ISBN: 0-812-50800-9
CAN. ED.: 0-812-50801-7

Printed in the United States of America

The manila envelope arrives in Mayberry's mail, addressed to a friend of a friend. Its contents were titled:

A POSSIBLE CONFIGURATION ENABLING FULL IGNITION OF LITHIUM-6 DEUTERIDE IN A MONONUCLEAR WEAPON

What Mayberry now holds has been the U.S. Government's most closely guarded secret for three decades.

What Mayberry doesn't know is how it was stolen, why it came to him, and who else is after it.

Mayberry's got to find out—if he wants to stay alive.

to Kris, if she'll have it

"Nuclear explosives have a glitter more seductive than gold to those who play with them."

Physicist Freeman Dyson

Part One

ONE

He didn't expect to be frightened, despite Zuckerman's warnings. Now he is frightened. The young man combs his hair again carefully with his fingers.

He closes the volume of *Nuclear Science Abstracts,* which he has opened randomly and stared into blindly. He picks up the attaché case. He feels a single cool globe of sweat break from his armpit and run like a plump little spider to his belt. Never mind. The tall stacks of the Reference Journals section shield him like arching cottonwoods. The young man delays a moment more. As long as he is inside the building, he promises himself, there is nothing to worry about beyond procedural complications, embarrassment, failure; possibly jail. No one is going to kill him, or even try, in the main library of the Los Alamos Scientific Laboratory.

Holding the small scrap of paper that Zuckerman has supplied, he walks toward the Circulation desk.

The sniffling man is still hunkered at his table between

Circulation and the staircase, head down over a magazine, handkerchief ready in one fist. His hanky is of the red bandanna type. His feet, huge cloddy hoofs like a Percheron's, shod in dusty brown wingtips, are crossed boyishly at the ankles. The sniffling man does not look harmless, he certainly does not look innocent, but he also does not look especially deadly. He looks like a bureaucrat's tame thug, a bumbler, slow of wit and foot, vicious eventually. He wears a brown tweed jacket that appears to have served a slightly smaller man well for years.

The sniffling man is pretending, with great stupid concentration, to read a late issue of the *Bulletin of the Atomic Scientists,* turning the pages from back to front.

The young man places the attaché case in sight on the Circulation desk, where it might contribute to the impression, if any, of his legitimacy. Another of Zuckerman's touches, the case, and it is only making the young man feel more conspicuously miscast. He wears suede chukkas with no socks and his jeans have survived a hundred washings, none very recent, but Zuckerman said that wouldn't matter. Zuckerman knew, among other things, the height and alignment of the desk. The young man's shirt came crisp from a plastic package. It still bears the factory creases behind which his sweat now dribbles steadily. From the waist up he might seem almost a scholar, the young man hopes; a disheveled one; or at least a student. He passes the square of paper, which is identical except for the writing with those offered in a trough near the reference journals, to a librarian.

"I'd like to order this from Reports," he says.

For no particular reason the librarian smiles, a pair of rodential incisors pushing out to daylight before her mouth is open. Her bifocals in their swooping turquoise frames resemble the spread wings of a Brazilian moth. She inspects the slip, guiding a pencil point over the lines as though it were her own near-sighted eyeball at the end of a slim wooden prosthesis, and chants as she goes:

"Hmm Teller hmm possible hmm 1363, okay. Yes, we probably have it. Are you an employee of the lab?"

"No."

"No. All right. It might be restricted to badge-holders. We'll see. Print your name here, please, at the top."

He prints, and when he has finished, she raises her eyes to squint at him with a new curiosity. She is in her late thirties, with straw-colored hair inexpertly baled, and the toothy smile is a vaguely rowdy one, suggesting she might be open to interesting offers of a sort she couldn't herself define.

"Jeffrey Jay Katy. That's you?"

"Yes."

"Why do I know the name?"

"I don't know."

"You're famous." Despite the grin it's an accusation.

"Um. No. Not really. You saw a magazine article, I suppose."

She snaps a pair of bony fingers in his face. "Aha." Her nails are apricot, matching her sweater. "The A-bomb kid. You built an A-bomb. For your college physics."

"Designed one. I didn't build it. I designed it. Possession of the actual materials would be illegal. Also dangerous." He says this as though he has said it often before, or memorized it. There is no trace of pride. "I did some drawings, and described a plausible method. Hypothetical exercise. It made sort of a splash in the newspapers."

"Yes it did." Smirking now like an autograph hound after a score, she glances again at the white slip. "Onward to bigger and better things?"

In acknowledgement of her drollery he produces, with effort, a polite chuckle. The young man is nauseated. Though she seems likely now to be helpful, this woman has greatly compounded his nervousness. Her gawkish good cheer, and the trace of sexual keenness behind it, make the young man—preoccupied as he is with thoughts of discovery and very sudden death—feel sloshy below the diaphragm, as though his belly were full of warm dish water. He wishes he could ask her to be more serious; stern and snotty and correct, the classic schoolmarmish way, what's wrong with that? An aging librarian in heat was not part of Zuckerman's elaborate programming. The chore for which the young man was hired finally at this moment seems to him awesomely serious, serious beyond expectation, and everything lesser beside it obscenely trivial. Like a soggy handkerchief in the spare hand of an assassin.

"Just library research. Mathematical stuff. I'm doing some consulting."

She punches four digits on her phone console and says a chirpy hello to the Reports librarian downstairs. She delivers the young man's request by its document number, ignoring title and author, then after a moment of silence she answers: "No. He does not work for the lab. Yes. His name is Jeffrey Jay Katy." A quick roll of the eyes, still enjoying her little discovery but not of mind to share it, and then she spells the last name, also the middle one. "Thank you, Fiona." To him she says: "They'll bring it up. If they have it. About ten minutes."

He stations himself in a carrel at the west end of the

stacks, a quite particular carrel, from which he commands a clear view across the magazine area toward—at different angles—both the photocopying room and the elevator. Zuckerman was explicit that only the westernmost carrel would do. From this spot he is also well placed to observe the sniffling man's pantomime of disinterestedness, but not even Zuckerman could have foreseen that.

Two other readers are working at the catalogue, both of them fortyish males with fastidiously trimmed goatees, both of them wearing cardigans from which clip badges dangle. A third reader somewhere in the stacks is getting loud instructions from another female librarian about how to trace his citation from the *Electronics and Communications Abstracts;* after a dizzying spiel about cross-listings and annual indexes and document numbers versus abstract numbers, her voice declares: "Of course this one we'll only have in Japanese." Meanwhile the young man waits, and the sniffling man glowers into his *Bulletin,* which might just as well be upside down as backward. Occasionally the sniffling man bursts out in a cacophony of mucous hacking. Occasionally he catches a large sneeze in the handkerchief, then pokes the dark hornrims back up on his nose. In between he snorts and chuffs quietly. Not once does he glance at the young man.

The elevator doors open, almost precisely on schedule, before a smallish chrome mail wagon and the dapper elderly messenger who pushes it. The messenger is a whistler: beautiful piercing clear tonal quality, and the musical soul of a teakettle. Today his selection is a string of notes roughly resembling the opening two bars of "Caravan," and repeat, and repeat again. The mail wagon's front casters catch, as they perhaps do every afternoon at this time, in the crack between elevator floor and foyer, and the messenger frees them with a deft little wheelie. He parks his wagon before the bronze bust of J. Robert Oppenheimer and continues on foot. All this time whistling. With an outpouring of courtly blarney he greets the ladies at Circulation, who are suddenly wearing their shoulders a little high, like earmuffs, and makes a minor ceremony of surrendering their bundle. By them he is humored but not encouraged. On his progress toward the Reference desk he dips his head cheerfully to the sniffling man, who is not quite friendly enough to scowl at him. Two minutes later the elevator doors close again on "Caravan." And a breathy voice over the PA system startles the young man with:

"Jeffrey Jay Katy. Please come to Circulation. Jeffrey Jay Katy."

When he sees the randy librarian waiting with empty hands and a certain negative line to her eyebrows, the young man feels a quick premature flush of relief. Well hooray: so they don't have it after all. It is unaccountably missing. Not available, upon more sober consideration, to anyone but badge-holders. Fine with me, he thinks, just as well. All commitments are thereby canceled. He can return to Taos before dark with no larger problems than disappointment and poverty. He hopes the sniffling man will agree with that reading. He presents himself at the desk, and she lifts the report out from nowhere.

"Sign this." Pushing forward a half-page form. "Bring it back to me when you're done. Don't take it out of the building. Don't make pencil or pen marks." Her curtness seems merely professional and related to the appearance of a document, precious document, any document, from downstairs. With a coy glance she adds: "Have fun." He carries the thing glumly back to his carrel.

It is simply two dozen pages printed on heavy cream bond, and a pair of staples; two dozen pages the information upon which has been, for twenty-eight years, the most jealously guarded scientific secret of the United States Government.

Julius and Ethel Rosenberg died over a handful of clumsy sketches that were bathroom graffiti compared to this. The young man is mildly wonder-struck that even bureaucratic drones, in their somniferous shuffling of endless papers, could be so reckless as to set such an item on the unclassified shelves of an open government library. But here it is:

A POSSIBLE CONFIGURATION ENABLING FULL
IGNITION OF LITHIUM-6 DEUTERIDE
IN A THERMONUCLEAR WEAPON

LAMS-1363

Written By: *Work Done by:*
F. de Hoffmann   E. Teller

April 3, 1951

LOS ALAMOS SCIENTIFIC LABORATORY

Timing, according to Zuckerman's coaching, is now a delicate matter. He has a window of not more than ten minutes for the next step. He spends one of those ten at his carrel, enduring a torture of impatience, while the IBM copier in its alcove remains idle. He can afford maybe two minutes of this waiting and just into the second a woman enters the alcove. When her papers are spread and she has begun copying, he moves. The report he carries open in one hand, as though to skim it as he walks. The woman, damn her, steps back apologetically.

"You go ahead. I'm not official."

A typed notice over the IBM says: *Classified material must not be copied on this machine. Laboratory-related copying has priority over other uses. A fee of 10 cents per sheet should be paid at the Circulation desk.* She is wearing black pants and high-heeled sandals, and has already yanked her résumé off the screen.

"I'm not either," says the young man.

"Oh. I have a lot. You want to go ahead?"

"No," he says. "That's all right. I'll use the one downstairs."

The sniffling man does not so much as peek at him when he passes. The sniffling man, looking authentically bleary, is busy with the bandanna. Also perhaps he knows that the only emergency door on the lower level is sealed with a lead lace and wired for alarm.

The downstairs machine is just at the foot of the stair well. For every page copied it releases a noisy mechanical groan, wafting upstairs, certainly audible where the sniffling man sits. The young man hears no coughing. He hurries. Snatching at the pages with moist jittery fingers, he makes a single complete copy. From the attaché case he takes a manila envelope, already addressed and stamped, and seals the pages inside. The mail wagon stands where it should at this moment of the day: before the downstairs doors of the elevator.

The young man slides the envelope into a file hanger on the mail wagon. He is mounting the stairs again, with the original and his case, when "Caravan" hoves back into earshot from the microfiche room.

The young man returns to his carrel, wipes both palms dry on his thighs, and pretends for several more minutes to read. Slowly his heart rate settles back toward normal. The sniffling man blasts a cornet note into his bandanna. And the young man now smells, close before him, success: victory to the clear of nostril. He is safe, probably. Or at least safer. The copy is gone, dispatched, beyond his possession and responsibility. Now there is merely the question of getting out. He counts off seconds until time to move again.

Rising distractedly, he leaves the original report in full view on the desk. He would prefer to leave the attaché case also, but Zuckerman said no, bring the case. The rest rooms are down a short corridor near the copier alcove. LADIES is second on the corridor, against the west wall of the building, with the transom window.

He bursts through that door and has the window unlatched in a motion. Out goes the attaché case, onto the silica gravel between a pair of shrubs, and the young man is hoisting himself with a knee on the sink, his nose aimed for the bleached polygon of clear New Mexico sky, when the door behind him flaps again, violently.

He lurches; the window gap is a tight fit and for a moment he hangs with his face pressing at freedom; then is yanked back like a doomed kitten. He tumbles, helpless, until his elbows and tailbone crack hard against the tile floor. Without pause he is hauled to his feet by a strong stubby hand that has wrapped itself into the shoulder of his white shirt. Buttons fly like popcorn. The sniffling man takes a firmer grip, at the throat, and thrashes the young man's head backward, slapshot, two more, against an electric hand dryer.

The dryer begins purring warmly. From behind him the sniffling man conjures out a long-barrel Ruger .22, a target pistol, and inserts the barrel deep into the young man's mouth. The high front sight scrapes his soft palate and he spasms for air. The sniffling man waits. Holding the young man pinned, both of them now still, the sniffling man carefully meets his eyes. The sniffling man seems neither angry nor insane. He pulls the trigger.

The action clicks. The young man gags again, his knees fail, but he is suspended erect by the hand at his throat.

"Bang," says the sniffling man. "Easy as that. So now you know I ain't fucking around." But on the off chance there is still doubt he smashes the young man's head backward again, then lets him fall. The dryer has given up. From his coat pocket the sniffling man produces a clip for the Ruger. He jacks up a round. Two hands gripping the gun, two fingers on the trigger, he steadies the muzzle two inches from the young man's right eye.

"What do you want?"

"Shut up," says the sniffling man. "Don't even bullshit me whatsoever. Your life is too short."

The young man shuts up. He lifts a fingertip gingerly to his adam's apple but is careful to avoid moving his head. "All right. I made a copy." Now he understands better what Zuckerman has anticipated, and from that takes faint faulty reassurance. "It's in the case. Out there." A gesture toward daylight. The sniffling man looks, and as he does so the young man thinks, "Jesus, I may not die."

With a hand restraining his ankle and a Ruger pressed to his rectum, he struggles up through the window. The sniffling man, surprisingly agile, follows easily. No one is passing between buildings and they are out of sight from the library's glass entrance, left to their own affairs, gawking about on the silica lawn like a pair of confused gardeners.

"What?"

"Shut up. You carry it. Down here, through the parking lot. We walk to a car." The pistol has disappeared beneath the sniffling man's tweed. "Test me. Any bullshit at all and I just kill you because it's less trouble."

"I won't test you."

The sidewalk leads down a set of concrete steps and then angles away along the building's north wall, from which a pair of large smoked windows overlook the parking lot. They parade past the windows, past the lot, still moving, the young man guided by a firm discreet grip at his elbow. The walk begins sloping downhill into a copse of ponderosas between the library and the road below.

"Where's your car?"

The sniffling man doesn't answer. His right hand comes out with the bandanna and he honks his nose.

Ahead in the copse is a wooden footbridge crossing a trickle of brook, and just beyond that the walkway forks. One fork swings back up toward the far edge of the library lot, and West Jemez Road, along which is parked a metallic blue Dodge van. The sniffling man seems unaware of the van, and the young man has forgotten it. Neither of them is looking that way when the shirtless figure detaches himself from the cab.

They do not notice this shirtless character until they are ten yards from the footbridge. By then he is ambling, with the calculated casualness of a panhandler, toward a point of convergence.

"Who is this?"

"Nobody I know," the young man lies.

He is also barefoot, the shirtless one. His jeans have

been largely reconstituted with irregular leather patches and from his yellow macramé belt hangs, before his crotch like a loincloth, a chamois pouch. He walks bowlegged with both hands in the pouch as though to cushion tender testicles or warm his fingers. Ring curls of black hair struggle to free themselves from under a leather vaquero hat. And of course he is smiling stupidly: a street gypsy, permanent citizen of a fantasized decade, a type the sniffling man and anyone else would have seen a thousand times, under a thousand different names, in Berkeley and Austin and Boulder and elsewhere, with always the same vacant ulterior grin. At the far side of the footbridge he stops, blocking passage. His head bobs in idiot's greeting.

The sniffling man lifts a forearm to brush him aside. Staggering back, the shirtless one does not cease smiling.

"Hey, man," he says; and when the sniffling man pauses slightly, head turning, mouth opening, the shirtless man's right hand flashes out of the pouch to bury a sharp stroke, with all the force of his skinny body and a sound like the crack of bone, into the sniffling man's left kidney.

The young man blinks back his shock at the quickness and the noise. The sniffling man crumples slowly. Limp at their feet, he continues to wilt away further, emptying of blood and offal, unspeakable slimes, life liquids which darken the wood of the bridge and dribble off into the brook. Cramped up in fetal posture, before many seconds he is seized with uncontrollable wheezing, like an asthmatic child. The young man, his eyes huge, is forced to step over with care on the slippery wood. By then he has seen the small bloody Beretta automatic in the shirtless man's hand.

"Walk," says the shirtless man. "Don't hurry yet."

"Jesus. Jesus." They move back up toward the van, the young man again simply following the tug at his own elbow. "You don't know how that guy scared me. Should we just leave him there? What's happening?"

"Yes I do. How were the arrangements?"

"Fine. Perfect. Everything except that he almost killed me."

"The mail went out?"

"Yes. It will. No problem."

"Good. You did very well."

"What's happening?"

The shirtless man doesn't answer. He has left the van parked for a fast departure, not in the lot but at the curb on Jemez, pointed down toward the traffic light and the truck road that winds down the back way off the Los Alamos mesa. When they reach the van he turns for a nonchalant glance back toward the footbridge. The sniffling man, head raised weakly, is attempting to gasp out a few smothered words to a small boy who has ridden up on a bicycle. The boy is frowning at him from a safe distance.

"Here," says the shirtless man. "You take this."

Shifting the attaché case into his left hand, the young man reaches to accept the gun, and the shirtless man reaches too, leaning, driving it viciously into the young man's stomach. Another loud slap rings and dies. The young man remains balanced on his legs, hunched slightly forward, face pinched in distant sadness.

His eyelids flutter. Then his mouth is spread wide by a torrent of vomited blood.

With the sound of the second shot the van door has broken open before another man. Also wearing dirty patched jeans, this one is totally bald across the crown of his head, with a halo fringe of stringy hair dangling like buckskin trim over his ears, and a faceful of graying beard. He lifts the young man's feet.

"Zuckerman!" he says. "Now. Let's go."

But the shirtless man, shaded under his leather hat, is staring absently back at the smoked windows of the library.

TWO

The yellow Civic comes to rest with both right wheels up on the curb but the dog in the passenger seat, long since inured to Mayberry's driving, doesn't flinch. Mayberry squints for an address.

The house is a white clapboard of eccentric design, a bay window that grows into an octagonal turret on the second story, a cyclopean porthole with leaded glass, wisps of bright chartreuse grass sprouting like foppish bangs from a mossy rain gutter and a sitting porch in the grand Southern manner sweeping the length of the front and turning the east corner. It is tucked back from Ross Street behind a wild overgrowth of yucca and pine and jacaranda, with a single magnolia struggling to top out through the wall of unruly privets that rise like a barricade at the sidewalk, thick enough to buffer a strident decade or two. The old lady clearly prefers privacy to pruning. The neighborhood is an affluent pocket of North Oakland, but the house itself would be more at home in

Memphis or Natchez. "This is the place," Mayberry decides. "You wait here."

The dog, gentle monster on tiny legs, obeys. A cross of golden retriever and Saint Bernard, with a head like a grizzly bear and eyes like Jackie Cooper, it watches Mayberry open a gate. Watches him roll the troubling manila envelope into one hand as he disappears behind foliage. And continues devotedly to watch, for the next half hour, that spot where he last was visible.

Two minutes pass after Mayberry's first poke at the bell. He is patient, determined to err on the side of deference. The woman of his telephone conversation was quick and keen and not the least deaf. Conceivably she is now away on some small emergency, or he has mistaken the agreed time. Such a fuddle-brained mistake is more than plausible, Mayberry well knows, given his usual state of disorganization as compounded by his current state of overwork. Or the woman has had second thoughts about tolerating his questions. Also very plausible. He hears a dull thud behind the door. Another, still faint and muted, but slightly louder. Someone desperately weak and knocking to be let out?

Then the door jumps open, just a few inches, just enough to reveal her in vertical section: a delicate cinder of gray old lady, crabbed at the shoulders and lean at the wrists, with darting azure eyes. At one time she might perhaps have been a stern European beauty; now she could impersonate, about as convincingly as Golda Meir, an addled Old Country grandmama. The eyes flick over Mayberry, once up and down, before she continues her battle against mortality and the front door.

She is scuddering painfully sideways, inch by inch, above an aluminum four-legged walker. She wears a white laboratory jacket, crisp and immaculate, no doubt her chief vanity, and beneath it a black Hattie Carnegie silk dress. One withered hand, a fist of buzzardy talons, squeezes down on the walker while she jerks again at the doorknob with the other.

"May I?" Mayberry opens the screen door for himself.

"You may!" A banked turn and already negotiating her six-legged retreat down the foyer. She pauses for deep breaths, taxed near exhaustion from the effort of crossing her house. "God knows you may."

"Dr. Broch?"

"And you are Dr. Mayberry." This is shouted over a shoulder, as though to be carried back to him on the wind.

"No, ma'am. I'm not a doctor." Two calicoes want out. He eases them back with a foot and shuts the door. "I'm only a third-year medical student. I just happen to be old."

She stops. Evidently her neck is more limber than the rest. "Ach!" The blue eyes narrow on him appreciatively. "I also just happen to be old. And for this coincidence you will call me Hannah. I will call you what?"

"Please call me Mayberry," says Mayberry.

"Yaa! So you were named for an uncle you despise, or Walter Winchell, or Milton Berle." Moving again, she scuffs toward an old-fashioned front parlor, mohair upholstery and doilies and sepia light filtered through jalousies, the sort of room that in Mississippi was once reserved to the entertainment of preachers and beaux. "I understand. Come along, Milton Mayberry. Match my pace if you dare."

He follows with dinky steps. After seventy years plus a few, her mind seems to be chafing and prancing within the decrepit body like a colt in an undersized corral. Emminent filthyrich surgeons of Mayberry's acquaintance tell stories of suffering her classroom sarcasm, and being rescued from dolthood by her relentless lucidity, at Stanford twenty years earlier. Her ankles are knobbled like oddity squash at a county fair.

"You knew Jeffrey Jay Katy." Mayberry does not make it a question. After an interval of feeble pleasantries, he is plunging back to the point where their phone conversation ended. A lean doberman only then pads in from another room to station itself silently at her knee. The doberman doesn't sit. Mayberry can almost hear the high whine of its metabolism. While it watches Mayberry with the dispassion of a butcher bidding on steers, Hannah strokes it absently. Elsewhere the room is done in cats.

"I did."

"You taught him physics?"

"No. I am long since put out to pasture, Mayberry. The victim of policy: mandatory senility at age sixty-five. I served merely as unofficial adviser to Jeffrey's infamous project. At the request of Dr. Linnemann, at the Stanford department. I critiqued Jeffrey's work. Though I did not encourage his fascination."

"He was fascinated by nuclear weapons?"

"He was. At one time I was. Many, many others, good scientists and in some cases good people, also have been. That is the problem, you see."

This is said with finality. But Mayberry *doesn't* see, and he admits it.

"That has always been the great problem," Hannah repeats. "The processes that occur instantaneously when such a device functions, they happen to be very interesting. They are in fact spectacularly so. The manipulation of those processes—it is not science. But it is fascinating to scientists. And not merely for base and shabby reasons."

"The bomb that Jeffrey designed for you, it was—"

She executes a strangely vehement arching of the eyebrows. "He did *not* design it for me, Mayberrry. He designed it for himself. For his own instruction and curiosity. My distinction may be specious but I shall cling to it."

"Excuse me. I understand. And your distinction is not at all specious." The manila envelope is taking an oil mark from Mayberry's palm but he feels it would be somehow presumptuous to set the thing on Hannah Broch's tea table. "This . . . device, then, that Jeffrey designed. With some supervision from you. It was a primitive A-bomb?"

"Yes. Primitive is a good word, I think. It was similar to the bomb that fell upon Nagasaki. Not much beyond that. These machines have been made literally thousands of times more terrible in the meantime, you understand. All of the scientific and engineering data embodied in Jeffrey's project were part of the public record by 1950. Much of it could be had from the report Henry Smyth published in autumn of 1945. And that Smyth report was fully sanctioned by the Washington mandarins. Jeffrey uncovered no secrets. What he performed was, more than anything, the work of an historian of engineering. Any bright student with similar training and access to a good library could do the same. It is this banal fact which the newspaper and magazine writers chose to disregard."

"The omission may have helped to get Jeffrey killed," says Mayberry.

"I agree. It is shameful. These newspapers portrayed him as some sort of scientific prodigy, who by demonic intuition or felonious prying had come upon the great 'secret' of the bomb. It was all a cartoon."

"I assume you heard the details of what happened."

"I heard the radio news report. With its lack of details. I heard he was shot down at Los Alamos and the body thrown into a truck. Who did such a thing, what reason, this I have not heard. A pitiful, ghastly waste. So misguided. But it is a ghastly and pitiful world, Mayberry, and we have no right at this late moment, certainly I have none, to pretend it might be capable of surprising us. And what about you?" So Hannah is not one to squander time clucking dolefully, fingering beads. Onward. "You were a friend of Jeffrey's?"

"Not really. I wouldn't say a friend. I knew him. I knew his brother much better. Paul Katy and I were in the service together. Fifteen years ago." Mayberry has barely resisted an impulse to mumble this last part into his shirt, and is a little embarrassed to have mentioned it at all.

"And where is Paul Katy now?"

"Dead."

"Ah. He died in Indochina? He was a good friend to you, and you are therefore loyal to his younger brother?"

"No. He died in an automobile on Highway 1, south of Carmel. Just after his discharge in 1966. I was lucky not to have been with him. He had almost gotten me killed any number of times before that. In Vietnam and Japan. Jeffrey's brother was a wild fool. Viciously egocentric and irresponsible almost to the point of criminality." Did Hannah Broch ask for this? Fingers spread wide with the tips touching, Mayberry's hands begin flexing rhythmically into each other, like a tarantula exciting itself on a mirror. "Just the proper companion for me in those days." He ducks his head and comes up again in the present. "My impression is that Jeffrey was quite different."

"Mine accords with yours."

"I don't want to waste your time, Dr. Broch, so let—"

"Hannah. I have told you once and now twice. Spare me excessive politeness, Mayberry. I can be trusted to say what I mean."

"All right. Hannah. Yes, I'm sure you can. I'll be more direct." He lets the manila envelope unroll itself in his grasp, studies it one more time, then holds it toward Hannah. She makes no move to accept.

"Is that Jeff Katy's handwriting?"

After a judicious scowl at the writing she says: "It could be. It seems to be." The envelope has been addressed, in precise felt-tip black print that Mayberry also recognized, to Jeffrey Jay Katy, care of Mayberry's Oakland street number.

"I told him he could use my house as a mail drop. Since he gave up his place in Palo Alto. He's been traveling."

Hannah is opaque.

"Take a look at it. Please."

With rickety fingers she slides the pages into daylight. Her eyelids go down in a weary blink, and stay down for the length of a sigh. Perfunctory glance at the second page, confirming what she dreaded and knew, then flip shuffle tuck, it is all back inside; back in Mayberry's oily hand.

"It arrived yesterday. I opened the envelope because I thought— . . . because I had just heard about the killing. I would have no idea where to look for his family. Or whether there still is any family."

"His family have no need of this."

"You know what it is?"

"I know quite well."

Mayberry sits forward but, still conscious of the doberman, not too suddenly. "Something to do with the H-bomb secret, isn't it?"

"Something." Echoing him with sardonic precision. "No, Mayberry. Rather worse. It *is* that secret. Merely the original working report, for internal use at Los Alamos, on Edward Teller's configuration for the superbomb. Or rather, what we have come rightly or wrongly to *call* Teller's. Merely that."

"And highly classified?"

"Highly classified is an understatement," says Hannah. Moments before so irrepressibly chummy, she is now managing only with careful effort to be civil. Hannah Broch is upset. "This information has always to the best of my knowledge been most zealously protected. And, notwithstanding the many stupid abuses of secrecy, in this case rightly so. But now apparently no longer.

"I will explain something to you, Mayberry. There has never been any such thing as a 'secret' to the A-bomb. The *A-bomb,* you understand. Despite the popular fantasies, despite the electrocutions. There was no great secret: there were only a thousand little secrets. It was chiefly a problem of industrial capability. But with the hydrogen bomb, this vastly more fearsome creature—" Hannah is making discouraging movements with her head—"it is otherwise. There is a genuine secret, yes. The feasibility of the hydrogen bomb depends utterly on a single ingenious idea. That idea is the subject of your report." The word "your" being pungently seasoned with irony.

"Not mine. Jeff Katy's."

"No. Not his either." She has ceased massaging the doberman's neck. Both hands are now clasped tight on her lap and she seems to have shrunken at least one dress size further toward cronehood since this subject came up.

"How in the world did Jeffrey get hold if it?"

"Because, I suspect, someone has made somewhere a

very grievous error. Someone in addition to Jeffrey Katy. Have you read the report?"

"Only a few words. But I couldn't make sense of it if I tried."

"Not all of it, certainly. But some. Broad principles, methods of approach. Shapes. You will be better off, believe me, if you do not take another glance. I advise you to give it over promptly to the interested authorities. Promptly, Mayberry. At once. Or perhaps better still, destroy it."

"Yeah," Mayberry says stupidly. "I thought of doing that. I don't want the thing. I don't want it lying around my house. But I wondered whether I might be destroying evidence involved in a crime." It occurs to him that this may be ambiguous, what with her intimations about espionage, so he specifies: "Jeff Katy's murder." Hannah Broch faces him stolidly. Evidently the untimely death of one precocious young man does not rank for her as a staggering tragedy. "I suppose I'll get on the phone to the New Mexico State Police. Or the FBI."

Hannah nods her approval. "This thing is an evil treasure, spawning always more evil. As though it has its own malign incubus. Not enough that it may one day incinerate a city. A world of cities. In the meantime I have watched it wreck friendships, reputations, careers."

"Whose?"

Now the head again goes gently side to side, though Mayberry doesn't know quite what it is to which she is saying no. "Edward Teller's friendship with Michael Zolta, for one. Eventually, Zolta's entire professional reputation. And the career of my own mentor, Robert Oppenheimer."

"Were you at Los Alamos with those people?"

"No. I never went to Los Alamos. I was not cleared. Later I worked at Livermore, the second weapons laboratory. After it had been founded for the private alchemies of Teller and Zolta, who could neither of them get along with the others. Not even so well as they got along together. Fourteen months I worked at Livermore, beginning in late 1952. Fourteen months and then no more ever. Better for my conscience now if I could say it was fourteen hours."

"You went there to work with Teller and Zolta?"

"Teller I barely knew. A brilliant man but very shy. Zolta? Not to work with him, no. One does not work with Michael Zolta. But yes: it was he who recruited me. With his characteristic mixture of vulnerable charm and blind icy self-certitude. Zolta served as the first director of Livermore. Badly miscast, and through only his own doing. Or chiefly his own: I think Teller knew better than to let *him*self be saddled with such a tedious chore. For two hours each morning Michael sat caged in a large office and dealt with, tried to at least, the mind-fogging details of budget, security, personnel. Then escaped for the rest of the day to a monkish cubicle in another building, where he could sit alone with a small blackboard and chalk. Dreaming wild ingenious dreams that would become other men's nightmares, and growing his muttonchops bushy. He was a little vain about them, his muttonchops. Rather like a Victorian dandy. Perhaps, so I suspected, they were to compensate for the thinning above. A meagerly thatched roof but beautiful shutters. Meanwhile I worked on problems involving directed shock waves. Trigger devices."

"Then you already know about Teller's gimmick."

"Gimmick. Yes, Mayberry. I have been among the privy." She turns her eyes again to the envelope, then away quickly. "I am spared curiosity."

"You mentioned the ruin of his reputation, this Zolta. But I've never heard of him. Not even that he was in disgrace."

"I said his *professional* reputation. By which I mean, among his peers. You are not a physicist. And Zolta was never a character in the newsreels. Not like Oppenheimer. Not like Teller."

"Who was he?"

"Michael Zolta?" Even the name she pronounces with special care, fastidious enunciation verging on mockery, as though the two words alone might reveal something. "A very amazing and difficult Hungarian. Refugee from the Nazis, like so many of these scientists—and from various other more personal demons besides. Probably one of the two or three most gifted mathematicians ever to work in this country. Teller's perfect complement and, while the friendship lasted, his frequent collaborator. Zolta, like Teller, was with the Theoretical Division at Los Alamos. In 1950." Hannah's face takes on a distanced abstractness as she rummages back.

"He was doing calculations for an earlier design concept of the hydrogen bomb, which at that time was still merely his and Teller's pet problem. The early design I speak of was Teller's particular child. Already for years then, since even the midst of the war, both Zolta and Teller had been fiddling with the idea of this much bigger weapon. Putting their heels down against other assignments, which they considered boring. Nagging the administrators to give them a full-scale thermonuclear project. Both of them Magyars, both asputter with the flame of genius, both quite impossibly stubborn. Zolta especially could be like a mule. But together . . . together they did some wonders. Always it was Teller the conceptualist, the creator, not strong on mathematical method but blessed with astounding muscles of scientific intuition; and Zolta the critic, the refiner, the shaper of rarefied ideas into practicable form. The mathematician. Teller proposed, Zolta disposed. A formidable pairing. Eventually they came to be called—though this was not usually to their faces—simply The Magyars. Even by such of us like me, and von Neumann, who were ourselves Hungarian. The epithet carried connotations of an exceptional gypsy intensity, burning dark eyes, you know, and a faint whiff of Asian horse sweat.'' Silently Hannah Broch issues a laugh. ''Mainly it was just our little joke on them, the name. Of course Zolta and Teller were rough horsemen in only the strictest intellectual sense. Teller in fact was a quiet gentleman of most impeccable manner. Zolta was Zolta.

''They had known each other, if it was not from Budapest, then at least since student days in Berlin. And always, for years, their working arrangement had been highly productive. Not to say in every instance harmonious. Then finally in 1950 Zolta laid hold of Teller's favored design, raced the computers with only his marvelous brain and a slide rule, and announced that the thing was worthless. It could not work.

''They were calling this bomb the 'Super.' Its conceptual essence lay in one extraordinary fact: that the secondary fuel component—the actual supply of hydrogen, you understand—could be increased without limit. I say without limit. The bomb could be made infinitely large. Blow up all of Russia, and set the oceans on fire, if we so desired. A single bomb. That was the attraction of Teller's Super. Then Michael Zolta looked up from a flurry of numbers and declared that it wouldn't work. 'No. Sorry. The Super is a fizzle,' he said. Zolta was never any master of tact. But from him even, discounting style, and the long record of fruitful skirmishing between those two men, it did seem very blunt. Seemed in fact like treason. Teller, no doubt, was furious.

"Yet by that time the whole thermonuclear idea was a focus of passionate disagreement. Not just between these two, you understand, but throughout the community of nuclear physicists and even among the military bureaucracy in Washington. Robert Oppenheimer was chairman of the General Advisory Committee of the Atomic Energy Commission, so he stood at the nexus of those groups. He and his committee had already recommended strongly against building the hydrogen bomb—or rather, against any frantic American crash program to build it. A bad idea for diplomatic reasons, they said. On moral grounds, equally bad. Militarily, bad again. A misallocation of R&D resources, because the bomb would have no practical use. It was too large. It dwarfed the targets.

"Furthermore, they said, it was an ungainly creature. It could not be put in an airplane. It required refrigeration, like a pint of ice cream, for the liquid hydrogen. And it was unreliable. There would be an incidence of duds. Altogether it was not, Robert said, in his impeccably condescending manner, *technically sweet*. Even if it might work, it was graceless. And Robert Oppenheimer could never tolerate gracelessness.

"For this flaw of character, and this official advice, he received his martyrhood. Small men with wounded egos whispered to Eisenhower that he was a Soviet agent. Michael Zolta gave testimony against him. Robert, detached and smug as a medieval saint, barely bothered himself to raise his arms against the flying stones. That was all later.

But in the meantime, for a while, there was to be no American hydrogen bomb.

"Then Teller had his idea. March of 1951. Or perhaps one should say, Teller and Zolta.

"You see some people claim that the crucial suggestion came from Michael Zolta. Zolta himself has so claimed. Teller's own version discreetly contradicts that claim—though he has been generous in his efforts to see that credit be broadly shared for the overall thermonuclear enterprise. Credit or, if you will, blame. Back in the middle fifties Teller published a little essay in *Science;* it was called, I believe, 'The Work of Many People.' Obviously intended to dispel the simplistic and no doubt embarrassing public notion of him as 'Father of the H-bomb.' Zolta specifically was held up for praise. Generally worded praise. But the idea for the configuration itself, according to Teller, that was his own. And his only.

"Of course he discussed it with Zolta. He discussed it with Freddy de Hoffmann, another mathematician still younger by quite a few years, who functioned as Teller's personal assistant. De Hoffmann did some computations, showing that this new design principle would succeed where the earlier version was faulty. Ignition would be instantaneous and complete, for any amount of hydrogen. It would even be elegant. Then de Hoffmann wrote a report. The loyal acolyte, and meaning no slight toward Zolta, he signed only Teller's name to it. By this circumstance the design secret became known—and who can say unjustly?—as the Teller configuration."

"And that's what I have here," Mayberry says.

"It was very deeply buried." With the sun lowering, Hannah seems to be taking a chill. "It has risen from the grave."

"And this new design was so clever, or so elegant, or whatever, that the technical resistance to an H-bomb program collapsed. And with that collapse the other objections—the diplomatic and moral ones—they were swept away on a hot wind of enthusiasm. Is that what happened?"

"It was sweet," Hannah says. "Yes. They all agreed." She pauses sadly. "Even Oppenheimer."

"Oppenheimer," Mayberry prompts.

She brings her eyes out of a far corner, the irises lit like votive candles.

"Oppenheimer," she repeats. "No. You must come back again if you would dare me to talk about him. You must come to tea, and resign yourself to a lost afternoon, and the dreary prospect of an old woman's nostalgia. In those days, Mayberry, I was in love with Robert Oppenheimer. More than a little."

As Mayberry lets himself out, the shadow of afternoon has crossed the parlor to lap at her ankles. Her hand is working gently again behind the doberman's ears. It might be a seeing-eye dog.

THREE

But still for a little longer Mayberry is permitted to think about medicine.

Having closely inspected the doorjambs to see whether his house might have been broken into and searched, also familiar patterns of shelf dust and paths in carpet pile, he comes up off his knees chiding himself for melodrama, a disease he had hoped was in remission. Then drives wildly off for Merritt Hospital, and barely in time is scrubbed and on call in the Emergency Room. Twelve hours later one of the duty doctors—a nervous brainy brunette, just appealingly emaciated, her eye sockets bruised with exhaustion—suggests they go up to Rockridge for breakfast. She is six or eight years younger than Mayberry, but a resident. She may be offering, and he is keen to the prospect of unwrapping her from her officious whites; but it isn't a sure thing; and Mayberry feels he can badly afford to waste even another twenty minutes of his life. Besides the dog will be waiting with full bladder. She grinds her heel on his demurral and he is home by 6:30 A.M. The first thing he sees is that his kitchen door has been turned into kindling, as though someone has driven a backhoe in from the patio.

The linoleum is strewn with shattered glass and a disgusting mixture of condiments, the cupboards hang open, the wet garbage has been dumped intentionally and spread like compost. The refrigerator, down on its side, looks especially alarming that way, like a terminal horse. Potpies are thawing in far corners. The stove top is horribly grimy, but that happens to be how he left it. The dog's water has been spilled, and it now occurs to Mayberry to grow very worried. The dog hasn't appeared.

The living room is worse. All of his books, the emptied drawers of the desk, his entire collection of four Rubenstein albums, records and jackets separately, have been thrown in a pile as though for burning. Old ballpoints and unopened power bills lay everywhere underfoot. A framed photograph of Mayberry's stepfather has been busted over a knee and the medical notes from three fat precious ring binders, no not the binders, yes the binders are sprung loose and scattered like sycamore leaves. The binders are almost enough to divert Mayberry's concern until he sees the blood. A light pattern of spoor on several books, then a sickening glistening smear.

Near the front wall is the dog's body. Great bulk of auburn fur relaxed in an awkward position that no living creature could find relaxing. But before Mayberry can get his own legs moving he hears that particular unmistakable snark: of a pistol hammer being cocked back.

The man is seated placidly at the end of the sofa. He wears a huckleberry-blue corduroy sport coat with all the tread worn off the elbows and a pair of robin's-egg doubleknits; also a jaunty vinyl string tie. His tortoise-shell frames are patched at the bridge of the nose with adhesive tape. The tape is dirty. The man is old. He looks like a shyster insurance salesman from Helena, Montana. His thin sandy hair has been grown long on the right side in a specious attempt to cover the dome; his hands have lately regained the freckles that once, probably fifty years earlier, disappeared from his face. He seems the patient, self-contained sort of fellow who, even in a room full of chattering people, would sit placidly silent at the end of the sofa. He hasn't moved since Mayberry entered the house, except now to raise the .38. He is the oldest man who has ever leveled a gun at Mayberry's sternum, though not too old to do it convincingly.

Stretched at his feet is another body, a human one, neatly intact but for the lack of a face.

Mayberry looks again. No face. A dangling jaw upholstered in black beard streaked with gray; a lonesome ear, in the lobe of which glints goldenly a small button earring; and a war zone of violently reorganized gristle and meat. Mayberry has seen something like it only once before, and not in the ER: above the neck of a black Spec-4 from Cleveland whose asshole bootlick lieutenant, outside Khe Sanh, ordered him down to inspect a booby-trapped tunnel. Mayberry was still watching when the squad pulled the Cleveland kid's body out by its feet. This number in his living room is wearing Mexican sandals.

"First of all, one thing," says the insurance agent. "I did not kill the dog. I tell you that for your own good and my convenience. Better for both of us if you deal with me coolheaded. I did not kill the pooch. I got here after. I'm not trying to sound chummy, it's nothing to me, but there you are. This yahoo killed the dog." He kicks hard but without anger at the thigh of the corpse, then rests his foot absently on the dead man's buttocks, where a chamois patch has been sewn into the faded jeans. "Him and another. The other is gone. And I want that one more even than you do."

Mayberry says, "Are you finished?" and with the stranger momentarily stuck for an answer, he crosses to squat over the dog's body.

Most of the blood on the carpet seems to have come from its mouth. The superciliary ridge has been crushed down over one eye, by a club or perhaps a rifle butt, and the upper jaw is fractured. The lower dislocated. Teeth chipped, teeth awry, teeth missing. Obviously the animal has died fighting. But then also, a clean bullet wound in the neck. Mayberry blinks once slowly and stretches his eyes wide. His fingers return to the neck wound, begin spreading sticky hair back from the hole, and at that point the stranger says:

"Sit down in the chair." The gun, Mayberry notices now, is still aimed. "Sit down in the chair." So he does.

"I'm ready to start hearing explanations."

"No doubt," says the man. "All right. My name is Albert Varvara. I'm a security officer for Rockwell International. I been waiting about an hour. I got some information for you about this mess, and I'll get some in return. But not here. I'm gonna stroll out your back door and across the alley to Lakeshore. You come around in your car. Pick me up there." As a testament of boundless good will, an afterthought, he lowers the .38.

"What if I don't?"

"What if you don't. Nothing. I won't come back. Stay here and clean house and think up a story for the police."

By pressing with both palms on his knees, elbows jacked wide, Albert Varvara levers himself up off the sofa.

Five minutes later, at the curb before Ray's Olde-Fashioned Yogurt Shoppe on Lakeshore, Mayberry swings open the passenger door of the Civic. Varvara's holster gapes indiscreetly from behind a huckleberry lapel as he struggles in but the gun itself is away, and he is now punctuating his instructions with a medicated toothpick.

"Bay Bridge. Then to the airport."

"Show me some identification."

Varvara digs wearily to produce a weary wallet. The Rockwell card is seasoned with enough pocket sweat to be genuine, or at least old; the Colorado driver's license expired four months earlier, on what it asserts to have been Albert Varvara's sixty-third birthday. Steering with his knees, glancing up occasionally, jabbing at the accelerator like Spike Jones at a top-hat cymbal, Mayberry forces them into flow on the MacArthur Freeway. The shock has burned off, some of the initial grief, and Mayberry is feeling irascible. Varvara has begun craning backward to scout for speeding cement trucks. Mayberry drops the wallet in his lap.

"Your driver's license is no good."

"I been busy. Watchit. All right. Now." He sits around forward. "What were they looking for, Mayberry?"

"I'm sure you already know."

"Tell me anyway."

"Military secrets. Classified blueprints for the doomsday machine. I keep a lot of that shit around the house."

"Good." Varvara seems genuinely pleased. "You're mad enough, we can skip some of the ballroom dancing. Okay. The Teller report." He untangles and then fastens the shoulder harness. "One copy got into the mail last week from Los Alamos. I'm not sure yet just how, but I know it did. I know it came to you. You tell me why."

"I let Jeff Katy take mail at my place," says Mayberry. "Why he wanted the Teller thing, how he got it—I have no idea. I haven't seen him in six months."

"That's interesting. Who said anything about Jeffrey Katy?"

"The envelope did, Varvara. Come on. It was addressed to him. The radio did, last week when he was killed. Suddenly Jeffrey is a big item again. But I only know him casually. Knew him. I'm not involved."

"You got a man's brains on your kitchen ceiling, Mayberry. Take my word, you're involved."

For five seconds or more that drag on like a minute, his face turned toward Varvara, Mayberry gradually squashes down hard on the gas; looks ahead then in time to wipe the soot off the rear license plate of a Cordoba as he swings into a narrowing gap in a faster lane. Immediately again his attention begins to stray. Traffic onto the bridge is heavy and sluggish with commuters waking up as they drive.

"He didn't find what he came for. The creep with the earring," Varvara says. "I did a little hunting, not stupid hunting like his, and I didn't find it either. Maybe you had time to hide it somewhere off the premises. Maybe you had advance plans for unloading it. Maybe even you're as innocent as you pretend. I got an open mind. But where's the report, Mayberry?"

After small deliberation Mayberry says: "No. Not until I know precisely what's going on."

"That's easy. What's going on is I been mild so far because I figured maybe it works better with you. All right? What's going on is a major violation of the Atomic Energy Act. You can talk to me like a decent guy and you can be subpoenaed. Also very possibly you can be indicted. Even if they don't get a conviction your acquittal still costs you a tall—" But this hypothetical line is interrupted when Mayberry lurches them back to the middle lane in front of a Greyhound and kicks at the brake. While the bus's horn howls like eleven elephants in a circus-train fire, Varvara seems to be holding his breath. He straight-arms the glove compartment as though expecting it to leap at him.

"I take poorly to threats when I'm in a mood," Mayberry explains.

"I see that."

"So who's the dead guy in my house?"

"All right all right." Albert Varvara exhales. "We'll start with my information." Clear now to Mayberry that this is a nervous old man, a December soldier, with a pension approaching and a low tolerance for freeway thrills. "You watch the road."

"I told you already I work for Rockwell. We operate a plutonium plant outside Denver. Called Rocky Flats. If you read the right magazines you think you know all about it. No reactors there. No weapon assembly. The metal comes in from other plants, we purify, pour ingots, and machine them into components. Components go out. Rocky Flats is really just a standard metallurgy factory, where the metal happens to be plutonium. The components," says Varvara with utter sincere blandness, "just happen to be core assemblies for thermonuclear weapons. All this is public.

"Rockwell has only had the contract since 1975. Before that it was run by Dow, and Dow was sloppy as sin.

Plutonium fires every couple months, decrepit safety equipment that fell apart while you were using it, short-cutting on health physics for technicians. Radioactive dust blowing toward Denver. Two-headed snakes in the parking lot. Tritium in the city water. It was a mess.

"Now Dow is out, Rockwell is in, but the Rocky Flats operation still smells like shit to a lot of people. My job, at least most of it these days, is to cope with those people.

"Mainly they are the same crowd that gathers at a Harrisburg or a Seabrook. Political Woodstockers. Casual thrill seekers, bored college kids who've heard secondhand what an ass-kickin' good time you all had in the sixties. Aging granola eaters who think they could run their Sony turntables off solar. Solar." Varvara wrinkles his nose derisively. "Some are a little more serious. Ban-the-Bomb types, Quakers and priests and other radical pacifists, the kind who bury a toy casket on the courthouse lawn and take a night in the county slam instead of a fine. All these different factions overlap pretty congenially. Except for a few cantankerous loonies.

"The loonies. You find some at the edges of any movement, I know that. Wiseguys with big ideas and permanent personality damage. Full-time societal misfits. Restless types who don't like the pussyfoot tactics. All right. One of the loonies, in my case, is a fellow named Chester Armatrading." Mayberry's stomach kicks like a fetus, but he remains silent. "More on Chester in a minute.

"Last summer we had big demonstrations, arrests, kids trying to climb in over chain-link fences. Armatrading drew a week with a year suspended, by the way, for breaking a cop's nose with a pair of heavy wire cutters. This winter they set up a tepee on one of our railroad spurs, and camped there for two months. A tepee, Mayberry. At first they were very cool, took down the tent and moved it whenever our flatcars needed to pass, put it right back afterward. Fine. We tried to stay flexible. Then some of them decided they wouldn't move. These are still the peaceful ones now, the ones who sit down in front of a bulldozer and close their eyes and hum. More arrests. Daniel Ellsberg was pulled in with this group. Armatrading wasn't, he was nowhere to be seen, and that itself made me uncomfortable.

"Just now things are quiet. The silly season hasn't got going. Or maybe it's that there's blood in the water back at Three Mile Island. I don't know. But Rocky Flats is due to see another large demonstration on Labor Day. We have their flyers. 'A massive national demonstration,' is the come-on. We're not pissing our pants, but we have to look ahead to these things.

"Now I'll tell you the truth, I been with Rockwell a long time, but I am no very big dog. I don't run the Security Division. I'm a glorified watchman who spends half his time as a gumshoe. And one of my small personal heartaches between now and Labor Day, I guarantee you it ain't my own choosing, is just to keep up on this Chester Armatrading. I say small and I say just, I mean it was like that until a week ago. We only wanted to know where he was, what he was up to. I'll tell you why."

But that isn't necessary. There can only be one Chester Armatrading, and Mayberry knows from the wire cutters that he is unchanged. Mayberry himself hasn't seen him since the afternoon in 1972 when Armatrading threw a photographer from the Washington *Post* through the plate-glass front window of a delicatessen on Dupont Circle. It was Armatrading's version of press relations, for whatever dignified protest Mayberry and the others had been currently choreographing. Long before that Armatrading was the first Beret of Mayberry's acquaintance to sell off his AR-15 in favor of an old Model 12 Winchester, a pump-action twelve-gauge shotgun, his preferred weapon for walking point in close jungle. Every Regular Army grunt in Vietnam was ready to mortgage one testicle for the chance to shitcan his M-16 and buy a Special Forces rifle, but Armatrading sold his own to a Chinese pimp in Saigon, and that was perhaps the first hint Mayberry had of Chester Armatrading's exceptional, ingenious talent for despicability. Mayberry is surprised, disappointed too in an abstract but vaguely portentous way, to learn that Armatrading has survived the decade. And is at large.

"On paper Armatrading is just a thug," says Varvara. "I know he rides a big Harley hog and carries a maul handle in the saddlebag. I know he smiles a lot. Somebody told me he is missing his two front teeth, but I found out he got those fixed last winter in Denver. I've talked to a lot of people about this guy and I keep hearing three things. First he is wacko. Unpredictable. Maybe insane. Second, deep down in his gut he is a mean bastard. Third, he has some brains. Not a lot, just some. He isn't Carl Sagan but he's much smarter than he looks, is the point. Thug or whatever, I can't afford to ignore him.

"He has a bad-paper discharge from the Special Forces and a record of small-time mayhem. His taste in trouble seems to run to the exotic. No bar brawls. One time in Monterey a pair of hippies put a scratch on his bike, he followed them down the coast on Highway 1, stopped them and ordered them out on the shoulder. They thought he was going to rape the girl. He tipped their minibus over the cliff with its own jack and went on. Another time he tried to walk in the Chicago Saint Paddy's parade wearing his Green Beret uniform and carrying a Viet Cong flag. Started a huge fight, of course. That sort of thing. Also he has a sizable dossier with the FBI.

"They liked him a lot in the earlier seventies, the Bureau. He was showing up at the fringe of various radical anti-war groups, including the Vietnam Veterans Against the War." Mayberry never at the time considered the VVAW very radical, at least not until the weirdness near the end, but he doesn't interrupt. "Nobody took Armatrading serious as a Political. Not then and not now. He isn't that coherent. But he was there, according to the Bureau's informers, in the councils. Always pushing, always a little ringy. Let's kidnap Kissinger. Let's assassinate the head of the Veterans Administration. Let's crash Tricia Nixon's wedding and moon the old man. Never quite serious and never quite not. They must have hated his guts. Let's seize the Statue of Liberty. Then in '72 a dozen Vets Against *did* seize the Statue, for forty hours of gaudy media. Maybe you remember." Mayberry is going cross-eyed, he remembers well, it was for him the second-last straw. "But Armatrading was in Bridgeport that day, trying to buy dynamite from the Mafia. They reported him to the Connecticut State Police, but there was nothing indictable.

"None of this much concerns me, except as part of a pattern. For a few years in there, after the war protests ended, his record goes blank. Maybe he was trying to hook up with the Hell's Angels. Getting rejected as antisocial. I don't know. Then in the summer of '76 something called Clamshell Alliance got organized, up in New Hampshire, and immediately they stormed the gates of the

Seabrook reactor. Almost two hundred arrested. Mostly for criminal trespass. One guy is busted for standing around with a pump shotgun under his coat. You can guess who.

"But lucky for Chester, the Clamshellers had a shark liberal lawyer. Or he was looking at five years.

"And now he's a regular on the anti-nuke circuit. Back at Seabrook in '77, jailed again, this time just for trespass and resisting. Then Diablo Canyon out here. Then climbing a fence at the Shoreham reactor on Long Island. Thirty-nine other fence climbers got picked up that day, but Armatrading was the only one carrying lock tools and a ball-peen hammer. Might interest you to know he killed a guard dog with the hammer.

"Our problems at Rocky didn't begin until last year. We were a quiet operation—no conspicuous new construction, no power-rate hikes or bond levies. Low profile. Minding our own little business for the Feds. No one outside Denver knew or cared much about that crap Dow had been pulling. Now it's different. Now we're a major target. Rocky Flats makes the bombs, Rocky Flats and the war machine, shut down Rocky Flats. Armatrading and others like him. Almost like him. He's been in the vicinity, off and on, for a year. Maybe he likes the climate. Maybe he's found a good dentist. Christ."

Varvara is tunneling fiercely into the pocket of his double-knits. What will this be, Mayberry wonders—a piece of evidence, a rumpled mug shot of Armatrading, an empty twelve-gauge shell? A pair of Chester's front teeth? Varvara hands him three quarters for the bridge toll.

"But you say he's gone now. Not in the last batch of arrests."

"Was gone," says Varvara. "Lately I don't know.

That's what bothers me. A month ago I had him traced to Albuquerque. Fine, there's trouble he could raise there, no skin off me. Sandia Corporation has a plant in Albuquerque, making the non-nuclear components, simple hardware, and anyway Sandia is not Rockwell. Then two weeks ago I get a report he's in Santa Fe. Drinking beer at a space games arcade three nights running, with a younger guy. A presentable kid, neat-looking, college type. This kid even wears a white shirt. Not Armatrading's usual style in beer buddies." Varvara leans back deeply into his seat. "The kid, unless I'm wrong, was Jeffrey Katy."

FOUR

"The ultimate in proliferation," says Mayberry. "Chester Armatrading gets the hydrogen bomb."

"This isn't funny, Mayberry. There are things he could do with that report. Straight around, stop at the South Terminal, opposite Qantas. Don't move till I get back."

Mayberry obeys. The impulse to drive off, leaving the airport, escaping Varvara, though strong is less strong than the impulse to hear more. But what next? A pair of dark parrot-nosed young men looking foreign and petroleum-affluent in natty brown leather trench coats float up slowly behind, peer in Mayberry's back window, stroll around to stare insolently through the windshield. Mayberry would be feeling trigger-happy if he had a trigger. Evidently the pair are just assuring themselves that his Civic is not a taxi; they load a colossal pile of Whip de Roma luggage into the first open cab and depart. After ten minutes Varvara shuffles out bearing two Styrofoam cups. One he holds toward Mayberry.

"Cream no sugar. I should have asked. Now circle back toward Oakland by the San Mateo Bridge."

"No thanks." The car jackrabbits away just as Varvara is peeking under his lid. "Things like what?"

"Like sell it. Ouch. Yow. Barter it. For guns and conventional explosives. To a marginal nuclear nation that wants to upgrade its program. Wants to turn a modest stockpile of smallish fission bombs into one or two huge thermonuclears. Understand, Mayberry, that's a difficult step. And the Teller report is extremely useful to any country hoping to make it."

"Who specifically?"

"Nobody specifically. I'm just speculating. The logical candidates would be India, Israel, maybe Pakistan. Maybe South Africa. They all have fission weapons, or close to it, or we think they might. But none of them has been able to build the big one. That report could buy Armatrading a lot of high-caliber mischief." Varvara is daubing coffee from his crotch with a paper napkin. "You got any idea what sort of poisonous cesspit is left behind if even just a suitcase of gelignite blew off, inside the right building, at Rocky Flats? Judas. Forget about Colorado for eight hundred years, Mayberry. If there's a breeze that day forget about Kansas and Nebraska. Anyway that's not the possibility I worry about most. It's too straightforward. Too mercantile. Doesn't have Armatrading's sort of crazy flourish. More likely I'm guessing he might *give* it away. Leaflet it."

"Leaflet it?" Then again Mayberry, quietly and more tentative, as though testing by nose an aging remnant of cottage cheese: "Leaflet it?"

"Sure," says Varvara. "Run off a quick ten thousand,

stamp in ten thousand staples, and hand out a copy of Teller's report to every man woman child and foreign intelligence stringer who happens to show up at Rocky on Labor Day."

"What does that accomplish?"

"Not a damn thing. As you and I can plainly see and Armatrading probably doesn't care. Disorder. Media attention. The Quakers and those others might go for it, thinking it makes some sort of point about government secrecy. Don't ask me what. It's dramatic. It gets them on Cronkite that night. And it leaves a lot of people in the Department of Energy looking like chimpanzees. More so than now. As a matter of fact, for his purposes, or what pass for purposes, it's maybe the smartest thing Armatrading could do with that frigging report. If he's got it. Or gets it. Which is why I suspect he'll do something else."

"How," Mayberry asks disingenuously, "did Jeff Katy get tangled with Armatrading?" And already knowing what must be the answer probably better than does Varvara: Paul Katy, the missing link.

Mayberry is passingly visited with a vision of Paul Katy and Armatrading and himself, piling sandbags and fighting tedium and Viet Cong and each other, at the scrubby little A Camp they called Dak To, circa 1966. The elder Katy's condescending but enthusiastic friendship for such a psychopathic baboon as Chester Armatrading had been a rare point of friction between him and Mayberry. Even Paul with all his faults and cruelties should have been able to recognize that Armatrading's vicious clodhood was of the unmitigated and irredeemable sort. Even Mayberry, even then, was willing to say so and that was one of the reasons—but only one—why Armatrading had always harbored such a blazing hatred for Mayberry. He has put the question now chiefly to see how far Varvara's research has led him.

"*If* he was," says Varvara. "I don't know. Not many people are aware that the Teller thing exists. Let alone its significance. A Jeffrey Katy would know about it. But not Armatrading. Not without a little bird. Maybe Ellsberg or someone like that. My information says the ACLU asked Katy to go down there. They had heard about this report being wrongly catalogued for public access. Which was exactly the little fuckup that started everything. He should find it, copy it legally, bring them the copy. Nothing about mailing out extras. Nothing about getting offed. The ACLU is fighting a federal case in Milwaukee over nuclear secrets. You heard about that?"

"I don't read newspapers, Varvara. No time."

"What exactly is it you do for a living?"

"I don't. I go to school."

Lips steadied on the rim of the Styrofoam, Varvara slides into a tiny malicious smile. "Continuing Education?" Mayberry does look his age.

"Medical school. As you well know, having searched my house. A late idea, but not the worst one I ever had."

Now Varvara allows himself to sound genuinely deferential: "Is it true what they say about bacon?"

"What do they say?"

"Cancer."

"It's true, Varvara, but don't let it bother you. You're too old to catch cancer from bacon. You don't have time. How many years did you say you had guarded plutonium?"

"Good. Never you mind. So, a small lefty magazine called *The Progressive*. They wanted to publish an article describing the H-bomb ignition mechanism. Don't ask me why. Making some point about government secrecy again, is what they claim. The Department of Energy got an injunction. The article is now locked away in a bank vault. It was just an amateur paste job anyway. Free-lance writer named Howard Morland, former Air Force jockey with a mental discharge, former dropout and bum.

"Morland was just another gypsy on the same anti-nuke circuit with Armatrading. Then one day he got hit by lightning and decided to make himself an expert on the H-bomb. The most classified technical details. Went to Oak Ridge, went to Los Alamos, came to Rocky Flats—covering all the stops, sitting through all the canned public info programs and then playing dumb but asking good questions. Teasing out threads from gullible people who should have known better. He has a year of college physics, this Morland. Definitely he is no scientific wonderboy like Jeffrey Katy. But he spun all the threads back together and evidently he hit it right. Or if not exactly right, close enough to cause large trouble.

"Morland swears he got it all from interviews, brochures, encyclopedia articles, other unclassified sources. Fine, says the government, we don't care if you got it from tea leaves at Madame Lola's, it's still a very big secret, and you'll shut up. Prior restraint against publishing the article, and everyone started screaming about censorship, fascism, the First Amendment. *The Progressive* collected a bale of affidavits from hot-dog physicists, liberals of course, arguing how you can find most of the same information at your corner library. Which is just bullshit, between you and me. But the affidavits themselves were seized and classified, wham, into the same vault. Not even Morland is allowed to see them. Only the lawyers. Meanwhile the government is starting to look like a kid with a squirt gun at the Chicago fire.

"The ACLU invited themselves in to help the magazine. Then I guess somebody tipped them about the Teller report, the original granddaddy horse's-mouth version. That it was out on the open shelves at Los Alamos. They sent Jeff Katy down to check. Why Katy? He had got all that press last year for his own kitchen-model nuke, he knew what he was looking for, probably Morland had already made contact with him. It doesn't matter. So Jeff Katy went to Los Alamos, on instructions to walk out with a perfectly legal copy of what the government claimed was the most secret of all H-bomb secrets. Which was supposed to prove that the classification officers at Energy, howling for suppression of the Morland article, were a bunch of hysterical geeks. That's the current story in retail form. I don't happen to believe it."

"Why not?" says Mayberry.

"First because it's being told. Second because it doesn't account for Katy being shot. And also because I happen to know that the ACLU never got what they paid for. Instead Katy mails a copy to you."

"To himself, care of me."

"Right. Whatever. That makes me think Jeffrey Katy had a new idea. Or a better offer. That he was trying to pull some sort of scam. Some sort. He hooks up with Armatrading, maybe. He goes to the library and dies. Beyond that I got nothing. It's a terrific annoyance to me, frankly."

Varvara remembers his tub of coffee, gulps deeply at it, scowls with masochistic satisfaction. "Ack. Now you. I been very generous. Let's hear what you know about this kid Katy. How come such an innocent hard-working guy as you got to be the mail drop?"

"Very little. Really," says Mayberry. "I knew his brother well, but years ago. From the brother I knew something about his family: the mother's inherited bucks, the divorce, the father's big reputation as a Caltech economist. Father's career had gone into the bag somewhere along the way, thanks to booze and the wife's money, I think. There was only the two sons. When I finally got here for medical school Jeff was just finishing as an undergraduate at Stanford, and I saw him a few times. Nice kid. Interested in what he was doing, the physics, and healthier in a lot of ways than his crazy wild brother. Also very bright. Very very bright. Cocky, but no more so than I had been at twenty. And with more justification. We had beers once or twice. Talked some about the lost brother, then quickly discovered we didn't have much else to say to each other. But I liked him. I got very busy, he did the A-bomb thing and then graduated. I haven't seen him but once since he hit the headlines. Couple times this past winter he came by the house, while I was working, picked up mail. Left a polite note."

Suddenly Varvara has conjured out a little drugstore ring pad and is scratching with a stub of pencil. His hands tremble at this chore, Mayberry notices, though they were steady enough with the revolver. He holds the half-empty cup clamped in his teeth. It covers his nose like a feedbag.

"What's the brother's name?"

"Paul. Save it, Varvara. I can't tell you enough to be worth writing down."

"My memory has turned to shit. For facts. Faces, I'm

still okay." Mayberry's name has become a page heading. Below it Varvara scribbles the words "Katy's brother," then an arrow, then the word "Paul," then a forceful dash that as far as Mayberry can tell means nothing whatsoever.

"How did you know his brother?"

"Vietnam."

"When?"

"Early. Sixty-four to '66."

"Not Special Forces."

Mayberry locks his molars. After a moment Varvara's fading red eyebrows come up, followed closely by the rest of his face. "Hello?"

"Yes," says Mayberry, and sighs. He glances at his watch. He has been awake since seven the previous morning and must be back on duty again this afternoon at five, but now forlornly he sees his precious midday sleep receding into unlikelihood like a missed Pullman leaving Bismarck at midnight.

"No shit. With Katy's brother?"

"Sure. Paul and I and a handful of other crazyass American kids. Running a band of three hundred crazyass Montagnards, in the high border jungle west of Kontum."

"And Armatrading?"

"And a weaponry sergeant named Chester Armatrading."

"Christ. Where is Paul Katy now?"

"Dead. Car crash in '66."

"When did you get out?" Varvara can't write this fast: he has miraculously regained confidence in his memory.

"Sixty-eight." Adding pointedly: "Right after Tet."

"Then what?"

"Back to college. Just as it went out of fashion. Everything peaches at first. But before long there was this very sour taste in my mouth. Delayed re-entry symptoms, I suppose. Or withdrawal symptoms, maybe more accurate. From the addiction."

"Drugs?" says Varvara. "You came back with a habit?"

"Adrenaline," says Mayberry. "I had a little warning as my attitude began to curdle. After one class I grabbed an assistant professor by his jacket lapels, slammed him against a wall and had words, because he had mocked a dumb question of mine during the session. That wasn't good. Then suddenly one morning I had thrown a toaster across the kitchen, kicked it, screamed at it and tossed the thing out a second-floor window. Because my muffin refused to stay down. About that time I got political. Stumbled around for the next couple years in the thick of the children's crusade, jabbing at ideological doors with my chin."

"Viet Vets Against the War?"

"Yes. All that stuff. But the VVAW came later. Not until 1970, '71. Before that it was the New Mobilization to End the War. In October of '69 I organized marshals for the great Mobe march in Washington. I drew coordinate maps of the Mall, briefed people who briefed other people, explained how to treat for tear gas and how to take a stick over the head. Rushed around between meetings looking crack and handing out armbands. Next day I stood on the back of a truck and hollered gentle instructions through a battery megaphone to a quarter million people. Loved every minute. Later I understood what that was all about: getting my battlefield commission in the Movement." He shows Varvara an embarrassed grin that is actually more of a wince. "The Movement was my methadone." Belatedly Mayberry fears that this outpouring has just refuted what it was meant to prove: the death of the past. "Anyway that's where I met Ray Wimmert, John Kerry, Shelly Sanzone and a few others, and got in with the anti-war vets."

Varvara by what seems powerful self-control has refrained from rubbing together his palms. "Are you still in touch with any of those people?"

"No. None. Determinedly not. Already in '72, around the time of the Republican convention, it was starting to get too flaky for my taste. Wimmert, our great charismatic chieftain, turned out to be a pathological liar. Had never done a tour in Vietnam, among other things. Then the Statue of Liberty gambit. That seemed to me large silliness, and counterproductive. But at least it was peaceable. Then another bunch of our guys got themselves indicted down in Florida, for stockpiling M-1s and walkie-talkies and slingshots, all sorts of ridiculous crap. Planning an action against the Republicans at Miami, evidently. What is this? I asked myself. Have I got time in my life for felonious street theater? No. The answer was no, so I got out. Stayed out. Spent a couple fuzzy years in New Orleans, watching the fall of Saigon on TV and not giving much of a damn either way."

By this point, certain switches having flipped, Mayberry can barely stop himself: "I've changed a lot since then. Right now I care about nothing except getting that medical degree. Before anything else diverts me. I want the paper, the one that says Mayberry is a doctor. After that maybe I'll get crazy again. But I want the paper, understand? I was very lucky to get into this med school, any med school, as a white male over thirty. I'm older than all of my classmates and dumber than maybe a third of them. I'm getting by on systems of self-discipline that still aren't habitual for me, and a fear of failure that is. If I fuck up this time, if I fuck up this time," Mayberry repeats himself with a tightening grip on the steering wheel, "the word is out on Mayberry. So there will be no fuckup. I'm going to finish it. The dull way. One foot in front of th—"

"Relax, Mayberry. I haven't even asked."

"I know. I just see it on your forehead like a drive-in movie."

"All I want is for you to make a few calls."

"No."

"Old war buddies. 'Hey, anybody heard from Chester? Where can I find him?' Easy."

"No."

Without vehemence Varvara throws his Styrofoam cup out the window. "All right, sure. Getting a license to cut hemorrhoids is important to you. Fine. So you'll do that. But meanwhile this little sucker on my hands is merely a life or death operation of huge goddamn international consequence. Possibly."

"Absolutely not."

"It's easy. For you of all people."

"I told you, Varvara. I'm rehabilitated. I'm doing medicine and I like it. I don't need to go near that other stuff. I don't need a SWAT-team call once a month to keep me down off the chandelier."

"Just calls, Mayberry. Easy. Nothing."

"No."

"What if it was Armatrading who broke into your house and killed your dog?"

"Don't try it. Don't be slimy with me."

"What if he killed Katy's little brother?"

"Where do you want to be dropped?"

"Anywhere. I'm just going ba—"

Mayberry has the car across two lanes to the curb. The horns are still yammering as he reaches over Varvara and flicks the door handle.

"Difficult. It could be difficult. It could be dangerous," says Varvara, smiling from the gutter.

Mayberry makes a U-turn without waiting for gaps.

FIVE

"Give me a sergeant," he tells the woman. "Any sergeant. No, wait. A sergeant in Homicide." She has scarcely gotten her nasal drone into rhythm when he interrupts: "Don't bother to ask that because I'm not going to tell you. I'll tell the sergeant."

Eventually a wet basso voice, making a noise like the forceful rearrangement of phlegm:

"Buski."

"Buski. My name is Mayberry. I have a dead hippie on my living-room floor. Most of him. The rest on my kitchen ceiling. This isn't a confession, it's a complaint. I want you to clean him up and haul him away. You might also find out who did it, and trashed my house in the process. I'll give you more information when you get here." Mayberry pronounces his address distinctly, then again. "Try and make it this morning."

"Wait a minute." Sergeant Buski sounds confused but bellicose, growling on principle, like a woken rhino.

"You slow down. Now. From the beginning. What's your name?"

"Mayberry."

"First name."

Mayberry hangs up.

The patrol car arrives in six minutes. Buski takes twenty, but the pace of his movements when he does appear suggests that twenty minutes from his desk chair to anywhere farther away than the station cafeteria probably constitutes reasonable haste. The third vehicle is a Criminalistics van, disgorging two uniformed technicians who carry lab kits and clipboards and cameras. They scamper ahead while Buski waddles.

He is a great pear-shaped endomorph with crocodilian eyelids, a dull smile, and a lower lip hanging full as a boiled bratwurst. Slight breathless snorts escape from his nostrils with the effort of walking, and he sways windward and lee for balance, as though under tow in a breezy Macy's parade. His hands are tucked away in his pockets. From a clip on his belt dangles a small electronic bleeper, like a remora attached to a whale. He drifts to the busy end of the living room, bumps a patrolman aside, and stares down with idle dismay at the faceless body. Blinks against the camera's flash.

Meanwhile he catches his breath from the exercise. One hand appears holding a white plastic bottle, several antacid mints fall into his dimpled palm, go from there to his mouth. A muffled but vehement crunch. Buski then turns on his moorings. Mayberry is waiting, seated. Another patrolman stands stiffly by, conscientious not to lean against clues. The scene of the crime has been, in the jargon, secured; but Mayberry has no inkling from whom or what.

"Mayberry."

"Yeah."

Buski regards him with roughly the same look he has given the corpse. "Smart ass." He takes himself on a tour of the kitchen, and Mayberry can hear glass shards popping underfoot. From around the wall:

"Who was he, Mayberry?"

"I don't know."

"What did he do to you?"

"Nothing. I never met him. He may be the one who smashed the place up, but I'm not sure."

"Then why do it?"

"Cut the crap, Buski. I told you, I found him like this. I told you that on the phone."

"Oh yeah. Slipped my mind. So how did he end up in your house?"

"He came in, and someone killed him, and so he couldn't leave."

The popping stops. Buski with hands pocketed orbits back into the living room. "*Why* did he end up in your house, smart ass?"

"I don't know."

"What *do* you know?"

"The phone number of the Oakland PD. We pay them to solve homicides. Also that I've been up all night and need sleep. I have just seven hours before I'm due back at work."

Buski, staring down at the dog's body, is silent; might as well be gazing stuporously at a magazine in a barbershop. Finally he says: "Your mutt or his?"

"Mine."

"Nice set of choppers. Christ. We should look for a guy with a limp?" Mayberry isn't amused. No one so far has touched the animal and Buski shows no interest in being the first.

Connoisseur of rubble, he now strolls to the bedroom. In addition to stripped-away sheets, slashed mattress, more scattered books, and a demolished Tourister suitcase, the linings have been wantonly torn out of two good tweed jackets. "Where are you when all this is happening?" From the sound, it seems Sergeant Buski is shouting into a closet.

"On a night shift."

"Where?"

"Merritt Hospital."

Buski reappears immediately, controlling his delight at, as he takes it, the chance of insulting a doctor: "Orderly?" And a carefully underplayed sneer.

"Medical student. Emergency Room clerkship."

Buski's woolly-bear eyebrows squash flat: another of life's niggling disappointments for a dyspeptic cop. "How old are you?"

"Thirty-five. I'm slow. But at twenty I was a lieutenant."

Ignoring that, Buski floats back. "So you come home from work to find somebody has ripped up your house and committed a murder."

"Or ripped up my house and then *been* murdered."

"Right. A mess and a corpse. Two messes. The deceased is nobody you know. A cat burglar. The Lone Ranger has wasted a cat burglar for you and ridden away on Silver. I hate this already. Tell me what's going on, Mayberry."

Mayberry imagines it. *Well, I got a thing in the mail; secret of the hydrogen bomb, see; a man named Varvara, an old doofus from the Rockwell company, he was evidently watching my house; then the dead guy, and another guy with him, I think, they came and . . . Stop me if you've heard this one, all right?* "Junkies maybe," says Mayberry without knowing precisely why.

"Junkies?"

"I'm vulnerable. I have a pattern of being gone all night every fourth night. Maybe he thought there would be hospital drugs. Maybe he's a dealer who owes big money to his connection. A Mafia punishment hit. I come home to find what you see. My dog dead. A corpse that I don't recognize. That I honestly have no faintest idea who he might be." This Mayberry stresses because it's the true part. But it all sounds ridiculous even to him, and meanwhile Albert Varvara, greasy fellow, is somehow eliding himself from the story. Very stupid, Mayberry senses, but he is still angry, now at Buski among others, and what good is anger if not to provoke outbreaks of rash stupidity? "I call the police, like it says to do. They send me Bert Lance."

Through his nostrils Buski makes a sound that almost resembles a snicker. "Junkie thiefs don't slash open mattresses, Mayberry. They don't look inside boxes of pancake batter. What time did your hospital shift finish?"

"Six A.M."

"Come straight home?"

Suddenly Mayberry is quite tired and wants his breakfast. "Yes."

"And you called us at nine-twenty. What were you doing in the meantime?"

"I went for a drive. I was upset."

"He was upset." Buski interpreting for the patrolman: "A lieutenant at twenty, but sensitive." The patrolman wears a delicate wince for the whole four seconds spent as confidant to Buski's sarcasm, and wisely makes no response.

"You stop any place for a doughnut? You got an alibi for the three hours?"

"No. None. I was cruising around. Run out and feel my engine."

"Never mind. What were they looking for, Mayberry? These junkies and mafiosos. I think they knew you. I think your house wasn't picked at random. What did they come for?"

His options are narrowing: he can now be believed, or lie, but not both. Buski's hands are stirring his pocket change like bingo balls. Mayberry says:

"I don't know."

"I'm getting dizzy. I think we need a stenographer," Buski says. "Let's go to my place."

So much for his sleep. Miserable but resigned, Mayberry rises. One of the technicians is by this time on his knees in the kitchen, sweeping up wheat germ and putting it into buff envelopes. The other, having climbed up to stand on the breadboard, is working near the ceiling with a large plastic jar and what Mayberry recognizes as his own spatula. "Tell them," Mayberry says to Buski. "Don't dispose of the dog. I'll claim it."

"Save the dog," Buski tells the lab man on the floor. *"Hey."* Now the man looks up. "Yeah, you. Save the dog."

But during the chauffeured trip downtown Mayberry's thoughts turn to the Head of Surgery at Merritt, a fiercely competent doctor and a good teacher and a total asshole, who once responded to an especially inane question from Mayberry with a blistering look (far more blistering than that from the assistant professor Mayberry had nearly mugged) suggesting he had read the back files and at that moment saw before him nothing else than an overaged dilettante upon whom a place in this class had somehow been wasted. The worst part was knowing that the Head of Surgery, asshole or not, might be very close to correct. Mayberry is oppressed at this moment by a suspicion that dealing with Buski could take a modest but disastrous bit of time. He missed one day of second-year classes with strep, and was badly late once during his Medicine clerkship when he drove the previous Honda into a guardrail, but so far Mayberry has never been blatantly AWOL. When they climb out in the lot behind Central Station, before moving toward the building, Mayberry says:

"Buski, look. I was making your life hard because I was scrambled myself. Confused, groggy, and pissed off. I'll tell you the real story now. What I know, at least. I'm not guilty of anything, I got connected despite myself. But frankly, I just can't afford to have you guys make trouble for me. You've got to understand one thing, though, in advance. This is kind of a weird situation. Some of it is going to sound like horseshit."

Buski says: "I wouldn't have it any other way."

And so Mayberry spends the rest of the morning in a small windowless room furnished with a green metal table, three green metal chairs, a stationery cabinet evidently in exile from more crowded areas, an asthmatic electric coffee urn, and a jar of Pream. There is barely enough open floor for Buski to pace. A middle-aged black woman in brass jewelry and what seems to be grapefruit perfume sits impassively taking shorthand and never speaks.

As he listens to Mayberry's recitation about the piece of unwelcome mail, Jeff Katy's death in New Mexico, Mayberry's own visit to Hannah Broch, Buski's face holds an expression of bored willful attentiveness. While Mayberry explains, or tries to, why an in-house report on the Teller configuration might be considered by certain people a large matter, Buski is feeding himself a palmload of antacids. Buski nods, masticates energetically as though on a mouthful of broken chalk. The black woman copes silently with the spelling of "thermonuclear." Mayberry feels himself sinking in swamp fog but when he comes to the part about Varvara, describes the old man, guesses the caliber of his pistol, even remembers Varvara's birth date from the license, Buski begins hovering alertly, avid as a trained porpoise.

Buski wants to know precisely where Albert Varvara got out of Mayberry's car. He wants to know whether Mayberry noticed any strange vehicles near his own house when he arrived home the first time. And everything Varvara said about the dead man. Everything, which was virtually nothing, he said about the hypothetical other, the dead man's accomplice who fled. Did Mayberry actually see this other person? No. Any reason, besides Varvara's statement, to assume there *was* another person? No, not that Mayberry is aware of. And again Buski wants Mayberry's full description of Varvara, to see whether it comes out the same. And then all that Varvara may have said about his connection with the Denver outfit, what, Rockwell. Can Mayberry remember any numbers or addresses from the company ID? Of course not; but Mayberry suspects that Rockwell International will not be too hard to locate. At that point Buski leaves the room for five minutes, presumably to start someone phoning Denver, and returns. He is not emphatically interested in Varvara's comments about Rocky Flats, demonstrations, some left-wing magazine in Wisconsin. Chester Armatrading has more appeal, and Buski makes sure the stenographer gets that name, at least for the sake of a check. Does this Armatrading have a felony record in California? Mayberry doesn't know but he certainly wouldn't rule it out. Eventually Busky says:

"Okay, Louise. Type it."

And follows her through the door. Mayberry kills another hour watching the coffeepot turn itself on and off. He has already been allowed his phone call to the surgical resident, explaining somewhat disingenuously that there has been a killing in his neighborhood, that the police have asked him to help them with certain information, so he might possibly be an hour or two late for his afternoon duty. The resident was in his standard brusque way understanding, and if Mayberry can just scream back to Merritt sometime before evening the Head of Surgery, pray God, might never know. Buski reappears holding four single-spaced typed sheets and an open folder containing some sort of completed form.

"You own a revolver, Mayberry?"

"No."

"What do you own?"

"Forty-five automatic and a bird gun."

The slight movement of Buski's lower lip says he already knew that but is placated by the veracity. "Your dog was killed with a .38. Non-fatal wounds with a blunt instrument. Probably was a .38 used on the John Doe also, but we aren't sure." The folder snaps closed. "We still don't know who he is. Varvara seems to be real, Rockwell admits to him. But as far as they knew he's on vacation in New Mexico. Which of course smells funny. If he killed this guy in self-defense or the line of duty or whatever, fine, that's one thing. But he should have called us. He's in some hot water. We'll pick him up. Your friend Hannah Broch doesn't answer her phone, but I sent a car."

"When can I leave?"

"Pretty soon, maybe. Then we'll need your phone numbers at work and home so we can reach you with more questions, when we think of some. Or for an identification."

"Of Varvara?"

"That shouldn't be a problem. More likely the dead John."

"I don't know him. I keep telling you that."

"I know you do. I appreciate your consistency. Here." He sets the typed sheets before Mayberry, also a black plastic ballpoint on which someone has been teething. "Sign this."

"No."

"It's only what you told me, Mayberry. Read it first, then."

"I believe you. And it's all true. But I won't sign."

"Why not?"

"Am I being charged with a crime?"

"No. Not so far."

"I gave you my information, didn't I?"

"Maybe. Some of it. Finally."

"Why should I sign anything in a police station where I'm detained without charge and against my will?"

"Against your will? That's not what this is. You'll know it for sure when we do that."

"Then I can leave right now?"

"No. Not yet. I want you to stick around just a bit longer."

"Then why should I sign?"

Buski seems genuinely puzzled. "To get out."

As they stare at each other Mayberry realizes that Buski at this moment is utterly without malice, struggling to understand what might compel Mayberry to be so masochistically refractory. Mayberry signs.

This time the wait stretches near two hours. After the first twenty minutes Mayberry gets up to check the door, expecting it will be locked, intending if by some chance it isn't to try walking pacifically out of the building and keep moving until he is arrested or brutalized. The door is unlocked. The bank of desks in the Homicide room are mainly deserted, except for Louise in a near row busy at her Selectric, and beyond her a man in rolled shirtsleeves, telephone pressed to his ear, listening on the line with a look of disconsolate boredom. He rolls his eyes at Mayberry, soliciting sympathy. Louise glances up.

"Sergeant Buski is downstairs. He'll be with you as soon as he can. Please take a seat."

She might be standing guard for a dentist. Mayberry draws back into the tiny room. Not having slept for a day and a half, he lacks the energy to rebel with panache. He dozes fitfully over the table, waking sometime later with sweat on his neck and a puddle of drool on his elbow. Like a Cheshire Cat in the doorway, Buski displays a smile that is wide and ominous.

"We got a read-out on prints from the corpse. And bells are ringing everywhere. His name is Sheldon Sanzone."

After ten seconds of gazing mutely and hopelessly into Buski's coy grin, Mayberry simply lowers his head back down onto his arm. There is nothing else to do. He feels it all gathered now like a sizable tight ball of horsehair resting weighty on the floor of his stomach.

"He was wanted for arson in Santa Barbara County," says Buski with large self-satisfaction. "That's how we made him so quick. Then I punched him into the NCIC computer, just for the hell of it, and a fire alarm went off in Washington. He's been underground for about seven years, you know that?" Buski inclines toward forgetting that Mayberry is not likely to share the joy of this good fortune. "Starring on post office bulletin boards from Miami to Winnemucca.

"He's still wanted in two states and by the FBI, for conspiracy to incite riot, conspiracy to foment draft resistance, criminal mischief, assault and battery. Conspiracy to get stoned and raise hell. Torching the Bank of America down at Isla Vista. And then for rigging that bomb in the chemistry building at Ann Arbor, where the woman died. You probably remember all this, huh? Sheldon Sanzone, Christ Jesus. So I'm on the phone to the FBI, and they pull his dossier. Just loaded with shit, I guess, all the way back to his service record and then the early protest days, when he was helping to organize the Viet Vets Against the War. And guess whose name happens to pop right off that particular page."

"Stop it, Buski. Mine."

"How long since you've seen him?"

"Seven or eight years."

"Nobody's going to believe that. Probably not even me."

"He had hair on his head then, lots of it. And none on his chin. He wasn't gray. I might not have placed him, even without the bullet. I know they aren't."

"The FBI will be over this evening or first thing tomorrow. They're very anxious to hear your stories. Meanwhile I also been on the phone with some high-karat assholes at the Department of Energy. They want to talk to you about this Teller thing. Before you get back on the street. Double emphatic underlined *'before he sees daylight,'* they say. And in the meantime I am not to question you any further. About stolen reports and bomb secrets, as though I wanted to, or anything. Total jerks. So anyway, here's the upshot, regardless of when the Bureau shows, it looks like I'm holding you here tonight."

"No you're not."

"Yes." Buski speaks with weary certitude. "I am. Call it material witness. Call it suspicion of aiding a fugitive. Call it whatever." From a pocket of his circus-tent trousers he produces a plastic bottle, which he finds to be empty of antacids, and tosses it at a green metal wastebasket in the corner, and misses. "We're off on the wrong foot, you and me. I can see that. But I been getting a nice earload from these hot-ass DOE guys. You're an item, Mayberry. They're coming in on the morning plane. What you told me about this report, it means nothing to me, and they tell me less than nothing. Fine. *Fine*. Maybe it's all federal." Buski pronouncing that last word roughly the way Comte would say "metaphysical." "With luck you might be out of here by tomorrow afternoon."

Mayberry is taken downstairs to a small holding cell not greatly more Draconian than the interview room, smelling of bodies and wine rather than bodies and grapefruit and cigarettes, also more recently cleaned. It is equipped with a wooden bench, a toilet, and a stainless steel drinking fountain, but the bench has with efficient perversity been designed too short for anyone but children or dwarfs to lie out on, so Mayberry sits on the floor and nods off again over his knees.

Half asleep he worries steadily about the passing time and his status, or imminent lack thereof, at the Merritt ER; and intermittently but more acutely about Shelly Sanzone's highly inconsiderate reappearance, as a dead burglar, in his living room.

Infamous Shelly Sanzone, Chester Armatrading's erstwhile partner in gonzo rebellion and the finer tactics of aligning opinion against yourself; more dangerous perhaps than Armatrading chiefly because he was more focused, and more dispassionate—Armatrading generally wouldn't hurt anyone until after he had found an excuse to get mad at them—and had served his hitch as a demolition wizard for the Navy SEALs; present with Mayberry and the cleancut John Kerry and a very few others at the creation of the VVAW. Sheldon Sanzone, whom Mayberry had himself otherwise barely ever known. Let alone harbored. But Buski was right: as a coincidence it was outlandish. Mayberry would have trouble believing it himself.

Late in the evening Buski is back again, with the duty officer, to jolt Mayberry from his torpor with the snapping of the electric lock. Buski looks embarrassed. Also, though, somehow amused.

"Yeah, hello. Forget everything. You're out of here."

Mayberry comes slowly up toward coherence, straightening his cramped neck and pushing against brain sludge to recall where he is, and why, and where else might be any better. The choppy naps are only making it worse.

"Your lawyer's here."

Mayberry squints.

"Your lawyer, Mayberry. Get out of my jail."

"I don't have a lawyer."

"Somebody's," says Buski. "Flashing papers and making the right noises to my captain."

"I don't want a lawyer. I don't like lawyers, Buski." Now he is awake. "Lawyers or insurance salesmen or fat cops."

"Loosen up, Mayberry." Buski grins forgivingly. "You'll like this one."

SIX

She is waiting upstairs, an unlikely decoration for the Homicide corridor, in her high brown boots and her brown suede skirt and vest, and a linen shirt tailored for the style-conscious Central American peasant. She is lank and leggy, with small breasts the nipples of which show faintly but not accidentally through the coarse cloth. At her side is a fine old leather briefcase that looks as if it might have come down in the family, with the collector's Blackstone and the blond hair and the money. Probably she is a Boalt Hall type and, before that, Pomona, and before that, a string of private swim clubs and snooty tennis camps. She holds herself so gracefully erect with an expression of such ferocious professionalism that the total effect must have been practiced in many courtrooms, and perhaps before not a few mirrors. Mayberry says:

"You're the first lawyer I've met who goes to Farrah Fawcett's barber."

"I'm afraid I don't take that as any great compliment, Mr. Mayberry."

"Then you caught the spirit. Excuse me," speaking past her to the frowzy brunette Cerberus at the information window. "How do I find the forensic lab?"

"Fourth floor," says the gorgeous lawyer, doing a rise on her toes. "Criminalistics." To which the brunette gives an indolent shrug of confirmation, as though she wouldn't notify either of them if they were on fire. Without invitation or further exchange the golden angel of jurisprudence accompanies Mayberry on the elevator.

She seems to know what he is after. They follow a tiled hallway to a frosted glass door behind which, despite God knows what the hour, a light still burns. Immediately inside, Mayberry's nostrils tick with recognition at the unmistakable caustic bouquet of formaldehyde. On the far side of the drop-leaf counter is a youngish man with Hispanic features, a Zapata mustache, and friendly brown eyes of puppy-dog eagerness. He wears a tan leather car coat, apparently because he has been waiting to leave. Raising the leaf, this fellow looks through Mayberry as if he's a dirty window and speaks to the woman:

"Yes. You can take it now. I rewrapped it."

"Thank you, Homer. You've been kind."

On a slab table in one of the workrooms lies the dog's oversized body, swathed in amber plastic sheeting like a huge holiday ham. With some difficulty Mayberry rolls it off into his cradling arms, more awkward but more respectful than over a shoulder. He staggers once, gets his balance and moves quickly to escape the two others, slams the leaf open with a pair of free fingers, crabs sideways around the glass door, bumps the animal's skull with unpardonable clumsiness against the door frame; then stops.

He is very weary. He is swallowing back peristaltic ripples of boyish emotion. Too much of his strength has been spent on self-control and anger, and one hundred pounds of inert dog now seem back-breakingly heavy. He feels owed: long overdue for some sort of cathartic interval, of pungent character judgments delivered at operatic volume, or knuckles cracking against someone's teeth, or perhaps just driving across Nevada at 110 mph with the radio deafening. He might need to put his fist again through the bedroom wall near that useful spot where the plaster still isn't repaired from the last time. Which way to the elevator? Why do they build these corridors so goddamned narrow? The woman pulls lightly on his shoulder.

"Mayberry. My car is in back."

He puts the dog in the trunk of a maroon Oldsmobile and settles himself limp into the passenger seat, and she is moving them confidently up Broadway in night traffic before it occurs to him to give her an address.

By the time his eyes open again, she has swung away from the lake and into his neighborhood, just passing the yellow blinking lights that spell OSCAR'S and beneath the towering iron frame sign of the Grand-Lake Theatre, long since turned off. At which point she says:

"My name is Karen Ives. I'm from the ACLU."

"My name is Mayberry. I feel like boiled shit and cabbage."

At his house he neither invites her to stay nor asks her to leave, simply walks away, shuffling again under the dog's carcass, toward a spot in the far back corner of his tiny scrubby yard, where the neighbor's barbecue patio and vinyl lawn chairs are mercifully screened away by the neighbor's redwood fence. He locates a garden shovel and borrows it from forty generations of garage spiders and begins digging. Impacted suburban clay and the roots of a dead plum tree, as useful in their way as a plaster bedroom wall.

It is a quiet warm night lit for him wanly by the half-moon and the lampshade of smog and the diffuse neon twitter from Oscar's, across the alley. He works for an hour digging a waist-deep grave. Then fills it, with no ceremony, or none apparent. The woman has disappeared.

He assumes she is gone. He has been rude to her, and without great regret, but he now feels a certain backwash of gratitude. Send her a note maybe, if he can recall her name, which he suspects fuzzily she has told him. He is punchy far beyond wondering how she happened to know the Oakland police were holding him, or why she cared. Teetering in from the yard, he finds his kitchen swept clear of all wreckage, and her, sitting cross-legged on the living-room carpet, one swatch of yellow hair dangling akilter as though a little sweat has made it ingenuous, rescuing his books into tidy piles. She has not touched either of the two bloodstains, or the bedroom. Best Mayberry can manage is a loutish "Thank you."

"I expect you're exhausted." She is already up on the long legs, putting herself back into the soft vest and the crisp persona. A graceful but precipitate exit. "Otherwise I'd ask you to come by my hotel for a drink. No interrogation. At some later point I'd like the opportunity to explain why I intruded. But that can wait."

"If you just offered me a drink," says Mayberry, "I accept."

He follows her in his own car. The bar at the Claremont is closed, as Mayberry knew it would be and she must have also. But she has, she announces—another triumph of efficiency, and at least she does not say, "I happen to have"—a bottle Cutty Sark in her room. She stops for ice. Despite the external grandeur of the Claremont Hotel, the mansard roof and the gables and the gleaming white stone all best appreciated under floodlight from a distance of half a mile, her room is plain and small, with as much cozy charm as an Edward Hopper painting. It is partially redeemed only by the sloped garret ceiling. Mayberry accepts the chair and she perches herself against a luggage stand.

"I do love San Francisco," she confesses though Mayberry didn't ask, "but I despise hotel rooms. Hazard of the job, I suppose. I've been out here for nearly a week. From New York. Running ragged by day and then coming back to a Gideon Bible and a TV. I used to live out here once upon a time. Not San Francisco, actually; down the coast near L.A. Lord, that was—" and so on. She isn't really this fatuous, she can't be, just working hard to keep things superficial, and meanwhile probably dying to attack him with questions. Mayberry's drink rattles soothingly in its plastic bathroom glass but all the rest is absurd.

"Berkeley. We're in Berkeley. San Francisco is over there. With the cable cars. Look, forgive my confusion," he says. "I don't know whether we came back here for a tumble in bed, or not. Certainly I'd enjoy that, but I'm not going to jump you. On the other hand I'm too stupid with fatigue right now to be subtle or winsome."

He endures a good twenty seconds of her cool spinsterish stare, then adds: "If I've insulted you horrendously, I apologize, and I'll leave." But by this time he almost believes that she is in fact only now making her decision. There is a hint of gentle bemusement entangling itself, especially near the mouth corners, with a challenged will.

"No, Mayberry. You haven't insulted me." Another sip

of her whiskey before setting it fastidiously on the lamp table. A mildly condescending smirk. And she begins to unbutton the linen shirt.

Mayberry is not in a state to be capable of much programmatic tenderness. Later he finds light abrasions toward the inside of both his knees, from leverage taken to pilot her across the sheets, drag her back with him, and again; presumably she ends with similar burns in complementary places. At one point she makes a noise and a gesture to let him know that her neck is crooked painfully against the headboard. Eventually he ducks under her left leg to reach higher within from the side, using her left breast for a delicate handle. Then he puts her onto her stomach, shifts fully behind, forces her rump up, her back arching like a ballerina's, and paces himself as her breathing rises into a rhythm of vehement shudders et cetera. Mayberry is asleep before he has wilted out of her.

"Mayberry." Some time later, he couldn't guess how long, but they are wrapped together in a more restful arrangement. "That was a distinctly pugnacious tumble."

"I apologize."

"Never mind." She sounds cheerful enough, and far more alert than he feels. "Under the circumstances, you're forgiven."

Hours afterward he finds a thigh sliding between his legs and they couple again and fall back, by which time Mayberry is nearly comatose. Again he sinks into deep gelatinous sleep and remains there almost totally helpless until well after the room has lit itself with morning. Not knowing what has stirred him he begins waking, but the ascent to consciousness feels like trying to surface from a long scuba dive carrying too many souvenirs from a galleon. He opens his eyes on blurred shapes of sheet and curtain, and then her beside him, cascade of blond hair tousled lushly, head on hand. She has been watching him.

"It's nearly ten o'clock, Mayberry. God-awful decadent late." Nevertheless she is smiling. "Do you suppose we could get dressed and have an elegant breakfast? And then a conversation?"

"I don't have it."

"Don't have what?"

"I turned it over to Buski at the Oakland PD," he lies. "Evidence. I didn't want any part of it."

"What on earth are you talking about?" Too early in the day still for Mayberry to detect the slyly concealed strain of panic, if there is one.

"Teller's report on the thermonuclear." He rubs a palm in his right eye socket. "That's what you came for, isn't it?"

SEVEN

First cheery words from the surgical resident are: "In your *neighborhood*, Mayberry?"

With a five-year-old daughter from his defunct marriage who sees him on alternate weekends, a late-model used Porsche with a balky ignition, a half share in a beach house at Bodega Bay, and a sizable trotline of imperious girl friends, the surgical resident should have a sympathetic view of life's potential for inconvenient complication. Generally he does. Also a wry sense of humor. What chiefly amuses him at present is how much serious trouble Mayberry is finding for himself so suddenly.

A pair of agents from the San Francisco FBI office have appeared at Merritt two hours before Mayberry arrives, which is three hours after he was due for the day shift following the afternoon shift he missed entirely. They were unmistakable in their FBI suits FBI haircuts FBI jawlines, pattern unaltered since 1962, asking questions and letting drop just enough information to gore Mayberry's alibi.

"They want me to call them as soon as you show up. Excuse me: *if* you show up, I believe they said. You'll try to let us know if you have to make a dash for the border, won't you? In the meantime, Mayberry, *you* call them."

From a quiet corner of the nurses' station, Mayberry calls. Special Agent Durso sounds neither gratified to hear from him nor annoyed by the delay, neither polite nor prosecutorial, neither surprised nor unsurprised. Special Agent Durso by telephone at least is impeccably free of nuance. Yes, they would like to interview him about the late Sheldon Sanzone. Now? says Mayberry. Yes, says SA Durso. Can it possibly wait until five o'clock? Durso ponders that for a millisecond and says no. Do they want to come back to the hospital? At your house, says Durso, would be preferable.

"For me too," says Mayberry. "Give me an hour."

This time the surgical resident listens with a skeptical glaze, purses his mouth like a barnacle, and responds with only a nod.

EIGHT

At home Mayberry is at once busy. He ignores the gaping kitchen door needing a sheet of plywood nailed over it, the dried bloodstains needing to be scraped and soaked, the bedroom chaos needing repair toward the unlikely contingency that he might ever again get the chance for a simple night's sleep. He does not even come in from the garage. With the hood of his Civic propped up and the engine still warm, Mayberry pops the clamps and removes the wing bolt that hold the lid of his air filter in place. From between filter and casing, he lifts out the copy of LAMS-1363.

Other than having been folded and then bent to fit the curved space, it is in fine clean condition: a low-mileage thermonuclear carburetor baffle. With the report in hand, Mayberry goes inside to wait. And only now, flipping pages idly, does he notice the fingerptints.

Not smudges, not smears of body oil or copy ink: photocopied fingerprints. They appear in the margin of page 24, the last page, which is perhaps why he didn't come upon them before. Vivid gray images of the distal two segments of each of two fingers, left middle and left fourth, photographed from beneath while the hand to which they belonged pressed a page—a page that was incorrectly centered—to the copier's glass screen. A nice set. Mayberry can read every whorl. It seems to him curious, and more than a little pathetic, that Jeff Katy photocopied his own fingerprints, just minutes before he died, and mailed them off as signature to this unlucky document.

Which Mayberry assumes the FBI will want, and knows for sure that he himself doesn't. Hannah, in whom the trace of superstitiousness seemed uncharacteristic, was right enough about a malign incubus. It has already brought Mayberry, who can't even read the thing and doesn't aspire to, cosmic aggravation and worse. For him it has only one value: as the white handkerchief tied to the rifle barrel that he intends waving at SA Durso.

Surely his voluntary, forthcoming, and immediate surrender of this precious goddamn report will buy him a little credibility on the subject of Shelly Sanzone. Concerning, specifically, Mayberry's lack of complicity with and genuine failure to recognize same. Or so Mayberry postulates. Surely it will. Here, I give you the Teller dinkum, source of all this ugliness. I give you Albert Varvara, gladly. I gave you Sheldon Sanzone, right? What's mine is yours, Durso. But SA Durso, very much out of character, is already twenty minutes late. At this moment the telephone rings.

And simultaneously something else happens that will prove to be equally disheartening. Jarred from his mental rehearsal Mayberry notices, while the phone begins its second ring, his Hermes portable typewriter. The machine is not where he last saw it, torn from its case and inverted under the desk. It is placed still more oddly. It is sitting upright on the living-room carpet at the center of the larger bloodstain. Threaded into the carriage is a sheet of white paper. He answers the phone.

"Mr. Mayberry? Special Agent Durso. I'm sorry for the delay and the inconvenience, I've just now gotten off the phone with Washington. You can go back to work. We won't be talking with you today after all. That phase of the investigation is being assumed directly by the Department of Energy. Two DOE men are coming out to see you. They'll be from the Department's Office of Safeguards and Security. I don't know their names. But they'll be arriving at the San Francisco airport tomorrow morning."

"I heard that yesterday." Mayberry has dragged the phone on its cord to where he can stand gazing down at the typewriter. "Where are they? I'm anxious to get this business settled."

"I believe there was a problem on the D.C. end." Durso clears a small FBI frog from his dry FBI throat and adds with the faintest reluctant hint of sarcasm: "I believe they missed the plane."

"I have material evidence," says Mayberry. "Very hot stuff. I want to turn it over to you."

"DOE will handle that," says Durso. "They'll handle it all. Good-by." And he is gone, vamoosed, rushing away like a Good Humor man with his truck double-parked in the sun.

Good-by, Durso. Thanks for everything. Setting the receiver back onto its cradle, Mayberry for a second time reads the words on the page in his typewriter:

MAYBERRY 40 GRAND FOR YOUR COPY
ZUCKERMAN

Who is this Zuckerman? Mayberry wants to know. Not, he hopes fervently, another old VVAW loony who is familiar with him by sight or reputation but whom Mayberry cannot recall ever having met. He never served with a Zuckerman. He never, so far as he is aware, protested with one. Obviously (if anything at this point can be deemed obvious) Zuckerman is the guy who came burgling with Sanzone and got surprised by Varvara and saw his buddy's face fly off like custard and then escaped. But came back. A guy who wants the Teller configuration very badly, forty thousand dollars' worth of badly, and can pay that much or thinks he can find someone else who will pay that much or at least thinks he can convince Mayberry that he might pay that much for it. Someone with a compelling use for the report—or, alternately, a market. Also he might well be the one who killed Jeff Katy, this Zuckerman.

"Zuckerman?" he calls aloud to the walls. "ZUCKERMAN?" But no, nothing. Mayberry is alone with his worries and his bloody rugs and his sheaf of photocopied pages. And with . . . ? Suddenly he rises and strides to the bedroom closet.

His house has been breached by so many strangers in the past two days, so many yahoos have been coming and going with so many ulterior purposes, so many long noses poking and greedy fingers rummaging, who knows what might be missing? But after a glance at the shelf—small surge in heart rate—then the closet floor, Mayberry is relieved. Alone with his worries and rugs and his .45 auto.

Jamming the folded report into the Civic's glove compartment, just for now, he weaves off at unseemly speed through Piedmont, toward Hannah Broch's house. So far she is the sole person in this entire affair whom Mayberry feels any slightest inclination to trust. Maybe

Hannah can tell him about someone named Zuckerman. Maybe she can tell him who to call at the Department of Energy. Maybe she'll make him a cup of tea and elucidate historical contexts and explain how in the real practical scope of things he, Mayberry, needn't be especially concerned. Maybe she has a coal cellar where he can spend a few days.

Again he passes her ramparts of vegetation and pushes her bell, but this time there is no long deferential wait. He knows that something is drastically wrong as soon as he hears the cats.

NINE

As he lets himself in, a small outrushing flood of manx and calico fur passes around his ankles. Ten feet down the foyer he finds the body of the doberman. It is attended by more cats, milling nervously about the carcass and raising their thin whiny voices with dolorous persistence, exhorting Mayberry to do something quickly about this distressing state of affairs; and by insects, tiny gnats in large numbers, that have nested and begun raising offspring in the corners of the dog's blank sticky eyes.

It has been shot twice in the head with a pistol of small caliber, and once low on the chest near the left leg. Evidently it was not easy to stop. Snagged between one upper canine and an incisor Mayberry notices several long white threads, possibly cotton, certainly not dental floss. Five feet away, glittering on the grayed Persian carpet, he sees a pearly plastic shirt button. The dog is cool, but not as stiff yet as it will be.

The rest of the house has been redone by the same decorator who did Mayberry's.

In the parlor where Hannah entertained him, the floor is covered with slashed cushions, loose woolen ticking, toppled and trampled philodendrons, potting dirt, and the remnants of a long-necked blue vase that Mayberry remembers from where it stood on a round stand, aloof and ridiculous and beyond the reach of time, holding a sprig of dried thistle. In the dining room a heavy blond china cabinet has been tipped off its matching buffet to smash itself face down over the oaken table, and that isn't the worst; the cabinet held a grand dower, or a lifetime's accumulation, of fine Hungarian porcelain. Now potsherds. This isn't rational searching, not even of the most frantic and ruthless variety, but sadism. Or possibly it was some sort of progressive emotional blackmail. Both padded trays of silver have also been dumped, the silver left where it fell. A Klee print has come down off the wall to be popped from its frame like a ruptured tympanum. All of which seems to have been just a warm-up for the study.

Not a book left on a shelf, not a file box of correspondence spared, not a drawer of the old roll-top desk still hanging in its slot. There is merely, on the tiny room's otherwise bare parquet, what looks like the landfill behind a foreclosed university. Seven decades of written and photographic memories, five decades of hard scientific labors, years of teaching and publishing, plus a dusty viola with its face crushed like a road-flattened grasshopper. The lining of the viola's case has been explored with a pocket knife. Snapshots and group photos lie scattered underfoot—of a handsome young European matron who might be Hannah, with a nondescript man and an infant of indeterminate sex; Hannah again, still youngish and in this shot dressed for travel, on a pier, and over her shoulder the benevolent arm of a tall burly dome-headed man whom Mayberry does not recognize as Niels Bohr; formal group portrait of twenty mugging older men plus Hannah, now middle-aged herself, and three faces to her left Bertrand Russell, whom Mayberry does recognize. At the end of an irregular trail of such mementos a telephone book has landed open side to the floor, like a gigantic yellow limpet, and Mayberry's attention is caught by a further photograph peeking out from among the pages, and a pair of sunken eyes that arrest him joltingly.

He stops to pull this photograph clear. For a moment he gapes at it. Even in the midst of homicidal chaos it is a startling and imposing thing.

On the back of the four-by-six glossy, evidently a print from the original negative, someone in a tight arthritic hand has scratched with pen point: *Princeton commencement, 1966.* It is a black and white portrait of Robert Oppenheimer, full face on, in plush academic robes that dangle from bony shoulders, and a proud austere mask of shrunken flesh, supporting himself over a cane. Taken—though Mayberry does not presently know it—eight months before his death from throat cancer. This man looks out of the picture with the bearing of a venerable Masai chief, a broken warrior meeting oblivion eye to eye, perhaps on the sixtieth anniversary of having killed his first lion with a spear.

The phone directory is for San Francisco, or was, vintage 1959, its white pages long since yellowed and its yellow pages going brown: the scrapbook of an old woman too unsentimental for scrapbooks. There are more photographs, and at least one more face recognizable by the bushy muttonchops that frame it, but nothing that for

Mayberry can match the dying man at the Princeton celebration.

Having found only more wreckage in the basement, he is searching for Hannah upstairs when he sees, out the porthole and down over the wall of privets, a police car sliding quietly up to the curb. From the passenger window protrudes a fat pink elbow that can only belong to Buski. For a moment Mayberry stands stupidly, thinking, "Good, saves me a phone call." Then a few small synaptic explosions prickle his brain and he is taking the stairs three at a time.

He darts down the foyer toward the rear of the house, moving as fast as silence permits, and lurches out of view into the kitchen. Struggles briefly with a bolt on the screen door, eases the door closed behind him, then turns to find himself cornered in a back garden no bigger than a squash court, hemmed fully around by a high post fence and more Amazonian overgrowth. No gate no path and Mayberry without a machete. Set out primly on a terrace of flagstones amid the myrtle, the only spot where sunlight might visit for more than an hour a day, are a steel music stand, empty, and a wooden chair. Farther, against the fence, is a hutch that must have belonged to the late doberman. Mayberry is on top of the hutch, hearing the heart-sinking crackle of failing plywood, when Buski hits the bell.

He dives forward over the fence, into a faceful of limbs from the neighbor's apple tree, and with apple branches slashing and snapping, then giving way, he lands on his back in a patch of blackberry. Christ, he thinks, these people and their vicious aggressive horticulture. But he pops out onto the sidewalk without having heard an alarm ring or a dog yap or a patrolman advise him to freeze.

As he crosses Ross Street again, two blocks away and doing his best to impersonate a respectable citizen, he can see a uniformed cop standing beside the squad car with the radio mike stretched out its window. Even at that distance Mayberry hears the radio's squawk of confirmation and knows that Buski has ordered in reinforcements. Also with a nasty shock he sees his own despicable traitorous lump of yellow Honda parked there on Ross—out of sight and mind from the upstairs window as he watched Buski pull right up behind it.

Mayberry wants to scream but this neighborhood is not zoned for scream therapy by innocent afternoon strollers. Too late, anyway, to do anything about the car. He hustles down Harwood for a quarter mile, then angles back to Chabot.

And ducks into the grounds of St. Albert's College when he hears the siren making its turn off Claremont. A pebbled alley leads back through the college grounds, on a promising meander past tennis courts and between ivy-draped stone buildings, until it comes to a blind end, naturally, at a locked chain-link fence. Mayberry vaults that at the NO TRESPASSING sign and runs like crazy through a thick redwood grove, trusting a trail that follows a landscaped creek and passes two different grotto shrines to the Virgin, dashing down several wrong spurs until he strikes a rear gate that opens toward the freeway, holy blessed freeway. He is striding out toward the BART station, hands in pockets and just nonchalant as all hell, when a vehicle pulls up at his heels. Trace of dust on the brake pads making them squeal. Now he does freeze.

"Get in, creep," says Karen Ives. "They'll be around this way again in a minute."

TEN

"Straight across toward Forest, then left on Claremont," Mayberry says. "To the ramp for 24. It's marked with a big green sign reading DOWNTOWN OAKLAND, but for Christ sake let's don't go there."

"Wherever you like."

"The city. Take me to the city, please. I need to stay clear of Buski's clutches right now. I need some time and some ideas. A sensible plan for getting myself extricated." He is rummaging nervously through the maps and manuals in her glove compartment. "You haven't by chance got a set of Groucho glasses?"

"What did you find at the house?"

"Mayhem. Another dead dog. This Zuckerman, or whoever the hell, he has a real touch with animals. No sign of Hannah. She could be kidnapped, or dead and disposed of. I can't imagine she'd disappear voluntarily and leave the doberman locked inside. Do you know about Hannah Broch?"

"I know about her," says Karen rather portentously. "She and I had a long talk three days ago."

Mayberry ponders the stretch of lost hours, the blurred pageant of his recent movements. "Three days ago was before I saw her. Funny she didn't mention you."

"No it isn't," says Karen.

"Why not?"

"Hannah is a complicated woman. Complicated even for a theoretical physicist. She's had certain difficulties along the way. Personal and political and combinations of both. Beginning in Hungary but even more so after she came to this country. And it all seems to have left her a bit, what, defensive. Guarded. Traumatized isn't quite right, and I'm trying not to say paranoid."

"What *are* you trying to say?"

"Hannah . . ." She stops to consider. "Maimed," says Karen. "And ashamed of it, maybe. I don't know. Anyway she is not inclined to reveal herself unnecessarily. She hides things. Injuries mainly, I think. I saw that much when I met with her. I had just read a thick file in which she figured prominently—as one of a handful of California scientists the ACLU tried to help, back in the high-riding days of McCarthyism. She had been quietly dismissed from the Livermore lab on a flimsy suspicion of pinkness. Ancient history. I alluded to her own past problems with security clearance when we talked, making some lame parallel with the object of my current concern. Just a passing comment, nothing for court, nothing I intended to pursue. But she would have had me believe that it never happened. Everything rosy between her and the Livermore management, her and the U.S. Government. And so it always had been. By her revisionist version. She wasn't aware, of course, that I had seen her own deposition from

1953, and the witless FBI report on her. She seemed to be favoring a wound. It was embarrassing. So I let it slide."

As does Mayberry, for the moment, storing that much away without gloss in his burgeoning collection of useless and unmatched facts. "What about Zuckerman?" He says. "Just a name to me, but I think that's who broke into my place. And now Hannah's. A dangerous maniac is haunting my life, and I don't have a clue what he looks like or where he came from."

"It's just a name to me too," she says. "I know by hearsay that he was in Los Alamos last week. Before that, total blank. But if he wants the Teller report, Mayberry, wants it badly enough even to kill for it, I'm afraid that does not necessarily make him a maniac."

"Everybody wants it but me." Mayberry is growing glum on this point. "Me and the FBI. Them and me, we just don't seem to be properly motivated."

Karen's eyes are suddenly flooded with tears. They sit facing each other across the oily Formica table, abutted closely on all sides by the elbows and backs of strangers, but in the general cacophony no one pays her the faintest notice.

"My God. What *is* that?"

"Do you like it?" says Mayberry.

"*Like* it?" She reaches in desperation for the can of Heineken and pours the last of it into her throat, then with a quick victory of gentility over instinct refrains from snatching up Mayberry's beer and draining that too. Mayberry waggles the empty can in signal to the waiter. By this time Karen has swallowed a cup of tepid Chinese tea and regained her voice. "Yes," she whispers.

"Pepper scallops with black bean sauce," says Mayberry.

"Grows on you, doesn't it. Here. Have some of the garlic chicken to relax."

"How on earth did you discover this place?"

They are in a tiny whitewashed room off Kearny Street. Behind the counter is a middle-aged Chinese woman in a filthy apron and steamed-over spectacles, standing with cosmic detattchment before two great blackened woks into which she throws diced meat and garlic in roughly equal proportions, also dangerous doses of Hunanese pepper sauce, generally without looking at what she is doing. She is more interested in the ceiling, the street window, the foolish menagerie of people waiting for tables. Beside her is a husky young man in a red baseball cap that reads *American Poultry Company*. With a cleaver the size of a tennis racket he is slicing celery into matchsticks.

"Henry Chung's number-two son came into the hospital one night with a stab wound. Nothing quite critical. God knows what he was doing on the prowl in Oakland. We got to talking, and now I never have to stand in line. That's Number Two in the disco shirt, at the cash register. So tell me. How was the rescue timed so opportunely?" On a move toward her mouth Karen's hand stops short. "Did you tail me to Hannah's? And then drop a dime to Buski?"

"You asshole." Meticulously laying her chopsticks across the bowl. "Yes. I did in fact follow you to Hannah's. After having swerved into the gutter, on the Piedmont hill, to avoid your careening yellow Honda. Nearly plastered myself against the side of a dumpster. And I was on my way to your house to *apologize*."

"Uh-oh," says Mayberry. "That was you?"

"The one with the horn, yes. I couldn't believe anyone but a psychopath would try passing a bus on that stretch.

Then I recognized the car, and of course it made sense. Now as long as we're trading recriminations, how about your having lied to me?"

"Lied to you? Lied to you?" But rather than deny it, which seems futile, he helps himself to the scallops.

"You have *not* turned your copy over to the Oakland police."

"No. Not hardly," he agrees. "But it seemed almost plausible at the time, didn't it? I wish I had. Now Buski wouldn't have it up his ass. Warned off by the boys in Washington. They're coming out first thing in the morning by Greyhound."

"Why did you lie to me?"

She is sitting very erect. He perceives dimly that at some sensitive spot in her character—and he did not suspect until this moment that she possessed either, a sensitive spot or a character—the small deceit has left a small bruise.

"Because I was worried I'd give the thing to you."

"I hoped you would."

"I know you did. I knew it as soon as I heard your professional initials. I didn't figure the ACLU had branched out into bail-bonding."

"Let me tell you about a case we're fighting, Mayberry. In Wisconsin. A simple press-freedom case. But it concerns the most blatant and ominous instance of prior restraint against publication since the First Amendment was written."

"Don't bother, I know about that too. *The Progressive* magazine wants to print Teller's secret, right? You think I don't read newspapers?" Mayberry is not letting this line of discourse dampen his appetite.

"Do you know that the report you received is a public

document?" she says. "At Los Alamos it was filed for public access."

"A public document? Or a classified document made publicly available? Through somebody's egregious fuckup."

"All right, the latter. But we will argue in court that there is no essential distinction between the two. Stamping 'classified' on a document is merely a fallible bureaucratic act. Assigning a document its library call number is likewise a fallible bureaucratic act. What's the difference?"

"I'm not a lawyer or a librarian or a Jesuit, I couldn't say. But here's a guess. Publishing the classified document in a magazine brings you a shitstorm of grief. The other doesn't."

"Precisely. *Precisely:* grief. It brings you government harassment. Which is why the ACLU has intervened. Our goal in this case is to neutralize the costs and the dangers of the official harassment."

"My goal also. Which is why I plan to hide from Buski till the DOE fellows get here, and meanwhile not give you what you want."

"When Jeff Katy copied that report, Mayberry, he violated no law. Not even when he mailed it to you. If that's what he did."

"Then you'll have no trouble getting your own copy."

Yellow hair sweeping and bobbing and coming magically back to position when she finishes shaking her head. "Not now. It may have stood on that shelf for twenty years, but no longer. Los Alamos suddenly got very wary. Slammed it back into the catacombs. Just as Judge Warren in Milwaukee has done to our expert affidavits, and the Morland galleys, even our briefs. It's all state secret now. Too secret to be printed. Too secret to be discussed in open court. Too secret to let the public know what's really going on."

Too secret to be sitting in my glove compartment with the car unlocked and parked on Ross Street in front of Hannah's house, he thinks. Now that a cash offer has been made for the copy by someone very possibly guilty of murder, and the ACLU has invested one night of carnal bribery, Mayberry quite earnestly hopes he will be able to hand his piece of evidence to the DOE people when they arrive, if they ever do arrive. Otherwise, as he well recognizes, the tale of his own innocence will be insultingly implausible. He dismisses the notion of going back to retrieve the report tonight, since Buski will certainly have a man in Hannah's shrubbery, and Karen couldn't be trusted to go for him. Maybe with great luck Buski will have the car towed.

"Your copy would be extremely useful to us in Milwaukee. Immeasurably useful. Because it shows that, whatever information Howard Morland might propose to give away, the Department of Energy itself has already been giving away the same thing. That their big so-called secret is already, thanks to them, in the public domain. It could well be enough to sink the government's case."

"That I don't doubt," says Mayberry. "Useful in Milwaukee, sure. Useful in Moscow and Pretoria and Tel Aviv and Kampala. Maybe of mild interest on the *Tonight Show*. But it isn't going to get there thanks to me."

"Not Moscow," she says lamely. "They've had it since the early fifties."

"Get some of this eggplant." He slides half a platter's worth into her bowl. "Fill your mouth. Have another beer."

"What is it that makes you so impenetrably stubborn?"

"Just fear," says Mayberry. "Fear and selfishness."

"You said something about being worried you'd give it to me." For this there is a sudden deft softening of tone, like an eight-track of Jefferson Starship abruptly replaced with Vivaldi. Corresponding adjustments in the line of her left eyebrow and the tilt of her head.

"I came to my senses."

"*Legal*, Mayberry. It's all legal." So much for Vivaldi. "You don't hear what I'm saying. There is no question of espionage. You've signed no Q-clearance oath. You came legally into possession of a few pieces of paper, and you have the legal right to dispose of them as you please."

"Fine. I'm not concerned about my rights. I'm concerned about trouble." The serving spoon from the eggplant goes into his mouth and emerges clean. "Look me in the eye, Karen, and tell me that there is no chance I'd be inviting some sizable trouble if I gave you that report."

She looks him in the eye. Hers are now dry around the edges, but the irises still blue as meltwater from a glacier. "I can't do that," she says.

"How old were you when you started law school?"

She blinks. "Twenty-seven. Why?"

"What before that?"

"I worked as a minor political aide for Ted Kennedy. Until I couldn't stand it."

"Okay, imagine you're twenty-nine. In six months you finish the law degree and turn thirty. Already you feel long overdue. Somehow the Teller report lands in your mailbox. Everyone is screaming and waving their arms and you have a Contracts professor with the personality of a guillotine. What would you do?"

"Contracts is first year," she says. Mayberry waits.

"I'd give it to the nitwits from the Department of Energy."
Then she waves down the waiter.

They are strolling past the corner over which Carol Doda presides timelessly, twenty feet tall and clad only in neon. The sidewalk barkers for the strip shows and live sex shows and two-oiled-hippos-mating-onstage shows are doing what they always do, haunting their doorways, straightening their bow ties, offering peeks, promising the unimaginable with no cover charge. Mayberry notes that the gender barrier for the profession has fallen: a girl in a black rodeo costume politely invites him and Karen to do their love life a favor and take a squint through her curtain. He spots a few other changes since his last pass through the zone but Karen beside him walks with her hands jammed in her vest pockets and mainly watches her feet. As though concentrating. She seems to be doing that too.

"I didn't expect you'd be such a problem," she says.

"I've heard that from several folks recently. Including the doctor in charge of my current clerkship. But from my point of view *you* people are the problem. Sanzone and Zuckerman are the problem. Jeff Katy getting whacked in Los Alamos is the problem."

"That *is* a problem," she says very much as though she deeply means it. Then again she is scrutinizing the sidewalk. "I expected you would be different."

"Different how?" Suddenly he stops walking. "Expected? On the basis of what?"

"Oh, I had this little image. The reckless wild Mayberry. The political Mayberry. Green Berets, then the anti-war movement, that combination. Plus a few other interesting bits and pieces. I thought it was all going to click, in our favor, and salvage the situation after that disaster in Los

Alamos. I couldn't imagine you'd find any reason to turn me down. Let alone a rather compelling reason." They are facing each other in front of a hole-in-the-wall shop that sells trilbys and gas masks and old leather flyers' helmets and tarnished silver canes. A man with a brown beard and poker-chip eyeglasses like James Joyce steps out, wearing a jaunty gray Mad Hatter topper, and tips it at them, controlling his nutty ingrown smile. He seems to be taking the hat for a test drive. "I can't argue that you should force yourself into bearing a big risk on our behalf. But I had the impression you did that sort of thing almost compulsively."

"Your information is out of date. But I'd still like to hear where you got it. Christ, what happened to privacy? All this week, I feel like my old FBI dossier has just come out in paperback."

"Paul," she says. "He had told me rather a lot. Then Jeffrey mentioned you, before he went down to New Mexico, and I remembered."

"Paul? You mean Paul Katy?"

"I also remembered you from the Mobe march in '69. But you were the big charismatic ex-Beret there at Washington, leading the troops to revolution. I was just a face and a pair of feet. A little radicalized war widow fresh out of college, working sweatshop hours at a Xerox service in Cambridge and getting away for a protest when I could. Paul was dead. At Washington I didn't even try to talk to you. I was tempted. Yes, Paul Katy. That's my link here, Mayberry. To Jeffrey and now to you."

"How well did you know Paul?"

"Not especially well," she says. "But for his last eleven months we were married."

A UH-1 gunship is shrieking along at ninety knots just

over the treetops, three rounds of tracer sweep up at it from the jungle, and so with one drastic motion the pilot pulls the helicopter up and away into a steep backward climb but Mayberry's stomach only reluctantly comes with it: that's how he feels now, more symptoms of vertigo, G-forces of time and memory dragging against his hold on the present.

"He talked rapturously about his buddy Mayberry," she says. "How flattering that you never heard about me."

"I heard something about a girl in Los Angeles."

"I was the girl. Only it was Riverside. And it was a wife. An eighteen-year-old child bride, left behind after a Christmas furlough in '65."

Mayberry's gaping dullard look must have given away at least part of what he is thinking, because she now sets her hands on her hips, enjoying the irony of the moment as much as he is not. "So tell me. Am I the first woman that you and Paul shared?"

He contemplates lying but cannot figure offhand what the meaning would be to that. It annoys him to have to consider the lie, and worries him slightly that it isn't worth telling. "No," he says. Then: "Sounds to me like you knew him well enough."

"I came to know him a little better afterward."

"After the wedding?"

"No. After his death. I got older and less smoke-eyed and I saw a few people operate who were very much like him. I count myself lucky. That may sound awful, you were his great good friend, but there you are. I was lucky. At the time, that accident seemed to me the cruelest and most hideously unfunny joke that fate ever played. Right there after I had just sweated him safely through the last hitch in

Vietnam. For a month I couldn't draw a deep breath. Now I thank the planets."

"You could have always divorced him. When the eye smoke cleared."

Her lips pinch down girlishly and this time the headshake is minute, a discreet signal only, the hair barely moving. "I wasn't just desperately in love. I was hypnotized. It would have taken me years. And cost me in ways that could never be recouped."

"All right. Then it's agreed, the world is a better place." She wrinkles her face into a question, so he adds: "As his great good friend, I was probably headed for a premature end myself. Or a long stint in the slammer. Come on, Karen. Let's have a drink to Paul Katy. And his considerate sense of timing."

She doesn't move. "It's Jeffrey that really bothers me."

"Jeffrey," he says noncommittally. "Yeah. Jeffrey was too bad."

"That was my idea." Without evidently being aware, she has fists hanging at her sides. "The little brother-in-law, whom I hardly knew. Hadn't seen him in a dozen years. Suddenly a famous prodigy for his bomb project. I got the brainstorm that he could be useful. It was me who called him. Asked him to go down there."

"Right this way." Mayberry risks putting an arm around her waist. "I know a very good bar."

They walk down an alley between strip joints to a door over which is a tin sign reading GOGGLES REQUIRED, though that is not the bar's name. Another sign reads ADLER MUSEUM CAFE, but as far as the regulars are concerned that is not its name either. Inside are many more signs. Also maritime signal flags covering the ceiling, antique seafaring paraphernalia, a set of shark jaws hanging by a wire above the bar with a dried puffer fish hung separately as though about to swim through them, a stuffed turtle on one wall, a stuffed pelican, a stuffed iguana, a stuffed armadillo in a glass case. They take a table beneath the iguana. While they drink overpriced Jack Daniel's she describes to him in tones of grim reminiscence her life on the Edward Kennedy Senate staff, then at Harvard Law during the mid-seventies, the great renaissance age of go-getterism. After an hour, that and the Irish Rovers music from the jukebox are quite enough, so they trek up Russian Hill into the hushed row-house neighborhoods for some cool fresh air. It's the best place from which to look over at Telegraph Hill and the tourists in the Coit Tower parking lot looking over the Bay.

"But he didn't tell you about Curaçao?" Mayberry says. "Paul. In his raptures."

"Curaçao?" She pronounces it offhandedly, as though deciding between that or Drambuie. "Yes. In fact he did."

"Then you're being very coy. No, coy is unfair. Very self-restrained."

She turns and leans back against a railing, so she can observe Mayberry, not the view. "Did it have anything at all to do with the accident, Mayberry? Or was that just coincidence?"

"Nothing at all. To my knowldge. Coincidence."

"Good. That's what I always hoped. More so after I met you. Yes, the Curaçao business was part of my composite Mayberry picture, I admit. But I wouldn't have mentioned it. That would have sounded like blackmail, and I don't want to blackmail you, for God's sake. I already feel so rotten about Jeffrey. This Milwaukee case is important, but it isn't worth people's souls. It isn't worth mine."

"There's a statute of limitations."

"See? See how defensive you are? Yes, a statute, and one on my feelings about Paul Katy also. Please relax."

He is beginning to feel comfortable with this woman. Moving again, along a suspended concrete walkway above exotic darkened back gardens, he makes an effort of shoulders and lungs and stomach to accept her advice. Then she says: "You aren't sure yourself, are you. That it was coincidence."

"Only intellectually," he says.

ELEVEN

Curaçao was really a small thing, another foolish youthful episode among a whole gallery of those that Mayberry can recall when he wants, which is seldom; a matter of one night's energetic drunken planning between him and Paul, and four or five days' execution. Daring idiocy forgiven by good luck—as it so often seemed to be for them in those days—and coming to nothing, almost. Mayberry would not even remember this skirmish more vividly than the others if it hadn't happened that the car Paul drove off Highway 1 also contained the money.

The cocaine had already been delivered and paid for. That was further good luck of a high order, in some sense for Paul perhaps, maybe even for the young widow, but mainly for Mayberry.

The money he didn't care about. He never much cared about the money, not from the beginning, though he is still unsure whether that made him less culpable, less wanton, or more. Anyway he was glad, for a broad range of reasons, that no cash was found in the burned-out Impala when they winched it up off the rocks. The money may have been incinerated with the car's upholstery and Paul's clothing, or it may have been pocketed by the Highway Patrol, or what charred scraps were left perhaps buried in the coffin with whatever else was left to be buried. Mayberry never knew, and there was no one to ask. He always rather hoped that the money burned but that Paul died quickly on impact. Not even the Monterey County coroner knew about that. And there was no one to ask. Mayberry was back at Tan Son Nhut and the funeral over before the news even caught him.

Curaçao: because that's where he met the connection to his connection. This fellow was a middle-aged French club owner on the island, called himself Philip without an *e* and the other French and Dutch called him Philip and he and Mayberry called each other Jack, spelling it mentally that way but pronouncing it *Jock*, which was their private mutual joke, derived from an initially antipathetic first meeting in a bar in Willemstad, across the island from Jack's own club. For Mayberry their acquaintance was just more of the careening half-masquerade lark he routinely indulged in during R&R passes, furloughs, any escape to the World, while for Jack it was evidently a compelling infatuation, not entirely unsexual. Without being churlish Mayberry was careful never to let Jack too near him, declining for instance when Jack announced he had ordered a gorgeous masseuse for the two of them. Nevertheless Jack was a big friend and patron to—in his choice of phrase, only partly facetious—the square-jawed American commando.

Eventually Mayberry learned that Jack was a part Algerian of natural gypsy and criminal and assorted other tendencies, native to Marseille, in exile from a certain branch of the French police. Besides the small casino he owned several charter fishing operations, and claimed to be mad over marlin. But he never offered to take Mayberry fishing. Jack also made frequent two-day trips to Barranquilla on the Colombian mainland. A cousin there, Jack explained; which meant nothing and might have stood for anything. Mayberry reached Curaçao four times during his last three years overseas. He had been pushing Jack's silken hospitality up his nose throughout the second and third visit before he ever, on the fourth, inquired about making a purchase. An ounce? Jack asked. Several ounces? No, in fact, what Mayberry had in mind was more like one or two kilos.

After a hammy performance with his eyebrows, portentous silence followed by a portentously softened voice, Jack allowed that it was possible. Yes. For the young American commando. Possible because he, Jack, had a cousin in Barranquilla. Jack at such moments reminded Mayberry of a charming cross between Cesar Romero and Sidney Greenstreet. But Mayberry knew it was all serious when suddenly Jack wasn't calling *him* Jack. Just this once, for effect, Jack addressed him as "Captain Mayberry."

In the upshot it was fifteen hundred grams of factory-outlet Colombian coke, ninety-five per cent pure according to Jack, who was almost certainly taking a brokerage fee from the cousin and had carried his own scale and other toys along to the Del Prado Hotel in Barranquilla to make some tests on Mayberry's behalf; very noble product, affirmed Jack. Mayberry wouldn't have known. He cached it all inside a hollowed madeira-wood statue of the Madonna, with what he considered great deftness, picking madeira to conceal the extra weight, and sealed back the statue's base along a fine undetectable line with wood glue. Then he packed the statue in a footlocker, purchased new for the occasion and bearing his name nowhere, along with a Sony tape deck, a backgammon set, and other plausible souvenirs. He had no trouble passing customs into the Canal Zone, and none again when he stepped off the transport flight he had hitched to Lackland Air Force Base outside San Antonio. Paul met him in a Mexican restaurant downtown.

Paul had taken his discharge three weeks earlier and gone back to the girl in Los Angeles. Or rather the wife, as Mayberry knew now, in Riverside. But this was just before Christmas of 1966, and Karen Katy was spending a few days with her sister and brother-in-law in San Jose.

"I didn't expect to see him until I got back to L.A.," she tells Mayberry. "I knew he was driving across to meet you in Texas. I knew why. I didn't want to be anywhere near until he'd unloaded it. Not because I thought there was danger. I just didn't like it. Instinct. Puritan upbringing."

"Don't apologize," says Mayberry.

"Then he decided to come up to San Jose. Evidently. With a flight bag full of fresh money. I suppose it was intended to be some sort of surprise. Probably he was anxious to begin squandering the profits. Take me out on a silly champagne bender or something. The first I heard of this was from the Monterey County sheriff. One of those wonderful 3:00 A.M. phone calls."

But first Paul had to drive the statue from San Antonio back to Los Angeles, and make contact with a friend in Long Beach, someone he and Mayberry had both known during their first tour, who was now a year out and already desperately bored with selling swimming pools and Jacuzzis and mediocre Mexican grass. The pool contractor claimed that he went to Rams games with Nick DeStefano of the Los Angeles Family, and had told Paul that DeStefano was very keen to move some high-quality cocaine, so that was the wholesale arrangement. It seemed very intelligent and professional to Mayberry at the time; later, insane. He and Paul would not put a cut on the coke, which they had no idea how to do anyway, and DeStefano would take the full one and a half kilos at factory purity. That also seemed to Mayberry a measure of their great prudence. The agreed price was forty thousand dollars.

Mayberry himself never left Texas, and spoke with Paul only once before heading back to Vietnam; that was when Paul had just reached L.A., before the delivery. So far as Mayberry knew, everything went off with exemplary honor and smoothness, until Paul celebrated by driving his car off the cliff. But who could say what treacherous improvisations might have occurred to someone like Nick DeStefano in a matter of that much cocaine? Or to someone like Paul Katy?

Not Mayberry. And there was no one to ask.

"Did you see the body?" says Mayberry.

"I wouldn't even look at the car. I was sessile with grief. I was jelly."

"Who made the identification?"

"Paul's father was bedridden from a stroke. His mother was in New York with a gigolo husband."

"I know that."

"It must have been Jeffrey."

"He was eight years old," says Mayberry.

Karen studies the toes of her brown boots; they are in fact faintly in need of polish. "Are you ready to go back to Oakland?"

"No," says Mayberry. "More booze."

TWELVE

They close a nice seedy local saloon on Vallejo that the tourists haven't found or don't want, a place so insistently local, in fact, despite being three blocks from the heart of North Beach, that even Mayberry feels like an intruder and a drunken woman at one point reels over from her stool to ask them who the hell they are. Exactly the sort of place Mayberry has been looking for. He wants to stay until the Sherlock Holmes movie on the television ends or the bartender throws them out, whichever comes first. At two-ten the bartender pokes his remote box, cutting Nigel Bruce dead in mid-sentence, and pours them a free one for the road. By half past Karen has them back on the bridge, pointed toward Oakland. Pointed toward Berkeley, rather: she swings off the MacArthur on 24 again, coming nowhere near Mayberry's neighborhood. Mayberry is hardly at ease with life but he settles more comfortably into the seat at this navigational development, thinking that things could be worse. Under the blazing flood-lights in the parking lot of the Claremont she turns off the car, then makes no move to get out.

"I want you to do me a favor."

"Sure," Mayberry says, but he must be leering slightly because she shakes her head and frowns like a gentle therapist for the mentally disinherited. He watches the blond hair sweep and bob, realizing instantly with a sad jolt that he will not be getting his hands into it this evening.

"No," she says. "A real favor. As between two recent acquaintances, of conflicting interests, who may possibly like each other. Not a big thing. And not a small thing."

"All right, Karen." He has caught the mood, though he doesn't know exactly what's coming.

"I'm not going to sleep with you tonight." That much he did know by now.

"All right. My loss."

"It isn't because of Paul Katy. Has nothing to do with him. Nothing to do with any of that ancient business."

"You want to say anything about what it does have to do with? I'm just asking. I'm not probing, I'm not fencing."

"Me," she says. "Last night was an aberration. Not the fact that I went to bed so precipitately. Not just. But that I did it with an ulterior motive. That's a new one for me. I'm not proud. A few hours ago I heard myself say that this bomb secrets case isn't worth my soul. Where that piece of good sense was last night, I couldn't tell you."

"Forget it, Karen."

"Exactly what I'd like you to do. Forget last night. That's part of the favor."

"Done." He smiles. "Reluctantly but cheerfully. Anyway, you're too hard on yourself. You had a little ulterior thing last night; I had one tonight."

She arches her back and blinks, looking faintly shocked

and quite earnest and even more beautiful that way. "You did? What was it?"

"Not wanting to go home."

She relaxes to a smile herself. "And you shouldn't. There's no point, Buski will just have you back downtown. We'll get you a room here." Now she climbs out of the car in a burst of enthusiasm for their collusion. Mayberry follows. "We'll have breakfast."

"Can I afford this place?"

Striding away toward the great white monstrosity, the briefcase in her hand, she is again brisk and almost lawyerly, but in a way Mayberry finds entirely acceptable. "Is that a request for a loan?"

"Probably. What's the rest of the favor, Karen?"

She waits for him to catch up; then hooks her free arm through his and they go on. "I want to start over. You and I. I want you to call me. All right Mayberry? Don't go away mad. Call me."

"Hello, Karen?" Pantomiming the receiver with an empty fist. "Are you free for breakfast?"

But he sleeps undisturbed until nearly nine and by then there is no answer on Karen's extension. He climbs two flights, follows the labyrinth to her room, and finds a maid's cart in the open doorway. The maid has already stripped and piled the linen. Holding a handful of bite-size soaps, she looks at him mutely. Mayberry runs for the elevator.

Karen is long gone. No, says the lobby clerk, who stands back an extra step behind his desk, suspecting correctly that Mayberry is just an ace from hoisting him out by his necktie: no, she had not left a wake-up call, and the room was reserved for another two days. Evidently her plans changed overnight. Then, still keeping out of range, this fellow hands Mayberry the sealed note:

Good morning. A rain check on the breakfast, if you will. I'm off to Santa Fe. Must try to learn something about what happened to Jeffrey. For the case; and for the soul in question. I will call YOU. *Karen.*

Mayberry throws his room key on the desk; but there is nowhere to hurry to.

THIRTEEN

Albert Varvara has been meanwhile vacationing, under an ambitiously peripatetic regimen of selective tourism, in the Southwest.

Three hours at Los Alamos, discussing the previous week's double shooting with the chief of the LASL Protective Force, then being permitted to interview a certain observant librarian; back down to the State Police offices outside Santa Fe for the rest of that afternoon, including a surprisingly useful half hour spent browsing through Missing Person files at the Records Section; roaring north again as far as Taos for the evening, and part of the next morning, to ring certain doorbells and then make certain calls from his motel room; finally a breathless connection by Texas International over to Austin, where he now sits at a rickety butcher-block table in a darkened and cavernous quonset hut eminent locally under the name Armadillo World Headquarters, drinking rum and Coke from a plastic cup and enduring loud electrified music.

Varvara is not entering into the spirit of things here. The building, vast inside and decrepit, a deconsecrated roller rink with a high stage at one end, is filled with bodies and lewd graffiti and fire-code violations and a grimy chartreuse neon haze. The concrete floor is padded with peanut shucks. Friday night, and the faithful are assembled in force. At the next table is a man almost Varvara's age with matted yellow hair reaching his shoulders, a tattered straw cowboy hat that looks as if it has crossed Wyoming in the spokes of a motorcycle, and a turquoise stud punctuating the lobe of his left ear; beside him is a consumptive Lolita, maybe fourteen years old, with a Marlboro dangling from her pout. Varvara, as focused as an old cart horse in blinders, is gazing toward the stage area. He is eager to have his conversation and leave, but after five rum and Cokes there is no visible prospect of relief. The young black man in the watch cap and fatigue jacket is still leaning placidly against a far wall.

The music is not rock-and-roll, small consolation in that, and not country-western of any mutant form recognizable to Varvara. For him it seems more like four longhairs and a strange salacious girl doing their faintly snide but energetic imitation of Tommy Dorsey. Or something. A sallow guitarist in a black velour blazer is taking most of the vocals while being upstaged, effortlessly and totally, by the dark-haired girl.

She wears a long purple silky dress, late 1930s vintage, something for Myrna Loy in her early vamping days, with slits down the short sleeves through which her milky deltoids peek deliciously, and on her feet Roman sandals with thongs wrapping upward out of sight. Her black hair is parted down the middle, bound back with ivory combs, and explodes beyond them in a broad wild thicket. Under the stage lights she shows a very pale indoor complexion flushed gaudy red just at the cheekbones like rouge patterns on a Raggedy Ann doll. But the red may very well be natural. She is playing the saxophone.

Tenor sax, and she is playing it in a way that, for a young woman of her nearly proper appearance, seems somehow gloriously, tauntingly indecent; playing it like a soiled maiden cast out of the oboe program at Juilliard for some startlingly imaginative act of moral turpitude. She isn't quite beautiful, though no doubt close enough for her purposes, if she has purposes; and she isn't quite a superb mesmeric musician, though again, close enough. Whatever the mix is, it works. During her saxophone riffs the whole motley noisy audience goes quietly dazed, like a deer frozen by headlights, and even Varvara's attention is held. He doesn't know what to make of the music, he doesn't know Boots Randolph from Tony Lama, but he can plainly see that this young lady is perilous medicine.

Varvara takes note of that fact, and without having to pull out his drugstore pad.

The pad has been filling fast enough anyway.

From the toothy Los Alamos librarian he has gotten a low-resolution description of the individual who shot Jeffrey Katy, a description short on detail but jibing roughly with what Varvara himself saw, of that second figure, in the darkness outside Mayberry's house. The librarian had only a brief distant glimpse, fifty yards off through the smoked windows of the library, and didn't claim to have seen much more than a murderous hippie in a flop hat. But she was emphatically definite about what she did claim.

From a Captain Harpenau at State Police headquarters

he has learned that the blue van which the librarian remembered had been stolen in Santa Fe on the morning of the Los Alamos incident, and later turned up abandoned on a county road outside Flagstaff. Inside the van were a hopeless collage of fingerprints, a trace of dried semen for which the van's rightful owner refused unconvincingly to accept credit, and a frustrating absence of any bloodstains; but the piece of shag carpet that covered the floor when the vehicle disappeared was by then gone, ripped out and disposed of. Presumably with the body, said Harpenau, but Varvara's pad was too small for storing presumptions. The other body, the man killed on the footbridge, had been indentified as Eugene Roy Rubens, thirty-eight years old, divorced, no criminal record, a security man and investigator employed by a private agency based in Dallas, who had been around the business for years with a solid unspectacular reputation, doing mainly industrial and insurance work. That much Varvara already knew. The Dallas agency couldn't explain why their employee Rubens was at Los Alamos, said Harpenau, but Varvara didn't need help with that either.

What he wished Captain Harpenau could tell him was how the stoned-out creep had managed to take a wary professional like Gene Rubens so mortally unawares. On this point Harpenau offered no theories. But he did correct himself on another: Eugene Rubens was not actually, to be precise, the *other* body. He was the only body.

Jeffrey Jay Katy was technically still just a Missing Person, since they had not yet found a corpse.

What the State Police *had* found, said Harpenau, was an eyewitness, the librarian, who watched from the window as Katy was gutshot with a .32 automatic at extreme close range, then carried away in unfriendly hands. There was some room to believe he might have survived with good emergency medical care, and no reason at all to suspect he had gotten it. So with Katy missing under such vivid evidence of foul play and such a strong presumption that the assault would have been fatal, said Harpenau, that case too was being conducted in all respects like a standard homicide investigation.

Not to mention the fact, said Harpenau, that the Katy kid's shooting had drawn a squirt of national media, which of course added pressure for an arrest. And besides, said Harpenau, the person who shot Katy was wanted on one definite murder charge anyway. Wait, said Varvara.

What did the captain mean by "in all respects" like a standard homicide investigation?

"The same vigor and thoroughness."

"Aren't all your Missing Person investigations vigorous and thorough?"

"Of course not," said Harpenau. He was a large direct man with red hair slightly shorter and softer than the bristles on a toothbrush. He folded his hod-carrier hands in an act of willful patience. "People go missing all the time. Any number of reasons. Other people report them. Sometimes after a year, sometimes four hours. For us it's a matter of judgment. The presumption, or not, of foul play. We got limited resources." Harpenau remained starchily polite as he reminded himself of these annoying realities. "We could piss away all our man-hours and budget just chasing husbands. Petty debtors. Stumbling through an endless mudhole of vindictive personal bullshit. If we were stupid enough to do that."

Which blunt confession struck a spark in Varvara's brain, not such a fireproof compartment as he often lets it seem.

He had the accidental advantage, over both Buski in Oakland and Harpenau in Santa Fe, of knowing about the corpse at Mayberry's house, even what it had looked like before the face lift, but of having left California before it was identified. Varvara now wondered fleetingly whether that deceased balding burglar might perhaps have shown up missing from someone's life in New Mexico. A long shot for sure, but he had no short ones. So from Captain Harpenau, Varvara troubled himself to learn a further thing: that the case files on Missing Person reports and investigations (when there were investigations), including a file for Jeffrey Jay Katy, were downstairs in the Records Section. Yes, he could look at them if he wanted.

He wanted. And this is what led him to a Pueblo Indian artist named Randy Ortiz, missing from Taos since the day of the Los Alamos incident, and eventually to a quonset hut in Austin, Texas.

The girl friend of Randy Ortiz had waited four days before calling the State Police, then supplied them with a snapshot and a few scraps of information before she left town herself. In the photo Varvara saw a much younger man than the one he had had to kill at Mayberry's, with not the faintest resemblance except perhaps color of hair, of which the dead man didn't have much anyway. Ortiz could more easily be taken for the other, the second man, the baboon who shot Rubens and Katy—though even that similarity was just a matter of weight and coloring. The only thing that made Ortiz worth a second thought, to Varvara, was the coincident date of his disappearance.

Harpenau's district investigator had punched Ortiz into the teletype and gotten back word of a heroin conviction in California, possession only, with alternate sentencing to a Bay Area rehab program called Walden House, followed by further probation still in effect; and that was the end of the Ortiz investigation. Harpenau's agents presumably had notice that they were not in business to track recidivist junkies who walked out on girl friends and probation officers.

The girl friend, Varvara learned from the case file, was named Tay Riordan. An address in Taos, but transient. Spent much of her time on the road with a country swing band called Lickety Split, for which she played flute and saxophone.

Varvara watches the dark-haired girl unclip her neck strap and set the saxophone on a stand. He watches her put a white handkerchief to her temples, mopping away some delicate mist that is invisible from where he sits, then tilt her head back and shake out her hair in the sort of pure equine gesture he doesn't recall having seen from a woman—perhaps through his own fault—in two or three decades. He watches her lean down from the stage long enough to exchange several sentences with the black man in the fatigue jacket, standing suppliant below.

She throws her head back again, still trying to fan some cool air over the nape of her neck, and smiles at the ceiling. Then, ignoring the black man, ignoring a word from the sallow guitarist, ignoring a cluster of footlight droolers, she walks upstage and down the steps and away.

The waitress has just delivered a fresh rum and Coke when the black man appears at Varvara's table. Varvara raises his cup in mock toast to the man, who is looming dourly.

"How many is that for you, Albert?"

"Three," says Varvara. "Never you mind. What did she say?"

The black man disappears. After a few minutes he is back, with a can of Lone Star, and seats himself at the table.

"Damn it, Jesse. What did she say?"

"She said no. She won't talk with us."

"Why not? Did you ask her about Ortiz?"

"I mentioned him."

"Did you tell her we might be able to find the guy?"

"I did. I tried. It was a short conversation, as you may have noticed from here."

"All right all right, it was short. Christ sakes, what did she say?"

"I told you. She said no. Unavailable for comment. She said scram." He concentrates on a careful first sip of the beer.

"Just like that? Those words?"

"Not precisely those words," says Jesse. "The lady is very direct, Albert. She made herself clear. But you couldn't have quoted her over the radio."

FOURTEEN

Mayberry is only bleeding slightly, from scattered cuts on the crown of his head and the backs of his hands, and these cuts seem to be the result of the flying window glass, not the shots themselves. He has been very lucky, he thinks; or else he has even now not yet recovered from that particular sort of training which allows you to make your own luck in such matters. His second thought, in a moment of distant sedate curiosity before climbing up off the bedroom floor, is this: I wonder if it's still the same Model 12 Winchester pump?

Armatrading's visit has come at the wrong end of another difficult day. During his first complete shift since Tuesday Mayberry has faced one basketball ankle, one stab wound that had nearly lopped away the entire left deltoid of a black teenager, two rather healthy snot-nosed kids whose mothers were worried over medium-high temperatures, a comatose wino whom he had seen three times before, a dead man with a .22 slug in his forehead whose friends flattened a trash can at the curb and almost drove their car in the Admitting door trying to get him there quickly, a back-seat maternity, a back-seat miscarriage, a psychotic LSD tripper who had attempted to cut his wrists with a *Brown in '76* campaign button, a chain-saw foot and, quite briefly in his oaken office upstairs, the Head of Surgery. Though it was not on his regular schedule, Mayberry then also stayed over into the night shift to make up some lost hours. This was just one of several compensatory measures firmly suggested by the Head of Surgery, a white-haired little man with Marine posture who reminds Mayberry too closely of Richard Widmark doing a good Princetonian accent. Besides vodka and Dexamyl Mayberry does not know a worse combination than Princeton and the Marines. On the night shift he helped put a tube into a heroin overdose, gave the man Narcan and rigged an I.V. on his arm, then was called over to look at the partially caved skull of a muscular college kid brought in by ambulance from the parking lot of a bar. The kid's girl friend claimed he hit his head on a car hood while checking the oil. The heroin OD made what he assumed was a fast recovery, pulled out the tube and the I.V., and while everyone was distracted slipped out the door so he could die in an alley somewhere when the Narcan wore off. At 3:00 A.M. Mayberry took a cab home with the idea of returning at eight. He hadn't bothered to claim his car from outside Hannah's, and no word from his friend Buski. All of that was the good news.

His phone started ringing before he had his shoes off, and with a quick hunch that it might be Karen he was foolish enough to answer it, but even that wasn't the bad news. Albert Varvara began hollering at him from an outdoor pay phone somewhere in Texas. Mayberry said: "What?"

"I been trying to get you. Hours now."

"I was at work. What time is it?"

"I figured that. Listen, I need your help. Don't hang up. Just hear me a minute. Nothing to do with Armatrading. All I want's information. One teensy question. Be a good Joe."

"All right. Then I've got one for you."

"What did you say? Talk louder, okay, I'm on a street corner and I been up to my ears all night with a noisy band and I'm going deaf along with my other senility."

"I said all right. But then I've got one to ask you. Things have been happening here. What's the question?"

Varvara was momentarily silenced. "You ever heard of a kid named Randy Ortiz? Indian painter, the art kind not the house. Busted for heroin back where you are. Did a therapy program in San Francisco as part of his terms of probation."

"Randy Ortiz?" echoed Mayberry.

"Yeah."

"No. Never. Why should I have?"

"No reason." Varvara's voice went glum. "Never mind. Just a flyer."

"Okay, now me. Do you know anything about someone called Zuckerman?"

"Nothing. Never." Reciprocally ignorant; he seemed to be pouting a little. "Zuckerman who?"

"Just Zuckerman. That's all I have. I think he's connected with Jeffrey's killing. I think he's the second of those two guys who broke in here. If you weren't lying about there being two."

"*That* Zuckerman. How do you know his name?"

"He wrote me a note."

"What did he say?"

"He wants to buy the report."

"Christ alive. Are you selling?" By this point both Varvara and Mayberry were shouting.

"No, damn it. Not selling and not giving. I'd just like to find out what's going on."

"Where's Zuckerman now?"

"I don't know. Not a trace of him here. That's why I'm asking you. He left the impression he would contact me."

"Are you gonna be at this phone most of tomorrow?"

"No. None of it. I'll be back at the hospital."

"What's that number?"

"Forget it, you can't call me there. What's the story, Varvara? What do you know about this guy? What the hell are you doing in Texas?"

"Music festival," said Varvara, and hung up.

Ten minutes later, despite the aggravation, Mayberry was asleep. He rested peacefully for close to an hour, then came wide awake in an instant without knowing at first what had stirred him.

But suddenly he was on his back, alert, listening. There was only the low steady gurgle of an engine, a garbage truck or a semi with a bad muffler and rough idle pausing somewhere outside on the street. Very near outside, perhaps right in front of his house. Not much room there for a semi. Garbage is collected when? After a long five seconds of mild puzzlement, pores opened and Mayberry was instantly damp over most of his body. The engine revved gruffly so it was not a truck with the driver dozing and not a truck at all he now realized but a Harley Electraglide: half a ton of steel and chrome like a rhinoceros balanced

FIFTEEN

"He's not here," says Mayberry. "He moved to a quieter neighborhood."

"Hello? Mayberry, is that you?" The voice is Karen's and the connection is bad, though not quite so bad as from an outdoor pay phone in Texas. Behind her are the murmurs and muted clinks of breakfast noise from a restaurant. "Is something wrong?"

"No, everything's normal. Thanks for your note. Somebody just tried to kill me a few hours ago. Or to scare me. Succeeded. I was fragged in my own bedroom, and now I'm lying here in rubble. How was your flight? How's the chili down there?"

"Mayberry, I don't understand. I need to talk with you. It's very important. Very distressing. But I can't tell whether you're kidding. Did someone really shoot at you?"

"Yes. An old war buddy, I think. He missed. Which probably means that he intended to."

"Have you called the police?"

"Not hardly." Mayberry is about to supply a reason for that but decides there are too many to single out one. "What's your news? What's so distressing?"

"I'm in a coffee shop," Karen says stiffly, and by which it is clearly conveyed that she means: *This is a public phone in a public place, I may be overheard, and I have good cause to feel frightened by that possibility.* "I can't say right now."

"Give me a hint."

"Jeffrey. I was in Los Alamos yesterday."

"What's more distressing about Jeffrey than his murder?"

"I think I may know what happened. Concerning that. Also, perhaps, Hannah Broch's absence." He realizes she is self-consciously choosing her words for their blandness. "Mayberry. Is there any chance at all that you could come down here?"

"Why?"

"I have information. A lead, I think. I could use help. And because I'm worried." It comes out sounding like an understatement, but he hears a strain in her tone that is other than pure selfish fear, and which Mayberry might rather label, without being clear just what the difference is, dread. "Besides, you have a personal connection to all this. Sort of. Like me."

"Can't you tell me more?"

"Not from here. Not now."

"Can I call you back somewhere?"

"No. I don't know. No, I'm going to be hopping around."

"It's suicide at the hospital if I leave now. Practically. When do you mean? Can I come when?"

"Right now. Today." A flat resigned silence travels up

from New Mexico to Oakland. "Then you'd better not come."

"Where are you?"

"My room is at the Hotel De Vargas."

"That's Santa Fe?"

"Yes. Near the Plaza."

"All right," says Mayberry. A large part of him, most of the past three years' growth, the bulky counterweight of stubbornness and fear of lost chances and good sense and well-annealed resolve, that part says no. No, very sorry, not possible. No. Karen Ives says nothing. "All right" says Mayberry. "If I make the plane connections. Tonight."

He doesn't bother—or more accurately doesn't dare—to call the surgical resident. He'll be back in two days and plead amnesia, kidnap, temporary insanity, anything. Rational premeditation will only be held against him, and in any case what could he say? He has an overnight bag stuffed with underwear and a few shirts that mostly seem free of glass fragments, several other necessities, when the phone rings still again. He can answer it or he can ignore it or he can kick the infernal thing across the room. He is trapped once more by the chance that it might be Karen, with a crucial afterthought, which of course it is not.

"Mr. Mayberry?"

"What."

"Is this Mr. May—"

"Yes. What do you want?"

"Ah." Taking no cue from Mayberry's impatience, the new voice settles itself, very much like a cat in a litter box, for leisurely conversation. "My name is Roger Ripley, Mr. Mayberry. From the Department of Energy. Office of

Safeguards and Security. I've been trying to reach you at this number for several days."

"I was told you would be. I was told you were flying out here."

"Right. That was the plan. Right." Roger Ripley is brisk but genial. "And so we did. Just got in. Still at the airport, in fact. We're very interested in this Teller thing."

"So are a lot of other folks. Who's we?"

"Beg your pardon?"

"Certainly. Who is *we?* You just said *we.*"

"Oh, of course." A self-effacing chortle escapes Roger Ripley, and Mayberry pictures the fellow slapping a palm to his forehead. "We. My associate, Bruce Guinness. Bruce and myself. And the Department. We're attorneys. Bruce and I. Functioning out of the Section for Threat and Risk Analysis, of the Directorate of Policy and Analysis, Office of S. & S. Excuse me, that's Safeguards and Security. The office has had communication from the Oakland police on this Teller affair. It's a matter of some concern, frankly. Understand you might be helpful. We'd like to talk with you." Then he actually swings away from the mouthpiece to say, "Isn't that right, Bruce?" and another voice, distant and hoarsely squeaky, answers. "That's right, Mr. Mayberry." They sound as seasoned as two kids in a photo booth taking their own snapshots with crossed eyes.

"Sure. Whatever you need," says Mayberry. He gives his address to Roger Ripley, who repeats it to his associate, who is evidently in charge of the ballpoint.

"Got it," says Ripley, meaning Guinness does. "Terrific. Is now all right? This morning?"

"Now is fine" says Mayberry.

"Wonderful. We'll be there in ten minutes."

"No you won't. You're at least a half hour away."

"Oh. All right. A half hour then. As soon as we can get a cab. Or a limo. Or a car. Is your place easy to find?"

"Better make it a cab."

"Right. Great. We'll see you soon."

"My pleasure," says Mayberry, breaks the connection, and dials for his own cab without having let go of the phone. Airport, he tells the dispatcher; get it here quick or not at all. Ten minutes later he is out the door.

Part Two

SIXTEEN

He catches a TWA flight at noon and climbs down in Albuquerque at four thirty-four, having learned when he bought his ticket that the Santa Fe airport is tiny and not commercially serviced, suitable chiefly for corporate Lears and the occasional recreational Cessna popping over from L.A. full of weekend shoppers. Mayberry rents a car at the Budget desk.

It is six years since his last stop in Santa Fe. Driving north through the scrub desert in its afternoon shades of russet, he wonders whether that town can still be as relentlessly, homogeneously picturesque as he remembers it: adobe and adobe and more bogus adobe. A man could grow very rich off the local concession in red mud and chicken wire. Notwithstanding the fact that uniform faked-up adobe might be aesthetically preferable to molded tin and sheetrock and bad phony Tudor halfbeam as perpetrated elsewhere, still, Santa Fe had quickly on that earlier visit begun bothering Mayberry. Not just the tidy appearance but the self-image, manifestly so smug. Then again Mayberry is not an architectural critic or a sociologist, thank God, and besides he is presently more bothered by something Karen said that morning on the phone.

I think I may know what happened, she said. *Concerning Jeffrey's murder. Also, perhaps, Hannah Broch's absence.* Mayberry is not even clear whether that constitutes one subject or two.

Amid all the hoopla in Oakland over Sanzone's body and Armatrading's résumé and Edward Teller's configuration, he has heard nothing more about the whereabouts or condition of Hannah. Doberman dead, cats starving, house shaken out like a dusty rug, but what has become of the old lady?

Mayberry is worried. She may already be stiff and cool, hosting new generations of blowflies, like the dog. If she wasn't killed outright, he can't imagine she will survive much rough handling as a hostage, but it may be the best to be reasonably hoped for: Hannah tied and gagged, heart still pumping weakly but steadily, perhaps with a broken hip, locked in some closet or car trunk like a septuagenarian Patty Hearst. That vision all day has been making Mayberry uncomfortable. In part because he liked Hannah, immediately and well and on the sole advice of his gut; in part because forty-eight hours have passed since he entered her wrecked house, and Mayberry still hasn't called Buski to trade information.

He wants to believe that this extraordinary crippled old woman will think up a way to escape from her closet. But Mayberry himself, as he is acutely aware, hasn't provided the dimmest flicker of help.

He already has an inkling, from Karen, of Hannah's considerable talent for survival and her experience in the matter of narrow escape. Karen got it all from the ACLU file, in particular Hannah's own 1953 deposition—10,000 words long and minutely autobiographical—and Mayberry has heard the tale thirdhand, between courses and arguments, two nights before in Chinatown. To him it was compelling enough, supporting his own first impression of Hannah. To Karen Ives, as obvious from her manner in the telling, it had the force of a parable.

She was born Hannah Csontváry, in Budapest.

Her father was Sándor Csontváry, an industrial chemist of solid bourgeois descent, employed at the Rimamurany Iron Works on the Danube; *his* father had been a lawyer and a liberal Jew, his mother a Serb. Hannah's own mother was a Viennese woman, also half Jewish, who came to Budapest as a governess in the house of Sándor Csontváry's cousin. Hannah was their second child, their first daughter. She was raised in a home filled with German music, German food, indifferent religious agnosticism, bland cultural Judaism on holidays only, and a fervid paternal devotion to Hungarian Social Democracy. This was still before Sarajevo. Her brother István, though demonstrably unclever, was sent to Budapest's finest private gymnasium, a school run by Piarist priests, which required the boy's formal conversation to Catholicism. Two years later Hannah began at the middling Marie Terezie Gymnasium, and was permitted to remain a Jew.

The Csontváry parents had noticed nothing exceptional about their daughter, in fact had barely noticed her at all, until at age eleven she began helping her older brother with his algebra. Then they consulted a mathematics professor who was a family friend, on his advice bought her a copy of Euler's geometry, later brought the professor around to talk with her; and eventually it dawned on everyone concerned that here was an exceedingly bright little girl. So far no one used the word "prodigy," let alone "genius." Hannah was thirteen and merely a model schoolgirl when her brother was shot dead in the street by one of Béla Kun's ragged soldiers, at whom he had evidently chucked a cobble.

The Revolutionary Governing Council ground its gears and produced a lame official apology to Sándor Csontváry. The soldier was disciplined, in an unspecified way, presumable corporal but not capital. And this event, despite the terror it caused her, despite her grief for a doltish brother she genuinely loved, became the first bit of crucial good luck in Hannah's life. From a month after the shooting, she was suddenly the focus of undivided parental pride.

Her family weathered the Kun regime—thanks in part again to István's death, and to the apology, which served them as a sort of safe-conduct—but not Admiral Horthy's reaction. Under the orchestration of Horthy, and the memory of Kun's worst abuses, Hungarian anti-Semitism rose like storm water in a clogged sewer and Sándor Csontváry ignored it for only as long as he dared. After two years he moved his wife and daughter to a family farm outside Szombathely, near the Austrian border, but continued in Budapest himself. For her eight months at Szombathely Hannah had no schooling. She read Kepler and Newton, and enough about Karl Friedrich Gauss to become aware for the first time of a place called Göttingen, in Germany. Then one day her father appeared back at the farm, looking exhausted and acting falsely cheerful, and hurried the three of them onto a train. Next evening they were in Vienna, sleeping on improvised pallets in the parlor of one of Hannah's maternal uncles. The arrangement was cramped and excruciatingly unprivate, also humiliating for her father, but after five weeks like that they moved on to Munich. Her mother's people had found Sándor a new position in the steel industry. Hannah was fortunate in already having the language, and wasted almost no time over the social adjustments of a displaced adolescent. At the Munich gymnasium she sparkled. She inhaled mathematics as if it was mountain air.

At age seventeen she qualified for university in physics and math, but there still was a problem. Sándor, having accepted Hannah's intellectual promise, found it harder to accept her choice. The vicarious ambitions he vested in the girl were now extreme, and he thought mathematics was a mistake. She would be squandering herself. It was a field without practical application, therefore also without prospect of adequately rewarding her gifts and efforts. Hannah was mildly puzzled by the concept of a gift that required further rewarding. She said so gently. Her father with deaf persistence hoped she would study chemical engineering, and to Hannah's mother this reversal by her husband, and the notion of her daughter as a process engineer at some great foundry, was ludicrous to the point of hysterical mirth. Hannah in her self-possessed way managed to be both a respectful daughter and a very stubborn one. In 1924 she left home to study mathematics at Leipzig.

Within four years she had done her degree in mathematics; come to be spoken of by her Leipzig professors, with condescension which they considered friendly, as certainly the most talented female math student within memory; been elaborately courted by, and married, a young medical graduate named Julius Broch; received her acceptance to begin study, still at Leipzig, toward the doctorate in physics; and found herself pregnant. In January of 1929, after five months of gestation and four months of physics, it was suggested by department officials that she withdraw from the university. Hannah politely declined. In February she was dismissed. In May the child was born, a boy, and named Isidor. In early June, returning on foot from a night call, Julius Broch was bludgeoned to death with a carpenter's adz by the angry father of a nine-year-old girl who, while under his care, had died of diphtheria. Hannah and the baby returned to Munich.

Now two years passed very slowly, two years of quiet motherhood under the roof of her own parents, while Isidor grew healthy and fat and Hannah grew desperate. Hannah's mother was still subject to fits of hysterical laughter; in fact these had grown more frequent, and no longer bore any correlation with moments of recognizable humor. Frau Csontváry's grip was slipping. Sándor had drifted into a permanent melancholy, stayed away long hours at the mill, and at home spent his time doting on Isidor. Hannah got hold of a book on the Special and General Relativity theories; when she tried to read a chapter while rocking Isidor asleep on her lap, her mother broke into a high liquid howl of maniacal laughter. The child woke and cried. Not long after that evening Hannah began writing letters.

Occasionally a letter arrived in reply, from the University of Munich, but Hannah was secretive. She still had not finished the Einstein book when she left the apartment one afternoon, and returned hours later, smiling thinly but irrepressibly. She had, she announced, wheedled permission to attend the lectures of the great physicist Arnold Sommerfeld. Attend as an auditor, she added. Her father looked confused but amiable, like an amnesiac under hospital care. Her mother left the room silently.

After one of Sommerfeld's sessions Hannah pushed together what remained of her courage and self-confidence, small precious pile of dry tinder, and climbed down from the rear of the auditorium. Sommerfeld was notoriously brusque to his students but she caught him at the door with a question about the Eötvös experiment and General Relativity that was percipient enough to snag his benevolent notice. Sommerfeld not only answered the question as though it interested him; he looked Hannah in the eye as he did. Afterward he evidently made inquires about her official status and found she had none, because when she next approached him, a month later, he handed her a five-page bibliography to guide her lonely study. The year following, against university regulations, Sommerfeld allowed her to attend his seminars. Meanwhile he wrote notes to several colleagues about the exceptional young Hungarian woman he had discovered, and in the summer of 1932 Hannah was notified of her admittance, again for the doctorate in physics, to Göttingen. Her father, squeezing Isidor against his unshaven cheek, shed two glittering tears of elation. Her mother was vacationing at a sanitarium, and the vacation was expected to be a long one.

Hannah's own tears of elation were saved until that day in September when she stepped out at the station and first saw the ramparts of the old Hanoverian city. In her 1953 deposition she said: "For a Muslim, it is Mecca. For a painter, I suppose, Paris. For a physicist, in those years—you must understand—Göttingen." She was to work under the renowned experimentalist James Franck. Six months after Hannah's arrival the new German Chancellor promulgated his orders dismissing Jewish faculty. James Franck left the country. It had all been snatched from her again, and beyond that there was a further concern: Hannah herself was a Jew. She mailed a long letter to her father, who with the help of a nurse was cheerfully caring for Isidor, then followed Franck to Copenhagen and Niels Bohr.

Bohr, watching carefully from across the water, had already formed a Danish committee to support refugee intellectuals, and was turning his own Institute for Theoretical Physics into a temporary haven for all Hitler's unwanted physicists. The Institute became a way station while Bohr himself conducted a zealous one-man placement service, writing dozens of letters to British and American colleagues who might be prodded to find space in their own university departments for some of the best brains in Europe. Though he had never heard of Hannah, Bohr welcomed her on Franck's word. She remained in Copenhagen through the winter and spring of 1933-34, bicycling across the city from her room to the Institute, working some small bit with Franck, taking part in great boisterous seminars, walking through Tivoli and exchanging ideas with men whose names were famous to her. Surrounded finally by brilliant scientists, and by this awesome evolving reticulum that was modern physics, she flourished. Her mind opened, almost suddenly, like a crocus blossom; her confidence returned, and she discovered in herself a vein of wry humor. Having hardly found anything easy before in her life, except mathematics, she now impressed and charmed whole roomfuls of strangers with barely an effort. The quantum theory—Bohr's own particular achievement, most radical and troubling of the new ideas, and of which Hannah had been almost totally ignorant—she took hold of like the boy Mozart sitting down to a keyboard. In July she left Copenhagen by steamer. On that occasion one of the German postgraduates commented, with what he had thought was generosity, that she might be the most promising woman physicist since Lise Meitner. Neils Bohr overheard. Six feet five of strapping Dane, patriarch of geniuses, forehead like the vaulted nave at Rouen Cathedral, with forgiving disdain he corrected the young German: "No. The most formidable autodidact, I think, since a Swiss patent clerk named Einstein."

Bohr had found her a place at Berkeley, in California, where the department was small and by European standards not greatly distinguished, but the people were eager. At Berkeley, said Bohr, they might well create something worthy. Ernest Lawrence was the star distraction, raising money like a speculator in minerals and building his endless progression of wildly expensive accelerators, but Bohr had guessed on Hannah's behalf, and accurately, that this sort of industrial physics was not her line. Anyway Dr. Lawrence was wont to describe himself in falsely confessional tones as "a great admirer of the ladies," by which of course he meant, said Bohr, a misogynist. There was in addition a single theoretician, a clever young man Bohr had met at Leiden. This one's name was Oppenheimer. Hannah would, Neils Bohr had predicted, find him interesting. And so she did.

Robert Oppenheimer during those years was teaching much more than physics. To the graduate students who clustered around him he was a total and irresistible paradigm, a hero of good taste and far-flung erudition. He read Plato in Greek, the *Bhagavad Gita* in Sanskrit, and Henry James in the original. He went to the symphony but could explain with informed sarcasm why he avoided Wagner. He knew where to buy the best fresh clams. He knew wines. He confessed to having written great quantities of bad poetry as an undergraduate, and refused to let anyone hear him practicing the violin, though it was established with near certainty that he owned one. He knew the best Italian restaurants in San Francisco and the most unlikely Mexican kitchens in Oakland, and when he went to either such place with a group of six or eight students, as often enough happened, Oppenheimer grabbed the check. He was a bachelor professor, only a few years their senior, with a good salary and family money beyond that. They were poor and callow and they worshiped him as the ideal of all older brothers. Periodically he would cook a mysterious New Mexican chili stew, making it so hot that his followers couldn't eat it without tears, but they ate it, washing the stuff down with a beer that Oppenheimer asserted was the only American brand worth drinking. Consciously or not, they copied his verbal mannerisms, his method of lighting a cigarette. His rumpled clothes and bad posture. His dogmatic preference in beer. Like him, and with him, they talked physics almost every waking hour. At the San Francisco restaurants, on the late ferry back, during long evenings of wine and nicotine at his apartment on Shasta Road, Saturday on a drive up the coast, Sunday after a concert: they talked physics. His lecture course in quantum mechanics was never attractive to large numbers but almost everyone serious enough to sit through it once returned and heard the whole series a second time; some came back again after that. He did not just make the quantum theory comprehensible; he made it seem beautiful, a glorious edifice constructed by man to describe the most improbable secrets of nature; and he was infectious with the excitement of its ongoing development. By personal style and the gracefulness of his own thought, he made physics elegant.

His immediate coterie at any particular time included

eight or ten doctoral candidates and four or five postdoctorals, all preternaturally bright and fervently devoted to their teacher. But in all this social and intellectual intimacy there was a certain one-sidedness. Oppenheimer gave. Besides companionship and adulation, also the deeper satisfaction of propagating ideas that he loved, he got very little back. His students had not much they could teach *him*. Hannah Broch was the exception.

He had never, until Hannah, known the exotic confusion of carnal passion with a person he truly considered his equal. And despite all the dabbling he had never, until Hannah, read Karl Marx.

During his own hearings before the review board that eventually withdrew his security clearance—this in April of 1954—Oppenheimer himself testified about his life at Berkeley: "I was almost totally divorced from the contemporary scene in this country. I never read a newspaper or a current magazine like *Time* or *Harper's;* I had no radio, no telephone; I learned of the stock-market crack in the fall of 1929 only long after the event; the first time I ever voted was in the presidential election of 1936. To many of my friends, my indifference to contemporary affairs seemed bizarre, and they often chided me with being too much of a highbrow. I was interested in man and his experience; I was deeply interested in my science; but I had no understanding of the relations of man to his society. In spring of 1936, those circumstances began to change. I can discern in retrospect more than one reason for these changes, but certainly it is fair to say that among the foremost was my acquaintance with a young doctoral candidate named Hannah Broch. Acquaintance is the wrong word." Notwithstanding "stock-market crack," Oppenheimer in this particular statement was striving carefully for the right words. "I had in fact been aquainted with Hannah Broch by then for more than a year. It was my intimate friendship with her, beginning that spring, which precipitated the changes. Helped to precipitate."

Asked later to define "intimate friendship," Oppenheimer said: "On several occasions we discussed marriage. But marriage at that point would have represented no substantive change in the character of our relationship. And Hannah for her own reasons was against it."

He had chosen to face the subject of Hannah directly, in his opening comments before cross-examination, because her name had appeared in the official letter of accusation against him. Hannah Broch was by then, 1954, an incriminating associate.

But in spring of 1936 she was merely a fascinating young European woman, and a physicist of high promise. After just a year at Berkeley as his most favored protégée, and before she had even received her doctorate, she became Oppenheimer's collaborator, on a theory explaining the results of certain experiments in deuteron bombardment that had been performed on the university cyclotron. The collaboration was a success, a monograph was published in *Physical Review* under their joint authorship, and something call the Oppenheimer-Broch Process concerning nuclear reactions, entered the professional vernacular. More importantly for each of them, also perhaps for history if not for science, they spent endless intense hours together refining the idea. Their paper, straightforwardly titled "Note on the Transmutation Function for Deuterons," was written during two long evenings at Oppenheimer's apartment. On the second evening Hannah never went home.

Oppenheimer had always until then observed a firm scruple against sexual or emotional involvement with any of his female students; until then it was never difficult, there was no serious temptation, since he had taught very few woman and those were lightheaded undergraduates with throbbing crushes on him. Hannah likewise had sworn to herself that no personal entanglement would ever again be allowed to jeopardize her pursuit of physics. But they hadn't counted on the transmutation function.

It was all highly inconvenient to their self-images and their predispositions (though not nearly so inconvenient as it would later become). It was also, in springtime of 1936, dizzyingly rapturous. Now there was one more place still to talk about physics: in bed.

The beginning of this affair with Hannah coincided, as he testified at his hearings, with several other changes in Oppenheimer's worldly consciousness. The others were in no way dependent on Hannah's influence—so he claimed, and plausibly—but the total effect upon him of these factors plus Hannah was, in his own characteristic phrase, "at least cumulative and probably synergistic." He explained: "I had had a continuing, smoldering fury about the treatment of Jews in Germany. I had relatives there, and was later to help in extricating them and bringing them to this country. I saw what the Depression was doing to my students. Often they could get no jobs, or jobs which were wholly inadequate. And through them, I began to understand how deeply political and economic events could affect men's lives. I began to feel the need to participate more fully in the life of the community." So Robert Oppenheimer became a giver and a joiner.

He contributed money to various groups providing medical relief to the Spanish Loyalists. He got involved with the local teachers' union and was elected recording secretary. He also joined the Consumers' Union, which seemed to espouse nothing more radical than Naderism before Ralph, and the American Committee for Democracy and Intellectual Freedom, a support group for refugee intellectuals along the line of Bohr's Danish version; both of which were later cited, by that forum for patriotic hysteria called HUAC, as "Communist front organizations." At the time of joining, Oppenheimer probably didn't know about any Communist link with either, and probably wouldn't have cared if he had.

He also continued to read Plato—now the political writings, and in translation for speed—as well as Thomas More, Bentham, Rousseau, and others, and to discuss notions of utopianism with Hannah. She loaned him a copy of *Capital* and he read every word in the course of a train journey from Berkeley to Chicago for a conference; handing the book back, he told her he found Marx more thorough than perceptive, more perceptive than persuasive, and more persuasive than humane. Marx didn't do it for him. Then on his thirty-second birthday, April 22 of that year, Hannah gave him a work in two volumes recently published by Sidney and Beatrice Webb. This was *Soviet Communism: A New Civilization?* It caught him, as Hannah herself had, from one of the very few angles where he was susceptible.

Hannah in turn owed her discreet but long-standing interest in Marxist theory and practice to the idealistic young physician who had once, briefly, been her husband. Julius Broch was the only man Hannah ever knew who could, even amid the press of his medical studies, read Lenin's dry pamphlets and emote. He had been just enough older than Hannah to remember the days of the Munich Soviet and the murder of Rosa Luxemburg (who had once been treated for a hemorrhaging ulcer at his father's dispensary), and those events had by some ineffable tempering process transformed his youthful liberalism into a fierce hidden sympathy for the Bolshevik enterprise. Julius belonged to the KPD, Germany's Communists, but kept it a secret during school and then decided the secret was best continued while he struggled to establish a Leipzig practice. There were by that time, after all, a wife and son to support. Then the stroke of an adz stopped him, just as another stroke stopped his idol Lenin, from seeing what an odd fruit would grow from the Bolshevik flower.

Hannah had kept his books with her during the two years back in Munich while her mother went mad. Sometimes, with the baby's demands momentarily met and no one watching to cackle derisively, she read them. Marxism for her was not at all like physics or mathematics: not beautiful, not the least fascinating, of no pleasure to contemplate. But it had a trueness, she felt. Beyond even the question of justice: it had a trueness. And that trueness seemed necessary to a world full of pernicious fallacies. She studied it further, not with any satisfaction but out of a sense of duty. Before the worst of the Munich period was over—before Sommerfeld's grace fell on her—she had learned how to get hold of, not just Einstein, but also *Tarsadalmi Szemle*, the underground review from the Hungarian Communist Party.

Oppenheimer, as of 1937, was a subscriber to the *Daily People's World*, a West Coast equivalent of the *Daily Worker*. Of course no American is ever guilty for what he reads, theoretically, but this subscription was just difficult enough to explain away that, at his hearings, Oppenheimer didn't try.

Through the winter of late 1937, Oppenheimer and Hannah attended together a number of small benefit dinners and concerts and auctions, in the East Bay area, gotten up by well-meaning folk to raise money for Spanish relief. The Spanish Civil War was then and always Oppenheimer's favorite leftist cause; to Hannah, who knew even less about Spain than he did (never having even dallied, like him, with Cervantes and Unamuno), that particular skirmish seemed slightly beside the point. But still she accompanied him to the benefits: they were determinedly sharing tastes in those months, and ideas, and everything else.

Hannah by then had her degree, plus a postdoctoral fellowship to remain at Berkeley, and their current collaboration involved the disintegration of high-energy protons. She kept her boardinghouse room but they maintained the formal fiction of separate habitation with not quite such careful discretion as before. Robert's older friends, who now saw him less, admitted grudgingly that, whatever the new thing was, it seemed to agree with him. She was hardly one to iron his shirts and remind him to comb his hair and cook him great soporific pasta dinners (in fact he did more cooking for her), but Hannah's effect on him was nonetheless unmistakable. Some of his edginess, the fast arrogant sarcasm that could be so cruel against those he considered second-rate thinkers, some of that was gone. He walked more lightly. He lost the nervous habit of breaking blackboard chalk into small pieces while he lectured. He smoked just as much, but without the same vehement masochistic intensity. The line of his shoulders relaxed a bit and he looked less like a grounded condor. It was Oppenheimer Refulgent, Oppenheimer In Love, and though for Hannah the external manifestations of this condition were not so pronounced, she had it equally. And for her it would last longer.

Sometime that winter she introduced Robert to Dr. Stephen Geddes, a kidney researcher at the Stanford Medical School, and a man who, like Robert, was fervidly sympathetic with the Spanish Loyalists. Geddes offered to serve as conduit for Robert's cash contributions for Spain, and promised that through him the money—unlike what was accepted by other relief organizations—would go directly to good use at the front. Robert was grateful, and began giving Geddes one or two hundred a month. Geddes explained that his short-circuiting was accomplished by passing the money through Communist channels. Fine, said Robert, whatever. Stephen Geddes later figured prominently in the edifice of accusation against Oppenheimer. For what it was worth, and in 1954 that amounted to rather a lot, Geddes himself was an active member of the Alameda County Communist Party.

Oppenheimer under oath could not answer the question of where Hannah Broch had originally met Dr. Geddes.

Hubert Jamisson was another East Bay Bolshevik about whom the subsequent questions couldn't be answered, or at least not answered so as to satisfy the official inquisitors, but in this case it was Hannah whose memory wouldn't rescue her. She was unable to give a tidy account, during her own personnel hearings after having been sacked from Livermore, of how she had first made the acquaintance of Hubert Edward Jamisson. It happened to be a crucial lacuna. Jamisson, a British petroleum engineer who had worked for Shell in the Soviet Union and then in the late thirties accepted a transfer to Berkeley, represented the foremost piece of circumstantial evidence in the kangaroo cases against both Hannah and Oppenheimer. No, she insisted in her 1953 deposition, after straining her memory for weeks she could still not recall where she had met Jamisson. An auction, probably. Perhaps through the

Consumers' Union. In a public gathering somewhere, anyway. It was simply a fortuitous event. Meaningless, innocent. The encountering of a new acquaintance, like any such encounter: how many of our acquaintanceships can we trace to the precise moment and place of their beginning? No, she could think of no one who might verify this claim. How can you verify a negative?

Hubert Jamisson had been the point on which Hannah's self-defense, her appeal of the Livermore dismissal, foundered. And in turn the point from which all Oppenheimer's most serious trouble sprang. Without the so-called "Jamisson incident," as compounded by his relations with Hannah, Oppenheimer was just another California intellectual who had passed through a phase of fashionable radical postures. But Jamisson only came later: more than five years after the dizzy days of Robert's political and romantic coming-out, after the discovery that an atom's nucleus could be split, after he was chosen to organize Los Alamos, long after his fascination with leftist causes—and likewise his fascination with Hannah Broch—had ended.

The ending evidently began, insofar as such thing can be traced, in 1938.

Concerning Hannah, it may have been her persistent refusal to marry him. They argued over this, sometimes epically. He had done the bachelor professor thing for nine years now and was tired of it, ready for what he described as some sort of fuller emotional regularity. That was a pitiful reason, she said, *regularity*. "Marriage, let me tell you, Robert," she declared from experience, "is no laxative." He accused her of insecurity about her work, about her ability, which she denied with such vehemence that she knew at once it was true. The threat this time was not that she might be prevented from doing physics; it was that her work would remain in the shadow of his; she would be too dismissable as "Mrs. Oppenheimer, who also in her own right . . ." et cetera. Hannah suffered badly during the period of these battles, as she watched nasty slashes being torn in the emotional fabric between her and Robert, rents that might be stitched but could never be rewoven, because she loved him as much as ever. They found themselves arguing, too, about Russia.

A pair of physicists Oppenheimer knew returned from a long visit to Moscow with word of purge trials, concentration camps, unbelievable restrictions against intellectual freedom, particularly as affecting scientists. Hannah may have met this with rationalizations. Robert on the other hand was sick of Communists, sick of the tedious drone of dogma and orthodoxy, even by now sick of Spain.

He and Hannah spent less time together but occasionally still had high moments, as high as before. They avoided discussion of politics. They began no further collaborations. Finally in August of 1939 came two other factors: the Nazi-Soviet Pact, which silenced even Hannah; and a new woman.

Robert met her on a patio in Pasadena. She lived there with her third husband, an enervated British doctor named Harrison. She was called Kitty. Kitty didn't know nuclear physics but she knew what she liked. On the first of November the following year, in Reno, she divorced Harrison and married Robert Oppenheimer.

"By which time Hannah barely noticed," Karen told Mayberry. "Or at least, so it seemed. To the people she worked with. People who later testified. She says nothing about that particular point in her deposition." Mayberry's contrary impression, based partly on what he heard from Karen, more on his own brief meeting with Hannah, is that she probably noticed acutely but very privately, and that the pain and bleeding over that injury simply had to be postponed, taken later in their turn. During the autumn of 1940 Hannah was spending too much of her attention on a quiet, terrified effort to locate Sándor Csontváry and Isidor Broch, grandfather and grandson. "They had disappeared from Munich," Karen said, "and her mother's relatives were not answering letters."

Mayberry as he picks through the outskirts of Santa Fe is still pondering Hannah's talent, putative, for survival and narrow escape. So far as anyone knew, it was not a trait she had got from her father or passed to her son.

He is impatient with Karen's tendency to assume that the old lady is stoic and indestructible, which he takes for projection more than perception, and wishful projection at that: Karen herself, feeling tough and self-sufficient, wants to believe that Hannah is even more so. *I think I may know what happened,* she said on the phone. *Concerning Hannah Broch's absence.* Right there, that was a curiously sanguine word, "absence." Why not "disappearance"? Karen might prefer to imagine the old woman hobbling off on some sort of lark but realistically Hannah would be lucky just now if she were a victim of nothing more than, say, kidnapping. Mayberry then remembers the fright he heard that morning in Karen's voice. And the fact that, in her own bearish way, she virtually begged him to fly down here and give her some help.

And he thinks, turning up the alley called Water Street according to Karen's directions, that a little such uncertainty, a little trepidation modulating her sense of competence, can only be good for her. It is one thought that, soon afterward, he wishes he could forget.

On the corner of Water and Don Gaspar is the Hotel De Vargas, a fleabag compared to other hotels near the Plaza, but a dignified fleabag, the sole place within blocks not peddling Old Santa Fe atmosphere at extortionate rates. In the lobby are two elderly men watching television and not a single turquoise necklace for sale from a locked glass case. The desk clerk looks tubercular. He wears an uncommonly ugly checked tweed jacket and smokes a cheroot, but he is very polite. Soft-spoken, with a trace of French accent. He registers recognition: Yes, Miss Ives is a guest here; yes, in fact, she has asked him please to direct Mr. Mayberry to a restaurant, the Ore House, on the Plaza. It is only two blocks. There is a carved wooden sign.

Mayberry sees the flashing red bubble as soon as he steps into the Plaza. He strolls on across the cobbles, then orients, then has to turn back toward the police cruiser and walk another few yards before he makes out, by the intermittent pulses of aqueous red reflected at close range, the wooden sign.

SEVENTEEN

A patrolman is stationed at the door. His offhand first statement to Mayberry is that the kitchen has closed. His second, punctuated with a straight-arm across Mayberry's path, is that no one goes in; no one comes out; Mayberry can wait here for his friend but Lieutenant Roybal will say when the people upstairs can leave. Mayberry ducks to pass under the arm and feels a hand catch the back of his collar, reining him up with a cheap choke hold. Mouth just behind Mayberry's ear, the patrolman is beginning his third statement, this one to be more personal and blunt, when Mayberry raises a leg to brace off the doorjamb and drives his head backward into the cop's chin. He snaps his torso around with a cocked elbow leading and makes lucky but quite solid contact in the vicinity of the mandibular socket. The patrolman falls in a sweet pile; Mayberry meanwhile is bent over double clutching his own funnybone, bobbing on his toes while cursing in foreign languages. He expects three more cops to leap out immediately and pin his arms back and beat him unconscious with flashlights, but that doesn't happen. So he climbs one flight of stairs to the restaurant.

Bestriding the threshold of the cocktail lounge is another patrolman, who looks at Mayberry with mild surprise. "Restaurant's lawyer. He said it was okay," says Mayberry, gesturing downstairs with the arm that isn't numb. Before this one can object, which seems imminent, Mayberry bellows across two spooky roomfuls of people who are sitting entirely too quietly looking entirely too sober:

"Roybal!"

A slender man in a gray suit raises his head. He is standing beside one of the dinner booths in a far alcove, where the rheostat has been turned up like a sun lamp. Near him are two other men, also plainclothes, and a sobbing girl in a leather apron. At their feet is Karen's body.

EIGHTEEN

The bullet passed through her liver on an upward diagonal path, missed her heart by a half inch, nicked a bronchial artery, and lodged in her left lung. Mayberry eventually learns that bit of cold fact from Lieutenant Roybal. Death was by suffocation or perhaps drowning, consequent from massive pulmonary hemorrhage, and either way was therefore quicker than if she had simply bled out her life onto the floor by the salad bar, but not so merciful as if the bullet had put a hole in her heart. The coroner will have more on this later; Roybal again is the immediate source of information. The gun was a small-caliber automatic, a .32, as determined from the casing they found near her feet. Evidently she was expecting to meet him—whoever it was—or at least she knew him, or something such, because he was able to sit down close beside her in the booth and get the snout of his pistol pressed flush against her right side, where it left a powder burn on her jacket by the entry wound. The sound of the shot was not as loud as it otherwise would have been. Nevertheless he wasted no time getting out. He didn't run; no one remembers him hurrying. The waitress was in the kitchen and the broiler man only thought someone had dropped a breadboard. Nobody else heard, possibly because the piano player in the bar was at that moment hammering out "Ob-La-Di." The waitress discovered her after three or four minutes when it was too late. Probably it would have been too late no matter what. All this detail comes from Roybal, though only long at the end of a horrible evening, when Mayberry is finally being talked to more like a witness than a suspect. And even then it comes quid pro quo.

Anything is an improvement. When Mayberry left the restaurant he was under arrest. The formal charge was Assaulting an Officer but the suspicion was Murder.

Roybal had immediately conceived the idea—only tentative, an operating hypothesis—that Mayberry might have killed Karen in some blood-blind moment of erotic rage, then returned in remorse a half hour later and throttled the first person who challenged him. It was plausible and Roybal was just getting oriented on the case. Mayberry had no solid alibi, since he could have cut twenty minutes from the Albuquerque drive by speeding. But at midnight there was a line-up and he passed it: four different witnesses from the restaurant told Roybal positively that Mayberry was not *him*. By that time too the teletype had informed Roybal that Captain Harpenau of the State Police, just ten miles away, was investigating a recent homicide at Los Alamos, probably two, done in very much the same style. Mayberry was invited upstairs from his holding cell and given bad coffee while Roybal for the first time showed careful interest in the story that Mayberry had been telling all night.

Until then Roybal had barely listened, so it seemed, though evidently he was alert enough to notice when one of the names from Mayberry's tale appeared also in Harpenau's wire: Jeffrey Jay Katy. Katy was missing and presumed dead, Roybal learned from the teletype. He was Karen's brother-in-law and the reason she came to New Mexico, Mayberry had said. Kidnapped, said the teletype, following point-blank assault with a .32 automatic. Eleven days earlier; "when I was verifiably in Oakland," said Mayberry.

Lieutenant Roybal is not a bullheaded man. He has already apologized for his suspicion. He has offered something resembling condolences. He is even inclined to forget the assault charge, with its mitigating circumstances, but as justification for doing that he will need Mayberry's cooperation. Roybal is too intelligent to be coy about the coercive offer, or to pretend that Mayberry should act grateful. Now Mayberry sits slouched in Roybal's private cubicle, looking indeed murderous, pondering chiefly that choking red flood during the seconds it filled Karen's lungs, answering questions but speaking only when spoken to.

"The telephone conversation this morning. Yesterday morning. Tell me again about that. Her exact words, if possible."

Mayberry tells him. He has rerun it enough in his own mind.

"By which she was referring to what?"

"Jeffrey."

"Why didn't she say that explicitly?"

"She did. 'Concerning Jeffrey,' she said."

"Jeffrey's murder," says Roybal. "Concerning the question of who murdered Jeffrey. Is that what she seemed to be saying? Or was it something else concerning Jeffrey?"

"Yeah," says Mayberry. "Jeffrey's murder. That's what she seemed to be saying."

"Why didn't she say it? 'I think I know who killed him.' Or did she? Is it just as possible that she phrased it that way?"

"No. I told you. It was 'I think I may know what happened.' "

"Then why the circumlocution?"

Mayberry stares blankly for a moment, his attention having wandered: he is trying to imagine Buski in Oakland using the word "circumlocution." "She was in a restaurant. At a pay phone. I heard restaurant noises."

"The Ore House maybe?"

"No. It was before 9:00 A.M." Mayberry is uncomfortably aware that Roybal hasn't forgotten this; that his own lucidity, or consistency, is merely being tested. "Some sort of breakfast place. A cafe."

"Do you know for a fact that the Ore House doesn't serve breakfast?"

"No. I'm guessing. Do they?"

"I don't think so," says Roybal. "We'll check. Why do you say a cafe?"

"I'm not sure. Maybe she told me that. Anyway it was all clattery, behind her voice. Spoons and cups being grabbed by a busboy. More cups than macramé. More spoons than potted plants. Nothing to absorb the clatter."

Roybal smiles faintly and makes a mark, probably only a doodle, on his yellow pad. He is working by memory, without a stenographer or, as far as Mayberry knows, a tape recorder. He has himself tipped backward in his swivel chair, feet on the desk blotter, as though he and Mayberry might be two cronies plotting strategy for congressional campaign. Occasionally, between questions, he even pauses to think.

"Anything else? About this cafe. Any music? Any street noises?"

"There was an espresso machine," Mayberry says suddenly.

"How do you know that?" Roybal looks dubious but interested. "You smell it?"

"I heard someone say the word. Like they were ordering an espresso. I think. I just now remembered it."

This is worth two or three doodles. Mayberry feels a small swell of satisfaction for having come up with the espresso, which is absolutely genuine, because he will need credit with Roybal soon when he begins lying. Mayberry has already decided that he will tell Roybal everything he can about Karen and Jeffrey and their purposes in New Mexico, also about the dead man back in Mayberry's own house, give him Varvara if Roybal wants that part, supply Buski as a character reference, all of it up to a definite limit: the name Zuckerman will not be mentioned. Zuckerman is for Mayberry alone.

Ten minutes more on the cafe, another half hour beyond that on the phone call until both subjects are exhausted several times over, and Roybal says: "Who do you know that might kill three people for this Teller report?" Roybal has shown no inclination, as Buski did, to wave the H-bomb business away from his head as if it was a menacing sweat bee.

"Who do *I* know? Nobody. Professional spooks. Cultural attachés with borscht accents and dangerous cigarette lighters. I can't give you names. I don't travel in those circles."

"Not good enough, Mayberry. The way I see it, you

traveled from Oakland to Santa Fe in precisely those circles. You knew Jeff Katy and you knew Karen Ives. You had talked to Karen about the *Progressive* case and the bomb design. She told you she felt responsible for what happened to Jeff." One aspect of Roybal's smooth informality that especially annoys Mayberry is his habit of referring to dead people he never met by their first name. "She must have had some idea who killed him."

"I don't think so. Not till she got down here. This morning, yes. I think she might have known."

"And that's why she wanted your company."

"Probably."

"And if you'd got here in time, she would have told you."

"Maybe. Not necessarily."

"But meanwhile you have no faintest idea what she had turned up."

"No. No faintest idea."

"Are you lying to me, Mayberry?"

Mayberry lowers his eyelids. It isn't enough to hold out against Roybal and mock the man and leave him balked; he must be persuaded. Otherwise Mayberry will lose precious time, maybe sixty days of it with the county for molesting a helpless cop. "No," says Mayberry. "Jesus. I want you to catch the guy." That performance seems to work.

At a quarter past three the phone rings and Roybal receives word, from the officer he dispatched earlier to wake people up at State Police headquarters, that the shell casings from the Los Alamos parking lot bear a pattern of magazine scratches matching those on the casing of the round that killed Karen Ives. The news is anticlimactic but valuable as confirmation for what he has already begun assuming, and evidently makes Roybal feel that a day's work has been done. At 3:30 A.M. Mayberry is released, with the usual admonitions to stay available.

His greatest immediate desire is to drink himself senseless and pick another fight but the bars have all closed. He feels more miserable at soul, more perniciously inadequate and directionless, than he has any time within memory, or a least any time in eleven years, since his final months of futile good intentions before the great terrifying distraction of Tet. His imagination keeps homing back on those awful first minutes for Karen, last minutes rather, in the booth of a trendy steak house, and on the thoughts that, unwilled now despite his acquired trick of practicing just such mental rehearsals, force themselves upon Mayberry's brain like the cortical spasms of a dark and ugly seizure: *All right into the trauma room, laryngoscope nurse open an airway, she's got blood in there lots of it, okay an endotracheal tube, put a light down, let's have an I.V. in the jugular with electrolytes then we'll want to know her blood type quick, now get that chest tube in and FOR CHRIST'S SAKE START SUCTIONING* at which point Mayberry sees himself cutting a horizontal incision between Karen's fifth and sixth ribs but the patient is already dead. He heaves his gut empty onto the tiles behind an adobe archway outside some boutique.

Then he walks to the Hotel De Vargas for a room. He manages no clear glimpse despite several acute turns and he doesn't want to be obvious, but he knows that someone picked him up outside the police station. He hopes it is Zuckerman.

His room is small and a bit shabby, with a bath that connects to the room next door, but the arrangement will suit Mayberry's needs. He stands in silhouette at the window to take off his shirt, then makes a few preparations.

The .45 and one loaded clip go from his overnight bag to the bathroom. He feels silly stripping down the blankets and then draping them back over two pillows punched up in roughly the shape of a body but not silly enough to disdain doing it; however risible and trite, he figures, it can't hurt. Mayberry is not deluding himself that he will have any foolproof logistical advantage. What he will have, at best, is first chance. He considers cutting the telephone cord to make a trip wire from one leg of the bed to his spot in the bathroom, and quickly decides that would be simply too dippy. He pictures Zuckerman stepping carefully into the room, glancing down at the cord, stifling laughter before he can proceed. The pillows are bad enough. Mayberry hasn't done anything like this in eleven years but he remembers the dull fact that there is no winner's percentage in being ornately clever. The thing is to have first chance and not bungle it.

Now he unlocks the room door again, hoping this itself won't be a giveaway, and feels a little surprised by his own indecisiveness and imperfect confidence. Fortunately he is still very angry. After another appearance at the window he snaps off the light and goes into the bathroom to wait. The .45 is tucked in his belt at the small of his back. Standing in darkness beside the toilet, he takes his own pulse.

Twenty minutes under such conditions always seemed long and Mayberry is out of practice. He has begun revising his estimates—what likelihood he was really followed; if followed what likelihood the person will try to break in on him; what likelihood Mayberry is making an ass of himself—when he hears a faint moan of hardwood in the corridor. Then nothing at all for at least another minute. Then the knob. Mayberry is breathing deep and silently with his mouth open like a choirboy holding a note. When the slim figure takes its third step toward the bed, Mayberry moves. He is fast but not very quiet, releasing an ursine grunt as he clubs whoever it is across the back of the neck with a tubular aluminum luggage stand.

And he is on top, pinning the other body with his, jacking back viciously on a chin, taking the neck to the threshold of fracture before he knows even whether the man is conscious. Mayberry himself gulps for breath. He reaches back after the pistol and puts it against the man's ear and about that time the room light flicks on overhead. Brightness like a klieg. Mayberry blind as a mole. He can only freeze. He wants to cry. Aloud he says: "Shit."

His head sags. But he keeps his grip despite general muscular despair. The man he has jumped is young and black, with gold-rimmed spectacles squashed down around his jaw. The other is behind him somewhere and Mayberry himself may as well be hog-tied.

"However you want it." This comes from Mayberry in a gasp, volume weak for lack of air, and beyond everything else he is mortified by his nervous loss of wind. The second person says nothing. The black man is indeed conscious, eyes bulging from fear or the blood pressure in his face, probably both. "I'll blow him away, I swear. You think you can stop my finger?" With fierce concentration Mayberry prepares to spend his last mortal nerve impulses, if necessary, on the act of pulling a trigger.

"*May*-berry." The voice is familiar. "Re*lax*. Judas. You got such a edge on you all the time."

First Mayberry reefs back again on the black man's chin, pressing hard enough with the gun muzzle to cause earache. Then he cranes for a glance over his shoulder. Flat-footed in the doorway is Albert Varvara, holding a fifth of Bacardi and a quart bottle of Coke.

"You'll wake up the whole daggone floor," whispers Varvara.

NINETEEN

Jesse goes back down to the lobby for ice. He is a little slow in warming to Mayberry anyway.

Varvara helps himself to bathroom glasses and eventually three rum and Cokes are made, of which Varvara drinks two because Mayberry has decided he prefers simply hitting off the bottle. He sits on the bed with his back propped to the headboard, shoes and socks now finally off, pistol forgotten on the night table. He stares toward the opposite wall. Jesse is settled onto the floor, working quietly to restore shape to his wire spectacles, and Varvara has come to roost on the radiator, chattering in a low voice full of urgency and suspect motives like a vizier at a levee. Mayberry listens but the bottle is two-thirds empty before he has much to say. For the bottle to reach that point of two-thirds emptiness, however, doesn't take many minutes.

"We wanted to catch you before you turned in," says Varvara. "But I was way the hell out at the motel. I had to scoot downtown after Jesse called. Did the Berets teach you that number with the luggage stand? Ever try that one in the paddies?"

"Asshole," says Mayberry. "You know, you might have got somebody hurt." At this use of the second person subjunctive Jesse lifts his face toward Mayberry, but forbears.

"Yeah. Wasn't that lucky," say Varvara. "Look, I'm glad you're down here now. It's very convenient. I mean, I'm sorry about the Ives woman, I know you had personal feelings. That was too shitty. I understand. Believe me." He mentions the name Gene Rubens, which Mayberry has never before even heard. "But it happens to be a good thing that you came down. It might work out pretty well."

"It's very inconvenient," says Mayberry. "It's working out pretty badly. Is this your only bottle?"

"I've learned something about Zuckerman," says Varvara, and though that turns out to be only marginally true, still it was the right thing to say.

"Now you have my attention," Mayberry answers.

"But I need more than that."

"Where he came from and where he's headed. Who he is and what he's up to. The problem we got is our total ignorance on both those counts. Right? Am I right? Among other problems."

"I guess so."

"Wrong," says Varvara. "As of yesterday. He contacted you in Oakland, okay. About a deal for this copy of the Teller report which through great stupidity on your part you still have. When was that?"

"He left me a note, yeah. Made me an offer. I haven't heard from him since. Thursday sometime. Or Wednesday night." Mayberry shrinks from recollecting too vividly because that was the night with Karen.

"Since then he's been working the other end," says Varvara. "Packaging up the rest of the deal. Now he has a buyer. Or at least he thinks he has. I'm not so sure they won't just take what they want and throw Zuckerman down a sewer. Which, the second half would be aces with me."

"How can you know about that? That he has a buyer."

"You're supposed to ask who it is," Varvara says coyly.

"Who is it?"

"The *Mossad*." In a tone of histrionic flourish, but the drama is lost on the audience.

"Who's that?"

"Israeli intelligence." As though Mayberry, showing such ignorance, must have spent the last few years in some sort of hermetic isolation; and for that matter he has. "The Israelis, Mayberry. They got a real hard-on for this particular merchandise. Two of their guys are in Juarez right now, just over the border from El Paso. Waiting eagerly. One is named Hod, a true butt-hole. The other I don't know. Zuckerman has talked to them four times by telephone."

"How can you know about that?"

"I know lots of things. Hah. They're in the Hotel Burciaga, five blocks from the bridge, in a neighborhood of ten thousand open-air taco stands." Varvara has demanded a stiff refill from Mayberry before it was too late, and now in a moment of weakness is showing off. Mayberry suspects that, at the bar of the motel, he got a lengthy head start. Jesse, beginning to look uncomfortable, folds his arms. "Hod is buying ivory. The other was fool enough to get some dental work done. They're calling themselves exporters. They both have the trots. How can I know. Hah."

"Albert."

"Shut up, Jesse. Anyway, that isn't all. I also found out that he has a girl friend, our busy Zuckerman. Or did have. Maybe. This is actually still just informed speculation. She plays saxophone and travels with a band. The rest of the time she lives in Taos. Right now she's driving back from a gig in Texas." He turns, placating lamely. "Isn't that what they call it, Jesse? A gig?"

"Does she have the trots?" says Mayberry.

"And this is where you come in. Miss Saxophone definitely has some tie with Zuckerman. She reacted very funny to the name. An old flame or a very new one or who knows what. But she won't talk to us. Not about Zuckerman, not about Taos, not about nothing. So we'll get her talking to you."

"Why should she talk to me if not you?"

Varvara smiles widely, delighted to be asked. "Because you're just returning Zuckerman's call. And you heard she might be able to help. With us, most likely, she was trying to protect him. If that was it, then with you there's no reason. He already contacted you himself, and all you want is to get back to him. What could be better?" The smile folds away. "Also because if she doesn't, we're stuck."

"Zuckerman's girl friend has a boy friend who isn't Zuckerman." Jesse, cold sober and logical and not evidently the kind to pout, speaking up at last. "The name we have is Randy Ortiz. Local Indian kid from the Taos Pueblo. I think Albert mentioned him on the phone: an artist; one heroin bust in California. Well, two weeks ago

Ortiz lit out on her. She was up in Durango for three days. A booking. Also she may have been sleeping with one of the guys in the band. That's only a guess. Came home to Taos and Randy Ortiz was gone. We have that from State Police files, not from her. She reported him missing, but there's no follow-up, not by the troopers or her either. No reason to assume anything except that he split. But she's still very touchy on the subject. That's how we started off on her bad side, I think. I went after her with questions about Ortiz."

"But *you* don't care bullwhack about Randy Ortiz," says Varvara a little wildly, and it's certainly true enough. "You just want to be put through to Zuckerman." Also true. The bottle of rum is empty and Mayberry has divined a message at the bottom: *Time to skulk home pathetically or else get reckless*, it reads. *Choose one*.

"All right," he says. "Sure. I'll go up to Taos and see her."

Varvara hoists his glass in a triumphal wave, then paddles the air with a free arm and, barely correcting his balance, avoids falling off the radiator. Mayberry drops the dead soldier in a wastebasket.

"You should be careful," says Jesse, though it isn't quite clear to whom.

TWENTY

On a hangover scale to ten he would claim for it no more than a six, maybe a seven, even despite his ingenious reversal of order, vomiting first and then pouring the booze into a raw empty stomach. He is able, just barely, to leave Santa Fe by noon. Sixteen miles outside town on the winding two-lane to Taos, Mayberry passes a small laconic green sign marking the turnoff that leads up onto the Los Alamos mesa.

He never noticed this sign on his last trip, concerned as he was with a very different set of destinations and purposes, though undoubtedly it had all been here then very much as now—the sign, the diverging road, the mesa, the laboratory. In fact by Karen's account it had all been here, lurking quietly on the mesa above Santa Fe, since early 1943. Except, of course, the sign. Bad gravel road, old Army trucks groaning up the terrifying switchbacks, and no sign. In those days Los Alamos was the most exotic secret America had.

In those days the country's pre-eminent nuclear wizards, native and immigrant, were tiptoeing out of their universities and disappearing with train tickets to the Southwest, not to be seen again for the war's duration. Or rather most of the pre-eminent wizards: not quite all. While the trains pulled out for Santa Fe Hannah Broch, due to circumstances only partly beyond her control, sat like a wallflower in California.

It had seemed as though things would be different. The American bomb project had been maundering along by way of committees and university physics departments since 1939; in October of 1942 Oppenheimer was asked to organize and take charge of the final-stage laboratory; but the first really serious work toward designing a fission bomb had begun four months earlier, at the start of that summer, in Berkeley. With Hannah Broch very much part of it.

Oppenheimer had convened a study group, inviting a handful of exceptionally keen and creative physicists to gather for a series of discussions on the technical problems. The group was small and select, chosen not for broad representation but for imaginative, agile thinking. They met regularly through the summer in an attic room of Le Conte Hall, a quiet garret with wire mesh over the windows and a door to which Oppenheimer kept the only key, where they could think aloud and amicably berate each other for obtuseness and posit, for the sake of argument, that this machine they were engaged in creating just might—if it did explode as imagined—ignite all the nitrogen in the earth's atmosphere, scorching the whole planet within seconds like a marshmallow in a campfire. The marshmallow was Oppenheimer's simile; and they examined that particular possibility, with earnest concern and slide rules, before dismissing it as unlikely. Besides Oppenheimer the group included Hans Bethe, Robert Serber, the dapper Swiss physicist Felix Bloch, Edward Teller, Hannah herself, and another young Hungarian, brilliant but dour, just lately arrived in the country by way of Germany and then England. His name was Mihály Szölta.

Szölta had come out for these meetings from upstate New York, where Hans Bethe had found him a place in the physics department at Cornell. Oppenheimer knew Szölta already from one or two gatherings in Washington but to Hannah he was a stranger, and she was fast impressed by the quality of his intelligence and the force of his obsessions. Impressed strongly but ambivalently. His mathematical powers were uncanny—in abstract computation he was ingenious and speedy far beyond anyone else in the room. His technical insight too could be terrifically penetrating without, usually, becoming inflexible. Then occasionally he would bore them for days with petulant harping on some fixed idea. He was thirty-four, two years younger than Hannah, and from Bethe she learned a little of his background.

Szölta came from a distinguished family of Roman Catholic gentry in Budapest, a family known by its reputation to Hannah herself, with a history of service in the mid-level bureaucracy stretching well back through the Hapsburg monarchy even before Franz Joseph. Mihály's own father had been a lawyer as well as a gentleman landowner, with two separate estates on the upper River Tisza and a fine house in the old cottage section of Pest, where Mihály spent his boyhood. The father had been active in liberal causes as a member of the Independence Party, and eventually rose to become Minister of Justice in the government of Count

Károlyi, charged especially with coaxing through Parliament a series of suffrage reforms. Minister Szölta was recognized and appreciated as a rare variety of man: the passionate democrat who happens also to be a large landholder, friendly in his dealings with socialists but implacably opposed to Communism. When the great Land Reform program began in the spring of 1919, Minister Szölta journeyed up the Tisza to be in personal attendance, and to add official blessing, at the parceling out of his own estates to his own former laborers. Then suddenly the Béla Kun episode had begun, and for eight months Hungary was engaged in its clumsy experiment with Communism. On a beautiful September afternoon of 1919, roughly six weeks before the collapse of Kun's rule, Minister Szölta was hanged. With his mother and three older sisters, all of them too terrified to attempt escape, Mihály remained at the house in Pest. They were, according to a seedy self-styled colonel who claimed to speak for the Revolutionary Governing Council, in no danger whatsoever.

Under Horthy's counterrevolution the Szölta family was treated with solicitude; Minister Szölta was even granted a posthumous pension; and so there was money for Mihály to advance his education abroad. He went to Leipzig and then later Berlin, working at the Kaiser Wilhelm Institute under Max von Laue on problems of Relativity. After Hitler had published his first racist decrees Szölta stayed on for three more years at the Kaiser Wilhelm, until finally the circumstances of trying to do physics in Germany became too inconvenient: Mihály Szölta may not have been Jewish but—so said the official censors of thought—Relativity was. He went on to the Clarendon Laboratory at Oxford and from there, in 1941, which seemed a good year for a nervous and gloomy person to leave England, to

Bethe's hospitality at Cornell. In fairness to Szölta it was not weakheartedness that made him so anxious to get out of England at that particular time, at least not weakheartedness in the civic sense; he was weakhearted that autumn because his wife of twelve years, a childhood sweetheart from Budapest whom he adored, had recently died of pneumococcal pneumonia, in the Radcliffe Infirmary, while waiting for antibiotics that couldn't be spared. When Szölta arrived with Hans Bethe in Berkeley, for the start of Oppenheimer's little conference, his precious Emmi had been dead less than a year and he was a rank newcomer now to his third adopted country. He showed no propensity to let his disposition reflect the California climate. He had not even yet altered his name.

Some days that summer Szölta seemed utterly disconsolate, all of his humanity locked away in a dank private chamber of despair; other days he rode buoyantly on the flow of ideas, his black eyes gleaming, like a man immune to any grief so mundane as the death of a wife. Sometimes in their study sessions he pouted or yawned, idly twisting the wiry overgrowth of his muttonchops into spiral towers. Sometimes he was rude—not in the way Oppenheimer could be rude, like a French marquis with a rapier, but as a child genius who knows his own gifts might make himself insufferable—though always toward Hannah, in the meeting room or elsewhere, he was impeccably polite. Even courtly. Even, in his own manner, gentle. Despite herself, and only outside the room, she liked him.

Sometimes, so she heard, this Szölta would go at 4:00 A.M. to a cubicle in the music building and hammer Mozart from a piano for hours. Sometimes he wouldn't appear for their sessions. Sometimes she worried about him. It was early July when he began talking about the thermonuclear.

They were wasting their time, and his, Szölta told the group bluntly, with this fuss over the technical details of a uranium fission weapon. The thing might be done, yes, but never mind, it was small beans. He and Teller had turned up a much larger, more interesting idea: use the fission explosion to trigger a fusion reaction in heavy hydrogen—*immense* quantities of heavy hydrogen—thereby creating a vast thermonuclear release. An explosion beside which their fission device would be insignificant. A *superbomb*, he said, coining the term in a moment's inspiration, but judicious enough to coin it in English, though everyone in the room also spoke German. Teller nodded to all this, diffident but in his own way equally firm, embarrassed most of all by Szölta's overbearing manner. Yes, it was true, Teller allowed: he and Szölta had talked through the new idea. No question that it was far superior. Of course it was, Szölta grumbled with the thick burr that five years in England had somehow barely touched: *Uff gourse*. They had even roughed out—that is, Teller had roughed out—a design concept for their thermonuclear beast, a bizarre and rather woolly set of technical hypotheticals which Teller was permitted to describe quietly before Szölta interrupted again with his vehement endorsements. Yes, there were too many good reasons why they should go after the bigger blast for them to dither about with mere fission, Szölta argued. He argued unrelentingly. Yet as Hannah heard him those reasons amounted to just three: the thermonuclear was possible, and therefore inevitable; hydrogen was cheaper than uranium; the thermonuclear, as a problem for them to work on, was more interesting. The word kept cropping up, *interesting*.

Two weeks of July were debated away over the matter. It was Oppenheimer who gave birth to the nickname, with his special talent for dry scorn, when he said in frustration that they might still make some small headway on the question of fission "if The Magyars would only let us." His logic against the thermonuclear was simple, not especially interesting, but required multiple emphatic repetition: *"There's a war on, Mihály, and we're in a big damn hurry."* Eventually Teller came around to the common view, if for no other reason than politeness. Szölta was silenced, but never convinced. After that, still attending sporadically, he took a less active part in the sessions. Late in August the group adjourned, Szölta disappeared with his Mozart and his hypothetical superbomb, saying no goodbys except perhaps to his friend Teller, and Hannah did not see him again until after Hiroshima. She would have assumed, wrongly, that in his demonic absorption with other things he had long forgotten her.

As Robert Oppenheimer, of such habitual mental neatness, evidently had.

Since his marriage two years earlier she had not seen Oppenheimer socially, not even in public, and hardly at all professionally either, because her Berkeley fellowship had finished and Ernest Lawrence had not wanted to keep her; she was now an assistant professor at Stanford. She had heard Robert give papers at several conferences. Once she asked a question from the audience, and while he was delivering a quite proper answer at the corners of his mouth there had been evidence of a smile, not the mocking sort but one of gladness. Gladness to see her, gladness to have her challenging his work. Kitty was seated that day in the first row, ignorant of the physics but very sensitive to the chemistry. Then nothing more between Hannah and

Robert until he had called, in spring of '42, asking her to participate in the summer sessions. She was saying *Yes, of course* mentally, or rather emotionally, before he had even described the subject; the purpose beyond the subject was not mentioned until they all finally assembled in the garret. She had been surprised by the invitation, and enormously pleased, though it was natural enough for him to want her in the group, if for no other reason than their bygone collaboration on the behavior of high-energy protons. She had also been surprised by the way her heart continued its boisterous drumming ten minutes after she hung up the telephone, and felt no pleasure over that. The man had shucked her away and married someone else. Discovering how much she might still love him was hard on Hannah's self-esteem. But very well then, that was just something she knew about herself, and so she would cope with it—or at least this was her attitude going into the sessions. Nevertheless the summer cost her: three years of distance. After the study group adjourned, in September and on into the winter, she found herself waiting like a bobbysoxer for his second call.

She knew he was recruiting for the new laboratory. She knew, from the summer sessions, that he still had a high regard for her brain. By Christmas she knew that Serber and Teller and Mihály Szölta were all joining the lab, wherever it might be, probably Hans Bethe soon also. She knew that her leftist activities during the late thirties would present a potential problem for security clearance, but she believed it could all be explained away rationally. What she didn't know was that Oppenheimer, in October, had barely passed his own security check.

As the bomb project began gaining momentum its grand high Pooh-Bah was General Leslie Groves of the Army

Engineers, a paunchy career soldier who had missed all the good wartime assignments and now to his vast frustration had been appointed caretaker over a menagerie of pointy-headed civilians. His personal responsibility, as he saw it, was simple: *Get one of these atomic deals built before the Germans do.* Grossly miscast as chief executive of the project, Groves made up for his total ignorance of nuclear physics by choosing very good scientists and then treating them like sneaky children. But this much at least he did right: when Groves liked a person, he supported him. Not *trusted*, necessarily, but *supported*. Robert Oppenheimer, for reasons far beyond anyone's comprehension, he liked. On the basis of several preliminary conversations and the instinct of his own gut, which was large and dear to him, he decided that Oppenheimer should be director of the final-stage lab.

Immediately the FBI was at the general's ear, twittering frantically. *Not only shouldn't you make this guy your director*, they told Groves; *you shouldn't let him anywhere near the project. He's red as a tomato!*

Groves did a canny thing. He thanked the FBI and accepted their reports and surveillance logs and told them to disappear. Then he held another conversation with Oppenheimer. There was no need to threaten or deal. Groves merely showed Oppenheimer what he had, and declared that for the time being he chose to be broadminded. Having accepted the directorship, even perhaps having wanted it, Oppenheimer from that date was subject to a very delicate sort of leverage from the fat general everyone else considered a boob.

The rest of the leverage presumably came from Kitty. New Year's passed, a semester began, colleagues were asking for leave, Oppenheimer was picking his team. Hannah received no call.

On the Ides of March, 1943, under what seemed all positive auguries, Oppenheimer left for New Mexico. Two weeks later he was joined by Kitty. The primary tasks at that point were construction—the Corps of Engineers was improving the mesa road, piping in more water, tossing up cheap wooden buildings—and recruitment. The latter was Oppenheimer's concern: scientists were arriving from Cornell and Columbia and Chicago, Berkeley and Caltech, but more were still needed. He wrote cajoling letters, he sent urgent telegrams, occasionally he went off to coax a man personally. He was one of very few persons who, having once seen the inside of the Los Alamos compound, were allowed to leave again on any account during the next two years.

And even for the director, when he was back at large in the world, there was surveillance. That he certainly knew this just made the Jamisson incident, to Groves and the later inquisitors, still more inexplicable.

With scientists in demand for other war research, and him prevented by security strictures from describing to an uncommitted prospect even generally what his project involved, or where it was located, Oppenheimer had hard times collecting a staff. First he thought a hundred top physicists would be sufficient, though he had no idea where he could find them; soon he realized that five hundred physicists and chemists and metallurgists was far too few. Hannah still received no call. In April, when enough technical people had been gathered to fill one large room, Bob Serber began giving a series of orientation lectures on the information that had been developed so far. They knew something about uranium fission, and Serber explained what; something about plutonium; something about a possible design for the bomb mechanism itself. But clearly they needed more specialists. Oppenheimer left in June on another recruiting trip, this time to Pasadena and Berkeley.

Late in the afternoon of June 12, 1943, he called Hannah from a pay phone on the Berkeley campus.

"Of course you can see me," she said.

"Not at your office," he said.

The letter of accusation, eleven years later, said:

> It was further reported that a British national named Hubert Edward Jamisson was approached, sometime prior to March 1, 1943, by a certain Pyotr Gerstmann, second secretary of the Soviet consulate in San Francisco, for the purpose of obtaining information regarding work being done toward a uranium weapon in the Berkeley laboratory, elsewhere throughout the American academic labs under contract for war research, or at a secret government laboratory then rumored to have been lately established; that such information was desired for the use of Soviet scientists; that Hubert Edward Jamisson subsequently requested the aforementioned Dr. Hannah Broch to approach you concerning the matter; that Hannah Broch did thereupon approach you, during private conversation on the evening of June 12, 1943, in connection with the matter; and that Hannah Broch finally advised Hubert Edward Jamisson that there was no chance whatsoever of obtaining the information from you.
>
> It has also been noted that you did not report this episode to the appropriate authorities until several months after its occurrence; that when you did finally discuss

the episode with appropriate authorities, in August of
1943, you refused to identify Hannah Broch as the
individual who made the approach; and that it was not
until several months still later, and then only under a
direct order to do so from General Leslie Groves, that
you identified the individual as Hannah Broch.

Hannah first read these words, eleven years later, in the
New York *Times*.

Until then she never knew she had been named. She
never knew why the Stanford department had gone chilly
on her, or why the assistantship was curtly withdrawn at
the end of her current contract. For years afterward she let
herself assume it was still Spanish war relief, and perhaps
the Consumers' Union, that prevented her from being part
of any goverment-sponsored research. Robert never told
her. She had not even known, though Oppenheimer himself must at least have suspected it, that by inviting him to
her apartment in Palo Alto that afternoon she had also
invited the FBI.

She only understood what Robert had said: that he was
in town for thirty-six hours, that he was exhausted, that he
was lonely these days and somewhat befuddled by his new
role, that it would be nice to talk. She agreed it would be.
Five weeks had passed since her conversation with Hubert
Jamisson, and she had nearly forgotten not only Jamisson's
proposition but even her answer: no, as things now stood
she could not possibly help. While Robert was finding a
cab over from Berkeley, she remembered.

"Hello, Robert. You look awful," she said at the door.
"Are you ill? Or is that just the uniform of an important
public servant?"

He grinned boyishly and went inside and eighty yards

down the block two special agents in a DeSoto settled in for their seamy little vigil.

At 7:00 A.M. one of the two agents scurried to a drugstore for coffee; the other made a log entry. At eight they followed Oppenheimer back to Berkeley.

And from there to the train depot, then on board the Southern Comfort for Santa Fe. A copy of their report reached Groves's desk in Washington within three days. The vice-provost at Stanford was only visited four months later, after Oppenheimer had been persuaded to use the names Jamisson and Broch in a single sentence.

TWENTY-ONE

But Mayberry ignores the Los Alamos turnoff, for now at least, under the mistaken impression that there is some urgency to his reaching Taos for a conversation with Zuckerman's girl friend. Albert Varvara has done nothing to correct that impression, though certainly he knew—or could have deduced with a little sober reflection—that Tay Riordan would be spending the next forty-eight hours on the road back from Austin, Texas. More than once during his wasted two days of waiting and walking and boozing Mayberry will curse Varvara for that oversight, if it was an oversight. The alternative is to begin wondering "Why should Varvara want me out of Santa Fe?" and Mayberry has made a silent vow to keep his paranoia within reasonable bounds. Anyway he had no real preference for doing the waiting and walking and boozing back in Santa Fe. As for Los Alamos: it is closed, at least that part of possible interest to Mayberry, on Sunday. Taos on the other hand is decidedly open for business.

The narrow streets of the old section are clogged with art shoppers, even art buyers, and other less stylish varieties of tourist. Mayberry abandons the car and finds a phone listing for *Riordan, T.*, but after twelve rings he hangs up. He has the address that Varvara lifted from State Police files, so with a map from a civic information booth he sets off on foot, the only person among hundreds not carrying a camera or a piece of pottery or a child. Within three blocks of the square he has passed a half dozen small galleries, each in a low adobe storefront, none of them showing anything signed by a Randy Ortiz. Alabaster Madonna heads with Indian cheekbones, desert scenics in red and ocher, welded bronze saguaros, abstract acrylics in red and ocher, firebird motifs and sun motifs and four-pointed stars, some of these in turquoise and green but more in red and ocher; no opium-poppy motifs and no saxophones.

He follows one street until the galleries and shops fall away to a residential neighborhood of dusty alleys and mongrel dogs taking siesta in the shade. It isn't far but the atmosphere has changed drastically. On the corner he has been searching for, where Burch Street forks away to the south, is an Iglesia Pentecostal. Burch itself is a drowsy lane that leads nowhere, three or four blocks of small old houses and dirt yards marked off with crumbling knee-high adobe walls, and made beautiful in a flyblown way by the concourse of great ancient cottonwoods lining both sides and arching into a canopy high overhead. The cottonwoods are full of squirrel nests. At the far end of this tunnel, one place short of a funeral parlor, Mayberry locates the address.

It is a pink adobe with a wooden porch swing. The screen door is ruptured, the windows are blank, and the cat-food bowl on the stoop is, but for a few crumbs, empty. The gravel driveway is empty. The mailbox is empty. The sound of his knuckles on the doorframe is very empty. The facing wall of the front room on the left, which Mayberry with nose to windowpane can see, is filled by a large gaudy canvas depicting, in oil, what looks like a slightly anthropomorphized angora goat. Concluding it must be the right place, Mayberry decides against leaving a note. He would rather take his chances than give a warning.

He gets a motel room and out of sheer orneriness eats dinner at a McDonald's on the edge of town, but even that place lacks the usual pyrite arches; instead, under compulsion by a zoning board or its own misguided agreeability, it is another parody of adobe, the ultimate parody, done in prefab aluminum paneling painted mud brown and complete with phony log beams pretending to jut from the lintels. Across the street is a Kentucky Fried Chicken in similar style. Mayberry is beginning to find it maddening, this narcissistic architectural uniformity to which the state seems so devoted, but then right now he has nothing good to say about anybody.

He retires for an evening of sullen soaking to a bar off the square and hates the decor there too, though without at first knowing why. Then he realizes. Low beam ceiling and white stucco walls and Navajo rugs and pots, *ristras* of red peppers and bunches of dried maize, dim lighting from cast-iron kerosene lamps, young Anglo waitresses and young Anglo clientele in a stagy Old Hacienda setting: it is too much like the Ore House in Santa Fe, of his brief but vivid experience, and he is oppressed by the association.

Karen has been dead twenty-four hours. Then twenty-nine hours, and Mayberry is still drinking. He is still listening inattentively to Muzak jazz from a softly electrified trio, bass and rhythm guitar and a dark woman on a Yamaha piano. And still, in his maudlin booziness, picking over a meager assortment of recollections. Mayberry didn't know Karen well, only quickly, but every minute, every word, now seems worth a second examination.

He talked rapturously about his buddy Mayberry. How flattering that you never heard about me.

I heard something about a girl in Los Angeles.

I was the girl. Only it was Riverside. And it was a wife. So tell me. Am I the first woman that you and Paul shared?

No.

From the bartender, an old acquaintance by now, Mayberry learns a few scraps. Yes, the bartender knows Tay Riordan, not well of course but who she is, it's a small enough town. And her group, yes, lately calling themselves Lickety Split; country swing and some vintage swing, also a little rock. Not that interesting, to the bartender's musical taste, except for Tay herself. Tay herself, Mayberry gathers, would be quite to the bartender's taste if an opportunity ever offered. No, they don't play this room. Too many of them, too much sound, too expensive. They play mostly the larger second-line spots in Santa Fe and around the region. Mayberry has heard they were just working in Austin: any idea when they might get back? No idea, says the bartender. Mayberry could ask Judy Ouray about that. Who's Judy Ouray? Bartender points to the dark woman behind the electric piano. The trio has begun what must be their last set. "Give me another. And one for you," Mayberry tells the bartender, but the bartender is a macrobiotic.

Sounds to me like you know him well enough.

I came to know him a little better afterward.

After the wedding?

No. After his death.

Judy Ouray specializes in breathy Latin-rhythm vocals, to which Mayberry through the whole evening has been at best indifferent. Now for twenty minutes he tries to make himself seem an appreciative audience. She is attractive in a severe cold way, with long hair hanging fine as black silk to her shoulders, straight-edge bangs, and a broad Indian nose. Mayberry approaches with gracious lies but she hikes a sneer into that nose at the mention of Tay Riordan.

"Who wants to know?"

"Just me. Friend of a friend."

"I didn't know she had any. Or is your friend maybe in love."

"I suppose that's what I meant." This is just to seem amiable, but Judy Ouray's moue says that she knew what he meant before he could even suppose it, and the whole matter is for her beneath comment.

"Austin. Yeah, they could be there. If you heard that, what are you asking me?"

"I was wondering if you might know when they're due back."

"Were you," says Judy Ouray. The other two have unplugged their instruments and disappeared, leaving the amplifiers in place; evidently it's here again tomorrow night. "That's a long drive, Austin. Two days, in a truck full of equipment. I've made it." As little sympathy as she shows for Mayberry's curiosity, she does want him to know that. "I've made it," she repeats.

"Can you tell me the best way to get in touch with her?"

"Tay Riordan?" She jerks her head in a small vehement toss toward one shoulder; an Italian farmer would make the same point by spitting on your shoe. "Not through me."

Did you see the body?

I wouldn't even look at the car. I was jelly.

Who made the identification?

Paul's father was bedridden from a stroke. His mother was in New York.

I know that.

It must have been Jeffrey.

Mayberry closes that bar and then, crossing the square quickly, another. He walks back to his motel without danger that the night air will sober him up.

What's so distressing?

I'm in a coffee shop. I can't say right now.

It was a coffee shop. When Roybal next runs him down, hindering, threatening, Mayberry can offer that tiny addendum: she called it a coffee shop.

Give me a hint.

Jeffrey. I was in Los Alamos yesterday.

The next morning, not early, Mayberry makes a perfunctory stop at the pink adobe on Burch Street. There is no change from the day before, still no sign of living presence, except now a skinny half-grown orange cat looks at him expectantly from beside the empty bowl. Mayberry would like to oblige but he is hurrying out of town, having decided to spend the day in Los Alamos.

TWENTY-TWO

After that morning she never saw Robert again, not in person, not even from the audience of one of those conferences for which he no longer had time and she no longer had credentials; only his face on the magazine covers. She was never asked to join the coven at Los Alamos. But for Hannah there were more pressing concerns. The problem of hunger, for instance, literal as well as intellectual. Beginning in early 1944 and for eight years thereafter, she had no job and couldn't get one.

Not in physics or any other field. Late in 1944 Hannah applied to the Office of War Information for work as a translator of German and Hungarian, and was considered, then rejected when her name failed to clear a routine security check through the Civil Service Commission. The next year she had another prospect, translating for the Nuremberg tribunals, and again was denied clearance. She had a minuscule bit of savings from the Stanford teaching but how she lived during those two years—even at her new standard, which in someone less naturally ascetic and self-contained would have seemed ragged proverty—was a mystery to her acquaintances in Palo Alto. She wouldn't accept much charity from the few former colleagues, at Stanford, who were willing to offer any: a meal with company, gladly; a can of coffee or a basket of fresh produce, if presented in the right nonchalant spirit. These two or three people who stayed in touch with her were of the faculty but not of the physics department. They suspected that someone else had to be giving her money—a tiny amount anyway—or her thrift-shop collection of furniture would have long since been in a pile on the sidewalk.

In 1946 she moved back to Berkeley, into a room above a bookstore on Telegraph, and began posting hand-lettered advertisements on the university notice boards. Eventually, after another year of that, she had a small steady trade tutoring graduate students privately in German and mathematics. She was exchanging afternoons of conversation in Hungarian, with an elderly refugee man as poor as she, for his instruction on the viola; and he was loaning her his second viola. She owned one dress bought since Pearl Harbor. She was a very busy woman with new friends, quite handsome at forty years old, and not unhappy.

She was first called to testify in 1947.

This initial instance was in Sacramento, before a body of the state assembly, something called the Senate Fact-Finding Commitee on Un-American Activities, and her appearance had not been subpoenaed. She was merely invited, and complied with the invitation, making herself (so far as she felt possible) a cooperative witness. There were no dramatic confrontations. The senators asked her about the Consumers' Union, and she described its activities during the late thirties with a wealth of innocuous detail, admitting readily that in those days she was a member, respectfully declining to identify others by name. The point was not pressed. They asked her about the American Committee for Democracy and Intellectual Freedom, and she told them volubly of its pot-luck benefit dinners and its rummage sales for Spanish relief. She was an active member of that organization, yes; she hoped the senators would allow her to speak only of herself. For some reason they did. It might have been her manner, deferential, hoping to please, careful not to provoke; it might have been male gallantry, or some bias of unconscious and less pristine motive in favor of an attractive, humbled widow; it might have been that this was still just 1947, after all, and the real smell of blood was not yet on the wind. Anyway they seemed to be after background information and not Hannah Broch. They asked her about the Communist Party of Alameda County. She had never been a member or attended a meeting, she told them, of that branch or any other; her brother, in childhood, had been killed by the Hungarian Communists. At which point the senators, slightly embarrassed, seemed to lose concentration. It was nearly five o'clock of a long day during which they had heard many witnesses. Hannah was dismissed. She had not been asked about Hubert Jamisson, Pyotr Gerstmann, or the man who by that time was America's most famous scientist.

Soon after this appearance Hannah filed an application with the California Board of Education, to teach physical sciences and math, at the secondary level, anywhere in the state. She never received a reply.

About the same time she was interviewed—also her first

such experience but not her last—by the FBI. The session was held at the Bureau office in San Francisco and lasted, with two agents in shirtsleeves questioning her by turns, for eleven hours. Hannah by the end of it was hoarse. The central theme of the interrogation was her relationships with Hubert Jamisson (portrayed by the agents as an espionage operative whose activities were well known to them) and with a minor official from the Russian consulate named Pyotr Gerstmann. The former relationship was casual, scant, and no, had never been intimate, she told them; the latter relationship was non-existent. In fact she told them this ten or twelve times and was still obliged to answer endless further questions based on their presumption that she was lying. Intermittently one of the two agents disappeared into another room, to answer the telephone or make a call out. After lunch, which was brought to her on a tray, they didn't for a while mention Jamisson. Instead they asked about Robert Oppenheimer, drawing no connection between the two. Hannah learned then, with a nauseating jolt only partly related to her political troubles, that strange men had been skulking nearby during the last night she spent with Robert. She was allowed to go to the ladies' room and be ill, though a female typist was sent in to watch her.

The agents revealed nothing to Hannah about Robert's own account of that night, if he had given one. She assumed he must have. If the authorities knew Robert had come to see her, he would certainly have been confronted with that fact, during the height of the war and the project, and would have had to say something. What would he have said? Maybe only a little, cleverly dismissive in his acerbic way. Or perhaps more than a little. She suspected that Robert's version might have included Hubert Jamisson and the proposition she had relayed—Robert might even have denounced her for attempted espionage. But while suspecting this, which was very nearly the truth, she continued by force of will and sentiment to believe she believed otherwise. Robert would have parried them.

Finally the agents left off Oppenheimer, questioned her briefly about her friendship with Niels Bohr, which they absurdly seemed to imply should be grounds for some sort of embarrassment, then came back around to Jamisson and Stephen Geddes and other East Bay Communists of the thirties. More hours on that line, more badgering questions about the poor tired old Spanish war relief effort and now it was dark outside the office window, but still they hadn't asked outright about any message she might have conveyed between Jamisson and Oppenheimer. Robert had beaten them, she was thinking; he had saved himself and her both. But apparently the agents were just waiting for her to grow weary, and orchestrating the whole ordeal rather adeptly. Jamisson had been picked up the same morning—as Hannah learned only a week later—and had spent all that day under interrogation at an office in Oakland, which explained the phone calls and more. They did indeed want Hanna's account of the Jamisson incident, but not until they could match it against Jamisson's own. Sometime after 7:00 P.M., quite suddenly, one of the agents said:

"Now tell us about the offer you carried from Jamisson to Dr. Oppenheimer."

"Robert was vehement. He was outraged at Jamisson," Hannah answered immediately. She sat back and rubbed her eyes. She felt relief, relief and not much else, even while realizing numbly that this relief only meant the agents had done their job well. "He would have no part of it. He was angry at me for speaking of it. In fact he clapped his hands over his ears, though that was merely a gesture, afterward, in his rage. I had been confused myself. Of two minds. I had never expected to see him, we were finished, and therefore I hadn't thought carefully about the ethics, about the legalities even, of such a thing. I had dismissed the idea when Jamisson asked me. Because I had never—you must understand—I had never expected to see Robert Oppenheimer again. Under those circumstances." Hannah bowed her head. She spoke to her own hands. "He was vehement against it. He shouted. I admit, I was to blame: I had not thought about it carefully. But I agreed with him at once. It would be improper. Of course it would. The subject was dropped."

"He was a married man," said the agent. "Employed on a government project of highest sensitivity. He was spending the night there with you. That wasn't improper?"

She didn't answer. She was waiting to be told she could now leave. Hannah still believed at this point that it was she who had caused trouble for Robert, not vice versa.

In the lobby is an oversized bronze bust of Robert Oppenheimer. In the library itself are a few men in goatees and cardigans and clip-on security badges, potting around at the catalogue and among the stacks. Mayberry has spent an hour roaming the building with nothing to show for it but the attention of a suspicious librarian, who has begun watching him as though he's a stumblebum browsing in a liquor store. Two murders in the parking lot week before last, and a cataclysmically dangerous document stolen: he supposes they have good reason to be a trifle jumpy.

Trying his best to look like a witless innocent tourist, he has inspected the photocopier in its alcove, read the notice above, waited for inspiration to strike. Nothing. He has done a little potting at the catalogue himself. With no idea what to search for. He has paced the stacks and gone downstairs and there discovered a second copy machine, at which for several minutes he frowns intently, remembering the vivid fingerprints on his copy of LAMS-1363, struggling in vain to formulate a precise question. "I'm missing something," he thinks. "Something that's right here, in this library." Knowing also that, whatever it is, Karen didn't miss it.

"Where do you keep your important documents?" He has gone directly to the suspicious librarian but realizes at once that, notwithstanding the forthrightness, this is a bad opening. She sucks her upper lip back from a pair of rodential incisors and glares at him over the swooping turquoise frames of her bifocals. "Unclassified," Mayberry adds appeasingly.

"Reports," she says. "In the vault." Her eyes have grown just a bit wide and wild; if she were a bank teller, Mayberry suspects, her foot would already be on the button. "Downstairs in the vault."

"Can an outsider get hold of one?" She does a slow blink while Mayberry bungles on: "Just to look at, I mean. Here in the library. An unclassified report. Unclassified."

"Exactly which report was it you wanted? The document number."

"I don't have a document number."

"The title then."

"I don't have a title." *I don't care which one you give me. I just want to see how your library works, you nasty* bitch. "Something in, say, the disintegration of high-energy protons." La-de-da, Mayberry.

"A non-staff reader may call up a report, yes," she admits. "But you'll need the document number."

And she directs him to the *Nuclear Science Abstracts,* in a far section of the stacks: five rows of fat black volumes filled with numerical indexes and coded cross-indexes and almost totally inscrutable to a normal ignorant human. It doesn't matter. Just to seem diligent Mayberry kills fifteen minutes in that quiet aisle, flipping aimlessly through one volume of the *Abstracts,* before choosing a title at random: "Criticality of the Water Boiler and Effective Number of Delayed Neutrons," which for him might as well be in Sanskrit. He also copies the document number and the author. Mayberry hopes the damn thing isn't classified. He trots back to the same librarian and hands her his scrap of paper. Then he watches. Already he feels positive that he is wasting his time.

She punches four digits on her phone console and says hello to the Reports librarian downstairs. She delivers his request by the document number, ignoring title and author. If she notices that high-energy protons have become delayed neutrons, she doesn't seem to care; it could happen to anybody. After a moment on the line she answers: "No. Non-staff. Yes," and reads Mayberry's name off the slip "Thank you, Fiona," she says, and that's all. No request for his identification. No questions about his affiliation or purposes. To him she says: "They'll bring it up. If they have it. About ten minutes." For ten minutes he leans there against the Circulation desk, watching her rustle paper in connection with other business. Then a pudgy Indian woman steps out of the elevator holding a slim eight-by-eleven pamphlet. This woman hands it to the bucktoothed librarian and returns as she came. The librarian sets the report before Mayberry.

"Bring it back to me when you're done. Don't take it out of the building. Don't make pencil or pen marks." She pushes forward a half-page printed form. "And sign this."

TWENTY-THREE

Mayberry almost wishes he hadn't come. He drives back to Taos feeling giddy with sickening vague suspicions and one very specific new worry. He is all the more eager to talk with the woman who knows a painter named Ortiz, an entrepreneur named Zuckerman. He wants to see what sort of enchantress might turn men into angora goats, drive them to break probation, perhaps even transform their signatures.

He leaves his car at the motel and walks, again, to Burch Street. Though the night is hot and starry with a crescent moon helping to light the countryside, under the long archway of cottonwoods Burch remains cool, silent, dark as a Kentucky cave. Still no vehicle in the driveway of the pink adobe house but now there is a lamp lit, and the cat's dish has evidently been taken inside. From the porch he hears neither conversation nor music. Tay Riordan answers his knock wearing a black terrycloth robe that hangs to her ankles, bundled as tightly around her as one terrycloth belt can keep it bundled. The collar is turned up.

She is barefoot. Her complexion is pallid as cream porcelain—from road-weariness, he assumes—except for the ruddy cheek patches, which look as if she has just finished scrubbing them hard with a gentle soap. Her hair is black and thick, kiting out in loose waves. Mayberry is not surprised by her odd vampy beauty, that much he expected after the gloss by Judy Ouray; what surprises him is that, at this point, he can feel the least susceptible himself. Her hands are jammed in the robe's pockets, and she address him unwelcomingly through a screen door.

"I can come back later," says Mayberry. Not that his curiosity isn't by now intense; but he doesn't want to spook her the way Varvara and Jesse did, and he believes that what she might tell him is worth waiting for. "Tomorrow morning. I know you've just gotten in from Texas."

"Why?" she says. "What's special about later? If the answer is no, it won't be yes later."

"I thought you might be tired."

"I am. What's that to you?"

He takes a full pace backward and clasps his hands behind him. "Look, lady. I don't want anything from you. Not how you think. I just have a simple question, and reason to believe you might be one person who can answer it. Maybe you can't. If you can, maybe you won't. Once that much is established, whichever way, I'm on the road back to Santa Fe. You don't know me, you probably don't know anybody who knows me. I only presume on you like this because, despite that, I think you and I might have something important in common."

"Do tell."

"I've got a missing friend," he says, though no longer so sure in what sense to believe it. "I'd like to discuss the matter with Zuckerman."

A slight movement at the elbows pinches the robe tighter against Tay Riordan's ribs. "Zuckerman?" Now Mayberry sees what Varvara meant by her funny reaction to the name: the rouge spots have gone livid. The woman is a chameleon.

"Yeah, I'm looking for Zuckerman. And I think he's looking for me."

"Then maybe you ought to be careful," she says. Which has a familiar ring. "Come in."

TWENTY-FOUR

For almost five years after the first FBI ordeal Hannah was left alone, with her tutoring and her viola and her Telegraph Avenue friends. The aged Hungarian man proposed marriage to her, unfortunately, and though she managed to decline him without losing the friendship entirely, still things were different afterward, and it seemed only proper for her now to buy a used viola of her own. She was without music for a year, scrimping, before that was possible. She consorted intermittently with a courtly Greek restaurateur, in an uneasy arrangement that from his side was dementedly romantic but for her was more cynically just a matter of hairy flesh and companionship, until he began embarrassing her in public with his simian displays of possessiveness. Also thanks to this Greek Hannah experienced her first and only black eye, which sent him down to a vast Mediterranean depth of abject remorse and led her to conclude that the whole affair, while interesting, was best not pursued further. The Greek was six years younger than Hannah anyway, and she was tired of the smell of olives. After that there were no further men. She drank coffee in the cafes with her tutees, or with a woman she knew from the Red Cross office, and had her meals in her room off a hot plate. She applied for no state or university or federal jobs. She read newspapers occasionally, German poetry often, Communist periodicals seldom, and *Physical Review* not at all. What she knew about developments at Los Alamos, or in the life of Robert Oppenheimer, came chiefly from the newspapers. In fact she was more completely detached from—excluded from—the realm of modern physics and physicists than at any time since space had been made for her in the back row of Arnold Sommerfeld's lecture hall. During those five years her freedom from visits by the FBI, from summonses by febrile fact-finding committees in Sacramento or Washington, was so total that it seemed ominous, under the circumstances, and destined to end suddenly.

She heard about *Joe* only when and as the rest of the populace did, though certainly she could extrapolate the details far better than most. *Joe* was America's name for the first Soviet A-bomb.

It was tested secretly in late August of 1949, detected by U.S. planes, and announced to the world several days later by an indignant Harry Truman; it came eventually to be known as *Joe One*, in distinction from its numbered successors. *Joe* was estimated to have been six times as powerful as the Hiroshima blast, and had arrived roughly fifteen years earlier than American defense thinkers—at least the loudest of those thinkers—had predicted it would. To the potentates of the Pentagon, among the high councils of the Atomic Energy Commission, to everyone at Los Alamos and not least of all Michael Zolta (as he was now calling himself), *Joe* was a monstrous embarrassment of the most terrifying sort. But Hannah was not taken much by surprise.

She knew that the Soviet Union contained its own modest share of world-class physicists like Kurchatov and Kapitza, all with full grasp of the principles of a fission chain reaction, and that there was no reason to suppose Comrade Stalin wasn't offering the industrial resources and the personal incentives, positive or otherwise, that could transform those principles into a working bomb. She also knew a bit, only at secondhand, about what had seeped out of Los Alamos by way of espionage; that wasn't much, but enough perhaps to spare the Russians a few blind alleys that Robert and his merry men had been forced to explore. And she knew that, despite the uproar, *Joe* more likely marked the beginning of something fearsome than the culmination. On the September day after Truman's announcement she sat on a bench in Berkeley reading of it in the *Chronicle* and imagining, among other things, how weary Kitty Oppenheimer must already be of hearing the telephone ring.

They would all want Robert's answers, Hannah knew; his advice, his reassurances, his proposals for action. The newsmen would want his pithy well-measured so-quotable copy. Serber and Bethe and others would want his guidance in technical matters, ethical ones too. Even Zolta—though Hannah wasn't aware of it then—would react to the shock of *Joe* by immediately calling Oppenheimer. And Robert would oblige them all. He had retired from active weaponry research, not to mention real science, for his prestigious and undemanding job as director of the Institute for Advanced Study, at Princeton, serving there as Einstein's zookeeper, but since 1945 he had mastered the corridors of Washington the way he had once mastered quantum theory, wines, Sanskrit, so that he was now the government's most revered and most adept consulting scientific oracle. He chaired the AEC's General Advisory Committee, the elite of nuclear planners, and Harry Truman would lead the list of people eager to hear that group's considered wisdom.

Hannah could imagine their breathless questions. *How did it happen, Dr. Oppenheimer? How so soon?* This was idle. *Who gave it to them? By what cunning perfidies have the Russians stolen our secret?* This was mainly paranoid. *What should we do now, Robert?* This at least was practical. The answer that they chiefly expected, chiefly wanted, was *We must begin a crash program toward Teller and Zolta's thermonuclear.* It was not the one he gave. To Zolta, as Hannah heard later, Robert replied:

"Slow down, Michael. Try to think about this with your brain, not with your gonads."

To Truman his answer was similar. Two months after *Joe* the GAC, meeting in extraordinary session, with Oppenheimer presiding firmly, delivered out its opinion that the superbomb was a lousy idea.

Under the current design proposal—which was nothing other than Teller's original suggestion, virtually unchanged since Hannah herself had heard it expounded during the summer sessions back in 1942—the superbomb probably wouldn't work. The proposed design was clumsy, full of brute stupid excess, unlikely to function as intended, wasteful of precious materials, unreliable. And if by chance it did work, so much the worse for humanity. "We believe a superbomb should never be produced," said the crucial GAC report. Certainly in October of 1949 this was unpopular counsel, perhaps also naïve, arguably even pernicious;

treasonous was another question, asked and answered only in retrospect.

The report itself became classified, and Hannah was not to see a copy until 1975, but she heard rumors, and could guess the substance of it from open clues. She knew, for instance, one unmistakable hint, that Michael Zolta was in transport of frustration and rage.

She knew this from Zolta himself, who called her in November of '49 from Los Alamos. She hadn't spoken with him in seven years and during that period the immigrant Mihály Szölta had become a naturalized citizen, a fervent patriot, and more: though not famous like Oppenheimer, he was now a valued adviser to multiple government agencies, a sophisticated student of the congressional budgeting process, and in his own discreet way a political warrior of broad contacts and dangerous skill. Also his English had marginally improved. The message that Zolta so effectively carried from hearing rooms to senatorial chambers, and back to the holier recesses of the Pentagon, combined implacable alarm toward the Soviet menace with vivid and well-informed technological recommendations in the realm of what loosely was called defense policy. Michael Zolta had become the greatest, or at least the most passionate and expert, of American weapons-mongers. Hannah was not yet aware of this flowering, and had neither reason nor occasion to be.

When he announced himself by the new name she thought for one disoriented moment that she must be speaking to an Americanized relative of the Mihály Szölta she had briefly known. But she was able to sort through that confusion and match person to voice, while he chattered on at her as though they had last spoken together just a week before. Zolta was angry, and Hannah for some reason had been selected to hear him out. In fact he was only a notch or two short of apoplectic.

It was the GAC report, and Oppenheimer. Zolta had just been in New York for a talk with Hans Bethe, he told her; had then gone down to Washington for more meetings, was now back in Los Alamos, and had only this afternoon seen a copy of the GAC recommendations. Unspeakable, he said, but certainly found no trouble speaking. Hannah could hear, even over the bad long-distance connection, that his hands must be in fists, his eyebrows jumping like crickets, the long overgrowth of his muttonchops twisted taut by nervous fingers. And while this voice rambled on bitterly, almost obsessively, about the disastrous influence of Robert Oppenheimer, Hannah was left wondering what Michael Zolta could possibly want from her.

Oppenheimer, said Zolta, it was all Oppenheimer: he was managing singlehandedly to thwart the superbomb program. Bethe had agreed to return and work on it, Zolta having finally persuaded him; then Bethe spoke with Oppenheimer, and now Bethe had changed his mind. Serber and the younger man were being swayed likewise. They wouldn't come. None of the best people would come, all were under Oppenheimer's spell. Even Fermi now. He and Teller could hardly build the damn thing just the two of them, could they? And who knew but that even Teller might cross over—this last worry being, for Hannah, the telling measure of Zolta's hysteria. Yes, it was Oppenheimer. His GAC had officially reviled the idea of a crash program—though a crash program was precisely the thing needed—and meanwhile Oppenheimer continued his personal campaign to alienate individual physicists, so that no one could be recruited who might help Zolta and Teller on even the lame little bastardized program of thermonuclear study that they were allowed. For example Hannah, she too had no doubt already been drawn into Oppenheimer's righteous circle. He couldn't be surprised at that, Zolta said, but he thought he would phone anyway since he had always considered her an uncommonly sensible woman as well as a fine scientist and only at this point did Hannah realize that Zolta hoped she, herself, would join him in his work.

"Michael. I'm sorry, you evidently didn't know. I haven't done physics for years."

"Why not?"

When she told him he seemed genuinely shocked. He pressed for details, questioned her with solicitous horrified curiosity until she had given him an account of her exile that was almost complete, omitting only a few significant items besides the night of June 12, 1943. Zolta then pungently expressed his hatred, which she knew to be sincere and long-standing, for mindless governmental security restrictions upon scientific creativity.

"Paagh. They should have anyway cleared you. Regardless. Oppenheimer himself, he was politically not so pure, I think. It was stupid. I suspected always something such, I confess it, Hannah. That you had this trouble. But I remembered your work," Zolta said. "And I thought it was stupid, so stupid, that you weren't cleared."

"What are you talking about, Michael?"

"In the war. Los Alamos."

"Clearance wasn't the problem then."

"How not? Then why wouldn't you come?"

"Michael, I was never asked."

"I had a bad feeling about him. At the beginning. Then that went away," says Tay Riordan. "Then it came back."

THE ZOLTA CONFIGURATION

"Zuckerman," says Mayberry.

She nods. The orange kitten is on her lap, luxuriating, accepting compensation for a week's neglect, flexing its claws down into the black terrycloth. Occasionally the woman arches her back suddenly, and with gentle indulgence unhooks a paw from the skin of her knee.

"When was this?" says Mayberry. "The beginning."

"February."

"Where did you meet him?"

"I didn't meet him, exactly," she says, "He sort of stalked me. He had been out here before, sometime last year. Last autumn, I think. He had heard me play then, with the group. Saw me play, I suppose is a more relevant way of putting it. Then he was back in February. In the audience. We were working the Sagebrush Inn, a big old place just south of here on the road to Santa Fe. And there was this guy. Zuckerman. He had a high awareness of me, apparently, before I had ever consciously set eyes on him."

"High awareness?"

"That's what I call it," she says. "Trying not to sound like a fool. Or a bitch goddess."

"You definitely don't sound like a fool."

"Get this much straight, friend," she tells Mayberry bluntly. "I am not either one."

"All right. I'm sorry. I didn't mean to imply otherwise."

"Yes you did," she says and Mayberry starts to be more impressed with Tay Riordan because of course she is right.

"Do you run into it often? This *high awareness* condition?"

"It isn't so funny. Yes, as a matter of fact," she says "More than I wish. I'm talking about something that's different from the average horny yahoo down there with one elbow on the stage and a dangling tongue. A little different. More intense, more determined. Greater attention span. Less good-natured bullshit. This kind I mean has a crazy steadiness in the eye. He comes back on the second and the third night, alone, sits at the same table, watches you with the same steady concentration. Sends you drinks. Really drawing a bead, you know? The standard hornies are just a nuisance at most, they don't mean anything. Take them to a movie and they reach for popcorn, to a bakery and they reach for sugar doughnuts, to a music bar and they reach for me. But this other guy, with what you mock me for calling the high awareness: he's different. Sometimes I like it, I admit. Sometimes I even play to him, and that helps me find an edge. God knows what it does to him. But more often he scares me, this kind."

"Did Zuckerman scare you?"

"No," she says. "Not at first."

"But you had a bad feeling. You said you felt he was stalking you."

"I had the same feeling about you just now when I answered the door."

"I'm not," says Mayberry quite earnestly. "I'm stalking him."

"It seems like everybody's doing that to somebody."

But Zolta, pessimistic as usual, had overestimated the power of Oppenheimer's spell while underestimating his own. The GAC recommendations were rejected, splashed aside by a great wave of nervous bellicosity that rolled across Washington, having gotten its early momentum from the crucial lobbying visit by Michael Zolta, and on January

31, 1950, Hannah heard Truman's announcement on the radio:

"It is part of my responsibility as Commander-in-Chief of the Armed Forces to see to it that our country is able to defend itself against any possible aggressor. Accordingly I have directed the Atomic Energy Commission to continue its work on all forms of atomic weapons, including the so-called hydrogen or superbomb."

Behind the bland and slightly confused language was a decision that, Yes indeed, we shall have a bust-ass program to get this thermonuclear deal built as quickly as possible.

How quickly that might be would depend mainly on The Magyars, Teller and Zolta. Hannah continued to hear from Zolta at irregular intervals, sometimes by telephone from Los Alamos at odd hours of the evening, less often when he turned up in Berkeley, for conferences with Ernest Lawrence's people. On one of the latter occasions he invited her to dinner, and Hannah by that time had sensed enough of his interest not be be startled. She accepted. They went to an unpretentious Hungarian cafe he had discovered in uptown San Francisco; he was excruciatingly gallant toward her and a little shy, with flashes of improbable self-deprecatory humor; Hannah enjoyed herself splendidly. It was years since she had spent any hours with a brilliant man and, by God, that was something she missed. They talked about Hungary, and about Leipzig, where they both had studied, and about the premise of her last published monograph, from 1942, which he seemed to know by heart. They did not—either that night or during the telephone calls—discuss his current project. He never mentioned the subject and she never asked. Only a few oblique references, barely more than shrugs, told her it might not be going especially well.

Though Zolta phoned her once in the last week of February, talked for five minutes and then brusquely hung up, she didn't know at that point about his latest computations, which had just demonstrated to all Los Alamos and the AEC leadership that Teller's original superbomb design was, and always had been, a worthless piece of conceptual scrap. She didn't hear until later about the weeks of controlled panic, during which it seemed that Oppenheimer's most priggish carpings about the design's lack of elegance were to be vindicated, after millions of tax dollars had been committed, by the sheer technical impracticability of making it work; or about how, during that period just after his merciless mathematical verdict, the Mozart howled out from Zolta's Steinway, at three or four in the morning, with more vehemence than usual. It came to sound like a she-wolf in mourning for its mate, the piano. All of that Hannah did hear eventually, from Zolta, who for her benefit lampooned himself with considerable wit, down to the deterioration of his already indelicate keyboard touch. But in late winter of 1951 she could not even be told, when it came, about the epochal bolt of inventive genius by which Teller—or Teller with a crucial suggestion from Zolta, according to which later version was accepted—solved the prohibitive technical problems and rescued the American superbomb. Zolta could not phone Hannah then and tell her about the new configuration because, of course, she wasn't cleared.

And she didn't imagine she ever would be.

Then suddenly Zolta was gone from Los Alamos: could not abide the place any more. He had been battling constantly with the current director over points of emphasis in the program, over lines of command, over the schedule of preparations for a full thermonuclear test. Now lately there was even the new tension between him and Teller. Fine: Zolta did not need it. He did not need the bureaucratic battles, or the more insidious battles of ego, or even perhaps the working partnership. Certainly he did not need professional credit to which he was not welcome. Anyway Los Alamos, Zolta claimed to believe, was in eclipse. The laboratory had done its job well enough during the war but today it was enervated, complacent, unimaginative, poorly administered, and inadequately funded; most grievous, it was insufficiently committed to the superbomb mission. The place was still that much Robert Oppenheimer's creature, responsive to signals of tone and perspective that could be passed, almost pheromonically, from as far away as Princeton, New Jersey. All right, then. They had their computations, the brilliant intuitive ones supplied by him, and others trickling in from their balky electronic computers; they had what they were pleased to think of as their Teller configuration. Zolta would now gladly leave the epigones to their own resources.

Hannah heard no word from him for months, into the summer of 1952. Last she knew, he was returning to Cornell. How amazing, how enviable, she thought: to be able to cast off one physics position at whim and snatch up another. How nice for you, Michael. She had sometimes been embarrassed by the emotional presumption behind his midnight calls, sometimes they were tedious, but now when none came for most of a year she discovered a small gap. Obviously he was very busy, or his needs had changed. When finally she picked up the receiver and it was Zolta again, Hannah felt herself go willfully cool. She made an instantaneous choice to be merely civil. At the same time she realized the unfairness of this, the silly girlish petulance, since Michael Zolta after all was not the person with title to her real bitterness.

"You must be in Berkeley, Michael. You sound close. Have you had a good visit?"

"I am in Livermore, Hannah. We drove out from Berkeley today. Teller and myself. We flew in last night."

"You and *Teller?*"

"Yes. Reunited. It seems." Zolta released a guffaw, evidently at the vagaries of his own Magyar disposition.

"How quaint," said Hannah. "What can there possibly be to amuse you two in Livermore? Is it like a honeymoon? Are you on a wine tour?"

So Zolta told her: the National Security Council had taken formal action creating a second American weapons lab, with endorsement by the AEC. Something Teller had been lobbying for, quietly, during the past several years. The land had been purchased, the funds appropriated. Livermore was to be the site, and Edward Teller to be the reigning wizard. Teller had asked Zolta to serve as director. A generous and conciliatory gesture. There was—Zolta explained to Hannah, only half convincingly—no abiding grudge. Beyond the members of Teller's own immediate group, Zolta himself would have full discretion in recruitment. He wanted Hannah to come.

"Come?"

"Work with me. In the Theoretical Division."

"Michael, you're dreaming. Or maybe it's me. There would be security checks, and you forget, I am a suspect person." Aciduously she added: "I once belonged to the the Consumers' Union."

"Paagh," Zolta said. "We will rehabilitate you."

* * *

"So he came out to see the group at this Sagebrush place." Mayberry is prompting. "To see you. More than once."

"Yeah. Second night, same table, like in the pattern," says Tay Riordan. "The reason for that, I think, is so you can recognize from onstage that it's them again. Then a funny thing happened."

After a moment, waiting expectantly, Mayberry is obliged to say: "What happened?"

"During the break before our last set I got myself a drink from the bar, and walked over, and sat down at his table."

"Why is that a funny thing?"

"Because I'm not a hooker."

"All right. You just felt like some new company, or what? I'm not sure I need to know this part. I'm not sure it's any of my business."

"None of it's your business," she says. "But this is the part where it turns into a long story."

"Give me the edited version. Leave out the bits that embarrass you."

She grants him a wry smile. "Then it would be a telegram. It wouldn't make sense."

Zuckerman, the thing was, had simply caught her at precisely the right moment. That afternoon there had been a culmination of pressures in her personal life, a hellacious argument—she had thrown bottles and put a paring knife through a canvas, actually—and a termination of sorts, or so it seemed. By evening she had settled down only enough to be looking for new mischief in a rather calculating way. "I was living with another guy then, see. Here. In this house."

"What was his name?"

"Randy Ortiz." She looks sideways at Mayberry. "But I think you knew that. Don't bullshit me. Don't be so goddamn coy."

"You're right. I know you reported him missing. I got your name and address from the State Police. And maybe *you* should know this: there were two murders this week in Los Alamos, and Zuckerman was probably connected."

"Oh God. Oh shit." Her voice is soft; the kitten is allowed to continue snoozing beatifically. "Are you cops? I knew it."

"I'm just what I said I was. Medical student with a lost friend. So you were pissed at Randy Ortiz. That particular evening. You got interested in a stranger. Nothing unnatural about that."

"Randy was driving me insane. It wasn't just that evening. Months."

"I won't ask why. It doesn't matter."

"Because he was indifferent," she insists. "To me. To most things, but me in particular. Emotionally he came and went, faded in and out. He lived in my house, slept in my bed, covered my back room with paint and turpentine. Didn't seem to give a great goddamn about me one way or the other. I mean, I believe that he really did. Does. But he just never seemed to be able to work up the energy, the focus, whatever, to show it. Or even to say it. He wasn't tomcatting around. None of that. Just slapping his paint on canvas. Watching TV. Strolling out to the Pueblo and wandering home ten hours later. He was comfortable here. And I don't think I was demanding a whole hell of a lot."

"Was he back on smack?" Mayberry asks this gently and now again has to wait while Tay Riordan stares at him, making decisions.

"No," she says. "I don't think so. Cocaine, though.

Lots of coke. It didn't seem to be any damn better for his focus, if you ask me. But that was just another symptom."

"And Zuckerman wasn't indifferent."

"Zuckerman was never indifferent," she agrees distractedly, as though reluctant to shift her thoughts back from Ortiz; but she does. "No, hardly. Like a wolverine, Zuckerman was indifferent. He was rapacious and possessive. God. For a while I loved it. About three weeks."

"So you took up with him that night. After the blowout with Randy." Hearing himself, Mayberry recalls what so annoyed him in Lieutenant Roybal. "With Ortiz."

"Wrong. Not that night. I'm not quite that fast. It was four or five days later. I met him for lunch and we spent an afternoon walking around town. Talking. Then before long, yes, we were going back to his motel. He was living in a motel. I wasn't sneaky about it. At least not in the obvious sense. I told Randy I was moving out. It's my house, I mean my name is on the lease, but I moved out."

"What does he look like?" says Mayberry.

"Who? Randy?"

"Zuckerman. When you first met him, that night at the Sagebrush. What did he look like?"

"Nothing special. That wasn't what attracted me. Although he was a little freakier than the average guy there, which didn't hurt. The Sagebrush crowd tends toward well-heeled grooviness, see. Young professionals and real estate moguls from Santa Fe and around here. Mainly Anglo, of course. Lots of nice cord jackets with wood buttons and sheepskin vests and Irish tweed caps. Money. Zuckerman didn't fit. He looked more like he had stepped out of the sixties: old jeans patched with leather and all that. He had plenty of money himself, as it turned out, but he wasn't spending it on his wardrobe."

"I mean physically."

"Physically? Don't you know? You're looking for him, he's supposedly looking for you, but you've never seen him?"

"I'm not sure," says Mayberry. "Maybe not."

She gives a rough description featuring the long curly black hair, the scrawny physique, the nondescript hazel eyes. Mayberry doesn't get much from that.

"What *did* attract you? He doesn't sound like a lady-killer."

"Good question. Partly the high awareness thing, like I told you. Flattery. But that was only a moment, at the very beginning—my impulse to sit down at the table and ask him why he was watching me. Also his intensity generally. That took a bit longer to discover. He was always coming and going, zooming from one thing to another with tight fists and blazing eyes. Grabbing me, grabbing an idea, grabbing something else. Grabbing me again. I found that exhilarating. Also—and you better know this if you say you're stalking him—Zuckerman happens to be very, very smart."

"You liked him for his intelligence." Mayberry at once regrets this gratuitous sarcasm, not calculated to aid his purpose, but evidently he just doesn't want to hear anything good about Zuckerman.

"I don't think I ever said I liked him," she answers clinically.

Mayberry is about to shift the discussion to other and more relevant matters when Tay Riordan adds: "Also he was convenient. Sure. Part of me wanted to hurt Randy. Not irreparably, just enough to get his attention. Make him jealous, you know. That was kind of shitty, I realize. I realize that. I thought I could use Zuckerman to help me with Randy. Sure."

"Did it work?" says Mayberry.

Eventually she raises her eyes and sweeps a hand through the air. "Do you see a thin Indian man here anywhere?"

Hannah joined the Livermore Laboratory in September of 1952. She had somehow passed the security investigation. Probably this minor miracle was a result of Zolta having made the same sort of desperate noises to certain AEC officials—about her absolute indispensability as part of the Livermore program—that General Groves had made about Oppenheimer a decade before. Hannah never knew for sure whether Michael had interceded (putting himself thereby at some jeopardy), but it seemed the only plausible explanation. He would not have said so, if it were true, and might not have admitted it if she cornered him: his manner toward her, while quite friendly, was still too professional and correct. That Zolta was a proud man, that he could be difficult, intractable, obnoxious, that he was ferociously brilliant, these thing Hannah had known from very early. During the past three years she had seen, in addition, that on political questions involving the Soviet Union he inclined toward a Manichaean simplicity. Certainly he carried his share of powerful hatreds and fears. Certainly he was self-righteous. Possibly even he was a little mad. Possibly he was dangerous. But at Livermore she began to see also that he was capable of small acts of self-abnegation, warmth, and even—for lack of a less anachronistic word—nobility.

Maybe Hannah herself *was* indispensable to Livermore, but she doubted it. Her work in the Theoretical Division concerned directed shock waves and the dynamics of turbulent fluids, as those matters would relate to ignition of the secondary trigger during the first few millionths of a second in the explosion of a superbomb. She was helping to refine practical details of the Teller configuration. To say that she found the work interesting would have been a large understatement. And her skills became keen again quickly; within five weeks she was proving herself, contributing valuable pieces of critical analysis, and counter-suggestions, to the search for a full trigger design. In a strictly scientific sense she had been, she knew, a good choice for this position. But not the only possible choice.

Back at Los Alamos, in the meantime, that lab was proceeding toward a test of the new design concept bequeathed it by Teller and Zolta. The test device consisted of a sixty-five-ton complex assembled on a small coral island called Elugelab in the Pacific, an elaborate arrangement including multiple tin sheds and gas-powered generators and gigantic reservoir of hydrogen, several heavy concentric casings, a fission bomb to trigger the thermonuclear reaction and a cryogenic unit like a large meat freezer to keep the hydrogen in liquid state. All this stuff collectively carried the name *Mike;* and though test names were generally cryptic if not entirely random no one was denying in this case an ironic fillip toward Zolta, who was resoundingly disliked among the Los Alamos people.

At the core of *Mike* was Teller's sweet little idea. *Mike* wasn't something that could be loaded onto a B-29 and shoved out the bomb bays. Wasn't a bomb at all. The accepted usage, on Elugelab and later in Washington, was to call it a *device*. More accurately it was a complete laboratory which its builders hoped to see vaporized. *Mike* had one purpose: to vindicate technically, or discredit, the Teller configuration. The test was scheduled for November

1, 1952. Zolta was invited to Elugelab for the occasion, as was Teller, but Zolta didn't go.

He told the Los Alamos people that he was too busy to leave Livermore, which may in fact have been the reason. Instead he and Hannah drove down to Palo Alto that day, and were admitted to a quiet basement room in the geology building, where they watched for *Mike* on a seismograph. Afterward they went back up the Bay to Zolta's favorite Hungarian cafe. Though he was clearly in fine spirits, he remained subdued, no trace of the gloating that Hannah might have expected from a bellicose man who had just done his part—acknowledged or not—to revolutionize the nature of war. Zolta seemed to be savoring his share of vindication in some more private way. He began to talk about his wife Emmi, who had died in England eleven years earlier, just a month before Hannah met him.

He began to describe his old dependence on her, his unplumbable devotion to her, this woman who had been his childhood playmate, later his first and only sweetheart, since early days in Budapest. He talked like a fierce and loyal lover whose bereavement was fresh. Toying nervously with a spoon, he spoke in wistful terms of the pleasure he had taken from doing physics during the years of his marriage, those years when each piece of his best work, each new paper, each professional victory was like a small nosegay of glacier lilies he could carry home to his Emmi, who needed no comprehension of the atom to share delight in his triumphs, to appreciate his little offerings. Hannah had not realized that Zolta was such a romantic but she felt it became him rather well.

Physics did not seem able to provide the same sublime gratification any more, he said. Not since Emmi's death. Hannah suggested that this might partly reflect the uses to which it had lately been put. And he agreed: their sort of physics was now mortally serious, a matter of national survival rather than just fascination and beauty. Only that wasn't all. For him at least, that wasn't all. It was not merely his innocence that he missed.

Certain things, Zolta said, are more important than innocence. More important also than any professional victories. Hannah suspected he meant the survival of Western democracy against the Communist monolith, and that this was prelude to one of those ardent political homilies for which Michael Zolta was notorious and which she always dreaded, but she followed the point anyway, faintly goading. What *is* more important to you, Michael? He appeared surprised that she should need to inquire.

"Work and love," Zolta said. "Both together. Only together." And then he asked Hannah to marry him.

It was an Old World proposal, humbly suppliant, formal, prolix, and though his voice had gone viscid with controlled emotion, he was not even so forward as to reach across for her hand.

Of course Hannah ought to have foreseen this but she hadn't. She realized now that the signals had been there for months, that Zolta had consciously postponed his bid, and she realized why. He had been waiting until she felt secure. Throughout the long personnel investigation after he picked her for Livermore, and the deliberations her name had provoked back in Washington, and his own efforts in good faith to influence those deliberations, he surely knew that it would have been unfair, not to mention improper, for him to push himself on her. But now she had her clearance, she had her job, she had earned the respect of Edward Teller and her other colleagues independently of Zolta. She might still feel some pressure of gratitude, which she would be sensible enough to discount, but there was no danger that she would imagine Michael was blackmailing her. He wanted her badly, and perhaps he had since the first long-distance call; badly enough to be so scrupulous about his means and so blind about his chances. Hannah weakened. This dour, harsh man facing her over the tattered tablecloth, she understood, was very likely a better friend than she had had for years. A better friend than, under the circumstances, she deserved or wanted. Delicately she told him no.

"Why not?" Characteristically blunt and peremptory, but then he waved that away at once as though erasing a mathematical solecism from his office chalkboard. "No, excuse me. A foolish thing to ask. It is of course simply a matter of your feelings, not subject to debate. My apologies, Hannah. I apologize for even suggesting this."

"Please don't do *that*. Don't regret paying me such a compliment. Michael, I have a terrific affection for you. Not just because of Livermore. Not just that. I like you. I enjoy your company. I treasure your good opinion of me. It is *not* simply a matter of my feelings. There is also the matter of my concern for yours. I would be doing you a very great disservice if I married you."

His head went side to side. "A very great favor."

"No. Disservice. A cruel, senseless disservice. Yes. Because for all our friendship, yours and mine—you must understand, Michael—I would still every day be loving another man."

Now Zolta lowered his chin and said nothing.

"It would be especially unpleasant, I think, Michael. For both of us. Especially unwise."

Zolta was silent.

"I mean Robert Oppenheimer."

"I know who you mean, Hannah," he said.

First at the motel in Taos, then back down in Santa Fe, where they got a room at the De Vargas, Tay Riordan stayed with Zuckerman for most of a month. A crazy time, she told Mayberry. Almost as though it were not a segment of time at all, not measurable and divisible that way, rather more like a unitary aberration: her Zuckerman incident. For a month she played no music, barely saw anything of her friends in either town, spent an ungodly amount of money in restaurants and bars, and bought new underwear instead of doing laundry. The money all came from Zuckerman, who seemed to have plenty. Lots of strange hours, staying awake till four or daylight for no particular reason, then sleeping into late afternoon. Lots of bizarre talk and good sex. Lots of crazy wild screaming arguments over small emotional matters, threatening mayhem and suicide back and forth only half jocosely, making up, more sex and sleep, then before long another big scene. Lots of Tay strolling around Santa Fe by herself, shopping for turquoise with his money and spending two hours over tea at The Shanty, while Zuckerman went off to do his business.

Mayberry sits forward. "What do you mean, 'went off'? Where did he go? What sort of business?"

She stares at Mayberry noncommittally, as though he is exceeding a reasonable allotment of questions. "Went off. I mean he went off." She shrugs. "Three or four hours. I didn't ask where. I didn't care. It wasn't like Randy. When Zuckerman came back, he was definitely back. Twitching with nervous energy, chattering about nothing, dragging me toward a fancy dinner or a movie or a bed."

"Did you think he was a little crazy?"

"What?"

"It's your word. Crazy screaming. A crazy time. Did you think Zuckerman might have been just a bit deranged?"

"No," she says. "Not at all. That was me. I was deranged."

Gingerly she lifts the cat off her knees and carries it, under one arm, out of the room. Mayberry fears for a moment that the interview has been terminated. He hears a refrigerator click open. "You want something to drink?"

"Thank you," he calls back, and expects she might sing off the options, but no. She returns with two tumblers of milk. The cat remains on the kitchen table, drinking noisily from a bowl; the glasses for Mayberry and herself, evidently, were an afterthought.

"Did you know where this flow of money came from?"

"No. Zuckerman's pocket, as far as I was concerned."

"Beyond that?"

"No."

"What was the business he went off to do?"

"That was always mysterious. I don't know. He met people."

"Met people."

"Yeah. 'I've got to go meet a guy,' he would say. 'I'll be back at midnight. You want to have a bite at the Ore House or wait for me?' If I waited, sure enough he'd be back at midnight. 'Hi, let's go. Tacos or pizza or what?' Any Mexican food whatsoever—you could be at La Fonda eating snapper by candlelight—to him it was all 'tacos.' 'Let's drive out to Chimayo for tacos.' And then meanwhile before you could ask, 'How was the meeting? How was the guy?' if you were gonna do that, which I wasn't, he'd already be launched on some dizzy spiel about how scientists had proved that rock music was creating a generation of deaf people. Or how if one Space Invaders machine was built with the same components they used in computers thirty years ago, it would have to be bigger than a two-bedroom house. That was the sort of crap he knew. And sometimes it was interesting, sometimes it was even pretty funny. He could talk like a trivia genius or a stand-up comic about anything—anything but himself. Himself, as a subject, was sort of off limits. Fine with me. I didn't push it. Mystery, disconnection, that's exactly what I was after."

"You must have wondered a little," says Mayberry.

"Sure. Didn't I figure he was some kind of criminal? Is that what you want to know? Definitely. Yes. I assumed he must be selling either coke or illegal guns, something on those lines. I never saw him sneaking around with extra suitcases so maybe it had to be coke. Also, in Santa Fe, there's probably much more demand for that."

Mayberry frowns. He suspects this is a false lead, less original and considerably less nefarious than what he has in mind, but asks anyway: "Cocaine. Is that something else he was treating you to?"

"No," she says brusquely. "I don't touch it. I don't like it." She gulps deeply at her glass, reappearing disguised in a white mustache. Despite all odds Mayberry sees some possibility, an intriguing possibility, that Tay Riordan is just what she pretends to be.

After about three weeks the hotel existence, she says, began to seem tedious. Bad enough to tolerate that sort of claustrophobia when she was traveling with the band; at home in her own neighborhood, she didn't need it. But she never said anything to Zuckerman. She never asked him, "Okay, what's next? What about us? Are we just gonna stay shacked up in this room for the next year while you go to midnight meetings, or what?" No, nothing such. They weren't communicating with that level of self-consciousness, she and Zuckerman, and besides, implicit to their arrangement was a certain mutual scorn of premeditation. Under the unspoken terms there was no "us" to be considered. It was all very much more—here Tay gropes for a word, finds it, pronounces it with faint derision—*existential*. And of course nothing is more existential, says Tay sarcastically, than harsh sex relieved by periods of tedium. So she reminded herself that she was a free and autonomous agent, who could leave any time, and then she stayed.

But only a week longer, as things turned out. After a month in all, her Zuckerman incident was suddenly over, ending as curtly as it began. She returned to the De Vargas one afternoon and was met with a message to call Randy in Taos.

"He had known where you were?"

"Yes, sure. The whole time. I told you, I wasn't secretive about this, I wasn't guilty of any discretion."

"And he was asking you to come back."

"No. He wouldn't do that. He may have wanted me back pretty badly—I like to think he did. Like to hope. But he wouldn't ask. He's not a persuader. He's a wandering planet. He was calling about the cat. She was having an asthma attack, and he needed to know where I kept the medicine."

"And that somehow changed your mind about Zuckerman?"

"Zuckerman schmuckerman. It like to melted my heart. I borrowed a car. I was back here within two hours."

"This was in March?" says Mayberry. "Three months ago now?"

"Yeah, March sounds about right. The Sagebrush job had been February. A month." Mayberry has calculated on the same basis. "Then Randy and I planted a garden. A garden, yeah. Very sentimental. Vegetables, actually, but still. Sentimental onions and peas. Really I planted it while he sat on the back stoop and watched. Typical. But I loved every minute."

"You love Randy Ortiz, don't you."

"Yes I do, God damn it," she says. "What's wrong with that?"

"Nothing. Not a thing. And so you haven't seen or heard from Zuckerman since sometime in March?"

"Christ no, I didn't say that," she says. "Judas. I wish it were true. Do I ever."

First came the phone calls. Evidently Zuckerman wasn't nearly so existential as they had both thought: he wanted her back. The telephone began to ring at unsettling hours of the night, waking her and Randy, and it was Zuckerman, calling to express in a variety of emphatic ways, some of them obscene, his rather vehement desire that she reconsider. He refused to turn loose of her. Come back to Santa Fe, he would plead, and then luridly describe what they might do when she did return, which was uncomfortably—for her—in the vein of what they had already done. Randy, always adaptable, to a fault, was understanding about this harassment but that made it no less excruciating for Tay.

During the early few calls Zuckerman seemed to be in a genuine panic, and perhaps now a bit deranged, yes, but after a week and then two had passed, his voice on the line at 3:30 and 5:00 A.M. was even more scary, precisely because it sounded so calm and sane. The obscenity by that time was gone. The mayhem and suicide themes had also been dropped. He was simply imploring her, mildly but with relentless persistence, to take pity, take courage, and give them back whatever it was they had had. What the hell so glorious was it we had? she wondered. Fun in an ugly room, and too many dangerous quarrels. She was not faintly tempted. She hung up on him. She considered reporting him to the police but she was afraid of some asshole cop who might sympathize with Zuckerman.

"Did he ever hurt you?" says Mayberry. "During the month. Did he ever strike you, or do something to cause physical pain?"

"No. Never."

"Did you ever feel he was capable?"

"Definitely. As a matter of fact, a couple times I was surprised. That he *didn't* smack me. Certain points in the woolliest of our scream contests, where I thought it had come to that. I would back off immediately—back off a little, at least—expecting it was already too late. But no. He never once touched me in anger."

"Though he threatened. And threatened again during the phone harassment."

"Right. He was always threatening. It was almost routine."

"Then the telephone threatening stopped."

"Right. And that's when I started getting worried. The threats stopped, the calls didn't."

But they came now during daylight hours, when she was home alone. Randy was doing a series of portraits of old women at the Pueblo, and gone therefore on a regular pattern, for most of each afternoon. The Zuckerman calls began to coincide with that pattern, and Tay suddenly had the alarming intuition that these were not being dialed from Santa Fe: that Zuckerman was in Taos again, somehow keeping track of her and Randy. She made the mistake of not mentioning the first several daylight calls to Randy, and then it seemed too late. She would have to admit not only the calls but also that she had concealed them. She didn't. As far as Randy knew, the night harassment had ceased, the ardor of his rival had waned, the matter was therefore satisfactorily closed. He held no grudge. Meanwhile two or three afternoons a week Tay was still forced to slam a receiver violently into its cradle, or beg Zuckerman to leave her in peace. And now she was hearing about the trip.

"What trip? What was that?" says Mayberry.

"He was planning this trip, he said. Something very exotic. Very dramatic. To hear him tell it, at least. Said he still hoped that I would go with him. I should be part of this trip, I would be sorry if I weren't. Didn't say where he was going and I didn't ask. Bullshit on his trip, what I wanted right then was just to stay home a lot. And not have to pick up the goddamn phone. Which I was thinking about having disconnected."

"Why didn't you?"

"I couldn't." She draws down a full breath and drops her shoulders. Mayberry has already heard enough to take her for an exceptionally sturdy person. "Because by this time I was lying to Randy."

She suffered quietly with the calls, and with the fear that Zuckerman was again in some sense stalking her, and continued to invent petty evasions that kept Randy Ortiz unaware, which became only less difficult logistically, more difficult emotionally, as he faded away into another of his episodes of remoteness. The portrait project, she heard, though not from Randy himself, had been abandoned. He still disappeared each afternoon but his brushes at the Pueblo were marinating undisturbed. Formerly his mood during these distanced periods had tended to be languid and sedate, inhumanly so; now he seemed, rather, morose. He was perhaps worried about something. She thought of calling his probation officer at the county—an innocuous man Randy still had to visit monthly and give a vague account of his doings—but dismissed that idea as too devious. Also probably unnecessary. She suspected the problem was she and Zuckerman. She had wanted Randy to care, now maybe he cared, yet things were no better. She had screwed up somewhere. She could not very well tell him, "Look, don't worry at all, it's over with Zuckerman, really, except by the way I've been talking with him a lot and I made sure you didn't know. So don't worry, see?" Not hardly.

In the middle of May she left for three nights with the band in Las Cruces. She had asked Randy to come along. No, thanks. So she told him a half dozen times on her way out the door how eager she would be to get back and see him on Sunday. She wanted him to trust her. She wanted him understanding that there would be no surreptitious rendezvous, no lost hours in Santa Fe, no Zuckerman. His response was: Sunday, sure, whatever.

Las Cruces felt wonderful, despite the soulless cinderblock barn on the edge of the campus where they played, because the students were whoopy from deprivation and, not having performed in almost three months, she was running a little that way herself. Her flute was awful but she had great fun with the sax, which always forgave her. She got to wear the old dresses. Desert cowboys in plaid shirts put their elbows on the stage and dangled their tongues. Friday the band played an entire set of encores while the crowd danced themselves sweaty as a chain gang. It was all glorious until midway through Saturday night, when she glanced up to see Zuckerman leaning against the side wall. She dropped some notes.

He had a new hat, a silly leather vaquero job that flopped down over half his face, not far enough that she might mistake him, not far enough to cover the smile. His arms were folded and he wasn't drinking. She readied herself, but to her surprise—and initially there was some relief—he did not approach her, neither between numbers nor even between sets. On each break she stayed close to the drummer or the pedal guitarist, except when she went to the john and emptied her stomach, but evidently she needn't have been concerned. Zuckerman through the rest of the evening only leaned placidly against his patch of cinder block. Small consolation. Everything about the way he was loitering, keeping his distance after coming all hell down to this part of the state, smirking out from beneath a stupid new hat—all of it gave her a bad feeling. Maybe she needn't fear him right now, needn't worry he might jump her behind the stage. Small consolation. He looked as though he already had what he wanted.

Immediately after the last set she browbeat the drummer until he would give her his car. Everyone was exhausted, she ought to sleep, and the notion of her trying to drive straight back to Taos was out of the question. No it wasn't, she said. The drummer knew only that she had seen someone in the house and that as a consequence she was very scared; he offered to trade motel rooms, to sleep on the floor of her room, to sleep outside the door of her room with a tire iron in his hand, but none of it would satisfy her. She couldn't explain. She had to get back to Taos at once. That was all. She wasn't concerned about being mugged or raped at a motel. She just had to get back to Taos. Do her this one favor or forget it. The drummer was a large goodhearted kid with linebacker arms who beat rhythm wearing a T-shirt and a Texaco cap and read Erich von Daniken during the breaks. All right, he would ride back in the van. Sleep for an hour when she got noddy and try not to drive his poor beater into a telephone pole. Tay left Las Cruces at ten till three with a quart of coffee on the dashboard.

It was almost noon when she opened the bedroom door. Not unusual for Randy to be asleep at that time, especially on a Sunday. He seemed fine. The sheet was tugged out at the bottom, clumped and twisted around him, leaving one brownish foot exposed below and a bare shoulder above. She could breath again with all of both lungs. Dropping out of the purple dress, she climbed in beside him.

"Hi, I'm back. I came early."

"Hi, kid." He always woke easily. He looped an arm over her neck and smiled: as though perhaps he was back too.

"I didn't notice the needle tracks then," she tells Mayberry. "It was a day or two later."

When circumstances for Hannah changed again drastically, she found that Zolta's loyalty had not. He testified strongly in her behalf at the first Personnel Board hearing. He wrote an impolitic letter to the AEC chairman. He offered another testimonial when she made her appeal. A good gauge of the political atmosphere in autumn of 1953, and of the sheer volume of trivial but damaging facts which had washed up in Hannah's security file, is that this time not even such a notoriously vigilant Russophobe as Michael Zolta, not even he, could rescue her. Let the record show, though, that he tried.

In that one respect, and in another, it was quite different from what happened to Robert. Hannah's case was very quiet. In fact the discreetness with which certain internal AEC bloodhounds managed finally to get her cast out of Livermore and exiled back to Telegraph Avenue, despite Zolta and one overworked ACLU lawyer, was silken. Robert on the other hand made front page of the *Times*. But then perhaps he could never have done that without, among others, Hannah. The Dergen letter was mailed on November 7, a Saturday.

It reached J. Edgar Hoover on Tuesday. Richard Dergen was an acrobatic young Washington lawyer who in 1949, not yet thirty years old, had become staff director of the new Joint Committee on Atomic Energy in Congress, and about the same time conceived for himself the personal mission to gather a large body of incriminating fact and innuendo about J. Robert Oppenheimer. After four years Dergen had indeed amassed the nation's foremost collection of this sort, public or private. But he had kept his data, and his theories about it, secret. Now that he was leaving Washington to accept a more lucrative job at Westinghouse, he had decided the day had come to make a bequest. To the chief of the FBI he wrote:

Dear Mr. Hoover:

This letter concerns J. Robert Oppenheimer.

As you know, he has for some years enjoyed access to various critical activities of the National Security Council, the Department of State, the Department of Defense, the Army, Navy, and Air Force, the Research and Development Board, the Atomic Energy Commission, the Central Intelligence Agency, the National Security Resources Board, and the National Science Foundation.

His access covers most new weapons being developed by the Armed Forces, war plans at least in comprehensive outline, complete details as to atomic and hydrogen weapons and stockpile data, the evidence on which some of the principal CIA intelligence estimates are based, and many other areas of high security sensitivity.

Because the scope of his access may well be unique, because he has had custody of an immense collection of classified papers covering military, intelligence, and diplomatic as well as atomic-energy matters, and because he also possesses a scientific background enabling him to grasp the significance of classified data of a technical nature, it seems reasonable to estimate that he is and for some years has been in a position to compromise more vital and detailed information affecting national defense and security than any other individual in the United States.

While J. Robert Oppenheimer has not made major contributions to the advancement of science, he holds a respected professional standing among the second rank of American physicists. In terms of his mastery of Government affairs, his close liaison with ranking officials, and his ability to influence high-level thinking, he surely stands in the first rank, not merely among scientists but among all those who have shaped postwar decisions in the military, atomic-energy, intelligence, and diplomatic fields. As chairman or as an official or unofficial member of more than 35 important Government committees, panels, study groups, and projects, he has oriented or dominated key policies involving every principal United States security department and agency except the FBI.

The purpose of this letter is to state my own exhaustively considered opinion, based upon years of study of the available classified evidence, that more probably than not J. Robert Oppenheimer is an agent of the Soviet Union.

So he had Hoover's attention. The letter continued:

This opinion considers, among others, the following factors:

1. During the period 1929 to 1942 he
    a. was contributing substantial monthly sums to the Communist Party;
    b. had no close friends except Communists;
    c. belonged to a number of Communist organizations, including the so-called Consumers' Union;
    d. had at least one mistress, Hannah Broch, who was a Communist;
    e. recruited only Communist scientists into the early wartime atomic work at Berkeley;
    f. was in frequent contact, through Hannah Broch and otherwise, with Soviet espionage agents, including Hubert Edward Jamisson and Pyotr Gerstmann;
2. In April 1942 his name was formally submitted for security clearance and
3. In May 1942 he either stopped contributing funds to the Communist Party or else began making his contributions through a new channel not yet discovered.
4. In June 1943 he made a clandestine visit to the aforementioned Hannah Broch at her apartment in Palo Alto, a visit of which neither his wife nor Los

Alamos security officials were aware, and remained with the Broch woman overnight.

5. Beginning in August 1943 and thereafter, he repeatedly gave false information to General Leslie Groves concerning the nature of that visit.
6. He was responsible for employing a number of Communists, including Klaus Fuchs, at wartime Los Alamos.
7. He was an enthusiastic sponsor of the A-bomb program until the war ended, at which time he immediately and outspokenly advocated that the Los Alamos Laboratory be disbanded.
8. Since 1946 he has
    a. used his potent influence against every postwar effort to expand capacity for producing A-bomb material;
    b. used his potent influence against every postwar effort at obtaining larger supplies of uranium ore;
    c. used his potent influence against every major postwar effort toward atomic power development, including the nuclear-powered submarine and nuclear-powered aircraft projects.
9. Concerning the H-bomb program,
    a. he was a vigorous supporter of that program until August 6, 1945, on which day he personally urged each senior individual working in this field to desist;
    b. he was remarkably instrumental in influencing the military authorities and the AEC to virtually suspend H-bomb development from 1946 through January 31, 1950;

    c. from January 31, 1950, to the present, he has worked tirelessly to retard the United States H-bomb program.

And even that wasn't all. When the invidious litany was complete, finally, Dergen restated his own baroque deductions:

1. Between 1929 and 1942, more probably than not, J. Robert Oppenheimer was a sufficiently hardened Communist that he either volunteered espionage information to the Soviets or complied with a request for such information; and
2. more probably than not, he has since been functioning as an espionage agent; and
3. more probably than not, he has since acted under a Soviet directive in influencing United States military, atomic-energy, intelligence, and diplomatic policy.

Within three weeks Dergen's letter had gone from Hoover to the Attorney General to Eisenhower. One other person who caught a sniff of its contents along the way was Joe McCarthy, and the President, more probably than not, flinched at the sound of the senator's snort.

On December 3 Eisenhower issued his "blank wall" directive: Dr. J. Robert Oppenheimer was to be immured in a chamber of presumed guilt, denied further access to any classified information, pending a full review of his security clearance.

And the subject of all this got the news himself in a brusque letter of accusation from the general manager of the AEC, a man he had known since Los Alamos days as a cold and toadying prick.

Oppenheimer found a lawyer, and the FBI wiretapped their private consultations. The AEC hired outside counsel too, a fearsome Washington courtroom shark named Charles Reese. The Personnel Board hearings in the matter of J. Robert Oppenheimer began four months later, April of 1954, in a small drab room, formerly an office, at the AEC building in Washington. By then, what was supposed to be merely an administrative inquiry had taken shape as a trial: there was a defendant, a bill of indictment, a defense lawyer and a prosecutor, a panel of three judges. There was a parade of witnesses. There was everything but due process. Due process wasn't required because, after all, this was not a trial.

From April 12 through May 6 Robert Oppenheimer spent each day in that room, delivering his version of things, answering questions, enduring scrutiny of the finest minutiae of his adult life, explaining, remembering, defending, later just listening to the witnesses. He had an old sofa at one end, by the door, facing up-room toward the Board. Kitty was beside him. The witness chair stood between, with its back to Oppenheimer. People came, sat in the chair, talked about a man's life: what they knew and what they thought. Oppenheimer listened and stared at the napes of necks.

Hans Bethe testified in his support. So did Enrico Fermi, Karl Compton, James Conant, and others among the United States Government's pre-eminent consulting scientists. Isidor Rabi gave the panel hell. Vannevar Bush, who had been FDR's chief wartime adviser on all scientific research for military application, proclaimed his complete confidence in Oppenheimer's loyalty, judgment, and integrity; Bush also added the unsolicited and unwelcome observation that a grievous mistake was being made here, by someone, in putting a scientist on trial for his opinions. David Lilienthal, formerly head of the AEC, endorsed Oppenheimer's character and praised his contributions to national security. Leslie Groves declared that Oppenheimer had done a magnificent job on the A-bomb project and that he himself was glad to have been responsible for pushing through the man's clearance. The current director of Los Alamos said that Oppenheimer's devotion to American weapons research, the decisions made, the advice given, were the best demonstration of patriotism that he could imagine. Even Edward Teller, no admirer of Oppenheimer either personally or politically, offered a few words: "I have always assumed, and I now assume, that he is loyal to the United States. I believe this, and I shall believe it until I see very conclusive proof to the opposite." Oppenheimer himself took the witness chair again. Kitty testified. Along toward the end of it all, on the third from the last day of the hearings, Michael Zolta appeared.

He had agreed to contribute to these proceedings, Zolta said, not only because he was asked to but also because, as an American citizen, he considered it a duty and a privilege. He bore no personal ill feeling against Dr. Oppenheimer and had high respect for him as a physicist, so if this were simply a matter of science policy, or of employment, he would prefer not to inject himself. But of course it was more than that. So he put himself at the Board's service. Furthermore anything he might have to say, he wanted to say it in the presence of Dr. Oppenheimer.

Such a rule happened to be already in effect. Zolta sat in the chair. His black hair was a little long across the back of his collar, and the wiry overgrowth of his muttonchops tangled outward on each side like solar flares.

Zolta's testimony was relatively brief. Five o'clock had

already passed when he was sworn. After the routine biographical preliminaries, the questions which each witness answered by reciting his résumé, Charles Reese asked: "You know Dr. Oppenheimer well, do you not?"

No, this wasn't strictly correct. Zolta had known Dr. Oppenheimer for a long time; he had met with him frequently concerning scientific matters since 1942; but known him well? No. Zolta hadn't done that.

The questioning turned to Los Alamos during the war, then to the thermonuclear in the days when that weapon was still just a wild idea in the minds of Teller and Zolta, finally to that decisive political juncture for the thermonuclear program and the adverse GAC report. Zolta had been mystified, he said, when he heard of the report's contents. Even more mystified later as he spoke individually with certain GAC members. Charles Reese seized on the word: Why *mystified?*

Zolta said: "Always I shall be mystified when, with the very existence of our nation at stake, intelligent men for complex and specious reasons tell us that the preferred course of action is inaction. And so they were telling us. I questioned Fermi, Rabi, Conant, in fact perhaps every member of that committee except Oppenheimer himself. I received various puzzling replies. We should not, on moral grounds, go ahead with this thing. If we did it, the world would hate us. If we didn't do it, the Russians might also not do it. It was too expensive. Too cumbersome. We didn't have the manpower. It was not *sweet*. Not *sweet*, mind you. Such were the arguments I was hearing, and they disturbed me."

"Did you ascertain," asked Reese, "the ultimate source of these particular arguments?"

Zolta said: "Yes. The source was Dr. Oppenheimer."

"How so?"

Zolta said: "He had done his usual uncanny job of persuasion. All of the logic in that report, to which Fermi and the others had signed their names, all of it was directly the reflection of Oppenheimer's own personal views. He had guided the deliberations utterly." Zolta paused. "It is more plausible, though perhaps no less amazing, if you know him. There is a magnetism. He can be the most exceptionally persuasive man."

Had Zolta ever suspected, asked Reese, that Oppenheimer had used his gift for persuasion in an act of disloyalty to the United States?

Zolta said: "An act of disloyalty. No. I have never doubted his loyalty. He believes fully in what he does. Quite fully. It is this very sincerity that makes him . . ." Zolta paused again, and then finished. "Dangerous."

"A corollary to that question," said Reese. "Do you or do you not believe that Dr. Oppenheimer is a security risk?"

Pushing against the chair arms, Zolta lifted his spine straight. He did not rush himself. Despite a dozen years in America and the five before that in England his speech retained much of the thick careful Magyar inflection, moving with the rhythm of yoked oxen toward a barn. "Let me simply say this. Dr. Oppenheimer is a complicated man. In some cases his actions, and so too his motivations, they have appeared to my view excessively complicated. Confused, yes, and complicated. For policy as for science the more complex is often not the better. Now security proceedings such as the present must involve, I think, not only the question of loyalty but another matter also. That is judgment. Judgment must be applied to technical and policy options but also—and no less importantly, I must stress—judgment is applied to people. The people one hires, the people to whom one delegates. The people even one surrounds oneself with personally. The people one chooses to trust. Dr. Oppenheimer's record in this regard is, in my view, something far short of reassuring." For no discernible reason the oxen came to a halt, as oxen do, and the hearing room was quite utterly silent. But he continued: "Good judgment in such matters, I mean the personal as well as the political, I do not in my own mind associate with excessive complexity of motive. Often the opposite is true. For these reasons I would say that I myself would feel more secure, as to the vital interests of our country, if those interests were not subject to the judgment of Robert Oppenheimer."

Evidently Zolta had declared that Oppenheimer's conscience was not technically sweet; but no one could be sure. By now it was 5:45 P.M. While the Board members were doing their best to digest Zolta's syllogism, Charles Reese said:

"In more simple terms, Dr. Zolta. You have spoken about trust. Bearing in mind what you've said, and what you know of Dr. Oppenheimer—would you trust him?"

"Trust him?" Zolta said. "You mean in matters of security?"

"Yes, sir."

Zolta said: "No. I am afraid I certainly would not."

Only that. In the upshot, the Personnel Board would agree rather precisely with Zolta's modest, ambivalent formulation. They would officially conclude that Robert Oppenheimer was a loyal citizen. They would find that his judgment had in some cases been faulty, that his conduct had often been mystifying, and in particular that his posture regarding the H-bomb program had been disturbing. They would revoke his security clearance.

Zolta, on his way out of the hearing room that late afternoon, lingered momentarily before Oppenheimer, whose face was empty as he accepted the handshake.

"I'm sorry," Zolta said.

"You must be kidding," said Oppenheimer.

Two weeks later, at the very end of May, Tay and the band had a booking in Durango, Colorado. Sometime that week, she wasn't sure when, Randy Ortiz disappeared.

Part Three

TWENTY-FIVE

Walking back, late on this warm night, under the high canopy of cottonwoods that admit so little starlight onto Burch Street, Mayberry feels like a lost tourist in the Carlsbad Caverns, strayed off inadvertently from the uniformed man with the flashlight and the floor plan: yes indeed, these other lonely uncharted chambers are spectacular, impressive stalactites, wonderful collection of bats, but how does a fellow GET OUT? Mayberry is burdened with ideas, unsettling new ones plus a few that have lingered, and though still inchoate, disordered, together they are nonetheless worrisome. For instance, *What's more distressing about Jeffrey than his murder?* That was one of Mayberry's own lines, to Karen, which now seems perhaps worth recollecting. The saloons on the square have closed so he heads to his motel. There he is immediately distracted from his elaborate and farfetched anxieties by something familiar, something that reminds him of home: broken glass.

The windshield of his rented Chevy has been bashed out with maniacal thoroughness. The safety glass has sprayed itself in bits like hard clear candy, and a few larger webbed swatches more on the order of peanut brittle, across the front seat and floor. Using even a good sledgehammer it must have taken someone ten or twelve minutes. No question here of a thief just wanting to get inside, there would have been much easier and quieter ways, and besides, the impression left is distinctly more rhetorical. The side and back windows, also the headlights, are untouched. Mayberry can't help but think of Armatrading and the Louisville Slugger he once liked to carry in the saddlebag of his great ugly bike. Varvara said something about a maul handle. Probably by now, though, Chester has switched to a hollow aluminum softball bat, lighter and more durable and in tune with the times. Mayberry is unhappy at the window's message, almost as unhappy as he is no doubt intended to be, but he doesn't delude himself. Only Armatrading could be just smart enough to track him to Taos and just stupid enough to batter out the entire windshield of an insured car with New Mexico plates loaned to Mayberry by the Budget corporation.

But in fairness to Chester's intelligence there was a point to be made, and Mayberry has grasped it. The point was no particular car windshield; the point was the bat, and Chester's eagerness to use it. And even the bat was, by Mayberry's reading, a metaphor. Chester will know that Mayberry would never let himself be bludgeoned to death, not by one person, not even one as well qualified for that sort of thing as Chester, and so he will presumably need to rely on some instrument more overwhelmingly lethal, like the old Winchester pump shotgun again, when the final urge comes. Evidently Armatrading takes Mayberry as having himself shot the face off Shelly Sanzone, Chester's valued playmate, thus Mayberry is down for a revenge killing, complete with these vainglorious gestures of prefigurement. Chester always did have the imagination of a character out of *Titus Andronicus*. Mayberry believes, prematurely, that his second death warning has been received and registered in full. And that he can therefore relax for a night's sleep.

Leaving the car till tomorrow, he goes up to his room. It is on the second level, at the far rear corner of the motel, away from the highway by Mayberry's own choice. He is only passably careful as he unlocks the door.

Late as it is, he takes a long shower, hoping vaguely to flush off himself and away—for a few hours at least—the disconcerting suspicions he has accumulated today, first at Los Alamos and then from the talk with Tay Riordan. He may as well be rinsing at slimy soap with very hard water. Standing dry and still naked, now also woozy from the hot soaking, ready to drop asleep within seconds, he snatches down the bedspread. The thing rests on his pillow, fastidiously placed, dark putrescent umber against the crisp white linen.

Mayberry feels a jolt of nausea before he even understands what it is, a bad shock to his stomach, based merely on the nasty color and the odd texture of this item, and the sense of violation from discovering it lurking on a clean pillowcase. A very ugly little surprise. His lips wrinkle back off his teeth. For the first several seconds his eyes tell him that he is, inexplicably, staring down at a sulfurous dried apricot, or maybe a peach; dried peach on a white pillow, like something from Salvador Dali.

But no. Mayberry focuses. What it is, he sees, is a human ear. An old one, presumably from Armatrading's renowned private collection. Probably, but not necessarily, Vietnamese.

Shelly Sanzone's death might serve as a handy excuse, but Chester's real homicidal fury at Mayberry seems to go rather a bit farther back.

TWENTY-SIX

Albert Varvara is closeted on the outskirts of Santa Fe for conferral with higher authority but Jesse, by no coincidence, is in the lobby of the De Vargas when these two men stumble through the door.

He hears one of them give a triumphal pop to the little silver desk bell. In only twenty minutes they have come all the way from the police station four blocks away, where Lieutenant Roybal drew them a map. They wear matching beige cotton suits but there is just the one briefcase. Apparently they share it.

Jesse is inconspicuous: sunk in a purple armchair before the lobby TV, and reading a copy of the *Christian Science Monitor* folded back to a single column as if he were knocking elbows on a crowded subway. He is wearing the same watch cap and fatigue jacket as in Austin. Though he doesn't glance up, except occasionally to scowl at Dr. Joyce Brothers, who is wagging her jaw from the sofa of someone's talk show, he can hear everything; the bag lady in the other purple chair is hypnotized speechless by the television. The two men wait while the desk clerk of the test-pattern tweed jacket takes a stately long time climbing onto his feet. In fact he delays first, insolently, to light another cheroot. If he hates the desk bell so badly why doesn't he just get rid of it, Jesse wonders, and tell his boss it was stolen by a guest? To the pair of chirpy men the clerk says, with a hint of autumnal Parisian accent:

"Help you."

"Yes. My name is Bruce Guinness. This is my associate, Roger Ripley." A billfold appears from an inner coat pocket and a hand flops it open toward the clerk, displaying some sort of identification certificate or badge; the billfold flops closed again and swish it is gone. There seems a very good chance that this fluid sequence of motions is the result of home practice. Roger Ripley, the associate, may have a billford too but he doesn't draw it. "Department of Energy. Safeguards and Security. Roybal of the city police steered us over here. We're looking for a fellow named Mayberry."

"And I am not him," says the clerk.

"We know that. A guest, we mean."

"You're the desk clerk here, is that right?" says Ripley. The clerk simply gapes at him, squinting in pain as though against the smoke of his own cheroot, and even the bag lady tosses over a contemptuous glance. Only Jesse is careful not to stare; and Guinness, of course.

"Saturday," says Guinness. "He may still be here. Or not. We hope so. It's a matter of considerable importance. We came out from D.C. to talk with him."

"By way of Oakland," says Ripley, faintly petulant.

The clerk does not recall Mr. Mayberry, or so he claims, but for gentlemen of such august badges he will certainly check the book. He lifts it out from below the counter: an old folio ledger of the sort most hotels have long since discarded for the charmless self-carboning cards. Ah yes, Mr. Mayberry of Oakland. Saturday, yes. Stopped over that one night. Then gone. Jesse slides a hand discreetly into his own right pocket where he is pleased to discover, as hoped, a dime.

"May we see?" says Guinness, and with a superior shrug the clerk obliges, turning the ledger around. It yields nothing helpful: Mayberry's slovenly signature which was made worse that night by the hour and the circumstances, his Oakland street address which they already know too well, the fact that he is representing only himself. His room was 322.

"Where did he go? Did he say anything, when he checked out, about where he was going?"

"On Sunday morning? It was not my shift. I do not know."

"Does he have a reservation to come back?"

For this the clerk does not require a ledger. "No." Reservations at the De Vargas are rare enough to be held within one idle memory.

"We'd like to see room 322," Ripley says suddenly, in a civil but firm tone he seems to have copied from Jack Webb. "Just for a look."

Guinness, taken unsuspecting by such an aggressively inquisitive proposition, blinks once at his associate before turning back to the desk clerk. "Yeah," he says.

"I'm sorry." The clerk pinches his lips and rocks backward a few degrees. "I've no one to watch the desk."

"You don't need to leave it," says Guinness.

"Give us the key. You can trust us. We're not a couple

of sleazy private detectives, after all. We're federal attorneys. Seriously."

"We work directly for the Assistant Secretary, practically."

"C'mon. Just a fast look. Maybe he left something that will say where he went. C'mon."

"We promise not to steal any towels."

As the desk clerk teeters toward acquiescence Jesse quietly pockets his newspaper and strolls for the door. Across Don Gaspar Street he finds a pay phone in the municipal parking lot. He pages through the book without haste in search of a number for the De Vargas. The clerk, his formulaic hello a trifle more curt than usual, a trifle more French, sounds freshly put-upon as beyond in the background Jesse hears the gate of the elevator clash closed. Jesse stalls until the machine has begun its groaning ascent; then:

"My name is Mayberry. I'm calling from Taos. I stayed with you on Saturday."

The clerk stammers politely and Jesse pictures him raising a finger toward the departing elevator. "Mr. Mayberry, yes. In fact there are just now—"

"I've got a pair of men I'm supposed to meet," Jesse says. "But my plans keep changing and I'm pressed for time. Right now I'm in Taos, at the Sun-God Motel. I don't want to miss these guys, they're traveling a long way. I'm here at the Sun-God but they might come asking for me to you. I wonder if I could leave them a message."

The clerk begs him to hold for a minute, only please hold, which by hindsight five minutes later the clerk fears Mr. Mayberry must have taken for preoccupied rudeness; when he gallops back downstairs, followed by Ripley who is followed by Guinness, the line is dead. And Jesse is seated again before the television.

The clerk having told them everything he can, Ripley and Guinness scudder off. Jesse hopes they don't know Mayberry by sight. If so they might be lucky enough to spot him, the wincing man behind the wheel of a Chevrolet with no windshield, when he crosses them on the road down from Taos. According to Mayberry's wild call this morning, asking Albert or Jesse to meet him, he should already be on his way.

TWENTY-SEVEN

Mayberry is just yards from the door of the De Vargas when he hears quick footsteps behind him and his neck muscles tighten accordingly; he readies himself in the instant for an effort of desperate ferocity against Zuckerman with the nasty little automatic or Armatrading with the Model 12; but it is only Jesse, who has evidently been watching for him from nearby. Not missing the flinch, Jesse spreads his palms up and open in a fast gesture of innocent intent. "Don't go in." He falls casually into step at Mayberry's side and they pass by the hotel entrance. "Let's just walk on down here and turn right. I have a car with all its windows."

"Is something wrong?" says Mayberry. "I mean, something more?"

"Yeah. Two guys from the Department of Energy were just looking for you. At the hotel. I figured we didn't need that. I sent them on a snipe hunt."

"Where's Varvara?"

"We'll see him. He's busy right now. We'll see him back at the room." Setting a pace, Jesse is silent until they leave Don Gaspar Street behind. "I hear you did well."

"I learned some things about Zuckerman. Scraps." Mayberry has in mind also the day at Los Alamos, the signature on a form at the library, but about that he plans to say nothing. "I didn't get shot up or beat on or cut. That's how well. Scraps, I think, were all she had. She was Zuckerman's honey for a while, like you suspected, but she barely knew him. What about you two? Where's Varvara?"

"We've been picking our noses," says Jesse. "Keeping up on the pair of Israelis in Juarez, but nothing doing there. No further calls from Zuckerman, according to our little bird. Which means among other things, unfortunately, that we don't have an inkling where he is. Might still be right here in Santa Fe, or long gone. And your buddy Roybal is getting nowhere with the Karen Ives murder. He has a description, is all, and a shell casing and a slug. But he doesn't have anything else on Zuckerman. Doesn't even have the name."

"You haven't given it to him?" says Mayberry.

"We're not really talking with Roybal. As a matter of fact he doesn't know we exist. That's how we'd like it to stay. What I just said about his getting nowhere, we only have that secondhand, office gossip. No, we haven't walked in to offer him the name. And I gather you didn't either."

"Not hardly. But isn't he talking to Buski in Oakland?"

"Yes. I think they've made contact over the wire. By way of the name Jeffrey Jay Katy, I suppose."

"Then Roybal knows damn well you exist. Or that Varvara does, at least. Because I told Buski everything I knew. About Varvara, appearing mysteriously, shooting my burglar in the face, chasing the Teller thing."

Jesse at this news shows sign of deep frustration. He even sweeps off the watch cap, evidently an annoyance, and pushes it into a pocket. With the same hand he absently fluffs his sweaty hair.

"Tell me something, Jesse," says Mayberry. "This has been nagging me. How does the Rockwell company tap a telephone in Mexico?"

"Pair of pliers and three feet of wire," Jesse says flatly.

"Where is Varvara?"

"Not in Mexico."

They drive out Cerrillos Road to that part of town where neon blooms in wild vigor on both sides of the drag and almost all pretense of regional decor has dropped away. Not even the hamburger franchises here are disguised, as in Taos, behind snap-on aluminum mud. In this zone of malls and drive-ins and two hundred motels new money is simply chasing newer, with little affectation and lots of shameless energy; it could just as well be the outskirts of Toledo or Harrisburg. Mayberry imagines there must be a comfortable measure of anonymity to be had out here, no doubt the reason for Varvara and Jesse so choosing. Beneath a sign on its hundred-foot pole, Jesse turns onto the lot of a Motel 6.

And there they wait, in a double room upstairs overlooking the growl and blare of Cerrillos. Jesse gives Mayberry the single chair, draping himself out across one of the beds. On the Formica counter is an unbroken bottle of Bacardi, another nearly empty, a six-pack of Coke in cans, and five small phials of prescription pills. Two suitcases rest open on the floor, one of them an old tan cloth-covered number with a flap latch, the kind of bag you see on an airport conveyor bound shut with a piece of clothesline. Varvara would have to have gotten it at Montgomery Ward during the Truman years. The television hovers blankly above everything, high on the wall like a security camera, but there is little in this room that could be stolen or vandalized. Varvara and Jesse have apparently been camped in here since Saturday; Mayberry thinks he might rather be shot at by Chester.

"How long?" says Mayberry.

"Not very," says Jesse. "Have a Coke."

"No thanks. Jesse, is there any chance Zuckerman has gone back up to Taos?"

"Sure. Some chance. I couldn't say how much. I told you, we've had no hint of his whereabouts since the moment Karen Ives was murdered. Even that's just an assumption, that it was Zuckerman who killed her."

"A safe assumption."

"Granted. It's a terrific annoyance, as Albert would say, but there you are: Zuckerman's scope of activity seems to be very limited right now, probably he's just laying up somewhere, and in consequence he isn't leaving any tracks. He's left precious few from the beginning."

"No tracks. Just corpses."

"Exactly right," says Jesse. "And stacking corpses around is one of the proven ways of making sure a secret stays secret."

"You think Zuckerman has a secret?" Mayberry proposes this in an ingenuous voice, as though the same thing has never occurred to him, and fortunately Jesse has his eyes on the ceiling.

"I do. Albert does. We talked about that. Why else would he kill the Ives woman in the particular way that he did? I mean, in such a public place. Why accept that extra risk? Not just to take possession of the report, if he thought for some reason she had a copy. No. He could have waited. He's still waiting now, if the news from Juarez, or rather the lack of it, if that's any reliable sign. No. He wanted her dead because he wanted her quiet. And he must have judged that the moment in that restaurant was his final chance."

"What about Jeff Katy? Another victim of Zuckerman's passion for privacy?"

"Could have been," Jesse allows judiciously. "Probably was."

"And Hannah Broch?"

After a tiny glitch of hesitation Jesse says: "Maybe. She hasn't been found, dead or alive, so far as we know."

"Then I'm worried about Tay Riordan. Sitting up there in Taos. She's a savvy young woman, she's tough and she's sensible, but she has no way to protect herself against the kind of thing that happened to Karen. She isn't even aware she might need to. I told her Zuckerman was probably involved in a pair of killings. I didn't say he almost certainly shot a woman in cold blood. And now Tay may know as many of Zuckerman's secrets as anyone who's still breathing. She could be the next corpse on the stack."

"Relax, Mayberry," says Jesse. "He's much more likely to come after you."

When Mayberry next glances out the window he sees Albert Varvara below on the traffic island, momentarily stranded among five lanes of cars moving four directions, and watching nervously for an opportunity to complete the crossing alive. Varvara's head snicks back and forth as his right foot gropes on the edge of a lane, risking amputation; he looks like a duck in the brush on the last weekend of bird season. He still hasn't changed out of the blue corduroy jacket or the doubleknits, it may even be the same shirt, and as he finally makes his break, through a gap in the traffic that seems more than ample until he finds a way to use all of it, and the horn of a Chrysler blats at him, and Varvara throws up his middle finger without turning back, Mayberry remembers that Albert Varvara is, in addition to whatever else, a sick old man. The tin knobs on his string tie bob with each creaky stride.

Mayberry wonders where he has just come from. On the far side of Cerrillos at the point of fording there is only more of the same, a Ramada Inn and a Denny's.

Varvara thumps the room door and is admitted, still sucking deeply for breath. He casts a glare at Jesse, then one at Mayberry, who does not offer the chair, and paces the length of the room twice, cooling out, before finding his way back to the rum bottles.

"We've been waiting about forty-five minutes," Jesse says pointedly, though Mayberry does not quite feel in on the point.

"Well pardon my whiskey breath," says Varvara. "I just got in from Butte."

"What's the consensus?" Jesse asks.

"Consensus?" As though the word could by no leap of fancy apply to whatever ideas Varvara has carried back from across the road, and Jesse should well know it. "The consensus is I want to hear Mayberry's poop."

Varvara consumes close to a half gallon of Coke and no small amount of Barcardi while he and Jesse listen to Mayberry's recitation; unclear still to Mayberry whether the man suffers from a serious sugar addiction or merely alcoholism. The three days of idleness in this room must have entailed a high volume of Varvara's favorite teenage cocktail, maybe even a crisis of restlessness that provoked a major binge just the night before, because the flesh of Varvara's face today has the look of a bar of orange soap left under a dripping faucet. His hands tremble as he scribbles into the ring pad. And moments before, when he popped a can and poured himself the first of the current sequence, Jesse spoke gently:

"Albert. Isn't it a little early?"

"Shut up, Jesse. Too goddamn early for you to start the mothering, yes."

Since then they haven't exchanged a word, though both are agreeable enough to Mayberry as he describes what Tay Riordan chose to call her "Zuckerman incident." Varvara is especially interested in the part about Zuckerman's midnight meetings with someone or other, conceivably several different someones, in Santa Fe. Mayberry explains that Tay, so she claimed, never set eyes on any of these mysterious folk, Zuckerman having always kept his business and pleasure carefully separated; and that he, Mayberry, believes her.

"So far as she knew he was dealing cocaine," says Mayberry. "It had to be cocaine, or maybe bootleg guns, she figured. From the money he spent and the way he operated. The way he looked. Cocaine seemed the more plausible."

"And right she was," says Varvara. "What this mophead is trying to pull off, I sure the hell wouldn't call it plausible."

Nor can Mayberry say, because Tay couldn't either, where Zuckerman went for these rendezvous. The only geographic coordinates at which he could be plotted in Santa Fe were a couple of Mexican restaurants, including the ranch out at Chimayo by the Los Alamos road, and the Hotel De Vargas. And now of course, since Karen, the Ore House.

"The De Vargas. Everybody stays at the De Vargas," says Jesse. "It's seedy but it's chic. And here we are at a Motel 6."

"Do us a favor, Mayberry," says Varvara.

"Not that again," says Mayberry.

"It's nothing really." Varvara's benign smile and tone of velvety reassurance are together maximally counterproductive. "Nothing difficult. Nothing especially dangerous. You maybe were planning to do this very thing anyway. I wouldn't be surprised."

"I'd be surprised," says Mayberry.

"Go back to the De Vargas, is all. Check in. Stay a few days. Hang out, see what turns up." As an afterthought Varvara adds, "I'm paying," and then he meets Jesse's sideways glance but the budgetary dispute is evidently left for later.

"You don't mean see what. You mean see who."

"Yeah. Sure I do. Our boy Zuckerman needs to know where he can reach you. Got to make yourself a bit more available, Mayberry. Stop all this charging around between cities and motels and jails. Sit still for a minute. Zuckerman wanted to buy something that you happen to have. He said so in a personal note, if I recall. Maybe he still wants to. Christ I hope so. Otherwise it means he's found himself an alternate arrangement, which is the last thing I want to hear."

"Bait," says Mayberry.

"Sure."

"He's got a problem with that, Albert," says Jesse.

Varvara's upper body cranks around as though mounted

on rusty Cat treads. "No doubt. But whose side are *you* on?"

"A pair of guys from the DOE showed up there not three hours ago. Asking for Mayberry. Lawyers. Out of Safeguards and Security. All right? You know what that means. As soon as they catch up with him, at the De Vargas or wherever, Mayberry will be totally neutralized. They'll wrap him in Cellophane. Maybe they've got an injunction to serve on him and even if not, there will be interviews and procedural threats and hopelessly clumsy surveillance. They'll just roil the waters up all to hell. And then no contact from Zuckerman. Not a chance. Mayberry will be worthless to us once those yoyos pounce on him. He'll be worthless to everybody."

This seems in Mayberry's judgment a little harsh but he lets it pass, saying only: "And that isn't all."

"Judas," says Varvara.

"I've also got Armatrading to deal with." He has told them already about the totemic message that accompanied his broken windshield. "If Zuckerman can find me, if even the two Tweedles from Washington can find me, then Armatrading can too. And he's looking to do more than serve me a process."

"Are you afraid of Armatrading?"

Mayberry ponders that. "Yes. If he knows where I am, and it isn't mutual? Yes. I don't much like the idea of sitting around, being passive and conspicuous while I wait for Zuckerman's approach, and in the meantime showing Chester an easy target." But even with all the qualification it rankles Mayberry badly as soon as he has heard himself say it: *Yes I'm afraid of him*. Armatrading is certifiably gaga, he'll do anything, he's utterly violently whimsical, and undeterrable, because he would never think of pausing to measure a fleeting whim against future cost to himself: any sane man *should* be afraid of Armatrading. Mayberry is surprised at himself, that such a sensible admission— *Yes I'm afraid of him*—could still seem so bitterly distasteful.

"Isn't that just the way things will stand anyway? He knows where you are and can choose his moment. I mean when you're back in Oakland again. Say you fly back there tonight and pick up your shifts at the hospital, tomorrow, the day after: what's the difference? Armatrading is still out in the bushes somewhere and you're in the open, right? Or do you plan to go into hiding?"

"Not hardly." The difference is, Mayberry recalls, that if he does precisely what Varvara just described the Head of Surgery will be less likely to flush him out of med school like a miscarried two-month fetus. But that's another whole framework of worry for which right now he barely has time. Not even a prudent and diligent thirty-five-year-old can finish a medical degree if he happens to be dead, gutshot with a Winchester pump on some Oakland street corner where such an event might seem almost routine, if a wallet were taken off the body, and not an ear. The thirty-five-year-old in question also cannot finish that degree, not now, he simply cannot, Mayberry realizes, until he has dealt satisfactorily with the Zuckerhead.

"So. You don't like the idea," says Varvara. "Got a better one?"

Arms folded and browline filled up with earnestness, Mayberry gives it some thought. Jesse watches expectantly. Varvara is more cocky: he turns away to pour another drink. Mayberry considers an immediate departure for Oakland. He considers the slim possibility that he might by act of will dismiss Zuckerman, also Armatrading, permanently from his consciousness; not to mention Karen.

He considers scampering back up to Taos and placing himself at the disposal, under the protection, of Ripley and Guinness. None of which seems remotely acceptable. What he truly wants is to face Armatrading and settle *that* dangerous silliness; then get both of his thumbs on the windpipe of this person Zuckerman.

He says: "No."

Then it's agreed. And Varvara will do the honors on Ripley and Guinness. "What's the name of this motel where you stayed?"

Mayberry tells him.

"They'll be there already, Albert," says Jesse. "It was three hours ago. They were on their way when they left the De Vargas."

"Maybe not. Maybe they stopped for a burrito."

"These guys were in a big damn hurry. They thought they had a hot trail. By now they will have heard that he checked out this morning and they're probably thundering back. They'll go straight to the De Vargas."

"Maybe not. Maybe they took a wrong turn." Varvara begins dialing the number of the Sun-God Motel in Taos.

"That's highly possible," says Mayberry.

"There *are* no turns. It's one highway the whole way. Don't you remember? Signs for Taos every ten miles." But Jesse is waved silent as a woman's voice answers on the far end.

"Hi, my name is Mayberry, I just left there this morning," Varvara tells her. Yes, with the busted windshield, right. Yes, it was breezy at first but he taped in a sheet of cardboard, thanks. Two men from the Department of Energy? No, the woman says, no one like that, no one at all has been by asking for Mr. Mayberry since he checked out.

"That's good," says Varvara. "Because I don't want to miss these guys. They're from back East, and I got to catch them before they leave again. They'll probably be at your door in an hour or two. But meantime I had to come up here to Durango, Colorado. Part of the same whole business. They'll understand. That's where I'm at now."

"Durango. You made real good time," she says.

"Yeah I did. So look," says Varvara sweetly, "would you give them a message for me?"

TWENTY-EIGHT

And so he is back at the De Vargas that afternoon. In the four days Mayberry then spends playing the role of visiting idler, contentedly adrift among the restaurants and bookstores and park benches of Santa Fe, he receives three further messages.

Two of these pass decorously through the rheumy French clerk who, like Varvara, evidently owns only the one jacket; the third arrives without intermediary yet entails a certain deft indirection all its own, more subtle even than a Louisville Slugger. But that is later. The first message is waiting for Mayberry, at the front desk, within hours.

Walking back from dinner, he is flagged over by the Frenchman with news that Lieutenant Roybal would like Mr. Mayberry to return his call or, better still, stop by the station for a chat. Roybal's telephone manners must have been good because the clerk makes no intimation that this could imply anything but respectable business concerns for an esteemed guest; or else he is accustomed to forwarding hooded threats from the police to his patrons. Mayberry calls.

"I gather you've been in a little scrape," says Roybal. "I thought we were going to keep in touch, you and I."

"What are you talking about?"

"Taos. Your car. Is someone after you, Mayberry?"

"I had bad luck with some vandals. How did you know?"

"Now *that*, please don't do that," says Roybal fastidiously, rather like an art teacher pointing his finger at lazy brushwork. "Don't ever presume you can dismiss me with that sort of facetious bullshit. It's just very irritating. It will only bias me against you." Roybal keeps tipping Mayberry off balance: *facetious* is another he wouldn't expect to find in the vocabulary of, say, Oakland's fattest sergeant. However, despite the verbal polish and the veneer of politeness—or the genuine politeness, as it may be—Mayberry by now is persuaded that Roybal will not hesitate to pulp Mayberry's testicles in a polite walnut vise if professional necessity should so require.

"All right, someone is after me, yes. It's a very old grudge. An Army thing. No reason to expect you'd be interested. It has absolutely nothing to do with the Karen Ives case." Which for all Mayberry knows might almost be true, although he doesn't believe it himself. "Do you want to be told about every car window that gets broken in the state of New Mexico this month?"

"No. Only yours," says Roybal. "An old grudge, huh. I *am* interested. Why don't you stroll over here and we'll talk about it."

"We can't do that by telephone?"

"What's wrong, Mayberry? I've asked you nicely. Are

you so busy? Are you embarrassed to be seen at a police station?"

"I'm on my way," says Mayberry. "Okay? God knows I wouldn't want to put a scar on your psyche."

Roybal, either a very confident man or having watched the street from a window, has two cups of coffee already poured and waiting, not in Styrofoam but white porcelain mugs. He offers a carton of real cream. The coffee is from a fresh pot made with stale grounds off a shelf in the supply closet, and as horrible as on Saturday night, notwithstanding the excellence of the service. Roybal closes his cubicle door. The idea, Mayberry gathers, is an atmosphere of amicable confidentiality; he half expects Chopin coming in by Muzak.

"Chester Armatrading," Mayberry volunteers. "That's who did the work on the windshield. I think. An old Army buddy of mine. Actually I was his CO at one time, and he has hated me nonstop since 1966. You could look up his police record. Violent but petty stuff. Not homicidal." Again Mayberry is hoping to preempt Roybal's curiosity, Roybal's suspicions, and avoid having to divulge anything about Zuckerman. "Smashing windshields is exactly the sort of thing Armatrading does."

"Mayberry, do you know Sheldon Sanzone?" Roybal asks in a mild voice.

"Barely. We once belonged to the same organization. Haven't seen him in eight years. But you've been talking to Buski in Oakland and you've heard Sanzone was killed at my house. It's true. Last week. But not by me. I was at work. Evidently they tried to burglarize the place. I've already told you about what they wanted: the Teller report."

"They," says Roybal, and Mayberry begins worrying.

"Armatrading and Sanzone." If Roybal now has enough

orphan facts and just moves the conversation around dizzyingly from one to the next, Mayberry will be hard put to keep a story straight with Zuckerman edited out. Maybe he shouldn't even try. "They were chums. Accomplices sometimes. Armatrading was in Oakland last week too. I know that the hard way, another broken window. Very possible that he was along the morning Sanzone went into my house." Momentarily Mayberry is relieved by this inspired variation on actuality.

"You told me that Armatrading had nothing to do with this case. Karen Ives and the Teller report."

"No I didn't. I told you his grudge against me had nothing to do with it. The windshield had nothing to do with it."

"What if Armatrading thinks you shot Sanzone? Couldn't that be why he's harassing you?"

"If Armatrading was there, he *knows* who shot Sanzone." I'm doing pretty well, Mayberry thinks, but it can't last.

"So who shot Sanzone?"

"I couldn't say. I wasn't there. I told what little I know to the Oakland police."

Pensively Roybal takes a sip of coffee. As if introducing a wholly new topic, though certainly he knows better, he says: "Albert Varvara."

"Claims he's a security investigator for Rockwell, the nuclear contractor. But I have my doubts." Yet Mayberry hasn't until now voiced these to anyone, not even Varvara. "He turned up at my house after the Sanzone killing. May even have been him who did it. Varvara was another one chasing the Teller report. I talked with him for about an hour, then blew him off. I did have a copy of the thing, like he thought, but I wanted to hand that directly to the FBI."

"And did you?"

"I tried. The FBI wouldn't take it. They referred me to the Department of Energy. And I'm *still* trying to make contact with those bimbos."

"Have you seen Varvara since that morning?"

"No," says Mayberry. He gives Roybal a long earnest look before lifting his own cup.

For the next half hour Mayberry struggles successfully to keep the missing character missing, to refrain from identifying that individual whose description alone Roybal has from witnesses at the Ore House; he also tries to weave just enough truth into his answers that Roybal might believe he is merely ignorant and foolish. At the latter, evidently, Mayberry fails, because finally Lieutenant Roybal lifts his feet out of his middle desk drawer, sets them on the floor, and says:

"You know what I think?"

"No, but I'd like to," says Mayberry.

"Two things. First, I think you yourself are not guilty of any crimes. Probably. At least not yet."

"Can I quote you if you take me to court for assaulting an officer?"

Roybal's face, quite stern, is transformed for a quick silent snicker, then back. "I don't plan to do that."

"I'm glad."

"But it isn't too late." Mayberry remains prudently mute. "I mean other crimes than that one."

"What's the second thing?"

"Obviously you are lying to me through your teeth," says Roybal. "Somewhere in all this. I haven't yet figured where. And I dislike that, Mayberry. Because it means you underestimate my intelligence. I'm just a city cop, brainpower negligible; meanwhile you're a big doctor.

That's the attitude I get from you. And it irritates me, you know?"

"I'm not a doctor. I'm just a medical student."

"In your head you're already a doctor. It's a class thing, really, a snobbery thing, this patina of snotty humor." Roybal is speaking with the dispassion of a sociologist; Mayberry is uncertain about his use of "patina" but it seems the wrong time to bring that up.

"In my head right now," says Mayberry, "I am definitely not yet a doctor. Excuse me for contradicting you, Lieutenant."

Roybal says: "Get out."

"Roybal is back. Asking me about Armatrading," he informs Jesse over the telephone.

"That's natural."

"And about Varvara."

Jesse grunts noncommittally. "What did you tell him?"

"I was a good soldier. I haven't seen Albert Varvara since last Wednesday morning. But Roybal could still prosecute me on assault charges. So you owe me something for that one."

"Why do we owe you?"

"You said it yourself, Jesse. That you want to stay clear of Roybal. Why you should be so shy, I don't know. I just know that, having done my bit, I am owed. Now I want to see you. Both of you."

"Already? That's a bad idea. After what you say about Roybal, especially bad."

"I don't care. Why is it so bad? You think he'll have me followed?"

"Sure. Maybe. Probably depends on his manpower. If

the division is having a slow week, yes. There might be one of his guys, watched you dial these digits."

Mayberry stretches his head out of the booth, which is in a far corner of the lobby of the De Vargas. The clerk is seated behind his cage, stroking the head of a fox terrier and devoting the rest of his attention to the last inch of a cheroot; the bag lady and a gentleman friend are watching *Masterpiece Theatre*. Otherwise the place is empty. "I don't think so," says Mayberry.

Nevertheless Jesse gives him an elaborate set of instructions for clearing his tail, on the chance it needs to be cleared, and appearing at the precise point in space and time where Jesse will pick him up. Mayberry recites back the instructions almost verbatim, to Jesse's approval, and then adds: "Should I wear a cloak? Should I carry a dagger?"

"Wear a Sam Spade fedora and carry a rubber chicken if that's what you want. Just take the precautions."

"You want to synchronize watches?" There is a vein of dry mockery, and failing patience, behind this sudden accession of sappiness. "My Timex makes it eight-fourteen. Excuse me. Twenty hours fourteen."

"Cut it out, Mayberry."

The place is on San Francisco Street fifty yards off the Plaza, just a storefront arrangement within that block dominated by the great adobe ziggurat that is Hotel La Fonda, and it calls itself, this small operation, The Bistro. Outside on the window, the name is in lavender neon script. Inside are cafe tables with round tops no bigger than a large pizza, a bank of pastry cases mainly empty tonight but for a few aging napoleons, a gas stove in the work area with a crêpe griddle beside it, a brass bar long enough for six drinkers to lean against each other's elbows, and behind that the clutter of bottles amid more gleaming brass, brass spigots and handles and high fat steam boilers like golden funhouse mirrors. Mayberry orders. He has already spoken the words when they play back chillingly to his own ear:

"I'll have an espresso."

Scanning, he sees the pay phone at once, no booth and not even a pair of acoustic wingflaps, just a lump of black plastic screwed onto the wall near the back door, quietest spot in the room on a busy morning but still not very quiet. He gawks around at the register station, the bar, the dirty cups and spoons on one deserted table, anything that could generate noise. He is positive, without proof, without flicker of delusion that it can matter now, that this is the phone from which Karen called him. Jesse's car passes down San Francisco two minutes later, almost precisely at nine-thirty.

The car doesn't stop.

Mayberry asks his waitress about rest rooms and follows her directions out the back door. This gives onto an inner corridor off the lobby of La Fonda. He finds the stairway to the mezzanine overlooking the hotel's garish indoor courtyard and then the men's room, which he ignores. On the southwest corner of the mezzanine is a stairway that leads down two flights instead of just one, to a basement hallway serving the boiler room, the storage area, and the loading dock. Mayberry is moving quickly but as though innocently lost. Beside the loading dock is a metal door, unlocked at least from inside. Mayberry busts through it before the maintenance man with the open mouth can challenge him. Down four steps and into the back seat of Jesse's car, which is idling, and they depart swiftly up Water Street toward the loopway.

"All right?"

"Fine," says Jesse. "But keep your head down for a couple more minutes."

After a series of squirrelly turns they are headed out Cerrillos again, but a half mile short of the Motel 6 Jesse unexpectedly pulls off, into the lot before a windowless cinder-block bunker that proclaims itself, in flashing yellow, Ramon's Lounge. At first Mayberry takes this to be still further evasive action until Jesse says, "Wait," and disappears into the building. He returns ten minutes later with Varvara, who is walking not so well. In fact Jesse, with a firm hold on Varvara's upper arm, has to guide him toward the car like a grocery cart with balky casters. Varvara climbs into the front seat and immediately sits up very straight, fooling no one.

"What is it?" he says without turning to look at Mayberry.

"I've just lied to Roybal again. He's curious about you. I told him I hadn't seen you since the morning we met."

"It's no felony, lying to the police. But a guy doesn't want to make it a habit." Varvara offers this in a singsong voice suggesting the incomplete participation of his brain. Jesse wasn't inside Ramon's long enough to have forced coffee into Varvara and now he shifts in the driver's seat as though he expects to regret it. He hasn't made a move to restart the car.

"Roybal asked me who you are. I told him that, so far as I knew, you're a security investigator for Rockwell International."

"Good lad," says Varvara.

"I didn't mention Jesse at all. I don't think he's gotten wind of Jesse."

"Jesse is very discreet," Varvara agrees, stiff as frozen turbot.

"Now I want to know the truth. I won't cover like that again unless you tell me. Who are you, Varvara? What's your real stake in this whole business?"

Inside their little space a crystalline silence prevails, suddenly, despite the herd of cars moaning and mooing along Cerrillos. Varvara clears his throat and then says: "CIA." Jesse covers his eyes with a hand.

As they drive back downtown Mayberry is perplexed. A bit of illegal domestic CIA interest, or something on that order, was exactly what he had come to suspect. The FBI had already had their chance, best offer of all to take possession of the report if not of Zuckerman, and the Rockwell story by now was stretched thin to the point of transparency. The CIA on the other hand must certainly have a counterespionage division that would not abide seeing the Teller configuration pirated off to Israel. Certainly they must. Even if the preventive steps entailed a small violation of their latest revised charter as handed down from Congress.

Mayberry is puzzled. That had all seemed quite plausible right up until the moment Varvara confessed to it.

TWENTY-NINE

Two days pass quietly, tediously, and then the second message.

This one is waiting for Mayberry upstairs, on the shabby blond table near the foot of his bed, delivered there evidently in full daylight, and not by room service. No words; it is rather a matter of what Mayberry in the outback of II Corps Tactical Zone used to call, punning, the plastic arts.

Chester Armatrading, heavy weapons sergeant and preeminent unofficial demolitionist on the Special Forces A team that Mayberry commanded, was—even Mayberry would grudgingly admit it—an inspired and masterly practitioner of the plastic arts. Picasso with rusty iron, Robert Rauschenberg with stuffed chickens and broken umbrellas, Armatrading with C-4 plastique and any other sort of explosive that came to hand. He was easily II Corps's most infamous booby-trappist. In just one and a half hitches of Vietnam duty, before his dishonorable discharge, Chester had probably devised more different ways to blow up an unsuspecting human than the entire Los Alamos Lab since the days of Oppenheimer. Often, though by no means always, the people blown up by his fiendish gizmos were enemy soldiers. He was good at this sidelight for several reasons, the main one being that he enjoyed it enormously.

Mayberry fails to notice anything out of order when he enters his room, not surprisingly so, since the blond table is off against a far wall and already cluttered with a few paperbacks bought yesterday, a *Newsweek,* a handful of change, and Mayberry is headed for the bathroom. Wanting a shower before dinner. He hasn't replaced the damaged car and his restlessness is growing acute so he will hike tonight or get a cab, to somewhere outside the old city center, a new restaurant, and then maybe a jazz bar. His shirt is unbuttoned, he is dropping a folded gallery program from his breast pocket onto the blond table when he sees something curious there.

The maid, in her insistent tidyings, has retrieved the dirty glass ashtray that Mayberry had banished to a window sill; but she hasn't bothered to clean it. And for some reason she has plunked it down, still grimy, atop one of his books. No, wait, wrong—not a book, something metallic, some sort of can. All this is being absorbed unprocessed into Mayberry's brain during the moment it takes him to raise an arm. He focuses eye and mind finally on the bland fact that the dirty ashtray is positioned neatly on top of what looks to be a sardine can and his hand is out, idly lifting the ashtray to see just what is beneath, before judgment and caution can intercept.

It is a sardine can indeed, an empty one inverted, which leaps into the air with a sharp and heart-stopping SNAP. Nothing more.

Mayberry presses a fist to his chest. He has no breath.

Muscles from the insides of his thighs to the back of his neck feel as though they have just been rudely spasmed by electroshock and he has no breath. The ashtray rolls unbroken across the floor to spin down dead on the hardwood with a vanishing yammer but Mayberry has no breath. Squirt of poison afloat in his stomach, a hot burst at the base of his medulla, and sweat everywhere. Mayberry's body and brain have taken a bad shock, which passes gradually as the seconds pass into a generalized queasiness like flu. Lying before him on the table, beside the upturned sardine can, is a small mousetrap. Risibly small. A Victor, the forty-nine-cent size. It had been cocked but not latched, pinned flat under the can, rigged to go when the weight of the ashtray was lifted. Ha ha.

He sits on the bed. He is breathing again, shallowly, pumping his chest like a sparrow. It isn't funny and it wasn't meant to be, Chester's ingenious little parody of a C-ration booby trap. Mayberry simply has not had a worse scare in eleven years. No hangover and no fever in that time has been more sickening than this afterflush. No nightmare has been more vividly reminiscent of his life's most frightening moments than that instantaneous realization just now, when it was too late to stop the spring, too late to call back his own hand. He may have to throw up. He had already planned to change his underwear.

Blasting shotguns, ball bats, all that loud and clumsy stuff he can deal with, even the idea of facing Chester at great tactical disadvantage in a real mortal confrontation. However deranged and dangerous Armatrading might be, Mayberry still has large confidence in his own capabilities. Not just his wit; even the purely martial skills, even after so much time. But this was different.

So quiet and meticulously placed, the mousetrap was

different. A booby trap, with its cosmic impersonality, was always different. And in the hands of Armatrading, it could be especially different.

Now Mayberry is truly worried. For himself. Now he will need to step carefully. Now he will be changing his way of opening doors, stretching his neck more, reacting to small sounds. The mousetrap—the clever progression from twelve-gauge to ball bat to mousetrap—is in that sense a big success. Chester has his attention.

Obviously Armatrading has given it all a bit of thought. He doesn't just want to see Mayberry dead. If he wants that, he wants equally to terrify and humiliate him in the process. It seems such a long leap—Kontum Province to the Hotel De Vargas, more than a decade, militarily legitimized murder to the free-lance variety—over just a question of souvenirs.

THIRTY

But then it never *was* just a question of that. The ear business figured less as a cause than as a manifestation—an especially focused and consequential one, true enough—of this rancor between Captain Mayberry and his own firepower sergeant. Mutual hatred had broken out much earlier, for a complex of reasons not all of which, Mayberry knew, were to his credit. One part of the thing, for instance, might have been jealousy.

From the moment Armatrading was rotated into Dak To, late in 1965, he and Paul Katy had become very chummy. Before long they were like a pair of snickering conspiratorial adolescents. Or so it seemed to Mayberry.

He himself had known Paul since Fort Bragg. More recently they had been operating together out of the A Camp at Dak To since February of that year, when Mayberry with a precocious swiftness that surprised even him had been promoted to captain, and sent up to the high western corner of II Corps in command of a team: twelve Americans and three hundred Montagnard irregulars with a mission of border surveillance and counterinsurgency. (Neat word for a Sisyphean endeavor, *counterinsurgency,* as Mayberry was painfully to learn.) The Montagnards were all Sedang tribesmen, from the village of Dak To and others in that area of the highlands. Dak To itself was just a cluster of bamboo longhouses laid out quite primly around a single well, and populated by maybe two thousand Sedang, counting women and children and the shriveled grandmothers too old to go anywhere without being carried. Twenty kilometers west was the Laotian border, along which wound a foot trail much favored by VC. Eight kliks to the northeast, in a bare clearing far from any village, was a leprosarium formerly run by French nuns. Nothing there now but a crumbling stucco building and a handful of woebegone lepers. Mayberry's own bit of turf sat on a knoll above Dak To, no more than two or three acres, rimmed with perimeter wire and containing a team house, mortar pits, an operations bunker, and a dispensary. The decor was plywood and sandbag and concertina, with filigree of sharpened bamboo. This American presence was still very welcome then to the Sedang of Dak To; Mayberry and his men were the great tall heroes who dispensed friendly bribes of rice and farm tools and breeder pigs, helped repair dikes and suggested improved design for community latrines. They shared in the local festivals, and several noncoms wore honorary Sedang bracelets. But no one enjoyed more esteem than Sergeant Katy, who wore only his tiger suit and a Rolex. Paul was the team's medical corpsman.

Mayberry, like the Sedang, viewed Paul's work with speechless awe; and, on his own, also some envy. Here were results. Here was a tangible and immediate effica-

ciousness of the most benign sort. A baby cleanly delivered.
Bad teeth pulled. Fractures set, old wounds dressed, tropical ulcers disinfected. Two hundred typhoid inoculations in an afternoon. Three days each week Paul held clinic for the Dak To folk in his camp dispensary; on alternate days he packed medicine and instruments onto his back and hiked off, with one other man as an armed escort, for sick call to the near villages; and every few weeks he got out to the leprosarium with Dapsone for unwanted men without fingers.

As often as duty allowed in that first stretch of months, Mayberry took his rifle and went along. Nothing cheered him so much as a walk through the sweltering brush to watch Paul work small medical miracles on grateful people. For safety's sake during those hikes they talked very little, even when stopped for water, but Mayberry had begun thinking of Paul as the single soul on earth to whom, for better or worse, he felt the fullest affinity. At Bragg during advanced training the duty hours had been long and their acquaintance was casual; now it had time to steep. The constant pressure of alien countryside surrounding their tiny compound pushed them closer. Also the moments of plain terror, and the appropriately professional measure of mutual dependence. Mayberry came to value Paul as a superior medic, a strong asset therefore to the team, but above all a rare friend to be held for better times. In fact he saw Paul in almost precisely the terms he preferred to see himself: crazy-wild young but percipient beyond his years; utterly irresponsible except when it mattered; obstreperous, but stubbornly decent. Paul Katy could stitch up the torn face of a child with tender dexterity, then bust ten kliks by foot back to Dak To while every step wary for ambush, pop open a warm Budweiser, tip back his head, and with a handsome boyish smile make the most hilariously crude profession of his lust for Joey Heatherton, or of his wish to deal violently with the rear-echelon motherfucker who had shipped broken ampules of penicillin. Not a saint, by Mayberry's assessment, but something better: a useful man you could trust and enjoy. In the security of the team house they would bullshit for hours about California hamburgers and women. Meanwhile Mayberry's own responsibility was the endlessly frustrating one of pretending to orchestrate *counterinsurgency* among a backwoods ethnic minority who had all reason to fear and despise Saigon as much as they did Hanoi. There were no small miracles to be wrought at that.

Captain Mayberry was twenty-two years old, and learning potent lessons about the worldly lack of neatness. Paul Katy was a year older. He was one of the lessons.

Mayberry could not pretend to believe in some dark change that was catalyzed only by Armatrading. He got his first hint one night in Da Nang, months before Chester joined the team. Standing not five feet away, Mayberry saw Paul break the nose of a bar girl with his open hand. It was a quick deft act and the result seemed unreal. Mayberry had to gape again at the tears and the blood before he absorbed it. But Paul had been very drunk in Da Nang and Mayberry dismissed the slap—the cruel words and lack of remorse that were almost worse than the slap—as an aberration. About that he was right. He was wrong only to assume that aberrations, from Paul Katy, should necessarily be rare. By the end of a full year at Dak To Mayberry knew better. By the end of that year Armatrading was with them.

Chester Armatrading came highly recommended as a weapons sergeant and demolitionist but nobody told

Mayberry that here was a charming fellow. At first Mayberry didn't care. Later he told himself that he *shouldn't* care. *This guy is not required to be congenial. We're trying to fight a war. The man is* GOOD. For all heavy firearms assigned to the camp—mortar, machine guns, Browning rifles, RPGs—Armatrading was a masterly instructor and curator. The Sedang weapons platoons he trained performed beautifully. Their weapons stayed clean and reliable. Chester himself could hit a caribou at sixty yards with one round of RPG. But it was all drone work to him; in the bush he preferred his own unmodified Model 12 shotgun. His real affection was not for weaponry but light demolitions: it wasn't his assigned specialty this hitch but with explosives, explosives of any sort, Chester was an eager genius.

He had a thousand tricks and extemporized more. Nothing was safe to touch after Chester had worked up an area, no place was safe to sit, you concentrated on each footstep and took a calculated risk when the weight finally went down. The flat rock or the patch of bare dirt beside it? Wrong guess and a friendly round had taken your foot, or worse. An oil drum concealed in a tree, a C-ration can left invitingly by an old cooking fire, the foot-spaces before a latrine, the tiniest wire strung ankle-high across a trail, a bush that must be brushed past, a cached sack of rice, a dead water buffalo still fresh enough to be salvaged by hungry VC: he could make any of these erupt, horrifyingly lethal. If war was an art, Chester was pure Dada. Give him a grenade and a rubber band, a bottle of ether and a jar of glue, a keg of construction staples and five ounces of plastique: he would devise a better booby trap. The Cong must have loathed him legendarily. They might have put a price on his head if they had known who, who in particular, was contriving this awful stuff. He loved the small intimate devious heart-sinking snap, the toe-popper mine by the drinking hole, the Bouncing Betty that sprang out of a shitpile and killed just one miserable soldier with his black pajamas down. That was Chester's special style. But equally he relished the occasional big screaming bang. Sometimes he would rig a night ambush with as many as four Claymore mines directed convergently on a single trail junction, and no one but Chester willing to stay near enough that sort of craziness to man a detonator, so having run the wires together he would blow it all himself, and then have to cope alone with survivors. Once he turned a box of laundry soap, fifty-five gallons of gasoline, and a Thermit grenade into the most amazing incendiary splash Mayberry ever saw: hundred-yard radius of jungle and a pair of humans on that stretch of trail, very possibly VC, burnt to creosote.

Chester had initiative. He would take an interdiction patrol out to the border, gone three or four days and when he returned the rest of the team would drag him to maps. *Where, Chester, goddammit? Where exactly?* No other patrol would willingly walk the same path for five weeks. That was interdiction, yes indeed, though perhaps not precisely what the staff planners rearward envisioned. Yet Mayberry got intelligence reports suggesting a VC trend to reroute themselves discreetly around his territory: as though the enemy had concluded that a madman, not a relevant adversary, was at large there. He wasn't sure whether to be pleased. For a bit longer he let Chester play.

The man trained his irregulars well, he killed people, he was fearless. Never disobeyed orders, not directly, merely circumvented them when he wanted to, like anyone. Armatrading by the fundamental criteria was a good soldier. Perhaps even the ideal soldier for this war, perfect mirror of the opposition, with lots of imaginative malice and little inhibition. What more could Mayberry rightly ask? Personal chemistry between CO and noncom was not supposed to enter into it.

Nor, God knew, was homophile jealousy. That went out with the fall of Sparta. If Paul Katy found the new weapons sergeant especially good company, for reasons inscrutable to Mayberry—fine. If Armatrading brought out the worst side of Paul, the side Mayberry had seen in Da Nang—too bad. No more than that. It wasn't Captain Mayberry's operational concern. Armatrading was doing his job, which was by its nature a vicious one. Mayberry might despise him, but could not conscionably punish him, for enjoying it too well. So he let Chester play.

Until the first of the ears. This was a legitimate tactical issue, the sort for which Mayberry as team leader was responsible, in light of the Sedang reaction. Mayberry, on behalf of the war effort, had to keep peace. He had in fact to keep much more than that: high morale among the irregulars and the trust of the Dak To villagers. Evidently he had been preoccupied, working too hard, insufficiently observant around his own men, because the village chief paid him a humble and embarrassed visit to make formal complaint before Mayberry had noticed anything himself. The chief curled his toes in the dirt and turned endless shy glances toward the interpreter but eventually it dribbled out. A matter of great delicacy, Mayberry could see. They were simple people, the Sedang, big friends of America, democracy they liked it very big, yes, and they wished to kill big many VeeCee, but still they were a simple people bound by certain sacred taboos and customs, very important. They held it for instance that when a man died, even Vee Cee, the ears should remain on the head.

Chester, evidently, had returned from the last patrol wearing three around his neck on a boot lace.

"No more ears. Hear me?"

"What are you talking about, Captain?" With the guilty grin, in someone else it might have seemed merely good-natured insolence.

"Don't bother to be coy. I'm not going to do anything." Distrusting his own motives, Mayberry was still leaning over backward. "Myself, I don't care. I don't happen to believe it matters, whether the maggots and rats get them, or someone else." This was nearly true. "But it won't do. You understand? For operational reasons. It isn't civic. We need these people to feel good about us. They won't, they just won't, if they see one of my sergeants wearing a lei of little brown ears."

"Yes, sir. First time I heard of a Montagnard so concerned about what happened to a Vietnamese. Sir."

"You're right. I agree." Mayberry, still trying hard to avoid an open rift, made a point of voicing sympathy with Chester's viewpoint whenever humanly possible, which was seldom. "I didn't say it was logical. I just said we have to deal with it. No more. Get rid of them. Or put them away in a box."

Mayberry should have known better. Chester had an idiot's cunning and this reprimand, halfhearted but unmistakably condescending, only made it a more interesting game. He was too smart to risk the consequences of outright insubordination and too something else—what was it? mischievous? evil? hormonally imbalanced?—to let Mayberry's word stand unchallenged. The necklace of ears disappeared, somewhere, most likely into an ammo box shared with other exotic war trinkets. For close to a month there was no further incident. Armatrading and Paul Katy took a three-day pass together in Saigon and returned with tales of epic debauchery and inspired misbehavior, which were recounted in private performance to various team members not including Mayberry, who nevertheless heard it all secondhand. Fine. That's what passes were for, that sort of thing. More and more now Chester went as the escort to Paul's outlying medical rounds; Mayberry less and less. Just as well, Mayberry was overtaxed by his own duties these days, with the expansion of civic-action projects to three other villages and the report of heavy southbound traffic on the border trail. Armatrading's protection would be at least as effective as anyone's. Also he noticed that Paul had begun carrying along his own rifle, in addition to the medical kit. Good: Mayberry had nagged him to make it a practice months ago. He only hoped they weren't stopping for sport shooting at monkeys. That sort of foolish racket could bring them a shitstorm of deadly trouble. And it wasn't civic.

Then Chester had his usual turn at interdiction patrol to the border, left the usual string of ugly surprises, made contact, and brought his squad back with one minor injury and a count of five definite kills. It was good competent work. Several days later Mayberry spoke with a Sedang intelligence scout who had also been near the border. In his rambles he had come across five NVA regulars, all of whom had evidently been killed with a pair of cleverly placed Claymores or in the firefight that followed, and all of whom had bloody holes instead of ears. Mayberry said nothing to Chester.

The next month it was more of the same. Increased movement of NVA regulars down the Laotian border trail along—but apparently not into—Mayberry's operational area. Increased contacts with VC between Dak To and the border, increased body counts from Mayberry's command. And for every ten certifiable enemy dead, there were accountable perhaps nine pairs of ears.

But Chester wore no fetishes. He did not flaunt. He smirked derisively at Mayberry no more than usual. Meanwhile the ammo box must have been filling like a hamper of mushrooms. It was a small wonder to Mayberry that, in the confines of the team house, such a little treasure wouldn't announce itself by smell.

"Of course he's taking ears. So what?" said Paul. "What's wrong with that?"

"What isn't. I ordered him not to, for one thing."

"Did you? I thought you just ordered him not to wear them."

"Have you *discussed* it with him?"

"He told me. That's what he told me. Don't wear them, says the CO. Put them away."

"Come on, Paul. He knew perfectly well what I meant."

"I see. When you give an order now, we're responsible for what you *meant?*"

"If I make myself clear, yes. Sure. And on this I made myself plenty clear. Come *on*. Leave that sort of goon shit to the Regular Army. How can you sanction it? You're out there trying to sew people back together. And here he is chopping them apart."

"I don't worry about dead bodies, I'm not a mortician. I got my hands full with the live ones. Besides, you go out on patrol with a rifle, jump a couple VC, what happens? That's not chopping them apart?"

"That's not gratuitous," said Mayberry, somewhat desperately, sculpting what he himself knew to be sandcastle logic. "It's a tactical necessity."

"So who decides what's gratuitous? In a guerrilla war."

Paul raised his Budweiser with the label facing Mayberry. "Is beer a tactical necessity?"

"No," said Mayberry, wishing immediately he could correct himself.

"No. All right. But it sure helps, eh?" As though in empirical demonstration he poured back a swallow.

"And cutting the ears off bodies does not. It hurts us."

"Maybe. Can't hurt the bodies, I tell you that as a medical man. And maybe it helps Chester." Paul was smiling hugely with pleasure over this line of inquiry. "He doesn't like beer."

"Then maybe we can't afford Chester." The smile dropped flat. Mayberry noted its fall, taking there one of the answers he had been after.

"He's damn good at weaponry."

"I know that. And demolitions, sure. But I can't tolerate the other crap. It spooks our allies. It's counterproductive to our entire effort. We're not a gang of barbarian mercenaries, for Christ sake. We're supposed to build something here."

Paul stood. "You mean it's not *civic*." Then he turned to go out for his sentry check.

"Yes." Mayberry, coming up off the bench, spoke to his back. *"Yes."*

At the door of the operations bunker Paul turned again. "Hey, why argue about it at me? I'm only a sergeant."

Still Mayberry did nothing, except squander a few hours on angry confusion that might otherwise have gone as sleep, and continue to question his own motives. He had the power to boot Armatrading off the team unilaterally but he was reluctant to do that. An arguable case of insubordination, over a matter that could be construed as petty: weak grounds for busting a man out. It would suggest, not that Sergeant Armatrading had failed in his job, but that Captain Mayberry was failing in his. And if he asked for a team vote on Chester's compatibility, the other procedural alternative, he might get a mandate but Paul would go against him, siding with Chester. How much should that matter? Mayberry didn't know. He preferred not to destroy his friendship with Paul in what might just be a misguided adolescent impulse to shelter it. He was annoyed with himself. He felt like a boy with his arms folded grumpily at the fringe of a high school dance. Ridiculous, and he was sick of the whole thing. Worst of all was the growing suspicion that Armatrading might be doing this, not for the souvenirs, not for the beer, not from genuinely demented blood lust, but for Mayberry's sake alone.

Flouting the order might be an end in itself. Chester might simply be lopping off ears and discarding them, feeding them to the beetles, in careful ridicule of Mayberry's authority; or, better still, to provoke Mayberry toward an ill-considered act of despotic leadership that could not be supported with evidence. Maybe there *was* no ammo box.

Could Chester be that bright? Possibly. That devious? Unquestionably. Could he marshal himself to such a piece of meticulous premeditation? Again Mayberry didn't know. The outside limit of Chester's premeditation, in matters of anger and hatred, seemed to be about five minutes. But then, wouldn't it just be a conceptual version of the C-ration can and the plastique?

"Seems I've still got this ear problem, Chester." The summons had been formal and Mayberry let him stand. Though the floor of the op bunker was bare concrete they both understood that Chester was on the carpet. He suppressed his grin almost completely.

"Sir."

"I have to believe it's you. But I can't prove that, and you know I can't. I'm not going to search your gear. I'm not going to repeat the original order because the order has already been issued, period. I'm not going to annotate it for greater clarity. You got anything to say about this, Sergeant?"

"No. Sir."

"Fine. So my assumption is that you're taking VC ears, contrary to a clear order. An assumption. But you're being discreet. You're right to do that. Okay. The practice happens to be acutely upsetting to our Sedang allies, the non-fighting ones at least, and I think you and I both know why. Not because of their love for the Vietnamese. Not because of tribal death beliefs. What makes them edgy is that, dangling around some American's neck, a Vietnamese ear looks very much like a Sedang ear. Their imagination gets going. They worry. Do you agree?"

"It's your theory. Sir."

"Yes it is. Sort of a domino theory I have. They don't trust us enough, not quite enough, not yet, to believe we really draw a line. Gook ears. That's what they saw on your neck. Not Vietnamese ears. Gook ears. You follow me?"

"Gook ears," Armatrading repeated. "Sir. A gook is a gook, if I hear you right."

"No, Armatrading, you don't hear me right. Christ sakes you got to do something about that shit in your own ears. A gook is precisely not a gook. That's what I'm telling you."

"A gook is not a gook."

Mayberry waited patiently.

"Sir."

"Now you've got it. All right. I haven't heard anything more from the village. Not since the first time. You're being discreet. Down in Dak To they aren't aware you're still hacking up bodies, or more likely they don't care, or at least they don't care badly enough to come back up here and, as they must see it, embarrass me—so long as they aren't forced to see the things waggling around your white American neck. So. Okay. I didn't call you in here to talk anthropology. Or to repeat an order I've already given." Mayberry stretched back on the bench to a more comfortable position. "I called you in to threaten you."

Chester wore the smile of a hyena.

"Be discreet, sure. Do that. As long as you stay that way, you'll stay on this team, maybe. But." Very casual, very offhand now, leaning into the wall corner Mayberry waved a single finger. "Take one Montagnard ear, Chester. One. Enemy or friendly. I don't care how cold the body is. Spy or sniper or sapper, I don't care, could be some guy shot on the perimeter wire at midnight with a straight razor in his teeth and a cameo locket of Ho Chi Minh, I don't care. One earless Sedang corpse: and you're gone, mister."

Step across this line. Mayberry was far from satisfied but it seemed the best he could do. The village might in fact remain placated. Or with greater luck, Mayberry thought, Chester might oblige him immediately. He should have known better.

Sometime, no way of telling exactly, in the next ten days. Mayberry saw the body himself.

A week and a half had passed and he was out on patrol, sweeping an area just north of the leprosarium through which an old overgrown French road led up toward the main highway to Chu Lai. Mayberry and his squad were avoiding the road, but at one point he brought them out of the brush to cross it. Two hundred yards back toward the lepers they noticed a small lump of green, a vehicle, evidently a jeep. It wasn't moving. Through his binoculars Mayberry could make out a figure at the wheel. That wasn't moving either. He sent two men to crescent around through the brush and take a closer look.

These two Sedang, when they got back, were oddly reticent. It was a jeep, yes, or the wreckage of one, which had apparently managed to trigger a Russian antitank mine. The floor of the thing was gutted out open. The driver, yes, he was a friendly. He had been dead for some time. Maybe a week, maybe more, judging from color and smell. Beyond that the scouts would say nothing. But they strongly urged that Captain Mayberry should go down for a look himself.

The skin of the face was umber and stretched taut, shrunken well back off the gums in a futile sneer; one week, to Mayberry, seemed conservative. The man was upright and stiff in the driver's seat with his left hand still clamped on the wheel and the other hand missing entirely, shorn away at the wrist when the gearbox flew into the sky. He had died in an instant, fragged up the ass and the spine by bits of his own jeep. His head was bare, the hat having no doubt been salvaged quickly by some passing VC with a sense of panache more developed than most, but Mayberry saw from the shoulder insignia that he was an Australian lieutenant. Must have driven down on some sort of business from an Aussie battalion of the Free World Military Assistance Forces up in I Corps. Besides the hat, his side arm and his boots were gone. Also his ears.

* * *

The next supply helicopter to lift out of Dak To carried Armatrading on board.

Paul always maintained that it wasn't Chester's work, the Australian; at least not directly. VC, argued Paul, in retaliation for their own. That was possible. Mayberry didn't care. In seven hours of fierce concentration he produced a report so impeccably bland, so seemingly dispassionate, yet so vivid, that Armatrading never saw another combat assignment in the Special Forces. First Chester was posted to a rear-echelon job at Hoa Cam, which worked out predictably poorly. Four months later he had his dishonorable discharge.

THIRTY-ONE

The sardine can has destroyed Mayberry's appetite. Instead there is anger and mortification and a sopping T-shirt. He abandons the idea of an evening jaunt across Santa Fe and sleeps with his .45 within reach on the floor. He feels as if he is under siege.

The unfinished business with Chester threatens to preempt all his concern about Zuckerman; threatens in fact to preempt everything. *Yes I'm afraid of him.* Any sane man, in Mayberry's position, should be. Small solace in that. Who will rid me of this baboon? Varvara and Jesse can't be counted on for much help. Certainly not Ripley and Guinness. Roybal won't even get interested until it's too late. Mayberry still imagines he will have to deal with Armatrading alone.

In the morning he recites a careful description—Chester as he was when Mayberry last saw him, with extrapolations for dental work and age—to the desk clerk. Regardless, Mayberry stresses, regardless of what he might say, this guy is not a friend of mine. Don't let him in the room. If you see him so much as pass through the lobby, please tell me. The Frenchman is most solicitous, promising vigilance. A full-service hotel. Graciously Mayberry omits to mention that Chester has already come and gone once. Then without bothering over breakfast he walks to a sporting goods store.

He buys bottles of gun oil and solvent and a cleaning rod and patches. The pistol hasn't been fired in eleven years. It has spent that span of time neglected on closet shelves and in steamer trunks. It might have passed the eleven years buried in cow shit and still, that particular model, the classic Colt, function perfectly; but Mayberry wants certitude. And he wants something soothing to do with his hands. On the way back, with his little brown package, he stops at the station for a word with Roybal.

His name is sent in but he waits twenty-five minutes, while the door to Roybal's cubicle remains closed. The lieutenant is not so eager this time to receive Mayberry. The lieutenant is busy in there, maybe, with his thesaurus. Finally the door opens before two men in Sears polyester blazers with guns bulges, evidently a pair of detectives, and Roybal between. Mayberry watches them talk for another five minutes, not idly but as though all their professional gears are engaged, Roybal ticking off statements authoritatively, the detectives answering tersely and nodding. They have their instructions, concerning whatever. Good, Roybal, get those boys cracking; if it's a hectic week, according to Jesse, Mayberry will stand less chance of being shadowed. By the police, at least. Roybal catches his eye now and waves him in.

"This is a courtesy call, Lieutenant."

Roybal waits. "Explain what you mean," he says dryly.

His expression is odd. For once he does not tilt himself crazily backward, fearless test pilot of swivel chairs; both feet on of all places the floor. He seems restrained yet expectant, like a fly fisherman. "I'm listening."

No longer much concerned about Roybal's sufferance, Mayberry starts to blather. The subject is Armatrading; the tone is acidulous and undiplomatic. Screw the assault charge, sixty days as a guest of Santa Fe County has fallen low on Mayberry's list of dreads. He stabs finger holes in the air, speaking fast and with vehemence, while Lieutenant Roybal sits taking it quietly.

Roybal, I give you notice, is what Mayberry says. I've just had what amounts to a threat on my life, he says. Here. In your town. Armatrading has arrived, the great geek with the baseball bat, and already done a breaking-and-entering on my hotel room, Mayberry says. That's a crime, right? Forget it, you're busy. You got witnesses to coerce in the Karen Ives case. He's looking for me, Armatrading is, stalking me actually. I'm *not* looking for him. Repeat, it's his initiative. I don't want trouble. But I'll defend myself, Mayberry says. That's why I'm here, that's what I'm telling you: I'll defend myself. I said before that he's not homicidal. Mean and loony and violent, sure, but not homicidal? Remember? Well, I take it back. I know this guy a long time, I know his language, and he's telling me that I belong in a box. I have good cause to fear for my life. You can't protect me, not against him. Okay, fine. So I got precautions to take myself. I'm taking them. I will be armed. This is just so you know, Roybal. You know in advance. I don't want trouble with Armatrading. But if he tries something serious on me, if he does that, I swear I will kill the cocksucker. Self-defense. You were notified. Mayberry stops for a breath.

"Then I guess you haven't heard," says Roybal.

"What?"

"We found your guy Armatrading this morning."

"Found him? Doing what?"

"Pressing his face into a plate of hashbrowns and eggs." Briefly Roybal savors Mayberry's mystification. "He's dead, Mayberry. Two hours ago. For a minute I thought you were here to confess."

It was much the same as with Karen. Armatrading died unobtrusively at an International House of Pancakes while the restaurant was full of people.

He came in alone. He ordered and began eating. Then evidently he was joined by another person. Somebody he knew? Must have been. Expected? Maybe. They were in a booth with high backs and plenty of overstuffed vinyl to muffle the noise. A small automatic jammed suddenly to his kidney, a sound not much louder than WHUP, and Chester went down into his breakfast. The place was routinely a madhouse of crashing dishes and harried waitresses and squalling kids at that hour of the morning; several people heard the shot but ignored it, thought it was a backfire, or perhaps just an explosion in the kitchen. No one recalls seeing the other man leave. No one took a close look at Armatrading—in this restaurant the face in the plate wasn't enough—until a waitress slipped on the puddle of blood and went down with a tray of orders. He was still holding his fork.

"I assume you've got an alibi," says Roybal.

By good luck, yes. At the approximate moment Chester died, on the south side of town, Mayberry was maligning him to the desk clerk.

"Will you make an identification?"

"I'd be delighted," says Mayberry.

On a slab table at the coroner's lab Chester lies naked, drained of color, already going quite waxen. His skin is more pallid even than Albert Varvara's on a morning after. He must have bled himself empty. Beneath his lowest rib, on the left side, is a darkened hole no bigger than a dime. Otherwise his appearance has changed remarkably little since Mayberry last saw him. The teeth are indeed fixed. The hair is still wild, and trailing down long over the back of his neck. He still wears the oversized flaxen mustache, like a biscuit of Shredded Wheat, that makes him resemble Nietzsche during the years of insanity, when Nietzsche's insufferable sister left the poor helpless man unbarbered for photographic effect. Armatrading had a sister too, Mayberry recalls vaguely, but at some point she married a respectable bail bondsman and told Chester to stay away from her house.

He looks more innocent, Chester does, than Mayberry ever believed possible.

After another hard hour with Roybal, Mayberry is free to go. His package of pharmaceuticals for the pistol now seems superfluous, but maybe not. Who is this, who in the almighty world, that could contrive to invest Chester Armatrading with a look of innocence?

Mayberry knows a name, but the name is no explanation. Dizzied with suspicion yet still uncertain, he walks back to the De Vargas, where his third message is waiting.

THIRTY-TWO

This one is handed to him, in a sealed envelope, by the Frenchman, who seems to be growing perceptibly more curious over the nature of Mayberry's dealings. Having relinquished it he continues, the Frenchman, to sight down his nose at the unopened envelope. So Mayberry thanks him blandly, without asking who made the delivery, and drifts back outside. The note is typed, all caps and no punctuation, like before:

NOW
40 THOUSAND FOR YOUR COPY
DOLLARS AND I HAVE IT
NO EXTRA CHARGE FOR ARMATR

There is more, logistical details concerning a signal by which Mayberry can indicate affirmatively, and receive directions for the actual exchange; a little stagy, Mayberry feels, but modest compared to the steeplechase he went through with Jesse. The prospective buyer does not want a meeting, evidently, until Mayberry has accepted the deal in principle. Anyway Mayberry is simply required to get an ice-cream cone and sit in the Plaza. The note concludes:

> NO MIDDLEMEN NO SILENT PARTNERS
> JUST YOU AND ME PAL
> ZUCKERMAN

No muss, no fuss, no greasy aftertaste. His first thought is to contact Varvara with the good news and submit to further coaching, but Mayberry thinks better. He does want to include Varvara, yes; possibly that's still wisest and probably he has no choice. Include Varvara, by all means, but not quite yet. Maybe the sequence of things can be more fruitfully arranged.

At one o'clock, as instructed, Mayberry is in the Plaza. He carries two scoops of German chocolate on a sugar cone: selected to communicate his wholeheartedness, and because he still hasn't eaten. The lunch-hour crowd is thinning so he has no difficulty finding a vacant bench. He works on the ice cream. With casual interest not unbecoming a bench sitter he surveys the square itself, the shop doorways surrounding, the cluster of tourists hovering over the open-air turquoise peddlers; more discreetly he watches the second-floor balconies, including that of the Ore House. He waits. He doesn't know what to expect. He is glad for his morning at the coroner's lab, his personal audience, because this sort of blithe self-exposure would seem foolhardy if there were any chance Chester might still be at large. He finishes his ice cream and keeps waiting. The Plaza is nearly empty. A boy about ten years old, an

Indian, crosses the cobbles on a straight line from somewhere, marching purposefully toward Mayberry on his bench. Arrives and mutely holds out another envelope. As soon as Mayberry's fingers close down, the boy gallops away like a kid with new money to spend. Inside is a highway map of New Mexico.

In black felt-tip a line has been drawn, a routing, back down through Albuquerque and south, along the interstate toward El Paso and Ciudad Juarez. Half an inch short of the Mexican border the line ends in a circle. Within the circle, just south of Las Cruces, is the dot for a small town called Mesquite. Beside the circle, a miniaturized fat black scrawl: "Danny y Tina's. Saturday 7 am. No silent partners."

Zuckerman is a cautious fellow. Today being Friday, Mayberry faces a busy few hours.

He first rents himself another car. He checks out of the De Vargas and hopes fervently never to see it again. He goes for a long drive through the outskirts of town, eastward on a scenic meander along the river, changing direction on dirt roads and in driveways until he is sure no one has followed. From the booth in a gas station he reaches a number in Oakland, charging the call to his own line. The voice, when it answers, sounds like a manatee with stomach gas.

"Buski. This is Mayberry. Remember me?"

"Hello, asshole. Where are you? You're under arrest. Where *are* you?"

"What for? I'm in New Mexico. Santa Fe."

"General principles. Aiding and abetting my ulcer. Also I might want you for unlawful entry, suspicion of kidnap, leaving the scene of a crime. Where's Hannah Broch? I towed your car, by the way. Costing you eight bucks a day in the city lot, plus twenty for the wrecker. In two weeks I'll auction it."

"It was parked legally."

"A technicality. I got a million questions for you, Mayberry. Boy, did you piss me off. Skating out of town like you did. I'm gonna put your butt on a skewer."

"Buski, I want to help you now."

"Good. Handcuff your wrists behind and beat yourself up."

"I'll fly back to Oakland tomorrow. I'll answer all your questions. I'll cooperate. For instance, have you heard anything more about that classified report?"

"Yeah. The Teller thing? Christ have I. Two jackoffs from the Department of Energy keep calling me. 'Where's Mayberry? We got to find Mayberry. Got to get hold of this report.' That's what it's all about, so I'm told. Sanzone and Dr. Broch and now your foxy lawyer friend, evidently. Too bad. 'Mayberry has the copy. Why'd you let his ass go? You stupid hick cop.' Except they say it like lawyers. Same exact guys who called me last week and told me not to interrogate you. Total jerks. Now they're desperate for anything I can tell them. Call me twice a day. You know they're looking for you in Durango, Colorado?"

"You want it, Buski?"

"Want what? I want you in a cell. I want a new stomach. Want what?"

"The Teller thing."

Silence out of Oakland. "Where is it?"

"I need a little favor," says Mayberry. "Just a little one."

"I don't make deals for evidence. Where is it?"

"Since when?"

"Where is it?"

"All right." From a gas station in New Mexico, with no friends and few assets, Mayberry has small choice but to take a chance. "It's in the glove compartment of my car."

After a second's delay, Buski guffaws. "Then I already *got* it."

"That's right." Mayberry tightens a fist around nothing. Please, Buski.

"God help you if you're bullshitting me," says Buski. "What's the favor?"

With Buski left to his task Mayberry's mind shifts along a logical nexus to Tay Riordan, back up in the house outside Taos, protected from Zuckerman's savage thoroughness by little more than a screen door and a terrycloth robe. Mayberry could have alerted her to the real dangers but he didn't. Took what she had to tell, in return left her ignorant and vulnerable and falsely expectant. He is unconscionably remiss, he knows, but for the immediate present that can't be helped. Even the simple phone call he owes her, a difficult one that he nevertheless much wants to make, would still be a few hours premature.

Instead he moves on, using a city map to pick a course across the southeastern suburbs toward Cerrillos Road without going back near the Plaza. He parks in the lot of that same Denny's he saw from Varvara and Jesse's motel window, and slides into the restaurant with his chin on his chest behind a pair of state troopers. At the counter he orders coffee. The telephone here is in the foyer. Through a glass wall he can easily see, on the far side of Cerrillos, at the near corner on the second level behind an iron railing, the door of their room. Mayberry dials.

"We've got our contact. Give me Varvara," he tells Jesse, who does.

Varvara happens to be sober. He is delighted with the news. He awards himself credit for devising the strategy whereby Mayberry dangled himself like a piñata at the De Vargas, and then presses for details. He wants all the details. Yes, it isn't much time, and yes of course Mayberry should meet with them before he leaves, that goes without saying, they'll need to talk it all through in person; but later, and meanwhile Varvara is greedy for the details. So Mayberry tells him. Straight and complete: every bit of what little he knows himself from the message and the map.

"Good. Real good, yeah," Varvara mumbles. Mayberry imagines him holding the phone with a crabbed shoulder, scribbling his cuneiform into the ring pad. "Except what's this Danny E. Teanuts? Who the Christ is that?"

"Danny *y Ti*—. . . Danny *and Tina's,* Varvara. Spanish. Probably a cafe."

"Oh. Okay, great." Further quiet while Varvara scrawls, no doubt, the words "Spanish" and "probably a cafe." "Now here's Jesse again. You and him set up another rendezvous. Later this afternoon or early evening. How long you figure it'll take us to get down there?"

"Long. Why not meet now?"

"Because I got to think is why. Got to work out a plan, Mayberry. Here, talk to Jesse." Before Mayberry can argue, the phone is passed.

"Where are you now?" says Jesse.

"A booth at the De Vargas," Mayberry lies.

The understanding is that they will simply repeat the earlier procedure, Mayberry in The Bistro when Jesse drives by at precisely six-thirty, meeting immediately afterward around back on Water Street. All right, six-thirty then, says Mayberry. He hangs up. He carries his coffee to a table by the windows. Not more than ten minutes have passed when he sees Varvara emerge from the room. This time Jesse is coming with him.

No move toward their car. Instead they dodge traffic out to the island in Cerrillos and for two seconds Mayberry suffers a terror of disappointment: that Varvara and Jesse are merely walking straight across here to Denny's for coffee. Coffee and innocent cogitation, just like Varvara said. Irrelevantly, Mayberry feels not only foiled but embarrassed. He can hide in the men's room, maybe climb out a window back there, but what does that accomplish? Wait, never mind. Varvara and Jesse clear the near lanes and peel away into the driveway next door. They haven't come close enough to spot him. They are striding out, busy men, people to see. Mayberry watches them disappear through a side door on the south wing of the Ramada Inn. He smiles.

An hour later they reappear from the same door. Mayberry steps out of his car, parked ten feet away in their line of return march.

There is no need for him to say anything. They both stop. Varvara takes on the discreetly tormented look of a man with a gobbet of bad lobster on his tongue and nowhere to spit. Jesse does what he has done before: covers his eyes with a hand. In fact he braces that elbow with the other arm, as though he might want to hold the position indefinitely. Varvara speaks first. He says: "Aw Jesus."

Mayberry toyed with the idea of bringing his .45, brandishing it at them while he made his demand; but he knew he could never use the thing, not in this instance, and knew they would know that too. Besides it would probably cause gridlock on Cerrillos. He wants above all right now to seem convincingly unswervable. Hands in his pockets, he feels relaxed. Hi, imagine bumping into you here. He feels unswervable.

"I want to meet your boss."

"We just came across for a swim," Varvara says hopelessly.

"I want to meet your boss. This is non-negotiable," says Mayberry. "We go back in there for a chat. You make introductions. And then we go to Las Cruces for Zuckerman. Or none of it."

"I can't do that," says Varvara.

"Then I can't go to Las Cruces. I'm unavailable."

Jesse unwraps his face. "Why, Mayberry?"

"Because I want to know who's who. I want to know who *that* is." Straight-arming toward the Ramada door. "Them. Whatever. I want to know who's directing this operation. God damn it, Jesse, Armatrading is dead." Which fact he deliberately withheld, saving it for surprise value and momentum. "Yes. This morning. Karen is dead. Zuckerman killed them both. My ass is going to be in the cross hairs next—because you need my help to trap him—and ALL I WANT TO KNOW IS WHO YOU GUYS ARE!" The shouting is not part of his premeditation.

Varvara hasn't moved. "I can't do it," he says.

"Then fuck off."

Mayberry turns his back. He has already started the car, bluffing furiously, when Jesse puts a hand on the window jamb. "Wait." Jesse speaks gently, over the hood, to Varvara who still hasn't pried loose his feet. "Make a call, Albert."

Varvara is silent, his jaw muscles are pulsing; for all Mayberry can tell he may be holding his breath and hoping to faint.

"We'll lose him, Albert."

"Christ," says Varvara. "Judas. I'll never hear the end of it."

From a desk phone in the lobby Varvara rings a room. He sidles three paces away from Mayberry and glances back ferally. After a longish wait he blinks and straightens his shoulders and says: "Mayberry is here."

Mayberry overhears nothing, the earpiece pressed like a gastropod to Varvara's head. Varvara says: "Yes. Here. Caught us flat-footed as we came out," and then listens, wincing.

Says: "He wants to see you," adding quickly, "No, of course I didn't. He was waiting. He wants to know who's running this. Wants to meet you. Otherwise he won't go along." More listening and wincing.

Says: "I *do* understand. I *do*. What can I tell you? Claims he just won't. No. Just won't. I believe him."

Says: "All right," cradles the receiver, and sighs. To Mayberry Varvara says: "Come on, asshole."

They troop down long corridors of orange wallpaper and chartreuse shag. It is a first-floor room in the back, very anonymous, very quiet, a number in the low hundreds. Varvara directs a last annoyed glower at Mayberry before knocking.

Behind the door Mayberry hears a dull thud. Another, still faint and muted, but slightly louder. He registers recognition of that sound just as the door jumps open, a few inches only, to reveal her in vertical section. The blue eyes flick up and down.

"Mayberry," says Hannah Broch, arched over her aluminum walker. "So. Come in if you must."

THIRTY-THREE

For the first moment he is simply mute. But after his brain has raced backward those thirty years, forty-five, reeled once around a pylon then forward again at speed over the same decades and facts and suppositions, back up to Ross Street in a quiet Oakland neighborhood and finally the Ramada of Santa Fe, a certain trimming against vertigo made, he manages: "I'm relieved to see you in good health."

"Ach! I am in terrible health." She speaks curtly. "Arthritis and cataracts and now at this moment, Mayberry, an acute dyspepsia. It seems I suffer a plague of stubborn young men."

"I had a touch lately myself," he says, in mind of Saturday night after the Ore House. "Dyspepsia. It's going around. Maybe the salsa."

"So." Exploiting age and station, she imputes to the little word a bullying sonority. "You could not heed my advice."

"Which was that, Hannah? I've been getting so much. All conflicting." Mayberry still cannot quite decide whether he ought to be chiefly angry, or startled, or what. "And most of it unheeded, I grant."

"Dispose of the report. Surrender it to persons of authority. Burn it. Avoid entanglement in matters that were not your concern."

"God knows you're right there: I could not. Did try, though, by the way. I made calls, offers, I was enormously responsible for a while. But no, evidently I just couldn't. Entanglement is putting it mildly."

"You have carried the copy with you?"

"No. Varvara knows that. I left it in Oakland."

"But safe?"

"But safe, yes, and no I won't tell you where. Sorry. Besides, you ought to be glad I held onto it. Otherwise you had no handle on Zuckerman. You and the Bowery Boys here."

"Otherwise perhaps there was no need. For any such handle."

"Maybe. But I did, and then apparently there was. Enough need to bring you all these miles. Incidentally, you know your dog is dead?"

A compact nod. "I do know."

"Stinking the house up pretty soon. And the cats are confused. You might want to make a call, if there's a neighbor or somebody. So anyway, I've been a nice helpful decoy," says Mayberry. "Tomorrow again. Convenient to your current purposes, which are a subject unto themselves. You could be a bit thankful, Hannah."

"For your cooperation, tomorrow, I will be thankful," she says coldly.

"Glad to," says Mayberry. "And there's just one little thing in return."

The blue eyes work quickly behind a mask of flaccid gray flesh, but Hannah says nothing.

"Tea and history," says Mayberry. "A lost afternoon, and an old woman's nostalgia, was the way you put it, I think. You said I should come back. If I would dare you to talk."

Furtive, and almost now seeming frail, Hannah watches him. Then with reluctance she pronounces the name: "Oppenheimer."

"And Zolta," says Mayberry. "And you."

THIRTY-FOUR

By midnight he has passed the bottleneck at Albuquerque, and from there the interstate stretches south like an empty runway, crossing arroyos, littered with curls of thrown tire tread and the carcasses of half-squashed armadillos, following the river toward Ciudad Juarez. Mayberry is alone in the front seat. Beside him lies the rust-colored accordion folder, so considerately furnished by Varvara. Two dozen sheets of blank mimeo paper, stapled in a corner, and the folder bound closed on them with a string clasp: to approximate one photocopy of LAMS-1363. It would give Mayberry something to carry—was Varvara's keen logic—and should seem convincing enough until Zuckerman actually opens it. Mayberry agrees. He figures the folder, all other things being equal, might keep him alive an extra four or five seconds. They haven't spoken since Santa Fe. He has scarcely thought about Zuckerman.

"How did she get into it?" says Mayberry. "Originally. Who recruited her?"

"You don't want to know that." Varvara's forehead and nose peek up from behind the passenger seat like a Kilroy drawing. "Christ. You had to get a Pinto. My spine."

"Yes I do."

"No you don't. Take my word, you don't."

"Was it Gerstmann?"

In the mirror Mayberry sees now an entire silhouette profile, faintly backlit by far headlights, scowling at his right ear. *"Gerstmann?"* Only a guess but evidently a good one. Mayberry has spent sixty miles remembering Karen's account, in Chinatown, of all the suspicions and accusations against Hannah. "What do you know about Gerstmann?"

"Pyotr Gerstmann," says Mayberry. "He was at the consulate in San Francisco. During the forties. A cultural attaché or something. No, a second secretary. Get your head down, Varvara. We made an agreement. Or else I pull over."

"Always threatening. Ultimatums. Can't you just ask?"

"Get it down."

"He isn't following us."

"We'll let Jesse determine that. Come on. No silent partners, unless they're invisible too."

Varvara's head, grudgingly, disappears. *"How* do you know about Gerstmann?"

"I read a file," Mayberry fibs. "Including the deposition she gave in '53, after the Livermore firing. Karen Ives showed me. So it *was* Gerstmann then? Or Hubert Jamisson, like they thought?"

"Jamisson was a flake. A nobody." The voice sounds more distant and reflective. Apparently Varvara is on his back again, cramped and jimmied onto the rear seat, speaking toward the ceiling upholstery, and maybe it's that position, so childlike, so soothing, the intimacy of a darkened car sweeping down miles of strange highway with only starlight visible through a window and only one other voice to answer his, that seems finally to be softening the edges of Varvara's wariness. Or maybe not. Maybe at this point it just doesn't matter to him how much Mayberry knows. "A dabbler. An amateur, stepping all over the heels of the professionals," and Mayberry thinks of himself until Varvara adds, "Jamisson. Turned out to be more trouble than he ever could have been worth." It has a terminal ring and Mayberry cannot recollect, if he was told, what became of Hubert Edward Jamisson after the FBI finished.

"But she dealt directly with Gerstmann," he posits gingerly.

"Sure," says Varvara. "Certainly not Jamisson."

"Sure. She was much better placed, I suppose. Than Jamisson. Was that it? She knew every top physicist who went to the project. And knew them as colleagues, not just socially." Glancing again at the mirror Mayberry sees nothing but headlights, and those a half mile back. "Knew Oppenheimer, for instance, better than *anybody*."

"She knew him well." Even now Varvara will not countenance the tawdry innuendo. "They had worked together on papers."

"How long did it last?"

Varvara hesitates. "With Oppenheimer?"

"No. With Gerstmann. Did she operate straight up through '53? I mean, after the whole first wave of investigations, the blackballing, eight years without a job—was she still passing information from *Livermore*?"

"None of your goddamn business." Mayberry wouldn't

dispute that but Varvara has put the point without any great heat of conviction. "No. No, Gerstmann had been recalled. Purged, we heard. I think that was about '49. September of '49, yeah. Gerstmann went home." Varvara the man with no memory. "For a long time we were out of touch. Anyway Hannah Broch didn't pass information. Not how you think."

"Why not?"

"Never you mind. Just a point of fact. She didn't."

"Because she never got to Los Alamos? Because no one but Zolta ever trusted her? And by then it was too late, with Gerstmann called back to Moscow and probably long since dead?"

"I didn't say Gerstmann was dead."

"Was Gerstmann dead?"

Varvara considers that possibility, presumably not for the first time. "Sure," he says. "Yeah, most likely."

"She was a recruiter herself," says Mayberry, and the notion has such a plausible feel, it holds shape so persuasively in the silence of the car, that he knows at once he is right. "She passed names. Not information. Names. She passed prospects along to Gerstmann. What do they call it? A talent spotter?"

"Now you're warmer."

"Did she spot you, Varvara?"

"Yeah." The voice from the back seat is full of roomy pauses. "Sometimes it wasn't what you'd call talent. Sometimes just a pair of hands."

"Where? Not in Denver. Rockwell probably didn't exist. Were you a physics student in those days?"

"Be serious, Mayberry. I was a machinist in Hayward. I met her through the Party."

"A machinist."

"At a tool and die shop. Making nose sockets for heavy rivet guns. I had all the strategic significance of a half bushel of potatoes. But then I got drafted."

"Let me guess," says Mayberry. "They sent you to Los Alamos."

"They needed machinists," the voice says by way of confirming. "I was in Fabrication. Turning out these casting molds for the high-explosive lenses. Oppenheimer used to wander in and ask me how it was going." The voice corrects itself. "This once, he did."

For five minutes or ten or perhaps it's fifteen Mayberry stares silently ahead at the road. Varvara watches the Dipper or reads messages off the insides of his eyelids. The nearest headlights in the distance behind may be Jesse, or they may not. Mayberry meditates on the themes of judgment and trust and betrayal.

Oppenheimer, from an early moment, must have seen her quite clearly. The reason she was never invited to Los Alamos. Zolta on the other hand, cast for public view as the cold genius and great right-wing ogre, loved less wisely than well. Refused to hear the FBI whispers, refused to look on the damaging pattern of circumstance in her dossier through a properly paranoid squint; or if he did hear, did look, refused to care. Past was past. Brain and heart together told him that Hannah Broch was a superb scientist and an exceptional woman. And as far as that goes, brain and heart didn't lie. Exceptional she surely was.

It is all bad enough, every bit of it, but Mayberry for his own sake would like to salvage one comforting belief: that Hannah did not spy during the year she was at Livermore.

Did not pass information, or names, or anything. Might have, possessed opportunity, but did not. It is all bad enough without that. Mayberry supposes he is asking a lot.

Hannah herself, at the Ramada, refused to say—shunned the entire subject of Livermore. Possibly, at best, that was embarrassment. Her very stoniness gives him a scrap of hope. Mayberry would like to believe she was asked, expected, ordered to betray that wildly unlikable dangerous generous man of the bushy muttonchops; but couldn't do it.

"Varvara."

The Kilroy drawing again. Obviously Varvara wasn't sleeping.

"One more question," says Mayberry.

"Isn't there always."

"Would you have told me all this," Mayberry asks, "if you were positive I'll still be alive this time tomorrow night?"

"Positive?" says Varvara. "That's too hypothetical, Mayberry."

Just before 2:00 A.M. they slide off the interstate at Socorro and find a gas station open. On Varvara's suggestion Mayberry pulls to the self-service island, so that Varvara can remain hidden and miserable on the floor of the back seat. The boy at the counter inside doesn't so much as glance up from his magazine. While Mayberry is replacing the nozzle Jesse drives past, vouchsafing a slow look but no sign of recognition; he is wearing the watch cap and fatigue jacket again, whatever that means; either he's superstitious or chronically chilly. Mayberry leans back in through the window as though hunting for his wallet.

"Okay, Jesse's here. I'm going to the john. I'll be quick."

Varvara has his aged body bent to a most foolish position and, like an ostrich, he has covered his head with Mayberry's overnight bag. "Take one for me," he says.

Inside the station, moving with all possible speed, Mayberry puts through a call to Buski. In Oakland Buski comes on the line within seconds. He has done his bit. The conversation takes less than a half minute, and Mayberry is back in the car.

They locate Jesse four blocks farther on, waving them into the lot of a Mini Mart from which he has procured three Styrofoam cups of ineffably bad coffee. "You're clean," he announces. "No one on the highway, no one here." Mayberry is glad to hear it. So is Varvara, though after a few minutes with his legs and neck straightened he folds himself stubbornly back into the rear of the Pinto. Varvara, this close to Zuckerman, wants no short cuts, nothing neglected. He shows a new level of focused resoluteness. Mayberry suspects the old man is feeling adrenaline. Mayberry is feeling some himself, especially since the call to Buski.

Back onto the interstate. They drive south through darkness and desert. The night, notwithstanding Jesse's outfit, is hot. Mayberry has opened all the windows and vents to let warmish air blast coolly across his body. He gapes ahead. There isn't much out here except red dirt showing gray by starlight. From the west, dry gulches cough out empty toward the river. Along the east is a low ridge of hills, and beyond it the Jornada del Muerto, a valley of desolate charms. Occasionally now Mayberry sees a stout girder tower topped with ears like an Amazonian bat: some sort of serious radar.

"Where's the pistol?"

"It's handy. I'll have it on me," says Mayberry, managing not to answer the question.

"How long since you used one?"

"Eleven years."

"Eleven years. Wonderful."

"But I cleaned it this morning."

"You cleaned it. Wonderful. Your gun will be cleaner than Zuckerman's."

"I thought I wasn't going to need it."

"Maybe not. I hope you don't. Me and Jesse will be very close."

"And you want him alive."

"If it's convenient," says Varvara, "yes. At least at first."

"How do you figure the dangers?"

"To you?"

"That's what I had in mind, yes."

"Pretty high, Mayberry. You know it. Pretty high. You're meeting an armed man and you gotta assume he intends to kill you. Gotta assume that. We know he don't have the money, for one thing. So what else is he gonna do? Ask you nicely for a line of credit?"

"You can't prove a negative, Varvara."

"Say again?"

"You can't *know* he doesn't have it. The money."

"We know he don't have it from Hod, in Juarez. And he's not gonna get it from Hod, in Juarez. 'Cause we know their arrangement now, and that ain't part of it. So how else is a guy like this gonna have forty grand? *Forty grand*, Mayberry."

"What's their arrangement?"

"An Israeli passport."

Mayberry waits. He glances back over his shoulder. "And?"

"And nothing. A passport."

"I don't get it."

"Good. I'd feel bad if you did because I don't get it myself. Alls we know is they meet on the bridge, midway between El Paso and Juarez. Five o'clock tomorrow. Just as it fills up with day workers. He's got the report. They got an Israeli passport in any name, with a space for his picture. That's it. That's the deal. He's letting them off very cheap. We don't know why, and it's a terrific annoyance, frankly."

"Why doesn't he just emigrate?"

"Ask him when you see him. But don't let it distract you, okay? Only way for him to be on that bridge, with his piece of merchandise, is to take it off your dead body."

"Or so he thinks. In exchange for twenty-four sheets of blank paper, Hod's not going to give him even a passport."

"Right. So he thinks. We think different. He ain't ever gonna see Hod."

"But he might have the money. From some other source than Hod. You don't know."

"Where?" Abruptly Varvara sits up, exasperated, pounding his palms upon his knees. "Nowhere! Forget the forty thousand, Mayberry. Dismiss it from your mind! If you shuffle in there with the idea that maybe this Zuckerman is okay, a man of his word, just wants to deal like he said he did—and then let him *surprise* you—Christ sakes, you'll be dead! And not just dead. *Stupid!*"

"No. Relax," Mayberry says. "I don't think he's going to surprise me."

Not since the call to Buski. As they drone down the highway it's still too vivid in Mayberry's brain, with its cold indisputable factuality, like a terminal diagnosis.

Buski? Mayberry. I can only talk a few seconds.

All right. We found it. It's genuine, yeah. Washington's

happy as geese and I'm a big hero, evidently. I got to thank you, for now.

Never mind. How are the prints?

They were fine. Real good, in fact. You can't hardly do better than that. Pressing the full hand to a Xerox screen.

Have you matched them?

Yeah. We were lucky. Much easier than it could have been. We had him right here in California.

Mayberry had suspected since his day at the library, even more so after the evening with Tay Riordan. Still he felt shock, harsher than he had anticipated. There was the basic emotional betrayal, acrid in his belly; and especially rankling, that bit of embezzled grief over the young man who died at Los Alamos, two weeks ago, after printing his fingertips on a classified scientific report.

Kid named Randy Ortiz, Buski said. *One conviction, for possession of heroin. Now on probation in New Mexico.*

Tomorrow sometime he will need to call Tay with the bad news. I'm sorry but you can stop waiting, your boy friend is dead. Tomorrow sometime, afterward, when there's time, and then with another dull jolt Mayberry corrects the thought: If he himself is still alive, he can call Tay.

Otherwise she will just have to work it out by herself.

They pull off for coffee again, at a truck stop, somewhere below Truth or Consequences. Then back on the interstate. For a few miles Mayberry sips nervously but even before the dregs are cold he sets this cup aside on the dashboard. Drowsiness is not a problem. Varvara might be asleep now, for all the quiet, though Mayberry doubts it. A little too quiet, an unquiet quiet, silence without tranquillity, like dead air over the radio. He supposes that Varvara's brain is just grinding away privately, no less febrile than his own. In fact Varvara may at this moment be pondering whether, if Zuckerman doesn't happen to kill Mayberry, he might himself be obliged to do it. For the protection of Varvara's own flank, not to mention Hannah's. And now finally, belatedly, a very distressing thought has taken form in Mayberry's skull: despite all the supposed concern for his marksmanship, despite all the unctuous assurances about how close at hand Varvara and Jesse will be, Albert Varvara might like nothing better than to stand patiently outside Danny y Tina's while Zuckerman murders Mayberry.

Dead air over the radio, he remembers, and snapping it on catches a weather report at exactly half past four: hot and dry for the KGRT listening area. No chance of precipitation. Well Christ what else could you expect, in June, in extreme southern New Mexico? KGRT wants to assure him that the Chihuahuan desert, at least for another few hours, will remain desert. Hot and dry also for tonight and tomorrow. Now *that* seems so far in the future as to be absurdly speculative. But then Mayberry is in a mood.

The country hits just keep coming, according to a canned jingle from KGRT: and indeed they do, for another half hour, growing only more sharply nasal as Mayberry approaches Las Cruces. At 5:02 A.M., with a wash of gray light leaking up out of the east, he clicks off "San Antonio Rose" in the very midst of a steel-guitar solo and eases to a stop on the shoulder.

Within a minute Jesse has pulled up behind. "Okay. Okay, we'll be nearby. Good luck," says Varvara as though he's a little embarrassed. Mayberry thanks him without turning around. "Remember. Signal us sooner, if you need to. Soon as anything gets funny." Mayberry declares that he will remember. The sky eastward is losing its color quickly.

"Go," says Mayberry.

Varvara unbends his body, falls out the door onto gravel, and goes. By the mirror Mayberry watches him climb in beside Jesse. And so they proceed.

Now again Jesse's car drops back almost a mile. Daylight is fully dawned—piquant as new morning anywhere except utterly and unmercifully dry—as they pass by the blight of Las Cruces. To the east, looming shadowed above town, Mayberry can see a high shark's-teeth ridge of naked rock, unmistakable landmark. He remembers it from his last trip this way; probably some Spanish Jesuit thought the ridge looked enough like Golgotha to inspire the city's name. Mayberry is not so poetically pious. What he sees are teeth.

Mesquite is sixteen miles farther, sharing its exit with another small village. He takes the connecting road and follows it two miles westward between wide dusty fields of early cotton. Eventually the cotton gives way to farm shacks, dazed burros, half-acre patches of pepper plants, and he passes downwind of a modest Holstein dairy: the local economy seems to feature a certain desperate diversity. From the last shallow rise he has a glimpse of houses and ramshackle trailers for perhaps five hundred souls, most of them no doubt Hispanic, and poor, and at this hour of day just walking up. Downtown Mesquite is a T-bone intersection opposite a rail spur. For a moment Mayberry sits at the stop sign, gazing left down the old highway that serves also as Main Street, then right, confused. There is nothing here. He didn't expect much. But there is not even that.

Nothing within sight that Mayberry might take for Danny y Tina's Cafe.

Just blacktop going soft in the morning heat, and a few pitiful buildings. Along the far side of the railroad tracks stretches a long tin warehouse, with a loading dock and a sign that reads "Santo Tomas Produce Association." Three blocks to the south, the flagpole of what must be a small post office. Postmaster rises early or has a bad memory, Mayberry notices, because the flag is up. To the north a grocery and a bar, each with its fading sign. Otherwise *nada y nada*. Mayberry turns right and parks at the bar, beside a Coors truck left with its door hanging open.

El Rancho Grande Saloon is a low blockhouse of crumbling whitewashed adobe. Across the outside front wall is written "Under New Management" in charcoal scrawl that might be five years old. The door of this place is also open.

Mayberry looks around. To the far range of view, up and down Main, he sees no sign of Varvara and Jesse. They were close behind when he came off the interstate but now they are being discreet. Somewhere. Good. And no sign of Zuckerman. All right. It is only six-fifteen, Mayberry himself is a little early. No sign of any other human. Except a beer truck with a door ajar. He decides to try El Rancho Grande, not failing to take the accordion folder with him.

In the soothing cool darkness he feels peanut shells snap underfoot and bumps a pool table before his eyes adjust. An hour after sunrise but El Rancho is nevertheless lit only with orange Christmas bulbs and a luminescent clock. From behind the bar a husky man in a black polo shirt is speaking Spanish with the Coors driver. This man acknowledges Mayberry with a flick of his dark eyes but does not interrupt himself. Mayberry waits. He is nervous, dopey from too many miles and not enough sleep, but mostly right now impatient. All he wants is a little information. Idly, he inspects the premises. A rest room at the back, a jukebox with a cracked face, another door into what seems to be living quarters, from which distantly emanate the sound and the smell of frying, a faint unhealthy grayish glow, and the smarmy voice of Gene Shalit. Behind the bar itself, atop an electronic cash register, Mayberry notices something more interesting. It is a family photograph in a gold plastic frame. The man of the black shirt is shown standing behind a comely black-haired woman, his hand on her shoulder, both of them smiling gravely, and clustered around her knees, three black-haired children. The press-on lettering across the top of the frame declares proudly: "Danny y Tina."

Suddenly Mayberry is hurrying. He scribbles his message on a blank sheet snatched from the accordion folder, judging that twenty-three should be no less convincing than twenty-four. Having had all night, he spends only a minute composing it. He folds the sheet carefully three times. And by then Danny has approached him.

"Yes, hombre?" Innkeeper making a ritual sweep with his bar rag, and forcing the day's first smile.

"You mean you're open?"

"Yes, my friend."

"A Coors," says Mayberry quickly. "And one for you?" Danny is grateful but does not himself drink before nine in the morning, he says; it is a principle.

"I wonder if you could do me a favor," says Mayberry. "A small thing but to me a very large service."

Danny frowns dubiously. "Just this," says Mayberry. Apologetic, he holds up the square of paper. "I'm supposed to meet a friend here at seven. A young man with dark curly hair. But I can't stay. So I wonder if you would give him this message."

Danny is relieved. "Certainly. Certainly I will do that."

"Thank you." The note is placed safely beside the cash register. Mayberry points to the picture. "You have a beautiful family."

Danny displays a broad unforced grin. "Thank you, my friend."

"Where is your rest room?" says Mayberry.

Twenty seconds later he is through the window and scampering between rusty burn barrels, around a chicken hutch, hurdling the four dismantled motorcycles in Danny's back yard. By a miracle there is no dog. Leaping the low cinder-block wall, Mayberry sprints away down the alley, folder in hand, hoping dearly that Varvara and Jesse are still concentrating their attention on the front.

He stays with the alley across town. Five blocks back to the flagpole and Mayberry is hawking up phlegm but he hasn't slowed to a jog. The building is a spruce little cube of red brick, newer than anything else in Mesquite, with a saguaro at one corner and the zip code across a wall in stainless steel letters. Mayberry has made a bet with himself. He has wagered that the best place to look for a vehicle left unattended with keys, in a small town, is outside the post office.

He wins. It is a Dodge pickup from the mid-seventies, with whitewalls and a gun rack and engine enough for an M-1 tank. Mayberry steals it.

THIRTY-FIVE

Sideswiping the saguaro, he rolls screaming back toward the interstate, then north again to Las Cruces. Fortunately the truck has a half tank of gas. He hopes that Zuckerman—in his mind Mayberry is still addressing that name, as he did prudently in the note—will be able to slip clear of Varvara and Jesse. Or at the very least, outrun them by two or three minutes. And that he will have no trouble with the directions. Mayberry himself has only been to the place once.

At Las Cruces he peels away, onto a state road that starts him climbing the eastern hills, almost directly toward that shark's-teeth ridge. He couldn't recall the highway's number and doesn't take note of it now, but a green sign whipping by on the right reassures Mayberry, and will tell Zuckerman, that they are on course. In a few minutes he tops over the pass and begins dropping steeply into a vast arid empty valley, a sunken basin, two thousand feet below the surrounding desert.

It is the nethermost extremity of the Jornada del Muerto, inhabited chiefly by soaptree yucca, kangaroo rats, and the United States Army. Lava beds, alkali flats, scant precious water, barbed wire, and stark gleaming white dunes of gypsum sand. Along the north side of the road runs a stern fence, and every few miles, affixed to a pair of posts, the identical notice:

> AREA CLOSED
> WHITE SANDS MISSILE RANGE
> U. S. GOVT. PROPERTY
> KEEP OUT

The sun is in Mayberry's face. He cheats against the speed limit but can't afford, not just now, to drastically flout it. The temperature must already be close to a hundred degrees. Some way out across the valley floor he starts to see sign of the gypsum: banked up intermittently along the left and barely revealing itself, a soft margin of stunning white sand. Elsewhere the desert is still brown and mundane. But before long the wave of white seems to be cresting, exigent, spilling beyond containment down toward the highway. Barbed wire is not likely to hold the stuff. Nothing out here to impede the wind, and these dunes are on the move.

Twenty miles short of the town of Alamogordo, at a break in the fence, Mayberry turns left. An old unmarked ranch road, but Zuckerman should find it easily. There is no other left turn. Mayberry drives in among the dunes.

He drives several miles, winding deeper into whiteness. The yucca disappear. The last gnarled dwarfed cottonwoods disappear. The scrub saltbush, and even the plain desert earth. Mayberry weaves on into the dune field, leaving behind all plant and animal life, all mineral matter that is brown or yellow or red. He has entered an extraordinary zone of soft lines and sterility, gorgeous and total absence of color. The road itself here is nothing but packed gypsum, drifted over at places like a high Montana pass in January; that blindingly white, and that silent. He rounds another bend, another, surrounded entirely now by white sand in dunes forty and fifty feet tall, wind-sculpted, shifting gently, creeping over themselves leeward with hushed and inexorable grace. Nothing else.

Mayberry stops the truck and gets out.

He slogs to the summit of a dune. Hazy in the far distance he can see a brownish-red face of mountains, below which crouches Alamogordo, but within his immediate area, for a radius of miles, only white. He sits. There is no sound at all but the wind, strong and dry, working. He waits. He doesn't move. He is feeling strangely relaxed with the situation, at last, and just a healthy bit curious.

He knows what to expect, and whom, if not precisely why. Or at least he suspects that he knows. But there is still the small matter of that coyly coincident figure, which for most of twenty-four hours now has been hovering at the periphery of his mind's vision, a second brown shape in the bushes, distracting attention: forty thousand dollars.

Mayberry has always believed that Paul died on impact and the money burned, but believing was always different from being sure. And there was no one, almost no one, to ask.

Certainly not Nick DeStefano. And not their mutual friend the erstwhile pool contractor, the tanned and pathetic former war buddy who had initially put Mayberry and Paul in touch with DeStefano, and who was himself, by the time Mayberry got home again, dead in Los Angeles of what was said to have been an accidental OD. Who then? Who else to consult but Paul himself? Mayberry might never have harbored the doubts, he might never have felt need to ask anyone, without that last telephone call between Lackland Air Base and Riverside, when Paul had just driven in with the Coca Madonna, and already seemed to be falling prey to dangerous ideas.

Have you called the Man?

Not yet.

Not yet? Christ sakes, what are you doing? Call him. Unload.

Relax. I will. I just got to see to a couple things first. Got some arrangements to make.

At which Mayberry felt the nastiest cool breeze of suspicion and, worse, dread.

Arrangements? You got arrangements *to make with DeStefano.*

Yeah. I know. Relax, man. It's all gonna happen. Just like we figured it. But one thing at a time, okay? Sometimes, I swear, you got an asshole so tight, it's like a sucking chest wound.

I want to know what you're up to.

Nothing. But then he laughed, a fluid joyless sound that Mayberry recognized too well. *I'm taking a drive up the coast. After I unload. Little road trip. Nothing.*

Be careful, Paul. My ass is in this too.

Yeah. Have fun at Dak To, okay? Give my regards to Charlie, Paul Katy said.

And so Mayberry boarded his transport feeling sure that Paul had decided, unilaterally, to put a cut on the cocaine after all. Lactose or procaine or something still better, from his little medic's pack of tricks. If he gave DeStefano just a fifty per cent cut-down version of what Mayberry had smuggled, still very respectable for the street, he could sell that kilo and a half as agreed, and then sell it again to someone else. Theoretically he could. If DeStefano let him.

It was exactly the sort of disastrous cleverness that might lead to a bad automobile accident. On the other hand Paul Katy might have been much smarter than Nick DeStefano: as Paul himself no doubt firmly believed. So the notion was not altogether beyond plausibility—almost, but not altogether, no—that Paul Katy could have somehow faked his own death, or tried, with plunging Impala and gasoline flames and the Santa Lucia cliffs for a perfect stage setting, simply to cover his trail.

There was only one person to ask. And when Mayberry finally did ask, last year in Palo Alto over a pitcher of beer, Jeff Katy gaped at him with a dull distant look that Mayberry at the time took for pure recollected horror.

Within a half hour his feet, to lee of his body, are covered with white sand. The sand is cool and soft. Mayberry has never experienced any place more peaceful. Or more unrelievedly white. He hears the car before he sees it.

A battered red Datsun wagon. From his point of vantage Mayberry watches this vehicle swing out dizzily around the last bend, slow at once with the sight of his parked truck, and glide to a stop nearby. He watches a young man climb out.

The leather hat and patchwork pants have been abandoned. The young man wears modestly faded jeans and a white cotton dress shirt, wilted, with the sleeves rolled above his bony elbows. His hair has recently been cut back short. He pushes his hands into his rear pockets and lets his mouth cock itself into a wide complacent smirk, as though he and Mayberry are sharing a vicious joke.

"Hello, Jeffrey," says Mayberry.

"Hello, Mayberry. Thanks for the warning back there."

"Not at all."

Glancing down coyly, Jeff Katy tries to rid his face of the grin but apparently cannot. "Are you surprised?"

"A little. I had an idea. But still."

"I suppose you've got a few questions."

"Not really," says Mayberry. "What's the difference now?"

"I didn't plan to get you so deeply involved. I'm sorry about that. I guess maybe there's some kind of lesson. About opening other people's mail." The thin snicker is not infectious.

"Jeffrey," says Mayberry, and then pauses to compose himself. The second time his voice is quieter. "I am definitely not interested in your apologies or your lessons."

"No. Well then." He moves to trudge up the dune.

"Stay there," says Mayberry. Jeffrey stops. His face is quite empty. "Do you have forty thousand dollars?"

Soberly Jeffrey shakes his head.

"Do you have a gun?"

Jeffrey nods but does not produce one. The little automatic would no doubt be tucked in the back of his belt. Mayberry is impressed by Jeffrey's level of sanguinary calm, and wonders passingly whether it is acquired or inherited.

"What time are you meeting Hod?"

"Three o'clock. Just come with me to Juarez, Mayberry. And I *will* get you the money."

"Stop it," says Mayberry. "You may be a good physicist. And a very slick killer. But you're a failure as a liar."

"Is that why you met me here—to deliver a character assessment?" Jeffrey looks back down the dune road, and around, perfunctorily. He does not seem to share Mayberry's appreciation of the spot. "Time's passing."

"No. No, of course not," says Mayberry. He picks up the accordion folder, pouring it clear of sand. He unwraps the string clasp. "I never realized that you were such an ardent Zionist."

"I'm not even a Jew. As you perfectly well know."

"Yes. So what's the point? That part still eludes me. Not money, I gather. Not politics. Or *is* there a point?"

"Call it professional ambition."

"I'm stupid. I don't follow."

The hands return to the rear pockets and Mayberry reminds himself that, from this position, a gun at the small of Jeffrey's back is easily drawn; but Jeffrey's thoughts for the moment are elsewhere. "They want *me*. That's our deal. Not just the Teller configuration. Me. I'm going to help them build it."

"It."

"Yeah. In a country where *it* has never been done. Fission bombs, maybe, but not this. Not the thermonuclear. We'll be starting from scratch." He casts a self-effacing twitch toward the folder. "Almost from scratch. Then boom." Jeffrey's tone falls quite soft; his eyes glow with the reflected luster of twenty-five megatons. "Boom. I mean, imagine that, Mayberry. Can you? You've seen newsreels. Can you imagine it?"

"Imagine what? The implications? The explosion itself?"

"No," says Jeffrey. "The thrill."

Mayberry says: "I think I've heard enough."

Reaching into the folder, he takes hold of the .45. He doesn't bother to pull it clear of the cardboard. He simply squeezes one shot into the center of Jeff Katy's chest. There is no echo.

Eleven years, and the Head of Surgery will not understand, but evidently it's what he is good at.

BESTSELLING BOOKS FROM TOR

- ☑ 58725-1 *Gardens of Stone* by Nicholas Proffitt $3.95
  58726-X Canada $4.50

- ☐ 51650-8 *Incarnate* by Ramsey Campbell $3.95
  51651-6 Canada $4.50

- ☐ 51050-X *Kahawa* by Donald E. Westlake $3.95
  51051-8 Canada $4.50

- ☐ 52750-X *A Manhattan Ghost Story* by T.M. Wright $3.95
  52751-8 Canada $4.50

- ☐ 52191-9 *Ikon* by Graham Masterton $3.95
  52192-7 Canada $4.50

- ☐ 54550-8 *Prince Ombra* by Roderick MacLeish $3.50
  54551-6 Canada $3.95

- ☑ 50284-1 *The Vietnam Legacy* by Brian Freemantle $3.50
  50285-X Canada $3.95

- ☐ 50487-9 *Siskiyou* by Richard Hoyt $3.50
  50488-7 Canada $3.95

Buy them at your local bookstore or use this handy coupon:
Clip and mail this page with your order

TOR BOOKS—Reader Service Dept.
P.O. Box 690, Rockville Centre, N.Y. 11571

Please send me the book(s) I have checked above. I am enclosing $_____ (please add $1.00 to cover postage and handling). Send check or money order only—no cash or C.O.D.'s.

Mr./Mrs./Miss _____
Address _____.
City _____ State/Zip _____
Please allow six weeks for delivery. Prices subject to change without notice.

MORE BESTSELLERS FROM TOR

- [x] 58827-4 *Cry Havoc* by Barry Sadler $3.50
  58828-2 Canada $3.95
- [ ] 51025-9 *Designated Hitter* by Walter Wager $3.50
  51026-7 Canada $3.95
- [ ] 51600-1 *The Inheritor* by Marion Zimmer Bradley $3.50
  51601-X Canada $3.95
- [ ] 50282-5 *The Kremlin Connection* by Jonathan Evans $3.95
  50283-3 Canada $4.50
- [ ] 58250-0 *The Lost American* by Brian Freemantle $3.50
  58251-9 Canada $3.95
- [ ] 58825-8 *Phu Nham* by Barry Sadler $3.50
  58826-6 Canada $3.95
- [x] 58552-6 *Wake-in Darkness* by Donald E. McQuinn $3.95
  58553-4 Canada $4.50
- [ ] 50279-5 *The Solitary Man* by Jonathan Evans $3.95
  50280-9 Canada $4.50
- [ ] 51858-6 *Shadoweyes* by Kathryn Ptacek $3.50
  51859-4 Canada $3.95
- [ ] 52543-4 *Cast a Cold Eye* by Alan Ryan $3.95
  52544-2 Canada $4.50
- [ ] 52193-5 *The Pariah* by Graham Masterton $3.50
  52194-3 Canada $3.95

Buy them at your local bookstore or use this handy coupon:
Clip and mail this page with your order

TOR BOOKS—Reader Service Dept.
P.O. Box 690, Rockville Centre, N.Y. 11571

Please send me the book(s) I have checked above. I am enclosing
$_____ (please add $1.00 to cover postage and handling).
Send check or money order only—no cash or C.O.D.'s.

Mr./Mrs./Miss _____
Address _____
City _____ State/Zip _____

Please allow six weeks for delivery. Prices subject to change without notice.